NIGHT
BLIND

NIGHT
BLIND

MICHAEL W. SHERER

THOMAS & MERCER

Published by Thomas & Mercer
P.O. Box 400818
Las Vegas, NV 89140

ISBN-13: 9781612184180
ISBN-10: 1612184189

To Roger
for planting the seed.

1

Gagnon pulled back into the shadows as a car passed, alert to the sights, sounds, and even the smells around him. The Quai d'Orsay was busy all the time—after all, this was Paris, the City of Lights—but he'd come at perhaps the least busy time of day, when one could best appreciate the city. Alive, but in repose, a slumber interlaced with dreams, even fitful nightmares, as traffic coursed through the arteries and veins of its streets and chimneys huffed clouds of breath into the night air.

Footsteps echoed faintly under the bridge, the Pont Alexandre III, and Gagnon hugged the wall, peering toward the sound. He'd been a fool to agree to meet so close to MAEE— the *Ministère des Affaires Étrangères et Européennes*, the French Ministry of Foreign Affairs. His contact had insisted, since it was convenient to his office, a short walk that wouldn't arouse suspicion, even at the late hour. And who would believe Gagnon would dare come so close to those in the foreign ministry who would have his head for the things he'd done?

Southeast Asia, the Middle East, Africa—he'd traveled halfway around the world on secret missions for France, ferreting out information and even killing to protect the French state. He'd spent most of his career in Algeria, Tunisia, and Morocco long after those places had been part of the French colonial empire, trying to foment the kind of unrest that would eventually produce the Arab Spring. He'd done the dirty work of several administrations for no personal or political gain, only his love for his country.

Fortunately, he still had value to DPSD, *la Direction de la Protection et de la Sécurité de la Défense*. He'd been their best intelligence agent for the past twenty years. Unfortunately, the branch of DPSD he worked for didn't exist on paper. His accomplishments went unknown to all but a few within the agency—and even fewer at MAEE—and if they chose not to acknowledge him or what he'd done, then he didn't exist, either. One of those men, he knew, stood on a precipice. For years, the defense minister himself had conducted an ongoing internal investigation to root out a small faction of devout Catholic right-wing officers intent on influencing national affairs. Among them were Gagnon and his contact at DPSD. Gagnon knew his superior was prepared to give him up to avoid discovery as a member of that cabal. He'd already planted the seed with someone at MAEE, though Gagnon hadn't yet discovered who.

A man's gaunt profile drew closer, the dim lights under the bridge barely illuminating the chiseled face, the aquiline nose. Dressed all in black, the man blended into the shadows. Were it not for the pale visage and the square of white beneath the man's Adam's apple, he might have been a shadow. Gagnon breathed a little easier now that he recognized Jules Baroche. How ironic that the monseigneur had the same name as the minister of foreign affairs at the time all this had started—if any of what Baroche had told him was true. Now Gagnon was about to find out. He stepped out of the shadows into the bishop's path.

Baroche flung out an arm. "*Mon Dieu!* Oh, it's you. You frightened me."

"*Oui, c'est moi.* So, my friend. What have you learned?"

Baroche looked in both directions and tipped his head toward the other side of the single express lane.

"Come. Let's walk."

Gagnon followed as the priest stepped over the guardrail and hurried across. The sidewalk on the other side overlooked the water beneath the iron trestles of the bridge. Gagnon sniffed the scent of algae and decayed fish and heard the lap of water against stone over the whir of traffic overhead.

"I verified the call," Baroche said as Gagnon fell in step. "The number traces back to Monseigneur Delacroix."

"And the message?"

"Passed on from the sisterhood in Montréal. The protocol, while out of use for the past century, was correct."

"Suggesting it's authentic."

"*Mais oui.*" Baroche pulled an envelope from an inside pocket of his sport coat and handed it to him. "This is what I found in the archives."

Gagnon stopped and opened the envelope. He pulled out a thin sheaf of papers, yellowed and brittle with age.

"*Alors, c'est vrai!* The legend is true after all."

"*Peut-être.* After all these years, who knows if anything is left? If there was ever anything of value on board."

"You think I care about what the Americans may have buried?" Gagnon said.

Baroche shrugged. "The sisters seemed to think—"

"I'm concerned only with what transpired between the captain and the sisterhood," Gagnon said sharply, his words echoing off the stone walls. He held up the papers. "This confirms their meeting?"

Baroche nodded.

"Who else knows about this?" Gagnon said.

"No one. My staff knows only that Delacroix called and passed on a message for Cardinal Villards. I searched the archives myself."

"And Villards?"

"Knows nothing yet."

"Good." Gagnon pocketed the envelope and palmed the Laguiole switchblade there.

"What now?" Baroche said.

Gagnon flicked the blade out, wrapped his arm around the thin man's chest, and drove the point under his chin. Baroche arched backward as if jolted with electricity, mouth stretched in a grimace of shock and pain. The knife sank in to the hilt, blood seeping around it, staining the clerical collar black in the darkness. Gagnon twisted his wrist and worked the blade up into Baroche's brain until the man went limp.

Gagnon dragged the body to the rail and flipped it over into the water below, pulling the knife out at the last second. He glanced around to see if anyone had heard the splash. At this hour of the night, only cabbies, prostitutes, and bums roamed the streets. Without bothering to wipe the handle clean, he dropped the knife into the Seine. Darting back to the other side of the street, he hurried out from under the bridge. He vaulted the low wrought-iron fence fronting the sidewalk and disappeared into the pedestrian tunnel that led to the Invalides metro station.

Soon he'd be safe. And if the papers in his pocket were real, he would possess the power to topple governments and lay waste to entire countries, if not continents. Let them try to marginalize him now.

2

The day Cole Sanders died, I lost my voice. I found it again the night of November twenty-fifth. Or rather, early the morning of the twenty-sixth.

People still read newspapers. Fewer each year, true, but they do. I know because I deliver them, one of two jobs I manage to hold down. It's not a bad job, really, but not one that many people aspire to, not like the career I'd had in public affairs once. And out on the street I sometimes witness tomorrow's newspaper news as it happens. This morning looked to be no exception.

Brake lights punctuated the darkness ahead. I let the car slow of its own accord in the tire tracks molded in the mantle of fresh snow, and lightly pressed the pedal. The car stopped with a jerk. Snow draped the green rhododendrons, laurels, and firs, even sticking to branches that had lost their leaves a few weeks earlier. Light trapped between snow and low scudding clouds cast an orange glow across the face of the city.

Another set of brake lights rouged the snow ahead of the car in front of me. Normally devoid of traffic at this late hour, the winding street was as clogged as a sclerotic artery. I sighed, shoved the gearshift into park, opened the door, and put one foot out onto the snowy road, slowly easing weight onto my bum leg. My knee ached like a bad tooth, the pain probing and stirring up the sediment of memory. I hung ungloved hands on the top of the doorframe, pulled myself out, craned my head above the roof, and squinted. Light as feathers, icy flakes caressed my face, melted quickly, and rolled like tears down my cheeks.

Limned in the headlights of the short line of cars, a late-model Lexus sprawled sideways, straddling the one-lane bridge, its nose up on the opposite curb. Outside the headlight beams, shadowy curtains of falling snow swirled into waves of amorphous gray ghosts, the scent of winter wafting after them. I gripped the frozen metal tightly to keep from flinching as dozens of sensory impressions rushed at me like the tumbling snowflakes.

"Fuck it, lady," an angry voice, heavily accented, called from the open window of the taxicab at the head of the line. "Just do it!"

Beyond the Lexus, a dark figure huddled atop the bridge abutment at the edge of an orange pool of light spilling from a lamppost. I stiffened involuntarily, throat constricting and pulse racing. More sediment churned, this time as if excavated by a dredge, the torrent of memories turbid with raw emotion, diffuse and indistinguishable.

Impulsively, I pulled the other foot out of the car and trudged toward the cab, my eyes on the stationary figure on the bridge. An hour earlier, when I'd been more focused, before the drugs had begun to wear off, I might not have gotten involved.

A nervous voice near my elbow asked, "What's going on?"

"Call nine one one," I said. "Get some cops out here. And an ambulance." I kept walking, the snow crunching under my feet.

"Christ, lady, make up fucking mind," the cabbie yelled. Russian, I decided, or maybe Ukrainian.

"Hey, give it a rest," I said as I came up beside the cab.

His head swiveled, mouth open in surprise. Dark eyes in an angular face narrowed. "Who in fuck are you?"

I stopped. "You're not helping matters. I'm going to ask you again, nicely, to be quiet. I'll go talk to her."

"What are you, cop or something?" He craned his neck and gestured dismissively. He dropped his gaze, looked past me, and yelled again. "Lady, move your fucking car or—"

My short, hard right jab to his jaw cut him off. His head whipped around, throwing drops of spittle onto the dash, the wet spots shiny even in the darkness. He turned back, eyes glazed. I hit him again on the point of his chin, aiming for a spot two feet past him. The blow turned his shoulders and pulled him away from the window. He fell forward, forehead hitting the top of the steering wheel with a heavy thud.

Ignoring the sharp intake of breath from the passenger inside, I flexed the fingers of my right hand and stepped carefully through the snow toward the figure across the road.

The woman on the bridge stiffened. She wore a dark wool coat, the collar pulled up around her chin. "Don't come any closer."

I slowed, my empty hands out where she could see them. "I just want to talk."

"There's nothing left to talk about."

"There's always something to talk about."

"You wouldn't understand."

An aliform shadow flapped heavily across the snow, alighting on my shoulder, cloaking me in her despair. I shuddered, her pain a vise grip on my heart. I did not want to lose this one.

"You're right. I don't know what it's like to be you right now. But I can guess you're in pain. You want to make it stop, and this is the only answer you can come up with right now."

Talking about it won't put the idea in her head; she's already thought about it.

For a moment she sat frozen, then her head bobbed.

I jammed my frozen hands in my coat, hunching my shoulders against the cold. "What made you decide to jump? You know, instead of some other way?"

She turned away from me and leaned back over the edge. I held my breath, the susurrant snowfall loud in the hush. I feared she'd go over, but after a moment she faced me again, giving me a glimpse of large, expressive eyes rimmed with dark circles above a delicate nose.

"It's okay if you don't want to talk," I said, "I'm glad you're here, actually. Because *I* need to talk." Her head tilted slightly. "I need to tell someone that I didn't get it before. I didn't understand the pain, how someone can look around at all this"—I spread my arms with hands still in my pockets, the gesture opening my coat—"the beauty of all this, the joy, and see nothing but bleakness. But now I do."

I pulled the coat flaps in to ward off the cold that knifed through the thin fabric. Then I took another step. She didn't react.

"I'm glad you're here because now I finally have a chance to listen. Understand, even. Maybe we can help each other. What do you say?"

In the dim light, inquisitiveness glinted behind the sadness in her eyes.

I stamped my feet against the cold, and waited. *How long until you know if you're getting through?*

"I thought it would feel like flying," she said.

I nodded. "Makes sense. But why this bridge? Why not Aurora Avenue?"

She considered the question—a good sign. "I didn't want to have time to regret it. You know, jumping."

"You mind if I sit down?" I hunched my shoulders. "I'm tired. Long day."

She stiffened. "Not too close."

I brushed snow off the cold stone abutment and perched a few feet away from her, the chill quickly seeping through the seat of my jeans. Sweat trickled down over my ribs. The falling snow thinned to random flakes. I turned away and focused on slow, complete breaths—*dirgha pranayama*. Darkness covered the Arboretum. The street below curved north. The drop was maybe twenty feet. Not much, but enough if she went over headfirst.

Most jumpers in Seattle pick the Aurora Bridge. The distance from the bridge deck to the water of Lake Union is 167 feet. Anyone falling from that height travels close to sixty miles per hour by the end of the journey. Hitting water at that speed is like hitting cement. It's pretty final. Taking a header off a bridge wouldn't be my choice, but until recently I'd never considered the options. And the woman had a point—a three-second fall from the Aurora Bridge could feel like a lifetime of regret.

3

Despite the cold, the air inside the car felt tropical, close, and humid, something fetid assailing his nostrils that he realized was his own breath. He leaned forward and rubbed a hole in the condensation on the windshield with his gloved hand. He'd waited long enough to steel his conviction to a fine edge, and now it carried him out of the car and down the street.

The cottage door beckoned. Despite the late hour, the window facing the street glowed yellow. Resolved, he went up the walk, the falling snow thickening now. He had to dissuade her from taking any further action. The old woman had stirred up enough trouble already, pestering the city with the threat of lawsuits. The fact that a well-known firm was even considering taking on her case made it clear that she posed a real threat. If she persisted, she could ruin everything.

He sweet-talked his way in, then argued with her, cajoled, followed her from room to room pleading his case. Now, after nearly half an hour, she asked him to leave, her voice firm, her meaning clear. That's when something in him changed, as if her obstinacy had triggered a pressure switch deep inside him, and he picked up the knife from the counter by the sink in his gloved hand. She had to be stopped, silenced.

His first swipe was hesitant, as if he meant to warn, not hurt, her. It drew blood nonetheless. She didn't seem to feel it, but he saw a black line well from her arm and drip red onto the kitchen floor. She slapped him, ordered him out of her house. The humanity disappeared from his soul, replaced by something primal. He struck again, more forcefully this time. Again she warded off the blow but felt the bite of the blade.

He drove her back through the door into the living room with more slashing blows. She caught his wrist in her grip and held the knife away from her, twisting his arm. Jerking away from her grasp, he struck again, a downward stabbing blow this time that pierced her shoulder, causing her to cry out in pain.

She was no match for his strength and the fury of his assault. She was old, frail, but her will to survive gave her strength she didn't know she had. She quickly hobbled into the kitchen, lifted a saucepan from the stove, and girded herself for his final onslaught. The old bird was tough, but he finished her quickly with a savagery that filled him with bloodlust. He almost let it overwhelm him, but he contained it, let it cool, his mind thinking through the variables now that he'd been forced into this course of action.

Once he came to a decision he moved quickly, pacing from room to room, taking stock, paying particular attention to the clutter on the old woman's desk. Then he retraced his steps to make sure he'd left no evidence of his passage, careful not to step in the blood that spattered the living room rugs, the kitchen floor.

When he was satisfied, he stole out the front door and down the walk to the street. His car was parked less than a block away, with a view of the house. He knew he should get far away from the scene as quickly as he could, but he forced his nerves to quiet down. He climbed into the front seat, took off his gloves, and blew on his hands to warm them. Looking back toward the house, he settled into the seat and waited.

* * *

"What did you say to the cab driver?" she asked in a small voice.

"I told him to shut up." I didn't think telling her I knocked him senseless would sound reassuring.

"Thanks."

"Sure. The guy was being an asshole. Pardon my French."

Hardly any traffic ventured out at this time of night, and the snow had kept even more people than usual off the streets. The oddity—snow—was notable for two reasons: Seattle seldom had any, and rarely any as early as Thanksgiving. That the jumper had managed to create a traffic jam here on Interlaken was a fluke. Far from being an arterial, it twisted up through the forest from Montlake partway up Capitol Hill, narrowing in spots to one lane, like this old stone bridge. The Lexus effectively blocked anyone from getting by.

Up close she looked to be in her early thirties. Dark hair spilled out from under her hat onto her shoulders like raven's wings. She twined gloved fingers around one strand, nervously preening the feathers.

"So," I said, "something's kept you from taking your life until now. Mind if I ask what?"

"Why haven't I killed myself before this?" She sounded miffed. "Maybe I was just too afraid to go through with it. Ever think of that?"

"Hey, no offense. I just meant that there must be something, someone you care about."

She shook her head. "Not someone, I can tell you that. Nobody gives a damn about me."

"I do."

She looked at me. "Bullshit. You don't even know me."

"Doesn't mean I don't care. For what it's worth, my name is Blake. It's nice to meet you. Why would I be out here in the snow with you if I didn't care?" I held up a hand. "Doesn't matter. What matters is what *you* care about. Humor me. Try to think of things that prevented you from taking your life in the past. Let's see if there's a reason to stick around awhile."

"Sorry, *Blake*. I'm done talking here. It's a waste of time. I think you should leave now."

"You might be done talking, but I'm not." Talking had kept her alive for the past few minutes. If she kept talking until the cops or EMS arrived, she had a chance. "Talking's only a waste of time for people who don't have anything to say. I think you probably have a lot to say. Maybe you just didn't realize anyone's listening."

Part of me wanted to take her by the scruff of the neck and shake her. A year earlier, I might not have had the patience to weather her histrionics, even may have commiserated with the cab driver and told her to get over herself. But the recent past had taught me how insidious depression can be, pervading every aspect of life, draining all the color and joy from it.

"Look," I said, "it's Thanksgiving. For some people that might mean stuffed turkey, mashed potatoes, and gravy at grandma's house with a ton of relatives. I used to love Thanksgiving. You know, eat until you're so full you think you're going to explode; play touch football out on the front lawn or down at the park; sit around and listen to all the stories about Uncle Joe and Cousin Drew and the funny neighbor lady down the block. I don't have family around anymore. It gets lonely. I can understand why you might be out here. It's okay, whatever it is. We all get depressed. That doesn't make it hurt any less. I know that."

She sobbed, a mournful wail that caught in her throat as tears trailed wet tracks down her face. And then she started talking, letting the words out slowly at first, then in a torrent. None of the details mattered, really—she had the usual problems: abusive boyfriend, uncaring mother, shitty job…what mattered was that I listened.

Don't judge; don't argue; don't give advice. It's not how bad the problem is, but how much it hurts.

Her breath rose in the cold air under the sodium street-lights like orange plumes of despair and anger, a cloud of flittermice taking wing in the night. I listened as if my life, not hers, depended on it. I didn't drift off, tune her out, take a mental walk. Not much, anyway. Gradually, the flow slowed to a rush and then to a trickle as she tired from the cathartic purge. By the time she wound down, I knew her as intimately as I'd probably known Molly—or anyone, for that matter.

Sirens wailed in the distance, then scrawked and went silent. The snow likely had caused more accidents than usual. The sounds, movement in the car behind the cab, shadows playing on the snow, stray thoughts—all tugged at my consciousness, vying for attention. I kept my gaze on the woman next to me, seeing the weariness in her eyes.

"I'm just so tired of it all," she said. "You know?"

"I know." Some of us just press on. Others find a way to take some R & R and recharge their batteries. A few—far too many—give up. *Don't.*

"What?" she said.

I focused on her face. "I'm sorry. I didn't realize I was thinking out loud. Don't give up. There is help out there."

She sighed. "I wish I could believe that."

Sirens burped again, much closer this time.

She frowned, suspicion narrowing her eyes. "What did you do?"

Her features pulsed red, blue, red, blue as a Seattle PD cruiser rolled cautiously down the street from the north, followed closely by an EMS bus and another cruiser.

"Damn you," she said. More tears rolled silently down her face. Her hand pressed against the hard stone.

I figured I'd lost her then, my quadriceps already bunching and shoulders tensing in anticipation. I jumped as she twisted toward empty air, black leather boots scrabbling for a purchase on the slippery stone. Arm outstretched, I grabbed a fistful of cloth as she launched herself up and out. I threw my weight in the opposite direction.

Shouts rang out from the street along with a high, sharp cry of frustration. My shoulder landed on hard pavement. I rolled onto my back, fingers still clutching the thick wool of her coat in a death grip. My weight and momentum jerked her around in midair, and she collapsed on top of me. She pounded my arms and shoulders and chest with small fists.

"Why, why, why?" she cried. "Damn you! Why couldn't you just let me go?"

I caught her wrists in my hands. Holding her arms, I rolled us over and straddled her with my knees, pinning her arms to the ground.

"You don't want to die," I said. "Trust me, the world will look different in the daylight."

"You all right?" a voice called behind me.

A uniform rushed up, sliding in the snow, nearly losing his footing. Another cop followed more slowly, picking his way in his cohort's footprints.

"She's okay," I said.

The first cop pulled up a safe distance away and peered at me. "That you, Legs?"

I sighed. "Yeah, it's me."

Not too many people besides cops got away with calling me that anymore. Charlie still thought it was endearing. The other cop hesitated, touched a finger to his forehead, and turned to give the ambulance crew an all-clear wave. He headed for the line of cars. I faced the woman beneath me.

"They're here to help you," I said quietly, the words coming as if from a script. "Don't be afraid. We need to get you some medical attention and some support. You showed a lot of strength out here. I know you can get through this. They'll make sure you find a way to feel good again. Okay? I'm going to let you up now. Just breathe easy. The EMTs will come down here and help you to the ambulance."

I tentatively let go. She lay unmoving, head turned to the side, a tear leaking from one eye. I stood and extended a hand. She ignored it.

"You're crazier than I am," she said at last.

"Could be." I gave my hand an impatient shake.

She took it, and I pulled her to her feet. Even in heeled boots, she still fit under my arm. Her knees wobbled. I stooped quickly, put my other arm around her waist to steady her, and walked her toward the ambulance. The officer fell in step and gripped her elbow. We took small, slow steps to keep our footing in the snow.

One of the EMTs met us halfway. "You need a stretcher?" he asked.

"I think we can make it," I said.

He walked alongside just in case. As we neared the patrol car in front of the ambulance, the officer let her go and pulled a spiral-bound notepad from a pocket.

"Hope you don't mind," he said, his voice apologetic, "but I'll jot down some notes while the EMTs take your personal history. Have to fill out reports, you know?"

Loud voices drifted over the snow. Over my shoulder I saw Charlie in a wide stance a few feet from the cab, hands on hips, getting an earful from the now-conscious cabbie. I handed the woman off to the second EMT waiting near the back of the bus and ambled toward the vitriol spewing from the cab's window. When I reached the Lexus, Charlie raised a hand to stop me without even turning around. I crossed my arms and leaned against the trunk. Charlie swiveled his head once to make sure I stayed put.

After the cabbie wound down, I heard the low murmur of Charlie's voice. The cabbie kept interrupting, but Charlie firmly quashed him each time. My thoughts drifted as the adrenaline rush dissipated, images and second-guesses tumbling in disarray. All that focus I'd worked so hard to maintain to keep the woman from going over the edge, gone.

Finally, Charlie turned, pointed a finger over my shoulder, and said through gritted teeth, "Go sit in the cruiser."

"I can explain—"

"Shut up. I'll get to you in a second."

"She was going to—"

"I know what she was going to do, but you should have let us handle it."

"There wasn't any time."

"She's not Cole!" he barked. "Now go sit."

The impact of his words numbed me as much as the cold.

The woman had left her car unlocked, keys inside. Charlie climbed in and started it up. He jockeyed it gently in the snow and straightened it out, then reversed it back toward the short conga line behind the cab. When it cleared the bridge, he swung the wheel and let it roll onto the shoulder. Brake lights flashed red on the snow and went dark. Before he climbed out, the cab pulled abreast of me. The cabbie leaned out, gave me the finger, and spat in the snow at my feet.

The other car eased up the road behind the rolling cab, the driver wearing a nervous expression. I waved and mouthed a "thank you." He kept his eyes on the road as he passed, both hands firmly gripping the wheel. I followed the receding sound of their tires crunching on the snow and climbed into Charlie's cruiser. The warm interior felt as comforting as my mom's kitchen. I rubbed my knee, trying to ignore the ache that had set in the joint like hardening concrete.

Charlie trudged up and yanked open the driver's door. He sat heavily, rocking the car on its suspension, slammed the door shut, and shuffled through a pile in the middle of the bench seat until he came up with a small notebook. Pulling a pen from a pocket in his insulated uniform jacket, he held it poised over the paper.

"Okay, let's hear it," he said.

4

Midge Babcock lived on the back side of Capitol Hill in a little two-bedroom house off East Aloha. No matter how small, the cottage still dwarfed her tiny, antediluvian frame. No one knew her real age—she said she couldn't remember, exactly, in which "aught" year she'd been born, and the church that had kept her baptismal records had burned down shortly after the Great War. She'd volunteered in hospitals as a Junior Red Cross member in that one. During the second War to End All Wars, she'd served as a Red Cross "Gray Lady." Those who knew Midge gently ribbed her that her merchant seaman husband, Cecil, now long dead, must have sailed on tall ships. The years had worn her down to brittle sticks wrapped in parchment. Although she looked as if she might crumble to dust at any moment, her outward frailty hid an inner strength that shone through bright, observant eyes.

I usually saved Midge's house for last. She'd given me her history over tea one or two mornings a week. She said I reminded her of her son at my age, whom she'd already outlived by a decade. I couldn't say she reminded me of my mother, and she was nothing like the only grandmother I remembered well.

Snow covered the vines twisting around the trellis that arched over Midge's walkway. Silence reigned, the city quieted by the unusual snow, which kept criminals and travelers indoors. The hush amplified small sounds—the slow drip of melting snow, the creak of rusty gate hinges—as I passed through.

The property looked far older and more decrepit than Midge herself. A blanket of white hid the worst of the wild growth in the yard, the untended gardens and shaggy lawn. Paint peeled in eczematous strips from the siding. A broken porch rail dangled precariously over a flower bed. A jagged black hole in the snow indicated where one of the front steps had given way to rot. The next dry spell, I would tackle some of the easier projects over Midge's loud protests. Big jobs, like house painting, would have to wait for spring or summer—and more volunteers.

Snow came down again as I went up the walk clutching a newspaper under one arm. I stopped, suddenly disquieted by a sense of something amiss. Peering nervously through the shifting curtain of white, I struggled to let the feeling take on definition. And almost as soon as pale indentations on the walkway caught my eye, falling snow filled and erased them.

Light and shadow. A trick of the eye.

The dark windows of the house stared emptily. The snow had thrown everything off schedule. I swallowed a mouthful of disappointment. I hadn't realized until then how much I'd been looking forward to talking to Midge. And for some reason that hovered like a mother hen in the back of my brain, I thought she had something to tell me. For the life of me, I couldn't remember what. Something she'd alluded to in the midst of a long ramble the week before. During which I'd tuned out, something I did from time to time. Not from lack of interest but a propensity for easy distraction.

I shrugged, stepped lightly up the stairs, and gently placed the paper between the screen and the door. Before the screen closed on my arm, I jiggled the door handle, an afterthought.

Locked. Already focused on the next stop, I didn't give it a second thought.

* * *

He watched Sanders come down the walk to the street and close the gate behind him. The tall man had shown up like clockwork. And what was it he'd seen on Sanders's face when the old woman hadn't answered the door? Disappointment? Sad—no, pathetic, really—that Sanders had relied on the crone for friendship. Too bad, now.

He watched Sanders get back into the beater at the curb and drive off without a second look. When the car disappeared around the corner down the block, he pulled out a phone and dialed 911.

"Nine one one," the operator answered. "How can I help you?"

"I think a woman's been murdered," he said.

* * *

A city as wired on coffee as Seattle ought to have had more places open late besides bars, the odd 7-Eleven, and QFC grocery stores. Aside from 13 Coins, which was too fancy and expensive, I could count the halfway decent all-night diners on one hand: Hurricane Café and 5 Point in Belltown, and Beth's Café up on Aurora near Green Lake. And they were too far away. For a while a fast-food joint on Broadway was about the only spot on Capitol Hill to sit and have a cup of coffee at four a.m, but it closed to make room for Sound Transit's Capitol Hill station.

Now the IHOP on Madison was the only place that served 24/7. What it lacked in ambiance it made up for in colorful characters, a veritable Rainbow Coalition of runaway teens, drag queens, panhandlers, and bar-hoppers sporting multihued tattoos and clothing. My kind of folks. These days, anyway.

I sat at a four-top and took a closer look at the morning's paper. The newsprint laid out on the table conveyed little joy, despite the front-page proclamation, "Happy Thanksgiving!"

Motion outside the front windows brought my head up. The two cops from earlier—Charlie Jones and Officer Downing—stopped just inside the door and scouted the interior. Downing's arm rose. He murmured in Charlie's ear, and the pair ambled over.

"Charlie." I nodded respectfully. "Officer Downing. Coffee? Paper?" I motioned at the empty chairs.

"We're on duty," Charlie said, his tone strangely formal.

Third watch had ended, I knew, yet they still wore uniforms. Charlie transferred his weight. Neither took a seat.

I looked from one to the other, trying to read their faces. "The girl...?"

Charlie shook his head.

"This isn't about the cabbie, is it?" I said. "The guy had it coming."

"Maybe so, but—"

"Impulsive, I know, but he wasn't helping, I swear. Might've goaded that girl into jumping. The man was rude. He—"

"Shut up," Charlie said. "Got a problem. We think you can help."

"Me? What problem?"

Downing cast his eyes on his feet, then at Charlie. I focused on Charlie. Bit my tongue to keep it from wagging unbidden.

"It's not the hack. We caught a crime scene," Charlie said. "On your route. Detectives think you might be able to shed some light on timing."

"You guys responded?"

"Should've known better," Charlie said. "End of the shift—shit, we won't finish the paperwork until lunch." He jerked his head. "You coming?"

Downing scuffed the toe of one shoe on the floor and glanced away. I tried to put my finger on it. Embarrassment, that was it. Something didn't feel right. I shrugged, shoved the chair back from the table, and stood. Their eyes tracked me all the way up, and they lifted their chins as I straightened to full height. Charlie led the way. Downing fell in behind me.

Outside, Charlie stepped off the curb onto the slushy pavement and opened the back door of one of the cruisers parked there. A few fat snowflakes lazily drifted to the ground like the last of the autumn leaves, larger and wetter than earlier, the air warmer. Snow would turn to rain soon, washing away any trace of Mother Nature's Thanksgiving surprise.

"Get in," Charlie said.

I eyed him curiously, but did as I was told, folding nearly in half to squeeze through the opening. Charlie swung the door shut behind me, leaving me snugged up in a warm interior that smelled of stale gym locker, old vomit, and fear. Downing peeled away around the nose of the far cruiser and backed out before Charlie settled heavily behind the wheel in front of me.

"What's going on, Charlie?" The calm in my voice belied the knotting in my gut.

"Just doing the job." His eyes flicked to the rearview mirror. "Look, it's a crime scene. Detectives say they want to talk to a witness, I go get the witness. That's you."

"I don't recall witnessing anything this morning. Other than the jumper, that is." I felt like a perp, not a witness.

He glanced in the mirror again. I shrugged and slumped down in the seat, trying to get comfortable. My knees splayed out more than half the width of the seat and still wedged themselves partway up the cage between front and back seats. I rested my head on the seat back and watched the lights of Broadway stream by. Less than five minutes later, the scene outside the dark window made me sit up. My stomach knotted. I didn't want to know what had happened, and couldn't seem to summon enough breath to ask if I did.

Four or five cars were double-parked on the dark residential street ahead. Downing had already nosed his cruiser into the curb beyond them and now approached us down the middle of the street, features illuminated by headlights. Light bars on two of the cars split the darkness with flashes of blue. Charlie pulled up behind the nearest cop car and climbed out. He waited for Downing, then opened the door and motioned me out. They escorted me up the walk—*light and shadow*—the snow trampled now to bare wet cement by the number of cops going in and out. As if mired in mud, my feet grew heavier with every step toward the house—Midge's house.

Downing babysat me on the porch while Charlie went in and spoke to a plainclothes cop visible through the doorway in the small living room. Downing surveyed the street, refusing to meet my gaze. Cops filled the cottage, making it look smaller than usual. Floorboards groaned as they moved about—taking pictures, making notes, measuring rooms—protesting the sheer volume of testosterone in the dainty surroundings. A tornado had already injured and insulted the delicate old furnishings, faded pictures in debilitated frames, and porcelain knickknacks, leaving detritus strewn in its wake.

The detective glanced at me, said a few words to Charlie, and gestured toward the dining room. Charlie waved me in and I followed him, pausing briefly to look past the detective into the kitchen. Ferruginous splatters of blood coated the pale linoleum floor like paint on a Jackson Pollock canvas. I tasted bile and turned away. Downing shadowed me into the dining room, standing a few feet behind me when I sat.

"Stay put until they say you can leave." Charlie spoke to Downing, not me. "I'll get started on reports." He glared at me. "You really screwed up big time, didn't you?"

My mouth didn't have time to flop open before he walked out, his words echoing in my head in a different voice, one from long ago. Downing had purposely positioned himself to keep me in check and discourage conversation. The detectives had a lot to do, but letting me cool my heels also was a useful ploy to make me nervous.

I tried to find a *drishti* that would force away the image of Midge's kitchen floor. I patted my pockets for the little notebook and pencil I usually carried. Remembered I'd left them in the car. Made a mental list instead of things I needed at the store, chores to do around the apartment. Laundry, wash the floor—*not that floor*—pay bills...

I sighed and looked up at my immediate surroundings. Large maritime paintings covered two walls. Brass running lights hung like sconces on a third wall above an old sideboard, flanking an antique world map. A beautiful brass ship's chronometer rested atop the sideboard. The whole cottage felt like the captain's quarters and bridge of a nineteenth-century square-rigger, the old ship's binnacle, sextant, and brass lanterns in the living room almost as familiar as my own possessions.

My eyelids fluttered. Five long minutes later, I opened them to the sound of footsteps. I'd already forgotten the things I needed at the store. A small Asian woman strode into the room, glanced at Downing, nodded, and directed her gaze at me. Through her open coat I could see a shield clipped to her belt. She pulled out the chair across the table and sat on its edge, leaning forward, pen hand poised over the notebook she placed on the table.

"I'm Detective Hiragawa. What's your name, sir?"

I gave it along with my address. I swallowed hard. "What happened here?"

"That's what we're trying to find out, sir." Her gaze flicked across my face. "Officer Jones says you deliver newspapers?"

I nodded. She waited, but I didn't volunteer more. My brain still wrestled with visions of what might have happened. I imagined the worst, but couldn't get my mind around the concept of someone vicious enough to terrorize an elderly woman in her own home. *So much blood...*

A flicker of annoyance crossed her face. "Is this one of the houses on your delivery route?"

"Yes. Midge Babcock. Is she...?"

The question hung there like stale breath. She ignored it. "There was a paper by the door. About what time did you deliver it this morning?"

I thought back. Midge hadn't been my last stop. The snow had thrown everything off. The *Times* guarantees delivery by five thirty. I finish long before that if I can. On a good night—light traffic, lots of vacation holds—the route takes a little less than two hours. Add time at the warehouse to assemble papers and travel time from there to the first house on my route, and I'm usually done in less than three, three and a half hours.

Trucks had been only a little late getting to the warehouse. The snow had just started falling. But the driving had been treacherous by the time I started out, and some of the hills had been tougher to negotiate. That—and the woman on the bridge, of course—had slowed me down. But a lot of Thanksgiving travelers had put holds on their papers, meaning fewer stops.

She watched me figure it out.

"Around three, I guess."

"Is that when you usually deliver the paper here?"

"A little later, actually. I changed my route this morning."

Her pen stopped writing. "Oh?"

"The snow, you know. Driving was tough." I hesitated. "Look, I'd like to know why I'm here."

"We just have a few questions."

I shook my head. "Not until you tell me what happened."

"Are you refusing to cooperate, sir?" She kept her tone polite.

They'd find out eventually. "The lady who lives here—Midge Babcock—is, well, I guess you'd call her a friend."

"You guess?" The thin, penciled brows arched.

"She's elderly. Gets up early. I've been delivering her paper for a year. I see her every once in a while. We have tea and keep each other company." I paused as she gave me a funny look.

"So you've been in the house bef—?"

"Sure, sure. Lots of times. She's a nice old lady. Came out on the porch one morning and thanked me for putting the paper by the door like she asked. She said the last carrier just tossed it. Half the time it landed in the bushes where she couldn't get it."

"And you got to be friends?"

I shrugged. "We chatted now and then. I was going through a rough patch; she liked to talk and, you know, reminisce, I guess. I usually put her last on my route in case she was up. We were acquaintances." I paused. "She's dead, isn't she?"

Hiragawa's expression wavered, then she nodded. "Did you notice anything unusual this morning?"

Light and shadow... My head wagged. "I was disappointed she wasn't awake yet. I could've used—" I changed my mind. "Some hot tea. It's frosty out there."

"But everything seemed normal?"

"The house was dark." I thought for a moment. "No, I didn't see anything out of the ordinary." No cars parked at the curb with motors running, no suspicious characters lurking in the shadows nearby, just a vague impression.

She cocked her head. "Nothing else comes to mind?"

The details replayed in my head. "I can't think of anything." The mother hen clucked a warning, again urging me to remember what Midge had worried like a rosary the week before. I fixed my gaze on Hiragawa. "What happened?"

With a sigh she glanced down before answering. "Looks like a home invasion. Probably someone trying to rob the place. She must have woken up."

It looked to me as if there'd been a struggle. Midge was so tiny and frail she would have blown away in a soft breeze, but she'd been tougher than she appeared. "Any idea who might have done this?"

"Not yet. We were hoping you might be able to help us." She pulled a card case from a pocket in her coat and handed one across the table. "If you think of anything else, please call."

I glanced at it and slipped it into my shirt pocket. "Sure."

Shutting her notebook, she rose to her feet. "Stay here a minute while I check with my partner. He may have some questions." She glanced over my head at Downing, turned, and left.

"Sorry," Downing said quietly.

I didn't turn. "About not giving me a heads-up?" I heard the bitterness in my voice.

"About your friend."

"Thanks." I glanced over my shoulder. "Not your fault. I know—you and Charlie are doing your job."

He shifted his weight, and his ears pinked, but this time he didn't look away. I faced the entry expectantly and drummed my fingers on the table, jiggled my knee. It was after six. The windows were still black, mirroring the bright yellow light from the glass globe lantern dangling from the ceiling and dim versions of Downing and me. When the sun rose in another two hours, the sky outside would only change to a lighter shade of gray. A clock ticked loudly in the quiet room. From other rooms came the muffled tread of footsteps, the occasional rumble of low voices through the walls.

Part of my brain skipped from thought to thought, a fly refusing to light on anything for more than a second or two, attracted instead to the gore in Midge's kitchen. I didn't let it go there, waving it aside toward some other subject whenever it tried to feed on the images.

"Did you get her name?"

Downing took a moment to reply. "Who? The jumper?"

"Don't call her that," I said quietly. "She didn't actually do it."

"Pretty damn close. If you hadn't been there…her name's Liz Tracey."

"She okay?" I looked at his reflection in the mirror and saw him shrug.

A man about my age poked his head around the doorframe. His gaze took us in before he stepped into the room. A head taller than Hiragawa, he had a round face punctuated by a sharp nose bent slightly askew at the bridge, as if broken in a schoolyard brawl. A dam of gel held waves of dark hair off his forehead. Black silk trousers creased to a knife's edge, soft Italian leather loafers, and a leather jacket cut roomily enough for a shoulder holster defied the wintry weather.

"You're the newspaper carrier?" he asked. "What's your name? Blake?" He stepped over to the table but didn't sit. A whiff of musky cologne floated across the table. "Detective Donovan. You told my partner everything looked normal here when you dropped the paper off at"—he checked his notes—"around three. You put the paper on the porch?" He went on without waiting for an answer. "Did you knock on the door?"

"Why would I? The house was dark."

"I just thought since you knew the victim—my partner says you were friends?—you might have knocked. Detective Hiragawa says you're upset the woman wasn't up when you got here."

"Disappointed. Give me some credit, Detective; we both know most people are asleep at that hour." I smiled to take the edge off the words. "And the victim had a name—Midge."

He tipped his head. "Midge, then. I take it she was a nice lady. I'm sorry for your loss."

"Thank you."

He waited a respectable beat before continuing. "So, you didn't knock. Did you happen to notice the door?"

"It was closed, if that's what you mean."

"Locked?"

"Yes."

He blinked, a small gleam in his eyes. "You tried it?"

I shrugged. "To make sure she was safe, yes." I felt heat color my face, and coughed, putting a hand over my mouth.

Locked. Midge never locked the handle. She used a deadbolt, hasp, and chain on the inside of the door, and she locked the deadbolt when she went out. She didn't lock the doorknob out of habit, for fear she'd lock herself out of the house when she stepped out for the paper or into the garden. She kept forgetting that I hid a spare key outside for her. Someone else locked it. *On the way out?* I feigned more coughing, eyes darting around the room again. *Robbery?* With Midge dead, a thief would have had all the time in the world. The paintings, the antiques—nothing seemed to have been taken, the only out-of-place furnishings in the rooms where Midge had struggled.

He regarded me curiously. "You all right?"

I nodded. "Fine. Thanks." Thoughts, questions kaleido-scoped through my head. *Tell him?*

He tilted his head and frowned. "Okay, that's it for now. I'll send in a forensics technician to get your prints. Officer Downing can take you back."

Donovan paused in the doorway. "Officer Jones says you two know each other?"

"I see him around on my route."

He waited, as if he expected more, then shrugged and disappeared.

The ride to the restaurant in the back of Downing's cruiser left me more discomfited than the trip to Midge's. I wiped my ink-stained fingers on my jeans. Images from both the bridge and Midge's kitchen indelibly etched themselves in my memory. But a suicidal young woman and an old lady's violent and hor-rible death weren't all that occupied me.

The two detectives had given me other things to think about.

5

Reyna peered at the monitor and absently chewed a nail. Captain Farley wanted an analysis of the HUMINT—human intelligence from a real person instead of an intercepted cell call or e-mail— they'd just received from an Iranian informant on a situation in the Gulf of Oman. She dreaded wading through the transcripts, but forced herself to concentrate since Farley had made it clear he wanted it by 0800 Friday. Which meant coming in today, Thanksgiving of all days. Good thing she didn't have plans.

Sadly, before Farley had handed off the assignment she'd wondered what to do with herself on Thanksgiving. She'd reluctantly accepted an invitation from Ross over in Fleet Support to join him and some friends for dinner at his home in Alexandria. She hadn't relished the idea of spending the day trying to make conversation with people she didn't know well and likely wouldn't see again. The work had given her an excuse to back out. Still, spending a holiday cooped up in her cubicle at the Office of Naval Intelligence outside Washington, DC, wasn't much better.

Try as she might to focus, the words kept blurring in front of her. After catching herself going through the same paragraph for the fifth time, she looked at her fingernail guiltily and pushed back from her desk. She stretched and idly moved the cursor on the screen. She clicked on her e-mail inbox. She didn't often give in to procrastination, but it was a holiday, after all. She scooted her chair in closer and opened the new mail that had arrived.

TO: Lt. Comdr. Reyna Chase, ONI
FROM: Daniel Jones, NHC
RE: Command Signal

5758
Ser NWD/SH/0750

ONI.PRTCL.A001: CLASSIFIED
EYES ONLY – TS/SCI CLEARANCE REQUIRED
Received request for information 1630 hours Wednesday re: USS *Anita* deck logs and Comdr. Selim Woodworth. Said request triggered command signal requiring ONI investigation.
Request initiated by William Royer, University of Washington, Seattle, 206-543-2100.
Please notify Cdre. Woodworth, Pacific Squadron, and advise of any assistance you may need.

Reyna frowned. The last thing she needed on top of Farley's deadline was a new investigation. And who else was working on Thanksgiving, anyway? She figured the distraction beat reading transcriptions, at least for a while. She filled out the Single Scope Background Information forms for an investigation of William Royer and put them on her assistant's desk to get started on first thing the next day. Then she pulled up a Pacific Fleet personnel roster online and looked up Commodore Woodworth. The navy had rescinded the rank of commodore back in the 1980s, but still conferred the title on senior captains in certain units—special warfare groups like the SEALs, Carrier Air Wings, and a few others.

She found no listing for Selim Woodworth. She tried again, narrowing it down to the personnel roster on Woodworth's ship, the *Anita*. No luck. She couldn't find a navy ship by that name. Since the command signal had initiated at the Naval Historical Center, she pulled up the NHC website on her computer for the hell of it and did a search for the *Anita*. No such ship existed. At least none by that name had ever been commissioned by the US Navy.

Irritated, she picked up the phone and dialed.

"Jones," a voice answered.

"What, you didn't get invited anywhere for Thanksgiving, either?" Reyna said.

"I'm having turkey dinner with my family later. Who is this?"

Reyna felt warmth rise in her face. "Reyna Chase. You just sent me an e-mail."

"Oh, Commander, sorry."

"That's okay. Say, what's the deal with this command signal you sent? I can't find any Woodworth in the Pacific Fleet, and there's no such ship as the *Anita*."

"Hey, I'm just the messenger."

"C'mon, Jones. Why'd this guy Royer call looking for the deck logs if there's no such ship?"

"All I know is that there's none presently commissioned. Could be an older vessel, in which case the logs wouldn't be here, anyway. They'd be at the National Archives."

"You're not helping. The archives are closed today." Reyna paused. "Any idea why this has been flagged with top secret protocol?"

"Sorry, Commander. Wish I could help. All I know is that when I started looking through the declassified records for Royer, the guy who called, the command signal popped up."

"You weren't curious?"

"I just do what I'm told, ma'am."

"You've got clearance, right?"

"Sure, but I'm an archivist, ma'am. I'll leave investigations to you folks at ONI."

"Thanks for the help, Jones."

"You're welcome," he said cheerily, ignoring Reyna's sarcasm.

"So, what'd you tell this Royer fellow?"

"What I tell everyone else who calls—give me a week and call back. If I find anything, they can order copies."

"A week, huh? Okay, if he calls again, let me know."

"Okeydokey. Have a nice Thanksgiving."

"Sure. You too."

She hung up. The best she was going to do in the way of a Thanksgiving celebration was a glass of wine and a frozen dinner. And she still had to write up the analysis for Farley. She sighed and started reading.

* * *

The woman at the information desk of Harborview said Liz Tracey had been transferred from the ER up to a room on the fifth floor. She steered me toward a bank of elevators. I wished her a happy holiday and set off.

Midge's murder and the questioning by Donovan and Hiragawa were deeply disturbing. But Liz Tracey was still among the living. And after what had happened to Cole, for the moment I was more interested in seeing her life saved than mine.

Signs on the fifth floor indicated an orthopedics unit in one direction and psychiatric ward in another. Gimps and nutcases— I wondered who was more afraid of whom. A sour-faced aid at a nurse's station checked a chart and told me Liz was in the "other" wing.

She pointed. "Down the hall. Take a left and go all the way to the end."

I backtracked and ended up on the west side of the hospital. The hospital hush was broken by a random cry from somewhere up ahead, a moan from a room behind me, an angry diatribe from another. Through open doors lay patients whose illnesses and injuries were buried in the deep recesses of the brain, not the body, making diagnosis—and treatment—difficult. In one room, a man lay slack-jawed and expressionless, his body just a shell, a residence with no tenant. His family surrounded him, smiling and chatting as if he didn't exist.

Liz Tracey looked up at the sound of my knock, and quickly turned her face toward the window. A barrier like a bulletproof sheet of Plexiglas went up in the space between us.

"Happy Thanksgiving," I said.

Figuring the silence for an invitation, I stepped into the room. The other bed lay empty, the bedside cabinet devoid of personal effects. She had the semiprivate room to herself. I sat, putting myself in her peripheral vision. Even with tousled hair, too little sleep, and no shower, she was prettier in the daylight. She wore two cheery pastel-patterned hospital gowns, one with the traditional opening in the back, the other over it like a robe. They, along with her turned-up nose and lack of makeup, gave the effect of a girl home sick from school. She looked almost young enough to be my daughter.

"How are you feeling?"

She squirmed uncomfortably, unable to look at me. "How do you think I'm feeling? They've got me in the freaking psych ward, for God's sake, along with all the fruitcakes."

"Funny thing, isn't it? They figure if you try to kill yourself you must be a head case."

She zeroed in then, anger in her eyes. "Did you ever stop to think that maybe people who kill themselves are the sane ones? Look around you. Anything's better than this."

I put a hand on my knee to stop the trembling. "Maybe you feel like shit right now, the lowest of the low. Like there isn't one reason you can think of to go on. But people choose to accept far worse every day."

Her lip curled. "Nobody *chooses* to feel like this."

"Bullshit. Think of starving kids in Darfur or Ethiopia. They struggle to breathe every day, but choose life with each breath. What about women in Afghanistan? Or the Middle East? They practically have to get permission to take a piss." The words tumbled out of my mouth. I couldn't stop them. "Hell, think of Holocaust survivors and what they must have endured just to see one more day. Don't tell me death is better than this."

The words reached out and slapped her, leaving two bright pink spots high on her pale cheeks.

"Sorry." Heat crept into my own face. "I shouldn't have said that. I'm in no position to judge. Whatever you're feeling must seem just as bad to you."

Her mouth set in a grim line. "Jeez, why don't you tell me how you really feel?"

Gritting my teeth, I fought the urge to do just that. To let the anger surge to the surface and bubble out. To tell her how selfish she was being, how wrong and mean and petty it was to simply give up, leaving family and friends and coworkers behind to grieve, full of pain and confusion. I knew what that felt like.

I looked out the window. "Does your family know you're here?"

"Christ, no. They're the reason I'm here in the first place. Why would I tell them?"

"It's Thanksgiving. They probably want to know you're all right."

She twisted a strand of hair in her fingers. "I told you last night, they don't care. And my so-called boyfriend went back to Oregon for the weekend. Even the shrink they assigned me said I should distance myself."

I shrugged. "Just shows you shouldn't listen to me, I guess."

She rolled her eyes. Mentally, she seemed healthy enough. If you overlooked her little escapade of the night before, that is. But if people with suicidal thoughts weren't so good at hiding their intentions, there wouldn't be so many victims every year.

"Did I mention he told me his high-school sweetheart was going to be there?" she said. "He said he couldn't wait to see her. They've probably already screwed each other's brains out."

Ah, the boyfriend. "He sounds like a loser, anyway. You're probably better off."

She burst into tears, and reached for a tissue. "What are you *doing* here?" she managed between sobs. "Why can't you just leave me alone?"

"No one should be alone on holidays," I mumbled. "You damn near told me your whole life story last night. I figured that at least entitles me to find out if you're okay."

The sobs stopped, but tears still left wet tracks down her cheeks. "Well, you got what you wanted. You put me in this loony bin, where I can't hurt myself. God knows when they'll let me out. So, you can go now. You did your job."

"I can't leave. Not until you promise me that if you ever feel like killing yourself again, you'll call me first."

She stared at me, wide-eyed, tears forgotten. "Why? Why you?"

"You remind me of someone," I said. "Someone I knew." Someone whose suicide attempt had been all too successful.

Her head came up. "Who? Your girlfriend? Your wife?"

"No." I considered the question. I certainly hadn't come visiting to see if I could get a date, but my concern didn't feel exactly platonic, either.

"Look," I said, "a friend of mine was killed last night. I don't know...I started thinking if I hadn't been able to keep you from going off that bridge she might have been around a while longer. You know, maybe fate did some kind of swap—her life for yours."

Her lower lip quivered.

I went on before the waterworks began again. "No, wait. I'm not trying to guilt-trip you. She was very old, and probably didn't have a lot of time left, anyway. I didn't put that very well. It's just…I wonder if maybe I was supposed to be there last night. At the bridge."

"Like it was your destiny to save me?" She rolled her eyes.

I took a deep breath, let it out slowly. "Let's try this. Today's Thursday, so promise me you won't try to kill yourself over the weekend. Get through Sunday. See how you feel on Monday, all right? One day at a time."

Her eyes searched my face. She nodded hesitantly.

"Okay. That's good. That's wonderful. See? Now you can make plans, like what you're going to have for dinner. Jell-O or turkey?"

"You really are a strange man." She seemed to be deciding whether to smile or call security. "What were you doing out there last night, anyway?"

"I deliver newspapers."

She laughed then, but it sounded harsh, brittle, like cold metal that's reached its stress point. "'Neither snow nor rain nor…' what is it? Isn't it just mailmen who are supposed to be out in that stuff?"

I shook my head. "People expect their papers. On time, no less. You'd be surprised."

"That's it? That's all you do, deliver newspapers?"

Something in her tone, not the question, drew another flush of heat up from my neck into my face. My jaw clenched.

"Seems to me," I said softly, "it's about liking what you do."

She quickly turned her head and looked out the window at the barren sky. After a moment she spoke. "I didn't think there'd be any traffic out there that time of night."

"Someone's trying to tell you something."

Her eyes lazily met mine. "I don't believe in God."

"Karma, kismet, fate, then. Call it whatever you want. Maybe you're supposed to stick around a while and see what happens."

She idly wound a strand of hair around her finger and toyed with it. "Maybe."

6

It was time to leave Paris. Nothing new. Gagnon had spent far more time in foreign countries during the past twenty years than he had at home in his beloved city. That was part of the sacrifice he'd made for his country, to do what he believed in, to protect *la belle France*. He trudged up the steps from the metro station to the street a few blocks from his apartment.

Dawn still had not shown its face, and the city was as quiet as it would ever get. He relished this time of day, felt his most productive before the world awoke, when peacefulness gave him room to think. The dark hour before dawn also was the time most people were vulnerable, either in the throes of sleep or, if awake, groggy and irritable. An ideal time to strike if on the offensive, or retreat in defense.

He spotted the first surveillance team at the end of his block. They sat parked at the curb, facing away from him, car pointed down the street toward his pied-à-terre. Smoke drifted out the passenger window, something he would never tolerate among those who reported to him. It was the easiest way in the world to detect a stakeout. He stayed on the opposite side of the street, in the shadows, and didn't alter his pace. Keeping his head down in case they bothered to look, he could easily have been someone on the way to work early, or on his way home, for that matter.

Alert now, he took the long way around the block and found another team at the other end of his street. A park fronted the street behind his, one of the reasons he'd chosen the location. It gave him greater access, but he had no doubt that they'd stationed one man there, if not two.

Several blocks away he found an open patisserie. He ordered a croissant and a café au lait, and called the one man he still trusted, a man with aspirations to become president of France.

"*Oui?*" a sleepy voice answered.

"*Pardon, monsieur,*" Gagnon said. "I must have the wrong number."

He hung up and sipped his coffee. Five minutes later, his phone rang.

"You should not have called me at this hour," the man said.

"They're watching my apartment," Gagnon said.

After a pause, the man said, "Who?"

"I thought you could tell me. Two teams of two men in cars. There are probably others."

The man sighed. "We both know who, then. I didn't think they would try to contain you so quickly, but it's no longer safe for you here, *mon ami.*"

"I suspected as much. I'd already planned to leave the city."

"Where will you go?"

"Better you don't know, but I've heard Canada is pleasant this time of year."

Gagnon heard a quick intake of breath.

"Ah, well," the man said. "*Bon voyage.* Do you need anything before you go?"

"I have everything I require." Gagnon patted the pocket that contained the papers he'd taken from Baroche.

"*Bonne chance.*"

Gagnon finished his coffee and rose to go. He left some money on the table, looked down the street in both directions, and made up his mind.

Within half an hour, he'd gone halfway across the city to one of the hidey-holes he maintained for just this sort of occasion. There he cleaned up, changed clothes, and took all the cash he had on hand, amounting to several thousand euros. Half an hour after that, he stood outside an apartment building in another part of the city, not far from the Latin Quarter.

He'd planned on this eventuality for years, knowing sooner or later he'd have to retire, or terminate himself before enemies or someone in his own agency did it for him. He'd opened Swiss bank accounts, salting away savings and side benefits from the job. He'd scouted potential locations where he might operate unhindered and find a modicum of peace and anonymity. Some time ago he'd run his own likeness through facial recognition software, comparing it to passport photos in the MAEE's database. Five other men had features similar enough to his that the computer had indicated a possible match. After careful investigation of each, he'd picked one and had gotten a forged EU passport under the man's identity.

Alain Dufours left his apartment building at precisely 7:32 a.m., just as he did most days. As always, he carried a briefcase filled with his lesson plans for the day, students' papers, and a small lunch. Tucked under his arm he held a copy of *Paris Match*. He walked five blocks to the Cardinal Lemoine metro station and descended the stairs. Gagnon had no trouble following and no concerns that Dufours might see him. As expected, Dufours looked neither right nor left, but walked purposefully, eyes ahead.

Gagnon knew that Dufours would board the last car of the subway train and ride two stops to Cluny station, where he would ascend to the street. Once there, he would buy a boutonniere from a flower lady, walk another block to a café for *le petit déjeuner* of café au lait and brioche. From there, he would walk to his first class at the Sorbonne. Professor Dufours was a bachelor who took a holiday in Portugal every spring but had few other interests beyond the subject matter he taught: history. Dufours would do none of these things today.

Gagnon sidled through the morning crush of commuters on the metro platform until he was directly behind Dufours. Dufours took the paper from under his arm and held it in front of his face. Gagnon pushed forward, bumping Dufours as he leaned out over the edge pretending to look down the tunnel for a sign of an approaching train.

"*Pardon*," he murmured as he stepped back.

Familiar with the jostle of the crowded platform, Dufours grunted and kept reading. Gagnon pocketed the wallet he'd picked from Dufours's trousers and waited, calming his nerves with slow, even breathing. He felt the vibration of the approaching train before he heard it rumble in the tunnel. Dufours folded his newspaper and tucked it neatly under his arm. Gagnon had one shot. He had to time it perfectly. He watched the mouth of the tunnel grow brighter as the headlamps came closer, gauged the increasing noise level of the rubber-tired train.

Dufours took a step closer to the edge of the platform. As the crowd around him jockeyed for position, Gagnon squeezed in tightly behind Dufours and felt a breeze caress his face as the train pushed air through the tunnel. He put one hand at the small of the man's back and the other on his briefcase. The moment the lead car broke through the opening into the station, Gagnon gave him a shove. Instinctively, Dufours let go of the briefcase and put his hands out to avert disaster. But he barely got them as high as his waist before the train rushed by, crushing his rib cage, smashing his pelvis, and splitting his head open on the shattered windscreen.

The train's brakes squealed as the driver tried to stop more quickly. A woman screamed, then another. Gagnon ignored the bedlam that erupted on the platform, calmly walked to the *sortie*, and climbed the steps to the street with the professor's briefcase in hand.

* * *

I left Harborview to join a small group of people in an office building a block from Green Lake. On the way, I remembered the white tablet in the pocket of my trousers. I dug it out, popped it in my mouth, and swallowed it dry. When I arrived, most of the group was already sitting under sterile fluorescent lights in a cramped conference room. Bud Monroe, a small, balding man, poured coffee from an insulated pot sitting on a credenza against the wall and took a sip. Judging from his expression, the coffee had been there since the day before. He sat down next to Jim McNamara, who sprawled in his chair, head resting against the high back, pen in one hand idly doodling on a pad of paper in his lap.

Two women lined up on the opposite side of the table in stark contrast, sitting primly, attentively. The dark-haired one wearing nylon sweats and a fleece vest with a bottle of Dasani in front of her was Cathy Cooper. The blonde wearing black silk slacks, a cream-colored blouse, and a choker of pearls was Adria North. All of them had lost someone they knew, someone they loved, to suicide. As had I.

Jeri Nolan sat at the head of the table, writing notes in a Day-Timer, unmindful of our presence. Casually dressed in jeans and a turtleneck, she raked her fingers through a utilitarian haircut, leaving it essentially unchanged. To balance out the table, I sat at the other end. The group numbered a few short of its usual complement.

Jeri looked up as I eased into a chair, and glanced around the room as if surprised she wasn't alone. She laid her pen on the open notebook and said, "I'm sure you've all got turkey waiting somewhere if you haven't eaten already, so let's get started. Anyone have anything they'd like to share?"

I kept my mouth shut. I wasn't ready to talk about what had happened on the bridge. Instead of focusing on the give-and-take around the table, I kept thinking about Midge. I wanted to talk about the unexpected hole her death had left, not the monkey I'd fed by hauling Liz down from that bridge. Celebrating a life saved was fine, but it somehow felt wrong without first mourning, or at least acknowledging, Midge's passing.

Suddenly, the real reason Midge weighed heavily on me scuttled through my head like a roach startled by kitchen lights. I went looking for it. Donovan and Hiragawa thought I was good for her murder. They could put me at the scene close to the time she died. I'd been in her house before. Their CSI techs would find evidence to that effect. Not good. I combed through mental filing cabinets for other signs they might come across that pointed to my guilt—and found one.

Damn!

Jeri's voice brought me back to the present. "Has to be able to trust you…and as Adria pointed out, you don't want anyone to think you're his or her only source of support. Questions? If not, then let's move on."

After the meeting, Jeri pulled me aside with a worried look. She shuffled papers, head lowered, until the last straggler left.

"You okay?" she said. "You're quiet today."

"Yeah, fine."

She glanced down and winced. "Ouch. That must hurt. What happened?"

Eggplant and blueberry splotches mottled the skin on the back of my hand. "I punched out a cab driver last night."

She touched my arm. "Look, anger is natural, but you've got to find a better way to channel yours, Blake."

"Anger's pretty low on the list of emotions I wish I could manage better."

"Don't let it run your life, okay? Come to meetings more often."

"I'll try." I forced a smile.

* * *

Frank Shriver's name popped up on my cell phone's caller ID on the way home.

I flipped the phone open. "Happy Thanksgiving, Frank. Working today?"

"Back at you, buddy. When am I not working? You doin' all right? Had your turkey yet?" The questions came in rapid fire.

"Nope, but I'll probably get some chicken strips, fries, and hot sauce at work."

"Poor excuse for turkey, mashed, and gravy," he said.

"What's up, Frank?"

"I can't call to wish you a happy holiday?" He didn't wait for the answer he knew was coming. "Police logs say they had a jumper out on Interlaken early this morning, a young woman. They say someone talked her down."

"Not really your beat, is it, Frank?"

"No, but the kid who caught the story said your name came up. That was you?"

I sighed. He knew it was. "Yeah. Look, do me a favor. Keep my name out of it."

"You know, if you started reporting the news, instead of making it, things would be a whole lot easier on you."

"Seems to me whenever you call, it's you who wants something. Not that I don't appreciate the fact that *somebody* from my former life still talks to me." I paused. "I'm not asking much."

The line went silent for a moment. I watched the wiper blades smear the small, sad rain on the windshield. Not one vestige of the early morning snow remained.

"What the hell," he said, "the cops are withholding the name of the jumper, so I guess I can keep your name out of it, too. Details?"

"Yeah, sure." I gave him the gist of it, letting him know that Liz Tracey had panicked when the cops had arrived and jumped. I'd just gotten lucky.

Shriver asked a couple of follow-up questions, thanked me, and rang off. I wondered how long it would take before he sniffed out the fact that the cops had questioned me about the grisly scene at Midge's house.

7

With no snow or Liz Traceys to slow me down that night, and a good number of customers with vacation holds still in place, my route was shortened considerably. It was barely three in the morning when the yellow crime scene tape outside Midge's house loomed in my headlights, stirring gently in the barest whisper of night breeze. The car rolled to a stop at the curb, motor rumbling softly. I peered out the window at the dark, empty cottage. It looked unkempt and decrepit without the snow. I wondered who would fix the porch step now that Midge was gone, then realized it no longer made a damn bit of difference to Midge if it were fixed or not. New owners would fix it, or simply tear the house down and start anew.

A block away, I found a parking spot and hurried back to the house on foot, alert for signs of cops. I held a newspaper in one hand as a lame excuse just in case, and let myself in the front gate as I had hundreds of times before. Half obscured by the foliage of an azalea under the kitchen window sat the fake rock I'd gotten for Midge when she first explained her fear of being locked out. The spare key was still there, never used. With a quick check of the street to see if anyone was watching, I lifted the crime scene tape strung across the front steps with a forearm, ducked under, and let myself in.

Carefully avoiding the debris still littering the floor, I made my way through the living room. Using the little penlight on my key ring, I searched the small secretary first, rifling through the old bills and messy piles of notes and correspondence. Midge's cramped, tiny script covered empty envelopes and scraps of paper like graffiti with reminder notes, observations, lists, notions, and half-finished cards. Somewhere in the mess was a letter Midge had written—a codicil to her will indicating her wish to name me a beneficiary. I'd adamantly refused her generous offer, pleading with her each time she'd brought it up to put the thought out of her mind. But if she'd ignored me and gone ahead with it, a codicil would give the detectives motive, the third leg of the stool they'd kick out from under me once they'd strung a noose around my neck.

I pawed through the piles a second time, then moved to check the kitchen, and from there upstairs to more jumbled stacks on the dresser and nightstand in Midge's bedroom. After nearly an hour of fruitless searching, I gave up. Maybe I just wasn't having any luck, but it looked as if she'd finally sent it to an attorney or thrown it away—or the cops had it. The odds of a bad outcome twisted my stomach in a knot.

* * *

Reyna drove into DC early to avoid traffic and arrived at the National Archives a little after seven. It never occurred to her that personnel might not be there on a holiday weekend. She suspected that bosses there overloaded minions with work just like at ONI. She found street parking and used the researchers' entrance on Pennsylvania. The Research Center didn't open for two hours, but Reyna rang a night bell and roused a security guard. He peered at her through the door and pointed to the sign showing hours of operation. She plastered her ID to the glass and waited. The guard walked up to look at it more closely.

"Open up," Reyna said.

"What do you want?"

"I've got a priority classified investigation. I need in, now."

The guard opened the door a crack. Reyna pushed her way inside.

"Anybody here yet?" she said.

"Think I saw someone back in microfilm."

She headed for the reading room.

The guard stopped her. "Ma'am, you have to go through security and get a visitor's badge."

"You're serious."

"Dead serious, ma'am."

"There's no one here. Oh, all right."

She walked through the metal detector and waited. The guard got her a badge. She clipped it to her belt.

"You need a research card if you want to use a secure research room," the guard said.

"I'm not planning on it," Reyna said.

She hurried to the microfilm room. At a computer terminal she did a quick search of the records catalog, jotting down some notes on scrap paper. She looked around for a warm body. A thin man in his early thirties with an austere expression peered through wire-rimmed glasses at a microfilm reader across the room. She composed herself, putting on what she hoped was a friendly smile, and walked over.

"I'm sorry to interrupt, but could you help me?"

He looked up and his eyes narrowed. "How'd you get in?"

"Security let me in. I have a research card." She held it up. "Look, I know you're busy or you wouldn't be here at this hour on a long weekend. I've got the same problem—boss wants a report by nine and I got a priority TS/SCI investigation handed to me yesterday. So, if you could—"

"Whatever it is, you'll have to submit a request to have whatever you want pulled. First pull time this morning is ten."

She glanced at his name tag. "McCann, is it?"

"Keith."

"Keith, do me a favor. Please. It'll take two minutes, and I'll owe you one. Whatever you want." She waved the slip of scrap paper.

"Two minutes?"

"I promise."

"Fine." He pushed his chair back and got up. "What are you looking for?"

"RG Twenty-Four: records of the Bureau of Naval Personnel."

"You want someone's service record. What's the name?"

"Selim Woodworth."

"Approximate dates of service?"

She shrugged. "I don't know."

"Right. Two minutes." He frowned and headed for the stacks. She trailed behind and watched him search for the file. He pulled a roll of microfilm and took it back to an empty reader. He threaded it and whirred through the footage. It took a minute before he slowed the film and scanned the images. He stopped it, then advanced a few frames and stopped again.

"Here you go," he said. "Selim Woodworth. Appointed midshipman in eighteen thirty-eight. Resigned in eighteen fifty. Served again during the Civil War."

"There must be some mistake. I received a command signal to alert him to this investigation. He's supposed to be aboard the *Anita* in the Pacific Fleet."

McCann scrolled through the film and stopped on another frame. "Pacific Squadron, not Fleet. Back then, anyway. Reported to the USS *Warren* in eighteen forty-seven in Monterey, California."

"You've got to be kidding." Reyna glanced at her notes. "Okay, look, NHC says they don't keep deck logs, but you do. Can you get me the logs of the *Anita*?"

"Look, I—"

"Whatever you want. Name it."

"Dinner at The Palm."

"A date?" Reyna winced. McCann wasn't unattractive, but the whole dating thing hadn't really worked out for her. Her career had always come first, which was why she was still single.

"Okay, fine. Just do it," she said.

McCann searched the archives online and went back into the stacks. Several minutes later he came back with another roll of microfilm. He hunted through it for close to ten minutes, frowned, and rewound the film.

"Problems?" Reyna said.

"Nothing I can't handle," he said.

He disappeared into the stacks and came back a few minutes later with another roll. He ran it through the reader. After a while he sighed and pushed away from the screen.

"Either the logs don't exist, or they were lost. We don't have them."

"You're sure?"

"I'm sure. Look, the sources I checked not only don't show a record of the logs, they don't even show a ship of that name."

"Impossible."

"Could be the *Anita* wasn't a navy ship. Back then, might've been a merchant vessel commandeered for a time by the navy. If it wasn't commissioned, there'd be no log on record."

"Damn. That's no help."

"You still owe me dinner." He grinned.

* * *

I dreamed of flying. I floated effortlessly in a blank gray sky over Elliott Bay, the same vacant sky outside Liz Tracey's hospital room window. A ferry silently glided past on the still, black water below, carving a trail of white in the surface. I heard the distant

51

rumble of thunder, another oddity in the Pacific Northwest, unlike the storms from my midwestern childhood. The thunder grew closer, louder, more insistent, pounding in my head.

"Open up! Police!"

The voice, accompanied by more hammering, roused me fully. I'd fallen asleep in my clothes again, an open book lying on my chest, the lamp next to my bed still burning. I rolled out of bed, book sliding to the floor, and stumbled toward the door. When it swung open, Donovan's raised fist greeted me, poised to rattle the hinges again. He let his arm fall slowly to his side. He'd replaced the leather jacket with a dove-gray sport coat over a snow-white button-down oxford dress shirt. Charcoal slacks and a different but equally pricey-looking pair of loafers completed the ensemble.

"Good morning, Detective," I mumbled. "I think."

Hiragawa stood to one side several feet behind Donovan. Her casual slacks and shirt under a fleece vest adhered more closely to the Seattle sense of fashion. A patrolman stood farther back, one hand resting on his holstered gun. Hiragawa pulled an empty hand from behind her back, casually resting it on a hip, face giving no indication of having been on heightened alert. I acknowledged her with a nod.

"We'd like you to come down to headquarters with us to answer a few more questions."

Donovan's statement brought my attention back to him. He smiled politely, but there was an edge to his voice and tension in the muscles along his jaw.

"Do you know what time it is?" I said, covering a yawn with my hand.

"About nine thirty."

"No, I mean do you have any idea what time it is?" I rubbed my eyes. "I just got off work a couple of hours ago."

"Sorry," he said gruffly.

I didn't move.

"It's important," he said.

Hiragawa leaned around him. "Please. We'd like you to come with us."

I sighed. "Wait here. I'll get my shoes."

He watched me slip on a pair of running shoes and take a coat from a hook by the door, and he moved back as I stepped onto the porch, closing the door behind me.

I patted my pockets. "Hang on a sec."

I went back in and lifted my wallet from the table next to the bed. I combed my fingers through my hair and fished in a pocket of the coat for a mint or piece of gum, already longing for a hot shower and a chance to brush my teeth. Sleep, apparently, wasn't in the cards, but I gave the two cops one last shot.

"You know, I comprehend things better when I get in a solid six or seven hours."

Donovan ignored the hint. "Got everything this time?" He stepped off the porch.

"We're sorry we woke you," Hiragawa said, falling in behind me as I followed Donovan around the house. The uniform brought up the rear. I doubted she'd been truthful, but at least she made an effort.

I tried another tack. "Any chance of stopping for decent coffee on the way?"

"I'm sure we can rustle up a cup for you downtown," Donovan said over his shoulder.

As we rounded the corner of the house, my landlord, Peter, stepped onto the front porch, holding the door close to block the cold air from entering the house. He watched us parade silently toward the curb, an unasked question on his face. I raised my hands as if to say I didn't know what they wanted. I tried not to think about it. If I started, I'd end up with an endless loop in my head that would provide no answers. It would just make me jittery and look even guiltier to the cops. Peter nodded and backed into the house, pulling the door shut.

Donovan skirted a couple of puddles, but didn't give the fancy clothes any other special consideration. They flattered him, accentuating broad shoulders and slim hips, and he wore them without self-consciousness. No runway turns or macho posturing. He opened the rear door of an unmarked sedan at the curb, a patrol car double-parked next to it.

"Nice threads." I put a hand out to touch his sleeve, eyes attracted to the soft gray fabric.

"Hey! Hey!" He stepped back quickly, slapping my hand away.

Hiragawa fell into a tense crouch and reached for her weapon.

I thrust my hands in the air. "Whoa, sorry! Just admiring the coat. Honest. Shit, sorry."

Donovan examined me through narrowed eyes as the uniform hustled up jangling a pair of cuffs. Donovan waved him off, and Hiragawa slowly straightened.

"The Rack," he said, referring to Nordstrom's discount outlet. "You oughta try it. Might have a few things in your size."

"Looks well made." I shifted my weight awkwardly, hands held high.

"Nice stuff just *feels* better, you know?" He took in my worn jeans and coat.

"I'm on a budget."

He jerked his head to the side. "Get in."

Neither cop spoke again until we were inside SPD headquarters downtown, and then only to direct me to a small interview room up on the seventh floor. Donovan found me a paper cup of what might have once been coffee, and then they let me stew. My juices had already started running, the fear that they'd learned of my scouting mission at Midge's—or worse, the codicil—dampening my shirt.

Hiragawa shuffled in ten minutes later, head bent, arms around a notebook and file folder. I half expected her to bow a greeting. Reminded myself not to get sucked in by her politeness.

"Sorry to keep you waiting," she said. "I had to return a couple of calls. Detective Donovan will be here in a minute." She paused and looked toward the door as if willing it to open. She gave up and turned back to me. "You all right? Want more coffee?"

I shook my head. "This will either keep me awake or kill me. But thanks."

She didn't smile. She opened her mouth as if to say something, then sat across from me and leaned back instead, folding her arms across her chest. My watch ticked off another sixty slow seconds before the door opened and Donovan entered juggling a briefcase, notepad, and manila file folders. He dumped it all on the table, shuffled it into piles, and sat heavily.

"Did Detective Hiragawa tell you why we want to talk to you?" he said.

"I assumed you wanted to ask more questions about Midge Babcock."

He lifted his chin in response, then gestured to Hiragawa. "Why don't you start?"

She leaned forward. "We're trying to figure out what happened to your friend. It would help if we could pin down time of death, so we're trying to get a sense of who might have seen her last and when. Would you mind telling us again what happened the other night?"

I thought carefully before answering. "I told you, I didn't see her the other night."

They'd taken notes; they knew this.

"That's okay," Donovan said. "Just walk us through it again."

Hiragawa threw him a look. "Take it slow," she said. "Try to remember everything you can, no matter how minor it seems."

My palms were sweating. I gave them the story one more time, starting at the warehouse, driving through the snow, the holdup on the bridge, delivering Midge's paper, trying the doorknob...

Tell them.

"Now that I think of it, I had a strange feeling when I got to her house. An impression..." *Too late. They'll never believe it.* I shook my head. "Never mind."

"No, go on," Hiragawa said. "It could be important."

A sympathetic expression on her face helped make up my mind. "I saw footprints in the snow up the walk. Faint, almost filled in. I think that's why I checked the doorknob."

Donovan frowned. "Why didn't you tell us this earlier?"

"It was an impression, a feeling. I know I saw them, but..."

Donovan looked up at the ceiling and sighed. Hiragawa stole a glance at him, gave me a smile meant to be reassuring. I should have known better. Morning meds would have helped. They hadn't given me the chance. I rubbed the tops of my thighs, hoping to feel the outline of a spare dose. Nothing. *Careful.*

"That's good," she said. "Impressions are good. What happened next?"

I continued, telling them about driving the rest of my route. Having a cup of coffee later, and minding my own business until Charlie and Craig found me and drove me to Midge's house. I included approximate times as well as I could recall them at each major point along my route that night. *That night,* as if Midge had been murdered in the distant past, not just a day earlier. Donovan scribbled in his notebook while I spoke. Hiragawa gave me her undivided attention.

"When's the last time you remember seeing the vict— Midge?" she asked when I finished.

I stared at a wall, a gut feeling admonishing me of the importance of getting this right. "Three nights ago. Well, mornings, I guess, to you. Early Tuesday. We had tea. Talked about flowers, global warming, kids' lack of manners, stuff like that."

"You're sure," Hiragawa said.

Donovan leaned forward to hear my answer.

"Sure, I'm sure." The room felt warm, stuffy. They didn't seem to notice. "I told you we talked once a week or so. Maybe more."

Hiragawa frowned and thumbed a page in the notebook on her lap. "Actually, you said you saw her 'every once in a while.' "

"Once in a while, once a week…what's the difference?"

The temperature in the room rose. My face felt flushed. The clucking sound echoed in the back of my head. *Midge had asked me if I could recommend a good lawyer.* The cooing didn't diminish. *No, that wasn't it. When was that, anyway? A month ago? Longer? Around the same time she mentioned putting me in her will?*

"We're just trying to get a sense of your relationship with the deceased," Hiragawa said evenly. "You say you were friends, but then you say she just wanted company. Which is it? For all we know, you're a scam artist who butters up old ladies and rips them off."

I shook my head no until she finished, stomach clenching at the thought they'd found the letter. "Not even close. Look, maybe I'm embarrassed to admit that a woman old enough to be my great-granny is one of the few friends I've got right now. Or had, anyway. But that's all we were, friends. We both needed someone to talk to, so that's what we did. We talked. I even bought her a box of tea to replace what I drank. I brought her cake, too. Those little petits fours from the bakery. She was old-fashioned that way. I kind of liked it. It reminded me of when I went to my grandmother's on Sunday afternoons as a kid. You know, all dressed up, using our best manners—or else Pop would threaten to take a belt to us later."

I turned to Donovan. "You have a grandmother like that?"

He shook his head. I looked at Hiragawa. She said nothing, but something flickered across her face. Recognition? Discomfort? I figured Donovan for having a fusty Irish grandmother, but maybe it was Hiragawa's elderly relatives who were sticklers for tradition.

"So you were just friends," Hiragawa said, interrupting the mental digression. "And you were there Tuesday morning, talking and having tea." She saw me nod, turned to Donovan and murmured, "That could account for the prints."

He leaned in closer to her and raised an eyebrow. "All of them?"

"Fingerprints?" I said. "Of course my prints are in Midge's house. I just told you, I was there. Many times. Tuesday morning, even."

Donovan's head moved up and down. "Right. You said that. Tuesday morning. See, the thing is, there were teacups and plates on the drain board next to the sink. Unwashed. With your prints on them."

"She was elderly," I said, my mind racing furiously. "Not the best housekeeper anymore. In fact, I usually washed up after visiting, but she told me to leave it that morning. She insisted. So, maybe she never got around to washing the dishes. Maybe she just didn't feel like it. Maybe—" *Shut up!*

They exchanged a quick glance. I couldn't read a thing on either face. A growl erupted from my stomach, the burnt coffee adding an extra kick to the churning acid.

"Tell us more about these teas," Donovan said abruptly. "When did they start?"

"About a year ago."

"Her idea or yours?"

"I told you—I told Detective Hiragawa—she was waiting at the door one day when I brought the paper. She invited me in."

He looked skeptical. "Why'd you accept?"

"She seemed lonely. People ignore old folks. Like they're no longer useful. I had some things I wanted to get off my chest." I shrugged. "It seemed like a good idea." I stared at the memories that hung somewhere in the middle distance between us. "I liked her. She was a sweet woman, a real lady." Donovan's face came back into focus. "She didn't deserve what happened."

"No, she didn't," he said. "What was it you wanted to get off your chest?"

I tensed. "I'd rather not say."

He leaned forward, eyes turning hard as coal. "But you shared it with her, with Midge."

"It's personal." I sat back, crossing my arms. "Nothing you need to know."

"Anything can help," Hiragawa said. "It's okay to tell us."

I shook my head. "If I thought it would help, I'd tell you, but it's got nothing to do with this. It's no big deal. I'd just rather not talk about it."

Donovan held the hard gaze a moment longer, then sighed and pushed back from the table. "Tuesday, right? Tea and—what was it? Petits fours?"

My gut tightened and sweat dripped down my sides. I wondered if they could tell. I'd missed something. My eyes flitted nervously from table to notebook to wall, synapses in my brain firing like a string of firecrackers.

"No, wait," I said, my voice a little too loud in the small room. "Tuesday we had cake. White with chocolate frosting and raspberry filling. The store didn't have any petits fours. It was the only cake left in the case."

"Funny you should suddenly remember that." Donovan reached into the briefcase and pulled out a sealed plastic evidence bag. He held it up so I could see. A black-handled kitchen knife, a chef's knife, weighted the bottom of the bag. The dry, brown substance coating the ten-inch blade didn't remotely resemble chocolate.

Donovan watched my face. "Strange coincidence," he said. "The only good prints on this just happen to match yours."

8

Reyna went into the office early. After fortifying herself with her third cup of coffee of the day, she got online and ferreted out every scrap of information on Woodworth she could find. The NHC website had more information on the man than that twit Jones had volunteered, and she found other sources with references to some aspect of Woodworth's life or career. She spent an hour assembling bits and pieces into a sketchy bio. One piece stood out. For two years after Woodworth's assignment to the Pacific Squadron, the navy had no record of him.

"Chase!"

Startled, Reyna saw Captain Todd Farley lean through his office doorway.

"Yes, Captain." She glanced at her watch and reached for the report on her desk. "Coming."

A moment later, she placed the report on Farley's desk. She stepped back and waited.

Farley looked up from the papers on his desk. "Something else, Commander?"

"Yes, sir. Yesterday a command signal came through NHC for a priority SSBI on a civilian, a professor at the University of Washington. It was marked TS/SCI."

Farley frowned. "Nothing unusual about that."

"What's unusual, sir, is that the signal included an order to inform an officer who's been dead for more than a century."

"No mistake? It's not a duplicate name or something?"

"No, sir. I checked. The ship the officer served on also dates back to the same period. Problem is, there's no record of the ship. At least no record of its activities."

Farley rubbed his chin. "So, it's an old command signal."

"Why would it still be in effect after all this time?"

"I wouldn't worry about it, Chase. Go ahead and conduct the SSBI, see if anything turns up."

"Sir, this predates ONI by several decades. The agency wasn't even in existence back then. Someone went to an awful lot of trouble to make sure we'd be alerted if anyone inquired about this ship."

"But there aren't any records, you said. So the same someone must have gone to equally great lengths to make sure nobody could find out what the ship was up to back then."

Reyna still felt uncomfortable. "It just seems pretty odd—"

"What were the command signal instructions?"

"Check out the caller—the professor—and alert the ship's commanding officer."

"You can't alert a dead guy. So do the background check and you're covered."

"Yes, sir."

"Anything else?"

"No, sir."

"Then we both have work to do."

* * *

Gagnon drove up the entrance road to a circle in front of the massive complex in Montréal's Cartierville neighborhood. The old convent in Vieux-Montréal had long since been torn down and turned into a small urban park. The religious order was big business now, with chapters all over the world running charitable works such as hospitals, schools, and shelters with operating budgets in the billions. The multistoried buildings in front of him housed the administrative offices for all those programs along with the Montréal motherhouse, a retirement home, and the order's archives. He parked and pulled his collar up against a cold wind as he hurried inside.

"Sister Constance Monfils, *s'il vous plaît*," he said to the receptionist.

"*Bien sûr, monsieur*," she said. "Is she expecting you?"

"*Mais oui*. Tell her Alain Dufours is here."

After a short wait, a small woman in a smartly tailored charcoal suit emerged from a hallway into the reception area. She wore her steel-gray hair short. Gagnon had expected an old woman in a wimple and habit.

"Professeur Dufours?" She greeted him politely, but there was no warmth in her eyes. "Come with me, please."

Gagnon followed her down several hallways and up a stairwell to an office in the bowels of the building.

"Excuse me for not taking the elevator," she said. "It might be faster, but I prefer to stretch my legs. One gets so sedentary in an office."

He murmured his assent, but remained silent until they reached a small office.

"I was surprised to receive your call so soon," she said, motioning to an empty chair.

"Monseigneur Villards indicated it was a matter of utmost urgency, and I happened to be here on vacation."

"You are acquainted with the Cardinal?"

He shook his head, watching her closely for signs of suspicion. He saw only curiosity. "His assistant, Père Baroche. We were schoolmates. A long time ago."

"And what can I do for you and the Cardinal, monsieur?"

"The cardinal is concerned, given the nature of the missive he received, that public health may be endangered."

"Surely that's not possible after all this time."

"Stranger things have happened, *non*? The Church can't be insensitive these days, what with all its other problems. You're familiar with the legend?"

"It is no legend. We have been trying to get Sophie Clare beatified for a century. The Vatican keeps telling us we lack evidence of her miracle."

"So, you have nothing here that points to where this evidence might be?"

"All we have here are letters from Sister Marguerite to the archbishop of Montréal at the time, Monseigneur Cloutier." She waved at a sheaf of parchment paper bound with ribbon on her desk. "I took the liberty of borrowing these from the archives."

"May I?"

She inclined her head. He reached for the letters and glanced at them quickly before setting them down again.

"You've read them, of course."

She nodded. "They reveal nothing. Only that she undertook a mission for Cloutier and discharged it faithfully."

Gagnon mused for a moment. "May I ask what prompted your call, sister?"

"To Monseigneur Delacroix? There has been a standing order here for the past one hundred and fifty years to inform our presiding archbishop of any inquiries into Sister Marguerite's journey if they reference the mission assigned her by Cloutier in any way."

Gagnon waved impatiently. "Yes, yes. What specifically?"

"A woman called. From Seattle. Raving about why we weren't doing more to help the chapter out there. That the order is sitting on untold millions of dollars in land, so why weren't we lifting a finger to help while the city takes it away from the sisters."

"I don't understand."

"Neither did I," she said. "But she said that she had proof."

"Of what?"

"Of a meeting between Sister Marguerite and a man named Woodworth."

"She said nothing else?"

"Little that made any sense."

"So, all we have is confirmation that Sister Marguerite's letters were truthful. Perhaps your chapter in Seattle has records that could shed light on the mystery?"

"It would have turned up long before this."

"I think it's worth a trip to find out."

"Perhaps, but you may be wasting your time. The convent moved out of the city years ago to a larger property across Lake Washington. The order converted the original building to a women's shelter."

"Even so," Gagnon said. "What was the name of woman who called?"

"Babcock," Sister Constance said. "Midge Babcock."

* * *

They arrested me and put me in a holding cell after two more hours of questions. Three hours later, Hiragawa offered me a courtesy call, usually reserved until after prisoners were processed. I used it to reach Chance Reno, my landlord Peter's partner, and ask if he'd take over my paper route for a couple of nights. He'd done it before, knew the route. And he didn't mind, or so he said, since he was a night owl, anyway. I asked him to call a kid I knew from Jeri Nolan's organization to fill in for me at the restaurant over the weekend—with an offer to double the kid's pay—and let the owner know. The cops didn't give me time to say more. Hiragawa let me buy a soda and bag of chips from a vending machine on the way back to the little holding room.

At the beginning of third watch, the detectives finally had a uniform drive me to the sally port at King County jail across the street. Before putting me in a yet another holding pen, bigger this time, a county corrections officer handed me a paper sack containing some sort of sandwich and chips. Hungry as I was, the smell in the cell turned my stomach. My two cell mates, a couple of vagrants, reeked of alcohol. The cheap booze did little to mask their body odor. I caught one of them eyeing the sack and tossed it to him.

The prosecuting attorney's office had time—seventy-two hours' worth—to decide whether to file charges. Arresting me on a Friday meant I couldn't get a lawyer to push for an arraignment and bail hearing until Monday, not that I could afford legal representation, anyway. And it gave the cops the advantage of time to gather more evidence, as if they didn't have enough. The odds of relegating the whole incident to a simple misunderstanding ranked right up there with Seattle fielding another NBA team anytime soon.

They processed me, took pictures and prints, then put me back into holding. Not long after, the county inventoried my belongings and issued me a wristband and an orange jumpsuit that was four inches too short in the sleeves and legs. From there I went into another holding tank with several other prisoners until we were sorted and assigned cells. Those who'd committed lesser, nonviolent crimes waited for court appearances in large cells with up to eighteen beds on lower floors. I rode up to a higher floor, guards leading me to a semiprivate cell. It wasn't anything like a hotel concierge floor. Go figure. My stomach grumbled, threatening to eat itself, and my head felt as if caught in a vise.

A skinny Latino kid on the top bunk watched me with narrowed eyes as they locked the cell door behind me. He mistook my pained expression for something else. Sitting up abruptly, he pushed the sleeves of his jumpsuit above the elbows, revealing colorful tattoos up and down both arms. Then he let loose with a torrent of Spanish, and followed it up with, "Don't fuck with me. I got friends in here, *pendejo*."

I didn't need the limited Mexican slang learned in the restaurant kitchen to figure out he'd called me half a dozen unmentionable names. I ambled over to the bunk for a little stare-down, keeping my expression neutral, maintaining eye contact long enough to see hesitation on his face. I had no doubt about his ability to stick a shiv in me if he felt threatened. But I wanted him to think twice before he tried.

"*No problema.*" I eased myself into the lower bunk.

The *problema* would be lasting the weekend without letting the impulse to clock the kid get the better of me. In the meantime, I had a lot of time to think about how to get the cops to look at another theory for Midge's murder. One that didn't involve me.

* * *

Chief Warrant Officer Janet Tolliver stood at Reyna's desk with her coat on, ready to go home for the day. Reyna leaned back and glanced at a clock on the wall, noting that the weekend had started at least an hour earlier for most people. She tucked a stray strand of hair behind her ear and wondered how Tolliver could still look so good—uniform perfectly creased, makeup flawless, hair in place—at the end of a difficult day.

"I have that SSBI report you asked for," Tolliver said.

"Thank you, Chief," Reyna said. "Top line?"

Tolliver shrugged. "He's clean. Teaches history. Tenured. Not a single complaint in his file. Apparently well liked by students and faculty alike. Looks like he was just doing some research and rang the wrong bell."

"Obscure topic, don't you think?"

"His area of expertise is the Pacific Northwest. You tell me."

"Thanks, Janet. Have a nice weekend."

"You, too."

Reyna fingered the report as she watched Tolliver turn away. She stopped the chief before she reached the door.

"Janet? Do me a favor. Check out the professor's recent phone records and financials. Let's be absolutely sure there's nothing going on. I don't believe in coincidence."

9

Gagnon passed the house a second time, from the opposite direction, and parked two blocks away. The crime scene tape was a deterrent, but not insurmountable. More disturbing was what it signified. And that was? Gagnon put all conjecture out of his mind. He needed to find out what had happened and why, quickly.

He circumnavigated the house on foot from two different directions before closing in on the rear of the property. A dog in one of the neighboring houses barked. Gagnon froze and heard a muted yell from its owner. With a few halfhearted woofs, the dog quieted, and Gagnon crept across the yard to a rear window. The casements were old, rotting in some places, and thick with several coats of paint. Using a thin-bladed knife, he pried the point up between the frames and popped the flimsy lock. He raised the window, forcing it noisily at one point, and paused until the night sounds reassured him no one had noticed.

After climbing over the sill, Gagnon stood still in the empty house, letting it talk to him, taking in the scents of liniment, camphor, lavender, and mildew, and the sounds of a ticking clock, a mouse scrabbling in the walls. He moved silently on crepe-soled shoes from one room to another to get a feel for the layout, noting the wear patterns in the oriental rugs in the living room and the arms of the chairs. He noted the crusted, flaking patch of blood on the kitchen floor, the dark splatters elsewhere, the faint scent of iron that still lingered. The old woman had been killed, but not without a fight. Did that mean someone else knew? Or had she been a victim of the kind of random violence so prevalent in big American cities?

Gagnon worked quickly, fearing that he was already steps behind. Methodically, he searched every room, starting with the woman's bedroom, moving next to the desk in the living room, and spending less time on the others. He needed to know what the Babcock woman had learned about Sister Marguerite's mission. Why had she called? He found nothing, just the normal bills, letters, and scribbles of an elderly person who held on to too many memories.

* * *

Monday morning, guards put me in handcuffs, leg irons, and chains and escorted me, shuffling in county-issued flip-flops, across the sky bridge to the courthouse. On the way in, the guards removed the restraints before sending me through a metal detector.

"It'll go off," I said.

A bailiff next to the X-ray screening machine grinned. "Then empty your pockets."

One of the guards gave me a shove. "Step through," he growled.

As I stumbled into the frame the metal detector beeped wildly, sending guards and bailiffs into high alert. I put my hands on my head and stepped clear. Two bailiffs each roughly grabbed an arm, twisted them up behind my back and shoved me up against a steel table, bending me over. One kicked my legs apart, steel-toed shoes banging a tattoo on my ankles, while the other squeezed cuffs onto my wrists.

"Whadya got?" someone asked loudly.

"Artificial hip," I said through clenched teeth.

The bailiff with the cuffs leaned down close to my ear. "Don't be a wiseass."

He brought a knee up into my gut, the move hidden from the guards by the man behind me.

I grunted and sucked in air.

"There's a card in my wallet," I said. My gut bubbled hotly with more than pain.

"Aw, for chrissake," said one of the guards. "That doesn't do us much good, now does it?"

"Wouldn't do any good even if you had it," said a bailiff. "Medical card, doctor's note, doesn't matter. It isn't good for shit." He stood up to look at me over the machine.

Another bailiff ran a wand up and down my sides. It squealed over my left hip.

"Stand up," he said.

The other bailiff roughly pulled me upright. I jerked my arm out of his grasp and stared him down. The first one tilted his head, listening to the start and stop of the electronic screech as he passed the wand over my left hip. He tucked it under one arm and patted me down. I stared at the X-ray screener, ignoring the hands roaming over me indecently. He stared back, unblinking.

"He's clean," said the one with the wand. "Must be true."

He set the wand on the table, fastened shackles around my ankles, and wrapped a chain around my waist. The other officer unlocked one bracelet and recuffed my hands in front while the first threaded a chain from my wrists down to my leg shackles. They walked me like a dog on a leash to a holding cell adjacent to one of the courtrooms. I waited on a steel bench with a half dozen other orange-clad county guests. Gang symbols and graffiti covered the walls, scratched into the cement block with cuffs and chains. I tipped my head back, closed my eyes, and concentrated on my breathing until someone called my name.

Inside the courtroom, a harried public defender barely looked up when the bailiff delivered me. He shuffled papers and file folders, finally pulled an arrest report out of a stack on the table, and compared the name to a list of scheduled appearances for the day. He glanced at me and craned his neck as if looking for someone else.

He held up the arrest report. "This you?"

I leaned in for a closer look. "Yes."

"You're pleading not guilty." He didn't ask. "I'll see what I can do about bail, but don't hold your breath."

"Damn straight I'm pleading not guilty. I didn't do it."

"Look, we can get into the specifics of your defense later. Right now I—"

The clerk called the next case number, interrupting him, and read the charges—second-degree murder. The prosecuting attorney introduced himself to the judge.

The judge turned to me. "You're the named defendant?"

"Yes, sir."

"Do you have representation?"

"No, Your Honor."

"You have no problem with the court appointing you an attorney?"

Before I could answer, the door at the back of the courtroom opened and a woman's voice rang out. "Sorry I'm late, Your Honor. Molly McHugh, representing the defendant."

A very tall, striking woman with copper hair cut in a bob, briefcase in hand, covered the ground to the front with just a few steps. A balding man in a gray suit trailed half a step behind. She towered over most of the men in the room, even in sensible heels. Her tailored black suit showed off an athletic body to best advantage, the skirt short enough to show off a half mile of legs without being immodest. The red hair framed a strong, oblong face with wide mouth, thin nose, and wide-set eyes the color of cornflowers. My pulse felt a little rapid—she'd always had that effect on me.

"The defendant just indicated he doesn't have representation," the judge said.

"He does now," she said, squeezing past me. Her colleague slid into the gallery row behind us. "If I could have a moment to confer, Your Honor?"

The judge nodded.

She turned to the public defender. "Sorry, Jed. Hope you don't mind."

The lawyer slid my file in front of her, sat down, and pawed through another folder.

"Molly, what are you doing here?" I whispered, face suffusing with heat. "You don't do criminal law."

She looked me dead in the eye, those blue headlights turned on bright. Keeping her voice low, she said, "I can handle a bail hearing. Did you do it or not?"

"What do you think? Absolutely not." I heard enough conviction in my voice to convince twelve of my peers, but her eyes searched mine for a second or two before she nodded.

"Okay, we'll get you out of here." She turned to the judge. "We're ready, Your Honor."

"Let's get on with it, then."

The clerk recorded Molly and her firm as my legal representatives; the judge asked for my plea, which I answered with a resounding "not guilty"; Molly asked for a date for a first hearing to air some motions, and we got around to bail. The PA noted the viciousness of the crime and asked for remand. Molly moved for PR. I could have used some good public relations about then, but personal recognizance was just as good. A few people still recognized me by name, but going unnoticed at my size isn't easy, anyway. The PA countered with a million dollars in bail. Molly hushed me by putting a hand on my arm.

"My client's in no position to raise that kind of money," she said.

"Is this true?" the judge asked me.

"She should know, sir," I said. "She got all my assets in the divorce."

The clerk quickly covered his mouth with his hand. The judge took it in stride. "Bail is set at three hundred and fifty thousand, cash or bond. The defendant will surrender his passport. Unless there's anything else, we're done."

Molly rose and gave my arm a squeeze. "I'll have you out before the end of the day, but we need to talk. I'll have a bailiff bring you to a conference room. See you in a few minutes."

With that, she breezed by, swinging the heavy briefcase as if it contained only one case file, and an easy one to boot.

* * *

Reyna hated Mondays. The world didn't take the weekend off. Work accumulated for two days while she wasn't even there, filling her inbox. She spent most of the morning catching up, but found it slow going. Her mind was elsewhere. Though she'd tried over the weekend, Reyna couldn't get the command signal out of her head. Someone had gone to a lot of trouble to protect Woodworth, or at least make sure he'd be aware of any inquiries about his activities. More specifically, activities while he was in command of a ship that didn't exist, at least not officially, according to the navy.

First chance she got after lunch, she renewed her search for the *Anita*. When she came up empty beyond the few facts she already had, she sat back and thought. She was a good investigator, and an even better analyst. So she started over and pretended

Woodworth was her subject. She reviewed her notes and ran another online search to see if she could glean anything more. When she finished, she wasn't much closer to an answer, but she'd narrowed things down a bit. Whatever had gone on aboard the *Anita* had happened between 1848 and 1850, when Woodworth tendered his resignation to run for office in California.

Reyna still couldn't figure out what the navy thought was important enough to create a the command signal for in the first place, never mind why it remained in effect so long after Woodworth's death. Time for a history lesson. She needed to learn more about what had been happening in California during that period, as well as what was going on here in DC. And she knew just where to start.

* * *

"How'd you know I got arrested?" I asked ten minutes later.

"Peter called me," Molly said. "Chance never would have given you up. Thank goodness Peter has some sense."

"You shouldn't be here, Molly. You've got your own clients to worry about, not to mention other partners who probably aren't too happy you took on your ex as a pro bono project."

"Who said anything about pro bono? You'll get a bill like everyone else."

"I can take care of my own mess." Maybe it was pride or simply embarrassment that my ex-wife had come riding to my rescue, but I'd already decided that my only way out of trouble was proving my innocence. Donovan and Hiragawa had no reason to consider another suspect. They had me. Vanishing footprints in melting snow wouldn't make much of a defense. Even Molly and the criminal attorneys in her firm, as good as they were, would struggle to defend me given the evidence. I wouldn't allow her to take on that burden.

"Is this your mess?" Her eyes bored into mine.

"Well, no. I just meant that I should take care of my own problems. Let the public defender—Jed, was it?—let him have it."

"Why do you have to be so stubborn? Did it ever occur to you that maybe I care about what happens to you?"

I tried to come up with a suitable answer, chewing on something that tasted like resentment. She went on before I found the words.

"This *is* a real mess. We were lucky to get bail, and luckier still that Judge Johnson set it generously low."

"Low? Three hundred fifty grand is *low*? Speaking of which, did you figure out how to change the setting on the water heater? I could come over and take a look. If you want."

"Damn it, Blake, focus! The PA wanted to file aggravated murder charges against you." She saw my blank look. "That's a capital offense, Blake, death penalty stuff. He still might."

"Why?"

A cloud darkened her pale, freckled skin. "You can't be that naïve. Maybe because the county prosecutor is still pissed he couldn't charge you with embezzlement? He still thinks you should do time for that business with Rafe's campaign fund."

My eyebrows and my blood pressure went up. "Rafe? I didn't know you were on a first-name basis. And you know damn well I didn't have anything to do with those missing funds."

Her nostrils flared and her lips whitened at the corners, but she kept her voice even. "I'm not sure of anything anymore when it comes to you. And who I'm on a first-name basis with is no longer any of your business. You saw to that."

A flash of heat went through me. "*I* saw to that? Like you had nothing—" I stopped and took a slow, deep breath before I said one of the hundred other thoughts that spun through my head like dust devils. When someone pushes my buttons, Jeri once told me, I react to something that happened in the past, not what was happening in the present. The more extreme the reaction, usually the further back the emotional trigger. I didn't have to go back very far this time. On days I felt like laying blame instead of taking responsibility for my own actions, I pinned most of it on Rafe Acasa.

"That wasn't fair," I started again, my tone softer.

The fire in her eyes faded. "You're right. I'm sorry." She looked away. When she faced me again, I thought I detected tears.

"What's wrong?"

"Nothing." She wagged her head. Her eyes cleared. "Are you still taking your—"

"My meds? Yes. Not in there, obviously." I grimaced and jerked a thumb in the general direction of the county jail. "Why?"

The long fingers of one hand toyed with the top button of her blouse. The gesture made me want to slowly undo that button, and then the next. I knew every freckle, every nuance that would be revealed as they came undone, could feel the softness of her curves under my fingers, smell her perfume, taste the sweet saltiness of her skin. I remembered the passion in her kisses.

"Focus, Blake!" Her words pricked the memory bubble over my head. "You're in serious trouble here."

"I'm okay, Molly, really." It came out a little harshly. I tried again. "I'll be fine."

"You just…you were so…" She gave up.

I nodded, anyway, with a good guess at what went unsaid. Her face turned somber, and she glanced at her watch.

"I have to get back. Look, I'll call you later in the week and set up a time you can meet with someone—probably Jeffrey. And I'll have my assistant call you before meetings and court appearances."

"Jesus, Molly, I don't have Alzheimer's. Just send me a list of the damn dates and times. I'll mark them in my calendar."

She examined the legal pad on the table, tapped her pen on the blank page a few times. "Let's just set up a meeting first and talk about a defense."

"You know I didn't do it."

Her eyes held something akin to pity. "That doesn't mean they won't try to put you away. This isn't going to be easy, Blake. The PA says the cops have an eyewitness now. Someone saw you come out of that woman's house."

"I *was* there, Molly. I *told* the cops I was there. I never denied being there. It's perfectly possible someone saw me at Midge's. I delivered her paper every day, for God's sake. But I never went in the house. I left the paper on the porch. Whoever saw me there saw me coming down the walk. That's all."

She shook her head. "You don't have to convince me. You have to convince a jury."

"If you don't think it's going to be easy, don't do it. Don't take this case."

Her eyes bored a hole in me. She finally relented. "At least the cops don't have motive. They have means and opportunity. But no motive."

She paused. My thoughts lit on the codicil still floating around out there somewhere.

She put the legal pad away and closed her briefcase. "We can talk about that later. Let's get you out of here first."

"I'll find a way to pay you back for putting up the bond money."

"I know you will, but there's no hurry. I can afford it." She stood and suddenly leaned over the table to kiss me on the cheek. "It's nice to see you, Blake."

"Even under the circumstances?"

She laughed. "I would have preferred a glass of wine at the Hunt Club. But it's nice to know you're okay. It's been a while."

"Thanks. Same to you. You look great, by the way. More beautiful than ever."

She blushed and turned for the door. "I'll talk to you later." And then she was gone.

10

Midge had volunteered at a women's shelter up on Eighteenth Avenue. She'd spoken about it often, but in general terms—how it helped so many homeless women get back on their feet and lead productive lives—never naming names or dishing dirt. Except that she'd been troubled about something recently. Ever since she'd asked me if I knew any lawyers, now that I thought about it. The last few times I'd seen her, she'd seemed tired, more frail somehow. I'd asked if anything was wrong, but, typical of Midge, she'd waved me off, giving me some line about being entitled to act crotchety at her age.

The large brick house, formerly a convent, sat on a corner lot across the street from a parish school connected to a large church farther up the block. The religious order—the Sisters of Mercy—had moved in first, then had helped establish and build the church. The nuns had moved out long ago, building a retreat on the east side of Lake Washington, and donated the building as transitional housing.

I stepped up onto the stone stoop to get out of the rain, wondering why I'd bothered to stop at home for a shower after leaving the courthouse. A brass plaque affixed to the wall next to the big oak front door read "Joyance House." The heavy door swung inward easily on well-oiled hinges. Inside, the scent of bacon, oil soap, and lavender couldn't completely mask the musty smell of old house. A sign in the foyer directed me to the office. A mousy woman in thick-framed glasses with small rhinestone butterflies on the corners looked up from a desk when I entered.

"Can I help you?" she said.

"I was a friend of Midge Babcock," I said.

Her face fell and she blinked back tears. "That was so sad."

I nodded and tried to make the lie I'd prepared sound convincing. "I wanted to say something at her memorial service, so I thought I'd talk to the people who knew her best."

She perked up. "Oh, there's a memorial?"

"Yes," I said, deepening the deception, "there will be."

"Well," she said, "this is the right place to come. Midge didn't seem to have any family or friends besides us," she said, "except for that gentleman from the maritime museum. He stopped by fairly often to take her to tea. Mr. Beardsley." She smiled at something unseen. "Nice man."

"She never mentioned him. A gentleman friend?"

She pinked. "Oh, no. I wouldn't think so. More like compatriots—more than acquaintances, but not exactly friends, if you know what I mean. Certainly not a suitor. They weren't romantic."

"You said he's with a museum?"

"I think that's how they met. You know her husband was a merchant seaman. A collector, too. I guess over the years he brought home a lot of nautical stuff. After he died, Midge gave some of it to the museum. Mr. Beardsley is on the board, as I recall. He's been very attentive for as long as I can remember. Takes—took Midge out for tea every Thursday afternoon."

I changed the subject. "I know she volunteered, but I don't know much about what she did."

Her head bobbed. "What *didn't* Midge do here? Goodness, she helped out in so many ways. She helped me here in the office with filing and such. She sorted clothing that people donated. But I'd say she probably spent most of her time in the kitchen."

"Could I talk to some of the people who knew her, get a better sense of who she was?"

She stood and walked around the desk. "Oh, sure. I'll take you back." She hesitated suddenly, frowning. "I'm sorry, but could I see some ID?"

"Of course." I dug out my driver's license and handed it to her. "Security, I suppose, for your residents?"

She rolled her eyes, cheeks reddening. "I almost forgot—you seem so nice." She looked at the license, then up at me. "Gosh, you're tall. Six eight? The view must be nice from up there." She handed the license back and stepped past me. "In a crowd, I'm so short usually the only things I see are guts and butts. I'm Jean, by the way."

I followed Jean to the back of the house, into a large kitchen upgraded with commercial equipment. Several women busied themselves at different tasks. Jean introduced me to a hard-faced woman in white smock and apron who was stirring the contents of a stockpot on the stove. Her gray hair was pulled back in a bun, wisps of it sticking out from under a hair net at the back of her neck. Thick arms bulged out of short sleeves.

"Alice, this is one of Midge's friends," Jean said.

Alice grunted. "Sweet old lady. Good worker, too. Worked harder than some people around here." She threw a piercing look at a pair of women washing vegetables. "Want some coffee?"

"Sure." I followed her to the end of a counter where she poured two cups. Alice took hers to a small table and sat down heavily. I took the chair next to her. "Is everyone here a volunteer?"

"Depends on how you look at it." Alice leaned back and crossed her ankles. "I'm paid. Some, like Midge, or Wendy over there, they're volunteers from outside. All the women who live in the house, like Joyce and Tamika at the sink there, have to chip in with household chores when they aren't at work. And they have to work if they want to live here. Chores are what you'd expect— housekeeping jobs like cooking and cleaning on a rotating basis.

"Midge, she was a gem. Not real strong. Who would be at her age? But she'd do anything you asked, and most times I never had to. She knew what had to be done, went and did it."

"Sounds like she was well liked."

"I'll miss her, that's for sure. I think most folks here liked her."

"She didn't have any problems with anyone?"

She looked at me sharply. "This isn't any charm school. The women who live here come from the streets. Most of 'em just caught a bad break—a divorce, usually, or they lost their job. But there's a few who are pretty rough around the edges. Midge was a lady. Stubborn, too. Sure, sometimes she'd butt heads with residents, but that's 'cause she was a stickler for manners."

I smiled knowingly. "She corrected me once or twice."

"Truth be told, I don't know what good half of it'll do these women. A little common courtesy may help 'em get and keep a job, but I can't see any of 'em needing to know the difference between a dinner fork and a salad fork anytime soon. A fork's a fork."

She leaned across the table. "Hey, Joyce! Come over here a sec. You, too, Tamika."

Two women at the sink, one black, one white, jerked up. The other woman across the kitchen shrank away. Joyce and Tamika shambled over, a mismatched pair, the black woman almost as wide as she was tall, the white woman a gaunt whisper next to her. A small, white-haired woman crossed the kitchen floor behind them, toddling over to the coffee brewer.

Alice followed her with her eyes. "Morning, Sister," she said with a curt nod.

"Good morning, Alice." The woman's voice was thin and reedy. She poured herself a cup without looking at us.

Alice turned and waited until the shuffling pair of women stood over the table. "Either of you know if Midge had trouble with anyone here?"

The two exchanged glances. Joyce spoke first. "Not that I know. Most people liked her okay. She could be a little nosy, but she was nice enough."

Alice focused on the black woman, her eyes narrowing. "That how you see it, Tamika?"

"She never got in *my* face, that's what you're askin'. But I wouldn't be takin' no shit from some old lady, anyways."

"You can't think of any reason why anyone would want to hurt her?" I said.

"Hell, I'd have liked to clock her a couple of times myself," Tamika said, a hand on her hip.

Joyce's eyes widened. "You think someone here might have killed her?"

"Well, it wasn't me," Tamika said emphatically. "I might've liked to smack her one upside the head. Never would've done it. Old lady like that?" She harrumphed, crossing thick arms in front of an ample chest. Her frown softened. "I know who might've, though, come to think of it."

"Who?" Alice's voice was sharp.

"The one who left. What's her name? Mary." Tamika twirled a finger in a circle next to her temple. "That was one crazy bitch."

"Crazy, how?" I said.

"Talk to herself. Look at you like you was some sorta space alien or somethin' like that."

"Oh, but she wouldn't hurt Midge," Joyce said. "Midge was really nice to her."

"I don't know 'bout you, girl, but I seen Mary light into Midge just like she done everyone else. Saying crazy shit, like Midge was some creature trying to steal her eyeballs or somethin'."

"But she wouldn't have hurt Midge," Joyce said. "I just know it."

"Why did Mary leave?" I said.

"She crazy, that's why," Tamika said. "Bitch been on the streets too long."

"She was asked to leave," Alice said. "I got some ideas why, but you'll have to ask the director about that."

"I'll do that." I saw the elderly nun turn and hurry out of the kitchen. I looked at Alice. "Anything else you can think of?"

She peered up at the ceiling. "No, but I'll ask some of the others who knew her pretty good. See if they've got any ideas." She looked at Joyce and Tamika. "Well, what are you two standing here for? You better finish up quick or you'll both be late for work."

Joyce bowed her head and turned away, but Tamika's face clouded with irritation before she lumbered back to the prep sink, thick arms swinging and heavy hips swaying with each step.

"Thanks for the help," I called.

Alice leaned over. "I didn't want to say nothin' in front of them two, but one other person didn't take to Midge was Gretchen, the director. Oil and water, them two. Heard them argue more than once."

"What about?"

"Couldn't say, but always seemed to be about money."

I chewed on it for a moment and rose. "Thanks for the coffee, Alice. I appreciate the time."

"You're welcome," she said. "Say a good word for Midge from us."

Out in the hallway, I looked for the white-haired nun who had scurried from the kitchen so quickly, but she'd disappeared. I stopped in the office on my way out, hoping to find her. Instead I found Jean talking with a heavyset woman in black slacks and blazer over a fuchsia silk blouse.

The woman turned abruptly when I entered and looked me up and down. "Who are you?"

I extended a hand. "Blake. One of Midge Babcock's friends."

She slowly lifted a limp wrist, making me step forward to take her hand. "Gretchen Nylund. I'm the director here. I really didn't know Midge all that well." Her voice was chilly. "We have so many volunteers, it's difficult to get to know them all."

"I understand she was well liked. I'd very much like to get comments from some of your residents to include in the memorial in some way."

The hand she waved jingled from the weight of several bracelets. "Oh, I don't think that would be possible. We try to maintain the privacy of our residents. For their own safety, of course. Many of these women have been abused by husbands and boyfriends. We keep male visitors to a minimum so as not to upset them."

"I see," I said. "There's something else you might be able to help me with. I heard there may have been hard feelings between Midge and a former resident here. Mary?"

"I wouldn't know about that," she said quickly. "Why do you ask?"

"I wondered if she'd made any enemies here."

Her eyes narrowed. "I heard they arrested somebody for Midge's murder."

The office suddenly felt warm. "I heard that, too. I also heard the police have no motive. Why was Mary asked to leave?"

Again her hand dismissed the question with a jingle. "It had nothing to do with Midge Babcock, I assure you. We have strict requirements for our residents regarding abstinence—from drugs, alcohol, smoking, and sex. Mary violated the rules."

"How long ago did she leave?"

"Last week."

"Do you know where she went?"

She looked startled, as if the thought hadn't occurred to her before. "Back to the streets, I suppose. But really, I can't imagine that she has anything to do with what happened to Midge."

I pressed her. "Do you have Mary's last name?"

"Jackson." She gave it reluctantly. "It won't do you any good if she's on the street."

"It might if she's been to a shelter for a meal. Can't hurt." I could see from the way she folded her arms that she wouldn't volunteer any more information. "Thanks for your time." She remained mute, jaw thrust forward. "I'll be sure to let you know when the memorial is scheduled."

"Oh, yes, please do," Jean said, stepping forward to shake my hand.

Her boss eyed me guardedly as I turned for the door.

11

I stood on the front steps of Joyance House and considered what to do next, trying to remember my conversations with Midge. There'd been a sister somewhere, but the two of them hadn't been close. A sister, though, could mean nieces and nephews, and their kids, too. I wondered if any of them had known Midge, ever met her. Midge hadn't mentioned anyone. Joyance House had occupied her time and energy, had given her a reason to get up in the morning. The people here had been her family, dysfunctional and screwed up like any big family. Strange she'd never mentioned Beardsley, but they sounded more like business associates than friends. I'd have to see if I could shed light on the rift between Midge and Gretchen, too.

The door behind me closed with a solid thud, and a small voice said, "Excuse me. Would you mind helping me with these stairs, young man?"

The white-haired nun who'd stopped in the kitchen for coffee extended her hand. She wore a trench coat and plastic rain bonnet tied tightly under her chin. Stout legs in opaque hose sticking out beneath the hem of the coat ended in sturdy black oxfords. "I'm just headed to the church, there, up the street, if you wouldn't mind."

"No trouble at all." I took her elbow and held her steady.

"I'm glad I caught you," she said when we reached the sidewalk. She craned her neck to look at the house, and leaned into me, patting my arm. "I'm Sister Florence. Florence Addison."

Mention of her name triggered the memory of what Midge told me the night I'd tuned out weeks earlier: "I'm worried about Florence. I may have put her in a bad spot." What had seemed like mild concern at the time took on chilling new meaning, given Midge's grisly fate.

"I lived in Joyance House back when it was a convent…a long time ago." Florence gestured up the street. "That's where I live now. In the rectory." She looked up at me again. "Midge was my friend. I didn't want to say anything in front of those other women. I don't trust them."

"Alice? Or the residents?"

"Any of them. They're all…I don't know, they're just shifty. They can't help it. Not a very charitable thing for a nun to say, I know. I pray every day for forgiveness for such thoughts." She peered into my eyes. "You cared about Midge, didn't you?"

I thought for a moment about what I'd felt for an old woman with whom I'd held middle-of-the-night discussions.

"She extended her friendship when no one else would," I said finally. "She didn't judge me. Yes, I think I cared about her a great deal."

"Do you think someone in the house could have harmed her? I heard you ask about it."

I shrugged. "It wasn't a random act. She wasn't robbed. Someone had a reason for killing her."

Florence nodded. "I'm afraid she might have brought this on herself."

"How would she do that?"

We stepped off the curb. The sound of an approaching car brought my head up. We stopped, letting the car pass.

"She was on some crusade, some nonsense about the history of the house. It was stirring up nothing but ill feelings."

I gently led Florence across the intersection. "Whoever did this to Midge should be caught," I said. "If there's anything more you can tell me, maybe it could help."

Her face held uncertainty. "What can you do? You're not the police."

"I have something the police don't—incentive." I told her about my arrest. "Anything you can tell me, Sister, anything at all, might help me find the person who did this."

Florence stopped walking. We stood opposite a courtyard between a school building and the church rectory. Landscaped hedges and other greenery, uncharacteristically lush for this urban block, framed a shallow circular fountain.

"Well," she said, "Midge recently became very interested in the history of the convent. Not just how the house happened to pass into the hands of the charity, but how it came into being in the first place. She asked me if I could help her look through the order's archives. Rather than make her travel to Bellevue, I brought it here in bits and pieces. She'd look at what I brought, ask me to keep some here, and return the rest. Not long after, I heard her argue with Gretchen."

"And you don't know what it was about?"

"They always kept their disagreements behind closed doors, but you couldn't help noticing. They argued frequently after that, and loudly. Gretchen is, well, opinionated. And Midge, bless her soul, was quite headstrong."

"Do you still have the documents that interested Midge?"

She nodded solemnly. "Midge insisted I find a safe place for them. She didn't want the responsibility of keeping them, and thought Gretchen might take them if she discovered them."

"Could you make me copies?"

"I...I wouldn't know the first thing about that. But perhaps you could make copies and return the originals to me?"

"That would be fine." I gave her my phone number and asked her to call when she was ready. "Thank you for telling me, Sister."

She gave me a shaky smile. "I'm sure Midge would have wanted me to. She spoke of you often. She trusted you; so shall I."

Midge apparently hadn't trusted me enough.

* * *

He watched Sanders walk the old nun up the street to the church and smacked the top of the steering wheel. He should have known something would go wrong. The call to 911 had been inspired, a perfect way to deflect an investigation into the Babcock woman's death onto an ideal suspect. Who knew a judge would be stupid enough to let Sanders out of jail? What a fucked-up system when pot smokers ended up getting life and murder suspects walked.

And now, worse, Sanders was free to nose around and try to clear his name. *Damn!* He should be at work, but now he'd have to make up some excuse. Maybe say he went home early because he was feeling sick. It wasn't far from the truth. With Sanders out on bail, he'd have to be more careful. First, he had to find out what Sanders was up to.

Sanders got into his car a few moments later and pulled away from the curb. He checked his mirror for traffic, pulled away from the curb, and followed.

* * *

A strange man lay in the bed of the room at Harborview where I'd visited Liz Tracey. I backed up quickly before he turned his head, and stopped at the nurse's station. The hospital had checked her out on Friday while I'd been sitting in a holding cell at police headquarters.

I found a quiet spot away from the front entrance of the hospital where no one would hassle me for using a cell phone and called information. The automated computer operator found one listing for E. Tracey in Seattle. A female voice rattled off the number and the computer connected my call. Voice mail kicked in after four rings. I didn't leave a message. I pulled a piece of scrap paper from my pocket and wrote myself a reminder to call her later.

* * *

Zipping up the field jacket and donning a warm pair of gloves, I locked the Toyota and hoofed over to Broadway in the cold rain. Weather kept some of the usual crowds away, but the street kids and panhandlers still roamed up and down the sidewalks, trying to stay dry under eaves and awnings. As soon as business owners came out and asked them to move on, others moved in to take their place. Restaurants still did decent business even at the late hour, catering to upscale urban couples out for the evening and locals looking for cheap eats. Every so often, people emerged through restaurant doors in a blast of light and heat, the bright cheeriness from inside, along with laughter and chattering voices that quickly dissipated on the dark sidewalk.

A block up, I spotted a homeless man who called himself King Ralph hitting up passersby for spare change.

"Your Highness," I said.

He spooked and looked up suspiciously.

"It's just me, the newspaper guy."

He barked and drew himself upright. "Bad form, bad form."

"Sorry. I need your help, Ralph. I'm looking for someone, a woman."

He cackled. "For the love of a good woman. They're everywhere if you've got enough beer tokens, lad."

He swayed gently, a willow in a soft breeze. I'd caught him at a good time, before he was totally lit.

"Not that kind of woman, Ralph. A specific woman. Lives on the streets. Name's Mary."

"As common as Smith. Lot of Mary around—Mary Jane." He sniffed. "I'm strictly a cognac man."

I pulled a five-spot from my pocket and held it up in the light. "Give me a break. Focus, Ralph. I don't want a dime bag; I don't want a hooker. I'm looking for a woman named Mary. She's an old-timer, but just spent some time at Joyance House."

His face lit up. "Bloody Mary, Queen of Scots," he said in his best Olivier with a sweep of his arm. At the very end of the flourish he tried to snatch the bill from my hand, but had enough alcohol in him to attenuate his eye-hand coordination.

I jerked my arm back. "Come on, Ralph. Give me something I can use. A Hamilton if you know who she is."

He looked hurt. "Bloody Mary, lad. That's who you want. Though Venusians are much prettier than Earthlings. I wouldn't mess with Bloody Mary."

"Where can I find her?"

He shrugged, the movement almost tipping him over. I put a hand on his shoulder and steadied him. He looked at my hand and raised his blurry eyes to my face, frowning. I held the money in front of his nose.

"You might try the park," he said.

"Which one?"

"Doesn't matter."

Conceding, I handed him the bill and dug another out of my pocket as promised, leaving me with nothing but loose change. I went in search of an ATM. If I found her, Mary would cost me at least the bottle of Thunderbird I'd picked up, maybe more.

Cal Anderson Park sat midway between two formerly state-run liquor stores on Capitol Hill. I headed there first. Four or five teenagers of indeterminate gender hung out on the sidewalk in front of a drive-in a block away, trash-talking and roughhousing. "Gutter punks," cops called them. Homeless kids who populated "The Avenue"—University Way in what used to be the commercial heart of the U District—were called "Ave rats." They could pass for students. These gutter punks generally were older, harder core.

Light drizzle sparkled on their clothes under the streetlight. A guy with a scraggly goatee carried a soggy piece of cardboard. On it he'd written, "Stealth bombers killed my friend. Need $$ for nukes." Two dark figures a little farther down the block caught my eye. An older kid, maybe early twenties, in a thick parka with the hood down pressed another teenager up against a darkened storefront. Something in his hand down low glinted as he brought it up close to the kid's waist. *A knife.* The kids behind me were oblivious. The sidewalk down to the corner was empty. Passing cars wouldn't stop, and the few people on foot across the street were too far away even if they noticed.

Something hot bloomed inside me and spread through my limbs. Just before I drew abreast of the pair, I changed direction. I saw fear on the kid's face now, heard the snarl in the older man's voice to "give it up," whether money or drugs. He sensed my presence and glanced over his shoulder, confident that the weapon in his hand would deter me from getting too close. I took one more step and threw a closed-fist tae kwon do punch at his face. His head snapped back and he staggered, hands flying to his broken, bleeding nose. The knife clattered on the pavement. Ignoring it, I advanced. He backpedaled, resoluteness gone without six inches of steel to harden it. When he got his feet under him he turned and ran. I spun around to see if the kid was all right, but he'd already hightailed it the other way.

"You're welcome!" I called.

He threw a frightened glance over his shoulder and didn't stop running.

Jeri keeps telling me I'm too impulsive. I squeezed my hand under my arm as pain from my bruised knuckles reached my brain. I pulled the glove off and brought my knuckles to my mouth.

Light glinted off the knife blade lying on the pavement. I picked it up. A sheet of newsprint fluttered on the curb, stuck under the wheel of a car. I ripped it out, wrapped the knife tightly, and slipped the bundle into a pocket. The gang in front of the drive-in laughed and dished dirt. There was no sign of the kid, and no one else seemed remotely aware of what had just happened.

The block to the park barely gave me time to walk off the adrenaline rush. The glove had cushioned some of the blow, but my hand ached. I'd hit the guy hard—my own form of anger management. I shrugged it off.

SPD had boosted patrols and increased manpower on Capitol Hill—throughout the city, in fact—as part of the mayor's push for "neighborhood policing," the old style of deterring crime. The city had redrawn precinct sectors and beats and put more cops back on bicycles or on foot. For all that, they couldn't be everywhere at once, and nighttime was a predator's milieu, when the cover of darkness hid furtive activities from cops and nosy neighbors.

Seattle's a polite city—polite, not friendly—which may be why it has only one cop for every eight hundred and some-odd citizens, compared to New York, with one for every three hundred or so. But Seattle isn't immune to crime. For the most part, locals feel safe enough to drunk-walk through Cal Anderson Park to the drive-in for munchies at one in the morning. The renovation a couple years earlier cleaned up the park but couldn't prevent it from becoming a stop on the circuit for those the cops kept rousting. And increased patrols didn't keep junkies and crank dealers from trolling for customers. The park's location—close to Seattle Central Community College and Seattle University— provided a steady stream of corruptible kids.

Construction between Broadway and Nagle for the Link light-rail station under Capitol Hill didn't help. When finished, the line would connect stations from the University of Washington all the way south to the airport with the sort of mass transit system the city should have built thirty years earlier. The light-rail line from downtown to Tukwila and the terminals at Sea-Tac Airport had recently opened. The construction zone across from the park, though, was one more magnet for indigents and hustlers, the jumbled mess of earthworks, materiel, and equipment a maze of hiding places for shady dealings or sleeping off a major bender even with the sound-suppressing wall and fence they'd built around the site.

I ignored the first meth head who sidled out of the shadows in the park. He quickly melted back into the darkness. A quick tour, however, uncovered little else out of the ordinary—a few late-night dog walkers, the end of a men's league soccer game down on the lighted playfields, some drunk Seattle U kids splashing in the fountain—as if a November night in Seattle didn't offer enough dampness—and a lone wino passed out on a bench.

A quicker way to find Mary popped into my head. I checked my watch. Late, but not too late to call an old acquaintance working the night shift. Pastor Paul ran a street ministry and emergency shelter placement service out of offices down near the International District. At night, the ministry's van took volunteer pastors to locations around the city—bars, shelters, and other gathering places—to talk and pray with the homeless. Paul or someone on his staff might have seen Mary or even know where she was sleeping most nights. A volunteer at the dispatch center put me on hold to go look for him.

A moment later his voice came on the line. "Blake. Long time."

"I know. I was out of circulation for a while. I'm doing a little better now," I lied.

"No need to explain," he said. "I understand. I said prayers for you. Good to hear your voice. What can I do for you?"

I told him why I was looking for Mary, said I was looking into Midge's relationships with the people at Joyance House. "I thought she might be crashing in the homeless camp under the freeway."

"Up on Capitol Hill? I've got a van going up there almost as we speak."

"Any chance I could do a ride-along?" Homeless people are no less territorial than the rest of us. They'd be suspicious and uncooperative if I showed up in their camp alone, but less so if I was in one of Paul's ministry vans.

He didn't hesitate. "I can have Dave pick you up. Where are you?"

I let him know where to find me, and after a promise to stay in closer touch closed the phone. As I slid it into my pocket my fingers bumped the hard handle of the bundled knife. I pulled it out and dropped it in a trash can.

* * *

He was tired, cold. For hours he'd tailed Sanders, to the hospital, back to Sanders's apartment, and now out on the streets. He wasn't sure what Sanders was looking for, but Sanders seemed intent on finding what or whomever it was. He found it worrisome. So, he'd followed, bored silly most of the time, the only real challenge keeping Sanders from spotting his car.

The last half hour, though, had gotten interesting. Sanders had interrupted a mugging. The sudden intervention had surprised him almost as much as the poor schmuck Sanders had laid out on the sidewalk. He'd underestimated Sanders, had considered him toothless, ineffectual. He knew what Sanders had been through recently, had studied him. He'd thought Sanders's personal setbacks had broken him. But Sanders hadn't hesitated even when the mugger had brandished a knife. The incident made him more wary, more alert.

When Sanders had entered the park, he'd found a place at the curb and had run across the street to follow. Now, after circling the entire park, he watched Sanders stop and make a phone call. He slipped into the shadows and waited until Sanders finished and walked out of the park. He stepped out to follow, but froze as Sanders paused to throw a bundle into a trash can. His pulse raced as he watched Sanders turn up the street out of sight. He quickened his pace to the street and cautiously checked on Sanders. He had to hurry. Sanders had already walked halfway up the block. He turned back to the trash can and rummaged for the bundle Sanders had thrown away. Tattered newspaper wrapped around...*yes*! The knife Sanders had picked up off the street.

He slipped the bundle into his own pocket and hurried across the street to his car.

12

The ministry van pulled up to a nearby corner less than ten minutes later. Ten minutes after that, Dave, a young minister named Sage, and I slipped and slid down the steep muddy embankment under an elevated portion of I-5 on the west side of Capitol Hill. Mimicking the world above, shelters of all sorts dotted the slope, from elaborate little cabins with furniture and carpets covering the mud to small tents, cardboard lean-tos, and plastic tarps flapping in the breeze. Their views of the lights along Lake Union and up Queen Anne Hill rivaled those of multimillion-dollar properties just a few hundred feet away. Not for long. The city had already announced plans to turn the site into a skateboarding park for area teens, displacing these people once again.

At any given time, between 7,000 and 8,000 people in the city of Seattle and surrounding suburbs were homeless. At least half of them had jobs or were looking for work. By day they gave the people around them no indication of their condition. They lived as they always had, getting by the best they could. But their best wasn't enough to cover all the bills and leave enough for rent in a city that had seen housing costs skyrocket with the growth of its high-tech economy. They were normal people confronted by abnormal circumstances—loss of a job, financial strain from divorce or illness of someone in the family, victims of domestic abuse. The list went on.

At night, most found temporary shelter on a friend's sofa or in one of about 4,000 spots in church, city, and county shelters. The rest had to make do. The majority slept in their cars or trucks. Some joined the tent cities that occasionally sprang up when a neighborhood deigned to allow a local church or organization to host one. A few people rode all-night buses to stay warm and dry.

About a quarter of those with no permanent housing had mental illnesses that in part had caused their homelessness. Vets with PTSD, people with bipolar disorder, schizophrenics, and those who were just plain depressed. Another quarter had what service agencies liked to call addiction disorders. And often, the drunks and crazies either didn't meet shelter requirements or distrusted the people who ran them. They were hard-core street people, squatting in abandoned buildings, living under roadways, sleeping in parking garages, alleys, doorways, and on park benches. Hundreds spent nights walking aimlessly, unable to sleep for fear of their own safety, waiting for daylight to find an undisturbed place to catch a nap.

The people here were the hard core. I hung back as Dave and Sage waded into the groups of huddled figures, mostly men, wrapped in layers of frayed, filthy clothing. The homeless would talk to a man wearing a clerical collar more readily than they would to me. I didn't look much different from the denizens of this hidden city, wool cap pulled down over the tops of my ears, torn blue jeans, shabby sneakers, and worn field jacket over a sweatshirt, plaid flannel shirt, and T-shirt to keep out the wet chill. Below me, a group of homeless people congregated around the two clergymen, presumably for words of encouragement and prayer. The roar of traffic on the pavement above drowned out the words before they reached me. The camp residents soon drifted off, and the ministers slowly trudged back up the slope.

"They say the woman you want moved in with a man they call Stitch," Dave said loudly as they approached. He turned and pointed to a different part of the encampment. "Over there. I'd break the ice for you, but Stitch isn't too fond of ministers. He was abused by a priest as a kid. All collars look alike to him."

"No problem," I said.

I headed for the tent Dave had pointed out. I stopped a few feet from the zippered flap.

"Knock, knock," I said. "Mary?"

The flap zipped up and a grizzled, bearded face popped out. "Whadya want?"

"I want to talk to Mary," I said.

"She doesn't want to talk to you."

"I think she does." I pulled the bottle of fortified wine out of my jacket.

The head disappeared, and a moment later a figure emerged. In the dark, Mary looked like all the rest, bundled in layers of clothes. All that set her apart was her smaller stature and the long, stringy hair hanging out from under her watch cap. She edged out of the inky shadow of the freeway into what little ambient light filtered through from the city below. A Rorschach blot of something dark stained the front of her coat.

"Who're you?" she said.

"Nobody. I just wanted to ask some questions. You're the Mary who lived at Joyance House recently?"

"Who's asking?" She squinted at me. "Don't tell me they sent you to bust my chops."

"No, nothing like that. I heard you made friends there with a lady named Midge, Midge Babcock, a volunteer."

She eyed the bottle in my hand and licked her lips. "That for me?"

"If you talk to me."

Her eyes slowly lurched up to my face. "I knew Midge. I wouldn't call us friends, but she was okay. Nosy old biddy, but harmless, I guess."

"Some people there think you and Midge might have had a falling out."

She made a noise that might have been laughter. "We never had a falling in."

"Why did the house ask you to leave?"

"Ask me? They threw me out. I worked hard to get on the list for that place. Stayed clean for nearly a year. I used to tweak all the time. I don't do that no more. Even got sober. Found a place that would hire me to clean and do odd jobs. What do I get for my troubles? Right back where I started."

"Did it have anything to do with Midge?"

She drew back a half step, face hardening. "What's with the old lady? I already told you we got along okay." She hesitated. "I don't think I want to talk to you anymore."

I dangled the bottle by the neck. "You sure? I'm not trying to get you in trouble. I just want to find out what happened to my friend."

"The old lady? Why? What happened?"

"Someone killed her."

She backed away. "Well, don't look at me. I didn't have any beef with her. I ain't seen her since I got tossed out. And that's all I'm saying."

I held out the bottle, and she stopped. I unscrewed the top and held it out again. She tentatively stepped forward, took it and tipped it into her mouth. She took two or three swallows before I pulled her arm down and grabbed the bottle out of her hand.

"Tell me the rest and the bottle's yours," I said. I screwed the cap back on.

"Asshole." She put her hands to her face, blew on them, and rubbed them together. "If anyone had a problem with the old lady, it was that bitch boss lady. The one that threw me out."

"The director? Gretchen Nylund?"

She nodded. "I heard her and Midge get into it a couple of times. Miss High-and-Mighty lit into Midge once or twice for sticking her nose where it didn't belong."

"About what?"

"I don't know, mister. All I know is they argued."

I eyed her silently for a moment. "Is that blood on your coat?"

She hugged her arms to her chest, covering the stain. "So what?"

"How'd you get blood on you?"

"Nosebleed." She sniffed.

"How'd that happen?"

She glared at me. With surprising speed she leaned in and snatched the bottle out of my hand and danced back a step, holding it tight with two hands like a basketball.

"None of your damn business," she said. She turned and squeezed through the tent flap, the ripping sound as she closed it defiant over the noisy traffic.

* * *

Toward the end of my route, I weaved crazily past an SPD cruiser on a quiet block across from the Arboretum. It didn't move. A lot of patrol cops recognize carriers' cars, so they don't hassle us when we crisscross the street to deliver papers. The cop's dome light illuminated the interior, and I recognized the officer at the wheel. I rounded the corner, pulled up to the curb, and backtracked on foot. Charlie's bent head hung over his lap, practically resting on the steering wheel. Cutting across the grass to the curb, I squatted next to the passenger door and rapped on the window. He looked toward the sound, startled, hand automatically moving toward his hip. His surprise turned to annoyance when he recognized me. The window slid down with a hum.

"What do you want?" he said.

I reached in, popped the door locks, and clambered in before he could object. "Saw your car. Thought I'd drop in and say hello."

"I'm working." He sat with a pile of papers on his lap, pen in the hand that had reached for his gun.

"So am I." I watched him fill out forms. "Whatever happens next," I said finally, "it would help if I knew what was coming."

He didn't look at me until he finished writing. "You know I can't tell you that, even if the leads kept me in the loop. Which they don't."

"Come on, Charlie. Whoever Molly's firm puts on my case will get everything from the PA's office, anyway. All I'm asking for is a little advance warning, just some idea of what Donovan and Hiragawa are looking at."

He shook his head. "Can't do it."

I considered him, wondering when he'd gotten religion. "Are they looking for dirt on you?"

His face went dark, and his jaw clenched. "I'm going to try to pretend I didn't hear you say that." He spoke so softly I strained to hear him. "Not once..." He raised a finger and shook it in my face. "Never in fifteen years have I done anything to disgrace my shield. Not until this minute, when I let you get in this car."

I blinked. "Me? You think *I'll* tarnish your rep with the force?"

"The stink on you is so bad it wouldn't have mattered if you'd killed that old lady or not. Now, getting anywhere near you is like stepping in a lake of dog shit."

A dozen snappy comebacks vied to come out. I shut my eyes, counted slowly, tried to hear the sound of my breath over the voices shouting in my head. Slowly, I opened my eyes. He still glared at me.

"You owe me, Charlie," I said evenly. "You wouldn't have had fifteen years with SPD if it hadn't been for me. Maybe you don't believe in bad luck. I know I don't. Shit happens. You deal with it as best you can and move on. Something stinks, all right, but it isn't me. I got set up last time. Could be I'm getting set up again. Or maybe I was just in the wrong place at the wrong time. Doesn't matter. *I* know that I'm as clean as your shorts on wash day."

He opened his mouth, but I didn't let him get a word in.

"Tell you what, you don't want to help, maybe I'll help you instead. People at the shelter say a former resident may have had it in for Midge. I talked to her tonight; she's got blood all over her coat."

Charlie was a good cop, but he was happy working patrol. He wouldn't pass the information on. I pulled on the door latch and extended one foot out onto the curb.

"You can believe what you want," I said. "But we were friends a long time. We went through a lot together. I'd have thought that might count for something."

I swung my weight out of the car. He called my name as I shut the door. I leaned against the window ledge. His eyes flicked around the car, gaze finally landing on my face.

"I heard the ME's office ruled out a sex crime," he said. "Donovan and Hiragawa are eliminating all possibilities that it could be anyone but you."

13

Sirens woke me before eight, bringing me grudgingly out of a troubled sleep. Dreaming they'd come for me, I sat up abruptly, sweating. The sounds faded in the distance, and I flopped back on the sheets, exhausted. But the sandman stole away in the early light, leaving me half awake and grumpy enough to take on a bear in springtime. A cup of coffee and a pill helped, but only a day job or a regular seven hours of uninterrupted sleep could offer a real cure. I wasn't ready to face the light of day yet, anyway. Darkness suited me better.

The reminder to call Liz Tracey sat on the coffee table. I got out my cell phone.

"It's Blake," I said when she answered. She didn't reply. "Blake Sanders. How are you?"

"What do you care?"

"Look, I'm sorry I didn't call sooner. Something came up. Are you in a program yet?"

"Why are you calling me now?"

Patience. I heard Jeri's voice in my head.

"You need to put together a support network. People you trust," I said. "I tried calling you yesterday, but no one answered. Where were you?"

"Over the weekend? Out of touch." I left it there. "Seriously, are you all right?"

She sighed. "Yes, I'm okay. Yes, I'm seeing a shrink, or therapist or whatever. It's all so incredibly humiliating."

"Try not to see it that way. You hit a low last week. You didn't see how things could get any better. But they have. Or you wouldn't wonder if they could get any worse."

A beat later she broke the silence with a small chuckle. "God, you're twisted." She paused. "I'm back at work," she finally said.

The "shitty" job in the city's communications department, I assumed.

"What the heck am I supposed to say when people ask me how my Thanksgiving went?" she asked. "Gee, it was super! I went out to play in the snow and tried to jump off a bridge."

I laughed this time, at the geeky tone as she mocked herself. "You're an odd duck yourself, Liz Tracey. I like it. Don't worry about it. Thanksgiving is old news, anyway. No one will ask you about your holiday today."

"Maybe you're right." Then in a mirthless tone, she said, "I have to get to work."

"Ah, reality. I feel like I just got off work."

"Right. Delivery boy. And I thought my job was bad. How can you live on that?"

"I can't. I have another part-time job, and pick up some freelance work here and there." I paused. "I didn't always do this."

"What did you do before?"

"Long story. Maybe some other time. Look, if you need anything, call me anytime. Day or night. I've got a helpline number for you, too." I made her get a pencil and rattled off the number for Jeri's organization. "I'd like to check in once in a while, see how you're doing."

"Yeah, okay, I guess."

"Good. I'll let you get to work, then."

Liz Tracey could be a real nutcase for all I knew, but I hung up feeling like I'd just eaten a good meal.

I tried calling Mr. Beardsley at the museum and got voice mail, so I spent the better part of the morning talking to street people. Trying, anyway. There are almost as many reasons why people end up on the street as there are street people. Each has a distinct patois that I'd never mastered.

I asked those who could carry on a conversation about Bloody Mary. Only a few acknowledged they knew her. Most looked at me vacantly when I described her. None could substantiate her story of how her nose had been bloodied. I wondered if Mary had conned me, too. Maybe someone else's blood covered the front of her coat.

By lunchtime I was cold, wet, and I'd had enough of crazies and grifters. Summoning the patience to coax anything resembling normal conversation from most of them had left me with a jaw that ached from clamping my mouth shut, and grumpy from the exertion. Tempted by the smells emanating from nearby restaurants, I almost abandoned my resolve to watch my budget. Instead I stopped in a market and bought an apple and a banana. I ate them slowly, lingering inside until the skin under my fingernails reverted from blue-black to a healthy pink.

Sister Florence surprised me, calling and asking to meet in the nave of the church where I'd left her. I told her to give me twenty minutes to make the walk.

I found her in a pew near the back. She glanced around nervously when I slid onto the hard wood a few feet away. She reached down into a cloth shopping bag at her feet and pulled out a bulging manila envelope. She placed it on the bench and pushed it toward me.

"This is everything I've been keeping for Midge." She said it so quietly I strained to hear.

I covered the envelope with a hand and pulled it next to me. "I'll make copies and get these back to you."

"Keep them until you're finished with them," she said. "I think they're safer with you than they are in Joyance House. Especially if they're what's caused all this trouble."

"If you're sure." I put the envelope inside my coat.

She nodded. "Just find out what happened. For Midge's sake."

* * *

Gagnon had never felt quite this far out of his element before. It unnerved him, a feeling completely foreign to him until now. He'd always been at home, whether in Europe, North Africa, or Southeast Asia. But perhaps that had been because in so many of those places—Tunisia, Libya, Morocco, Vietnam, Laos, Thailand, Cambodia, Indonesia—there were still signs of French influence. He'd been able to communicate, blend in better. Even Canada had a large, and partisan, French population. America was different, a vast sea of homogeneity. In the polyglot neighborhoods of an urban area like Seattle, English was the lingua franca, and rudeness the order of the day. Not rudeness, perhaps, so much as a sense of entitlement, an assumption of superiority. Not unlike Parisians.

He'd wasted an entire day driving to eastern Washington. He reminded himself that the trip hadn't been a waste, but a necessity. He was sure he could have gotten what he needed in the city, but the lower his profile here, the better. Instead, he'd traveled to a rough, woodsy area near the Idaho border north of Spokane to meet with a gunmaker. A skinhead. A member of one of the many white supremacist groups that dotted the forests in the American West like mushrooms. Groups that funded their paranoia and hatred by dealing meth and firearms. An unsavory lot, but in some ways not too many degrees away, ideologically, from the cabal he had recently served.

The gunmaker had offered him the most beautiful .32-caliber semiautomatic pistol he'd ever seen. Small and light, it came with a custom sound suppressor, a feature that led Gagnon to approach the man in the first place. After Gagnon had tested it on a range in the woods behind the man's double-wide mobile home, they'd gotten down to business. The gunmaker had asked for an even thousand, and threw in a box of .32 ACP, 78-grain ammo. Gagnon had agreed the price was fair, shot him in the eye, and left.

He'd spent the morning driving through the sleepy suburbs on the east side of Lake Washington looking for the Sisters of Mercy convent. When he finally found it, he hit another dead end. The chapter did have an archive, but the information it contained on Sister Marguerite mostly concerned her good works after founding the mission in Seattle. The sister with whom he spoke offered one helpful tidbit. One of the sisters, Florence, had recently gone through the archives. Semiretired now, she lived in the rectory of the church near the old convent and served the parish priests. She might know where to find any information the convent had on Sister Marguerite.

Gagnon cursed. He needed something—a map, directions—anything that would give him a better idea of where to look. He could not have come all this way, destroyed what was left of his career, for all this to come to nothing. He'd played his hand, putting everything at risk, and now he was on the run. A step or two ahead of his own people, surely. They would catch up eventually, but not for a while. He was more concerned about being a step behind someone else. Someone had killed the old woman because of what she knew, or what she might have discovered. And that put Gagnon at a disadvantage.

He pulled up to the curb not far from the church. Perhaps the nun had found something of value in the archives. That must have been how the old lady had learned enough to prompt her call to the motherhouse in Montréal. He waited in the car while he considered how to approach the nun. He couldn't afford to arouse her suspicions. Dufours, however, had given him the perfect cover.

He reached for the door handle, but paused when he saw an elderly *religieuse* exit the church on the arm of an exceedingly tall man. They spoke a few words, and the man took the nun's arm and helped her down to the street.

* * *

Exhaustion set in when I got back to the apartment, but curiosity overcame it. I flopped down and gently slid the envelope's contents onto the coffee table. I carefully thumbed through the stack of papers—some yellowed, wrinkled, and fragile as old parchment; some white and crisp. In the middle of the stack was an aged, slim-bound volume, the spine brittle and frayed top to bottom. The cover was blank.

Intrigued, I opened it gingerly. A page of florid penmanship confronted me, faded to gray on paper that had mellowed to cream. The handwriting appeared indecipherable until I realized the author had written in French. I flipped through the pages. Dates appeared on some, in chronological order, as in a journal or diary. Early entries dated back to August 1856, and the date of the last entry was May 16, 1857. The author had run out of pages.

My rusty high-school French was still adequate enough to pick out words and simple sentences. With enough of those translated, I reread passages for an overall sense of subject. Though slow, the process revealed the gist of preparations for a mission. Drawn in by the challenge, I deciphered more.

The author, Sister Marguerite, had been in an order in Montréal. She'd lobbied for and taken a small contingent of her fellow sisters to the Washington Territory to establish a mission. I got as far as the group's departure for New York via ship before my eyes bleared and my brain short-circuited. I stifled a yawn and placed the journal on top of the rest of the stack of papers.

About to succumb and take a nap, I pulled out a page midway into the stack that had caught my eye. It was a copy of a letter written on Joyance House stationery, addressed to a familiar law firm—the one I'd recommended to Midge Babcock, the firm my ex-wife Molly worked for. And Midge had signed it. If Nylund was aware that Midge had sent out letters on the shelter's letterhead, it might explain why they argued. In the letter, Midge referred to legal action she wanted the firm to take on behalf of Joyance House.

I pinched the bridge of my nose and rubbed my eyes. Paging through the stack again, I found several pieces of correspondence from Midge and a couple of replies from the firm. I made note of the signatory and phone number on one of the replies and got up to find my phone. The call dumped me into voice mail. I hung up and redialed, this time choosing the option to transfer to an associate. A pleasant female voice told me that Scott Williams was out of the office, but would be back shortly. I asked if she could schedule an appointment for me. She reluctantly gave me fifteen minutes with him at the end of the day.

I unscrewed the bottle of meds, shook out a tab, and dry-swallowed it, grimacing as it went down. Doctors had likened my taking pills to getting glasses. No one likes the sobriquet "four-eyes," but I couldn't afford to lose my focus. Not if I had to spar with a lawyer.

14

Tolliver stood outside Reyna's cubicle. Reyna swiveled away from her monitor, frazzled from hours of reading and analyzing transcripts of hundreds of conversations, most of them on cell phones, some intercepted and recorded by naval operatives, and others passed on by the NSA or CIA.

"Phone records came in on that SSBI subject, Commander," Tolliver said.

"And?" Reyna immediately regretted her tone, but Tolliver didn't seem to notice.

"Royer received several calls from one number in the past two weeks. The calls were made by a woman named Margaret Babcock. Might be nothing, except she was murdered last week."

"You're running it down to see if there's a connection?"

"Yes, ma'am. Also, the police arrested a suspect. A man named Blake Sanders. He was released on bail yesterday."

Reyna tapped a finger on her desk. "Okay, check him out. Get me everything you can find on him. I hate to make more work for you, Janet, but it looks like this won't go away. And it was marked top priority. We don't have much choice."

"I'll keep you posted, ma'am."

Reyna nodded and sighed. She pushed herself out of the chair and walked down to Farley's office.

* * *

I still owned a suit. A couple of them, in fact. About the only places I could buy them off the rack were big-and-tall stores. The two in my closet I'd bought in better days, and they'd been tailored to fit. I'd saved them for formal occasions. In Seattle those were few and far between—funerals, weddings maybe, and charity auctions if they weren't black tie. Grunge, which Seattle invented, had become the new office casual. My daily outfit, cast-offs scrounged from Value Village or Goodwill, usually jeans and a sweatshirt, suited me just fine most of the time. A visit to a law firm warranted one of the suits.

I waited in the large reception area on a high floor of a downtown office tower, finished in polished maple, stainless steel, and frosted glass and dotted with comfortable leather furniture. Plush commercial carpeting blanketed the hallway floors leading to the offices, but rich Persian or oriental rugs with colorful patterns resembling Buddhist mandalas covered the hardwood floor in reception. Every inch of it said "money" without being ostentatious, money made from the misfortunes of others, reminding me that I had to find a way out of my mess before the legal beagles Molly put on my case started the clock. Otherwise, my defense would cost more than the median price of a Seattle house.

A dramatic two-story wall of glass offered a hazy view of Beacon Hill to the south, the docks and Elliott Bay to the west, and a slice of First Hill to the east. The sodden sky, already darkening, leached the colors from the landscape, leaving everything a dull, bruised, muted gray. The glass reflected movement behind me. I turned to see a man dressed like me descend the sweeping staircase from the floor above.

A few steps from the bottom he spoke. "Blake?"

I met him a few feet from the stairs with an outstretched hand. "Hello, Scott."

"My secretary said you wanted to see me."

He showed me to a small conference room and offered me coffee. When I declined, he eased into a chair.

"What can I do for you?" he said, his expression guarded but friendly.

"A friend of mine wrote you about a lawsuit she wanted to file. I know you can't divulge information that might violate privilege, but can you tell me generally what it's about?"

"You're correct in assuming I can't tell you anything." His smile remained, but curiosity prompted him to ask, "Which client are you referring to?"

"Midge Babcock is the person with whom you corresponded, but she wrote on behalf of an organization called Joyance House."

He frowned for a moment, then his expression lightened and the smile was back in place. "Oh, sure, I remember. I'm afraid I wouldn't be able to tell you anything about that case even if I could. I passed it on to another partner."

"I'd like to speak to that person, then, please."

The smile stayed in place, but his tone turned impatient. "I doubt he'll be able to help you, either. I'm afraid you've wasted your time."

"Midge Babcock is dead," I said. "Murdered. I believe whatever she hired your firm to do may have led to her death."

The smile faded. He looked at me thoughtfully, then rose and moved to a credenza along one wall. He picked up a phone, punched some numbers and waited, then murmured a few words before hanging up.

"That's a serious charge," he said as he took his seat. "I don't know the exact nature of this woman's complaint, but I've asked someone to bring the file in."

We waited in silence for a minute before a knock came at the door as it opened. An all-too-familiar redhead took three steps inside the room and stopped dead when she saw me.

"Molly?"

Her look of surprise switched to annoyance, which she quickly smoothed into a bland mask. "What are you doing here, Blake?" The words were measured, calm.

"Trying to prove my innocence."

A quick rejoinder died on her lips as she glanced down at the file in her hand. "This? This is her?" She saw me nod and glanced at Williams. She pursed her lips. "Of course it is."

He gave a little shrug. "Have you read it?"

"Skimmed it on the way down," she said. "You gave it to Roberts; he'll just end up shoveling it off on me, since I gather it's more up my alley than his."

Williams smiled guiltily. "And you'll give it to an associate. Nice job on the Chemco case, by the way. Brilliant close. Saved the client several million, I heard." He glanced at me. "Wrongful termination case."

Molly gave him the barest tip of her head before turning to me. She held up the file. "You think this has something to do with her murder?"

"I don't know," I said. "All she had was that shelter, Molly. The woman was damn near a century old, and she still got up every morning and tried to help people. Something about the place got her dander up not too long before she was killed. Plenty of people heard her argue with the director about whatever the problem was. You're the one who told me the cops don't have motive. Maybe something in there provided one to somebody." I pointed at the file in her hand.

Molly glanced at the folder again, then at her colleague.

"Go ahead," Williams said, standing. "Tell him what you can. I'm sure you can handle this without me. I have a meeting to get to." He appeared eager to leave.

Molly slid into the seat Williams had vacated as the door closed with a soft click.

"You look better than you did last time I saw you."

"That's not hard." I gestured toward the file again. "What's the case about?"

She idly thumbed a corner of the folder. "I didn't have time to delve into it. It's a pro bono case if we take it on. I seem to have enough of those already." A smile crossed her face so quickly I wasn't sure I'd seen it. "And Scott was right. I'd have foisted it off, anyway."

"Anything, please." I rested my hands on the table, palms up. "Give me a hint, at least."

She opened the file as if to refresh her memory, but didn't look at it. "Okay, in general terms? It looks as if your friend Midge wanted to sue Sound Transit."

"Why?"

"You know the Link light-rail project? Midge apparently thought ST should pay the convent for an easement for the property under the halfway house."

"I still don't get it. Why would Sound Transit need an easement?"

"I don't know, Blake. Like I said, I just glanced through the file on the way down. The notes say she wanted to file an injunction to stop the tunnel construction. Maybe she thought it would damage the environment, or maybe she was suffering from dementia. We won't know until we look into it a little more."

"We? I need you on this, Molly. Take the case."

"I don't know if I can, now. This might be a conflict."

"You're not on my defense team, though, right? So take this. Please?"

She looked thoughtful. "You say she had words with the director of the shelter about this?"

"Apparently, Midge took on this crusade by herself. People tell me Nylund—the director—was furious with Midge for butting in. Midge was a volunteer, not staff."

"And she contacted us on the organization's letterhead?" She riffled through the file and looked up with consternation on her face. "Blake. Oh, honey, I think maybe we're all getting snookered by a sweet, eccentric nutcase."

My ears burned. "She was sharp as a proverbial tack, Moll. She must have had a reason."

"You're a dear man, but God I wish you'd outgrow that cornpone gullibility."

I bit the inside of my lip, tasting blood, and swallowed the ten retorts that strained to leap out of my mouth. Better my blood than hers, which was what would spill if I let the words strike their cutting blows. She'd once appreciated my midwestern sensibilities and childlike spontaneity as a complement to her cool lawyer's intellect. The right words might come to me in a day or two.

"Please, Molly," I said softly. "Just look into it, see what was bugging Midge. For me?"

She pursed her lips and heaved a sigh. "I'll read the file and get back to you, okay?" She pushed away from the table. "I have to get back to work. Jeffrey Cabot has agreed to take your case, by the way. Arraignment is in a week or so. He'll let you know. Anything else?"

I shook my head and stood. "I appreciate the help. I really do."

Her manner softened. "I know. It's just…I worry about you." Anger flashed in her eyes then vanished. She lifted a shoulder and walked to the door.

I took three large steps and beat her there, opened it for her. She passed through without breaking stride. A dark-haired man in a pewter silk suit that probably cost more than my job paid me in a month turned as we came out of the room. His face broke into a thousand-watt smile as he strode across the carpet. Molly changed direction. Somewhere around forty, he had the dark good looks of a Latino actor I'd seen on television— square chin, generous mouth, chiseled nose, black brows over smoldering amber eyes, short black hair with a pinch of salt at the temples.

"Rafe," Molly said. "Good to see you."

He took her hands, leaned in, and bussed her on the cheek. "How are you, Molly? Just the person I was looking for. Have you got a minute?"

I ambled up and waited politely until Rafe turned his head. "Rafe."

I caught the warning shot that leaped from Molly's eyes. She looked worried. I practiced better manners than that, though. Usually.

Rafe didn't lose the smile—a true politician. "Blake, what a surprise. You're looking great. Things going well for you?"

"I'm hanging in, thanks. You?"

"Terrific. I dropped by, in fact, to go over some policy issues with the lovely and brilliant Miz McHugh." He turned that radiance on Molly and I watched it paint the skin under her freckles a bright shade of rose.

"We were just talking about one of your pet projects, Rafe," I said. "Link light rail."

Rafe Acasa was a city councilman and head of the council's transportation committee. He'd been part of the Sound Transit team of local, county, and state officials that lobbied the federal government for funds for the light-rail mass-transit program. Seattle had put off building a good mass-transit system since the idea was first broached in the 1970s because voters didn't want to pay for it, and legislators in Olympia didn't have the guts to raise taxes over their protests. As a result, we were paying several times more, even accounting for inflation, than we would have if we'd bitten the bullet thirty years earlier.

Acasa, a smart political animal, had played the transportation issue to his advantage. And I'd helped him. In the process I'd learned that his political ambitions were as voracious as his ego. He had his eye on the same path others had taken to the governor's mansion, through the job of King County Executive. If he made it as far as Olympia, he probably wouldn't stop there.

"We're finally making progress," he said. "Think of how many cars we'll take off the freeways when the University Link is completed. Imagine the positive impact on the environment. And now we have Sound Transit Two to look forward to."

He made the years of disruption and traffic snarls ahead due to mass-transit construction sound like an eagerly anticipated vacation in the tropics.

I glanced around. "No cameras, Rafe. You ought to save the sound bites for the voters."

Molly gave me a look designed to zip my mouth shut if not outright kill me.

Acasa's smile barely dimmed. "You still vote, don't you?"

"Sure, but maybe you forget I've heard it all before. Aren't they giving you any new material these days?"

A small tic pulled the corner of one eye and his lips twitched. He laughed. "Maybe not as good as yours, but they treat me pretty well."

Molly, I suddenly realized, brought out the worst in me as well as the best. I yanked the green monster's leash.

"Glad to hear it. No reason you shouldn't still be getting great counsel from the company."

"No argument here." His expression softened. "Just so you know, I've got no hard feelings. What's done is done."

I reflected some of his radiance back at him. "Spilt milk and all that? It's behind me."

"Glad to hear it." He glanced at Molly. "I won't keep you. I'm sure you have better things to do than stand here and gab with me."

Molly quickly took up his cue. "We'd better talk quickly, Rafe. I've got a meeting soon." She turned to me. "If you don't hear from Jeffrey by next week, call me. I'll look into that other thing we discussed and get back to you." Her look indicated that class was dismissed.

"Right," I said. "Nice to see you, Rafe."

Acasa had already turned, placing his hand lightly in the small of Molly's back for a moment as she led him back to her office. An innocent—and chivalrous—gesture. Any lower and some might call it sexual harassment. My own hand tingled from the memory of touching her that way.

15

I hustled uptown through Pike Place Market. Years had flown by since I'd been there last, and the creaky wooden floors, funky shops, and picturesque tenants brought back forgotten memories—a lunch date at a French bistro with Molly early in our marriage when we still couldn't keep our hands off each other, pressing her up against a wall in the dark corridor outside the restaurant, fingers roaming, touching the secret places on her body, our mouths locked in a hungry kiss; the delight and wonder on our little son's face upon seeing the astounding array of devices and tricks in the magic shop; leaning against Rachel, the market's big bronze piggy bank, to take in the show of ten-pound salmon flying across the counter at the fish market; strolling past the flower stalls on Sunday mornings in spring before breakfast. The happy visions stood in stark contrast to today's bleak, cold, soggy darkness as night descended.

Rather than waste the suit, I quickly walked up Western to the loft building that housed Bellnap & Dreier. The receptionist had gone home, but the offices were still open. A smattering of men and women in business attire walked the brightly lit hallways, most so absorbed in work or focused on where they were going they barely acknowledged my presence. One or two unfamiliar faces looked at me questioningly as they passed, but didn't voice their curiosity. I looked as if I belonged and knew where I was going. Once upon a time I had.

Nick McIver glanced up from his desk and scowled at me as I stood in his doorway. His eyebrows arched in surprise, then knitted as worry creased his forehead.

"Blake! Jesus, you surprised me." He jumped up and rounded the desk. "You look good. How the hell are you?"

I reached for his outstretched hand. He leaned past instead and swung the door shut.

"I'm okay," I said. "How about you?"

He went back to his seat, propped his elbows on the desk, and gestured to an empty chair. His suit coat hung on the back of his chair. His tie was loose, the collar of his powder-blue dress shirt unbuttoned. He'd rolled the sleeves up, exposing thick, muscled forearms, but he looked haggard, much older than I recalled.

I eased into the chair.

"What are you doing here?" he asked.

"Visiting an old friend," I said. "How's Peggy? And the kids?"

"They're good. Now cut the bullshit, man. What do you want?"

"This is how you treat the guy who stood up for you at your wedding? I haven't seen you in, what, a year?"

He sighed and leaned back. "People have long memories. You know that, Blake." His face darkened again. "Did anyone see you on the way in?"

I shook my head. "No one who knows me. Christ, you *are* paranoid. You had nothing to do with it back then. Why the concern?"

"Where have you been? Don't you read the papers?"

I snorted. "You didn't know? I deliver them now."

He shook his head. "You were arrested, right? For murder?"

I waved a hand. "Oh, that. Don't believe everything you read. Arrested, yes. I didn't do it." I watched his face, but it gave nothing away. I got to the point. "I came by to see what you know about the University Link."

"What do you mean?"

"I mean what gossip are you hearing down at Sound Transit? Project running into any problems? Have any unions threatened to walk? Are contractors delivering on schedule? Has anyone reported safety concerns? Have you heard about inspectors on the take?"

He held up a hand. "Whoa, brother. Slow down. And you call *me* paranoid. Why all the questions?"

I weighed whether or not to level with him. "It could be important," I said finally. He waited. I decided to leave myself out of the equation for the time being, instead telling a big white lie. "Molly got tapped to file a temporary injunction to stop the tunnel boring."

He sniffed. "Well, it can't be a noise complaint. The TBM is a hundred and sixty feet down." He looked at me. "Unless it's the Capitol Hill station they're complaining about."

"It isn't noise," I said. I'd seen the huge tunnel-boring machine, though—TBM, Nick called it—and wondered if people directly above it didn't at least feel the vibrations as it gouged more than twenty truckloads of rock and dirt from deep underground each day. "Something to do with easements. Molly's looking into it. I just didn't want her to get blindsided, that's all."

His eyes narrowed. "Why are you involved? I thought you two were on the outs."

"If by that you mean divorced, we are." I paused, wondering exactly what Molly and I meant to each other these days. "We're still friends. I still care about her, Nick."

He shrugged. "I guess that's not hard to believe. I see guys getting divorced who end up bitter, but I never quite understood why you and Molly broke up in the first place."

I stared at him until he looked away in discomfort.

"Okay, I get that you hit a really rough patch," he said, "but I would've thought what happened would have brought you two closer together, not driven you apart."

"We all handle things differently, Nick. Molly and I...well, I—we—couldn't find a way to connect during all that." I shook off the recollections before the bad juju soured me more than the depressing weather.

Nick glanced at a heavy gold watch on his wrist. "I'm not sure what you're looking for, but as far as I know, everything's sweet as peach pie at ST—at least as far as the University Link is concerned. Is that it?"

An overhead light reflected off his forehead, shiny with perspiration. His hairline had receded too, I noticed. Pressures of the job, no doubt. I knew from long experience that working at a public affairs agency was sort of like public relations on steroids. Dealing with policy issues and government bureaucracy on behalf of clients felt like being in crisis communications mode half the time. Living on adrenaline and caffeine took its toll.

"Yeah, that's it," I said. "I'll be sure to steer clear from now on."

He looked as if he'd had a sudden gas attack. "Give me a break, will you? I've got less than six months before I finally make partner, Blake. And I'm sorry, but it just wouldn't look good hanging around with you. You shouldn't be here."

"Congratulations," I said softly. "You worked hard for it." *So had I.*

"Aw, don't do me like that."

I turned away and shook it off. Rising, I looked down at my dress shoes, spattered with dirt and water spots from walking the wet streets to his office, then lifted my gaze.

"It's no problem, Nick. You do what you have to do."

He opened his mouth to reply, but froze at a knock on the door. Before he could respond it opened and a man poked his head through. The surprise on the man's face matched my own.

McIver gestured impatiently. "Get in here, Dan, and shut the door for shit's sake."

Dan Whiting stood just shy of six feet. Thin and taut as a tuned piano wire from cycling twenty to thirty miles a day, rain or shine, Whiting had close-cropped sandy hair and a face like a whippet's. When I first met him, he'd had puppylike eyes to match, which had made him appear guileless, naïve. I'd quickly learned that the lost-puppy-dog look hid quickness and an instinct for the chase. Now in his early thirties, he'd been hardened by maturity, which had turned his face almost vulpine.

"Dan." I tipped my head.

He stared at me. "What are you doing here?"

Nick stepped in before I could reply. "Dan, you hear anything down at Sound Transit that might suggest things aren't as peachy as we make them out to be?"

The question seemed to startle him. Whiting turned to Nick, taking his eyes off me for the first time since he'd entered.

"Why?" he said. "What's going on?"

Nick relaxed his shoulders. "It's no big deal. Blake stopped by to say hello, and mentioned he heard rumblings at Molly's firm about the possibility of a lawsuit."

Whiting's head swiveled, his gaze ping-ponging from Nick to me. He rubbed the back of his neck and shifted his weight. His face smoothed into a genial mask.

"Haven't heard a thing out of the ordinary." He turned to me. "I took over the account from Roger Sutherland. He left shortly after you did. I'm on site every couple of days for updates, photo ops, that sort of thing."

"Moving up in the world," I said. "Must have learned something from me."

He grinned. "More than you know."

Armed with an undergraduate degree in poli-sci from UW, Whiting had earned a graduate degree in public administration before joining the company as an intern. He'd ended up assigned to me. He had the formal graduate education that I lacked, but I'd had the benefit of experience. He'd learned from that, quickly. Most of my business had been sports related, my client roster consisting primarily of a few minor league teams. I was glad we'd lost a pitch to the Seattle Sonics. The team's whiny owner had tried to blackmail the city into building a new stadium—when taxpayers were still footing the bill for new homes for the Mariners and Seahawks. He ended up moving the team to Oklahoma City. I wouldn't have wished that public relations nightmare on anyone. Whiting wasn't a sports fan, and his talents were better suited to big issues—public policy and politics. But he'd cut his teeth on my accounts.

"Glad to hear things are going well," I told them, then looked at Nick. "Must have just been rumors. Thanks for indulging me. It's great seeing you, Nick. My best to the family."

"I'll walk you out," Whiting said quickly.

Nick stopped him. "Did you want to see me about something?"

"Yes, but I forgot the file. I'll go get it."

Whiting gestured toward the door. I preceded him out. He shut it behind him and put a hand on my shoulder. I stopped and faced him.

"I never got a chance to tell you how sorry I was about what happened," he said.

"I was listed. The phone never rang."

He reddened but held my gaze. As he opened his mouth a young associate glided up to Whiting's elbow, short black hair neatly parted and gelled in place. A rose-colored tie and matching suspenders accented a pink dress shirt with white pinstripes. The shirt looked freshly starched. He'd just put it on, or weathered the pressures of the job with refrigerant in his veins.

He leaned in close and murmured, "I hate to interrupt, but I need your help."

Whiting looked annoyed, then saw something that changed his mind. He excused himself and followed the associate to a desk in an administrative assistant pool, bending over to look at some papers. Whiting nodded as the man spoke, and pored over the text, absorbed. I watched the associate straighten and shift his gaze from the desk to Whiting, eyes slowly walking up and down Whiting's lean body, his eyes suddenly lustrous, face transfigured by hunger. I pondered a moment, then turned away, repelled by my own voyeurism.

As I did, I caught sight of a door opening at the far end of the hall behind them. A silver-haired man turned to shut it behind him—Dreier, one of the senior partners. I turned my back and hurried around a corner, heading for the elevators before he had a chance to throw me out.

16

He prowled the dark streets and alleys, eyes searching intently like a feral cat stalking a meal. Sanders was asking too many questions. He had to be stopped, but killing him was too risky. No, he had to find another way, and Sanders had handed it to him on a platter.

He'd followed the ministry van that Sanders had gotten into, had watched in the dark on the hillside under the freeway while Sanders plied the homeless woman with liquor. He'd waited until Sanders and the two do-gooders had left, and had approached the tent with a bigger and better incentive—cash. He'd found out what she'd told Sanders, and more.

Now he hunted. He felt the familiar hunger take hold, fueled by his anger. Almost sexual in nature, it made him squirm with anticipation. The knife's weight in his pocket felt reassuring. He caressed it with a gloved hand, a thrill of pleasure coursing through his body. Yanking his hand from his pocket, he narrowed his focus and peered down an alley. There would be time for that later, but he had a task to complete first.

Forty minutes later, he spotted a ratty pair of athletic shoes sticking out from under a sheet of corrugated cardboard halfway down an alley. He approached quietly, careful not to disturb the person sleeping under the impromptu lean-to. The stink of rotting garbage wafted up. He peered under the opposite end from the shoes, and his pulse quickened when he saw the tousled hair and youthful face. This was more like it. Gently, he pulled the box away from the sleeping kid. He lay on a thin bedroll, a backpack scrunched up under his cheek. The backpack was the right color, but then he was trusting the word of a homeless, meth-addicted wino.

Checking both ways, he nudged the kid's foot with a toe. The kid jerked awake.

"What the fuck?" He sat up, blinking. "You a cop?"

"Shut up and listen. You get into it the other day with a woman? Bust her in the nose?"

The kid rubbed his eyes and screwed up his face. "Why you wanna know?"

He squatted down next to the kid and flashed a C-note. His eyes widened.

"She wants to apologize. So, you the guy or not?"

"Sure, I'm the guy." The kid tried to snatch the bill, but he held it just out of reach.

"Not so fast. What'd she do that she has to apologize for?"

"Tried to take my stuff, man. She was gonna rip me off."

"You're the guy all right," he breathed.

He gripped the knife in his other hand, excitement spreading through him. The kid's eyes were on the money. He never saw the blade flash up and just as quickly disappear into fabric, flesh, and muscle. It slid easily between the kid's ribs, the point slicing into the right ventricle. The kid gasped, and he watched the boy's eyes dart frantically to the hand that plunged the knife in his chest and back to the money he'd never be able to spend. He watched the light go out of the kid's eyes, felt the whisper of the kid's last breath on his cheek.

He closed his eyes for just a moment, savoring the feeling. Then he stood and quickly walked out of the alley, smiling to himself. Sanders's prints were on the knife. Let him try to get out of this.

* * *

Those who work the dogwatch aren't normal by most people's standards, but they're indispensable. Cops, nurses, firefighters, airline pilots, ER doctors, truckers, bus drivers, factory workers, power company linemen, grocery clerks, security guards—they all keep the wheels greased, the lights on, and the streets safe for everybody else. Some do it for the money—overtime, time and a half, or as a second job. Some, like me, prefer the pace and the peace.

But something about having to permanently alter my circadian rhythms made me fearful of yielding to the night's dark secrets. Or worse, mutating into something out of a George Romero film. Instead, like bartenders or jazz musicians, I straddled both worlds, seeing enough daylight to keep my pallor in check but spending my most productive waking hours in darkness, blending in with night dwellers, finding solace in concealment.

Wednesday, after too little sleep, I called Liz Tracey at work and asked if she was free for lunch. The phone went quiet. I thought she'd hung up. In a hesitant voice, she said, "Sure," and we agreed to meet outside a little teriyaki place near her office at noon.

I walked up to the front of the restaurant five minutes late. Liz stood on the corner, gazing at the ground near her feet with occasional furtive glances at her surroundings. She spotted me and quickly scanned the sidewalk in both directions before acknowledging my approach with a halfhearted smile that vanished as quickly as it appeared.

"Sorry I'm late," I said cheerfully. It didn't seem to put her at ease.

She snuck peeks at me from the corner of her eye on the way into the restaurant. We ordered at the counter and found a table in back. She sat primly and put her hands in her lap.

I sat across from her. "You seem uncomfortable. You okay?"

She shrugged and glanced around the noisy room. Finally, she met my eyes. "I feel like I'm a kid again. Like I've been grounded and people are checking up on me all the time."

I raised my eyebrows. "Me?"

"I'm not going to do it, you know," she said. "You don't have to worry."

"Look, I'm not here to babysit. I have to trust you'll reach out if you feel like that again. I just figured you could use a friend, someone who'd shoot straight with you."

She grasped opposite elbows. "That's all?"

"I'm not your father." I paused, realized that I didn't feel at all paternal toward her, and quickly said, "I'm not looking to be your boyfriend, either, if that's what you mean."

She chewed on that for a minute, then picked up her napkin, draping it across her lap. A waitress set plates of steaming food in front of us. Liz peeled the wrapper off a set of disposable chopsticks.

"How's work?" I asked after taking a bite.

She grimaced and swallowed. "What do *you* think? It sucks."

"How much do you know about what goes on at Sound Transit?"

"Some. We all work in different areas—I'm in planning and development right now, so we have to interact with folks at Metro and Sound Transit on a regular basis. I mean, everyone talks about Sound Transit projects—new park and rides, HOV lanes, and light rail—but buses still move most people around—a hundred million riders a year."

"I'm curious about the light-rail project. I understand how they try to use public right-of-way wherever possible, but what about when a route or a station takes up private land? They purchase the land, I assume?"

She nodded. "Sure, far as I know. Where it encroaches on private land, they get easements."

"What about tunnels, like Beacon Hill or the new one under Capitol Hill? That's still private property, right? Those tunnels must go under a lot of people's houses."

She tugged a wisp of hair loose and twisted it with a finger. "Sort of, I guess. Property owners own mineral rights to the land beneath their lots. ST pays for easements to tunnel."

"That must cost a bundle."

"Not that much. I think the going rate is a few hundred dollars per homeowner."

"What if someone doesn't want to give up their mineral rights or grant an easement?"

She laughed. "You're joking. No? People who hold out for more money? The ones who won't grant an easement right away? ST exercises eminent domain. They condemn the property and claim the rights. The property owner is out the money. Sometimes even loses the property."

"That's harsh."

She smiled, the first time she'd been truly animated since I'd arrived. "Welcome to the wonderful world of government bureaucracy."

I walked Liz back to her office after lunch. She seemed lighter somehow, as if a small candle had been lit from within. Her cheeks were flushed in the chilly air, and her eyes had lost their dullness. Her gait was more confident.

From there I hoofed it over to Metro Transit, a modern building wrapped in white steel and glass across from King Street Station, the old but refurbished train depot. On the station's other flank stood the stylized brick-and-green-glass building where Sound Transit leased office space. Both were iconic, if not ironic, choices of location for transit administrations. There, I picked up some brochures that looked helpful. On the bus home, I called Molly.

"It's only been a day," she said. "I have real work to do, you know, for paying clients." She paused. "As it so happens, I have learned a little more. Your friend Midge wasn't trying to prevent Sound Transit from digging the tunnel."

I pressed a finger against my other ear to block out the street noise. "Then why the talk about a temporary injunction?"

"You didn't let me finish. The suit she wanted us to file is only about getting paid for an easement. Filing for a temporary injunction is just a saber-rattling technique."

"But wouldn't that have the same effect? Wouldn't ST have to stop digging while it sorted out the easement question?

"Not necessarily."

I thought of what Liz had said. "Eminent domain?"

"Among other things."

"And there's no evidence this came from Nylund, the director?"

"No," she said. "Everything originated with Mrs. Babcock. Question for you, Blake: Why would a sweet old lady, if she was as sharp as you claim, think there was a chance in hell she could scam Sound Transit?"

I blinked. "You think it was a con? You think maybe that's why she was killed?"

"You tell me."

I said thanks, closed my phone, and shuffled the brochures on my lap until I found one with a map of all the Sound Transit projects. Tracing the route of the University Link with a finger on the map, I followed the tunnel as it looped from downtown Seattle under Pike up to the Broadway station now under construction, then gently curved north-northwest and headed straight for the Montlake Bridge. From there it swung north under the Montlake

Cut to an underground station just west of Husky Stadium. Joyance House wasn't anywhere close to any of it.

It didn't make sense, no matter how I looked at it. Midge hadn't cared about money. She'd cared about people. Could she have cared about the people at the halfway house so keenly that she would scam the transit agency to generate funds to support the shelter? Whether or not a nonagenarian had had the presence of mind, let alone the criminal intent, to shake down a multibillion-dollar governmental agency was moot. Someone had killed her. If it wasn't a simple home invasion, then that person had something to gain or something to hide. Or both. I thought about it the rest of the ride home but couldn't come up with a plausible explanation for Midge's involvement in a land spat with ST, or who would want to kill her—until I turned the notion around. When I considered who had the most to *lose* from a major transit snafu, one name quickly came to mind—Rafael Alphonso Acasa.

* * *

Gagnon knew the old nun had lied to him. He just didn't know what to do about it yet.

He sat in his car up the street from the church and considered his next step. He couldn't very well beat the truth out of her. At least not now. But he had to find answers quickly or all would be lost.

The nun said she'd found nothing of value in the archives. He believed her incapable of telling a bald-faced lie, but she was withholding something. He'd searched the Babcock woman's house, so he knew that whatever had compelled her call to Montréal was no longer there. Which meant her killer probably had taken it, whatever it was.

Gagnon looked at the aged, brittle letters on the passenger seat. He picked them up and read through them again, searching for some clue he might have missed. The first, dated 1845, written by a lowly midshipman on an American ship to the French cardinal in Rome, spun a fantastic tale of a French *religieuse* named Sophie Clare. She'd survived a terrible illness aboard a slave ship off the coast of Africa. The American ship had intercepted it, taken the survivors aboard and quarantined them, then had burned the slaver to the waterline.

Unsure if she would survive the journey, Sophie Clare had entrusted the sailor with a talisman of some sort, one that she claimed had saved the slave ship's other survivors from becoming ill. In the letter, the sailor vowed to protect the talisman, just as he'd promised Sophie Clare. The major events of his story, minus the details about the talisman, had been corroborated by others aboard the American ship when it finally landed in New York. Sophie Clare had gone on to Montréal to found a new order. She had died a few years later, but her story had spread, and eventually she'd been venerated.

The second letter had been written in 1852, shortly after Sophie Clare's death. By then, both the cardinal and the sailor had become politicians—Cardinal Bonald, a member of the French Senate; the sailor, Woodworth, a member of the senate of the new state of California. Gagnon slowly deciphered the script.

Your Grace,

I received the news of the Reverend Mother's death with great sorrow. Surely, the world will miss her ministrations, but God has called her to a higher cause and she now sits with Him in Heaven.

I assure you that I have not forgotten her bequest. I have found occasion to place her talisman in a location of utmost secrecy, protected by the full weight and force of these United States of America.

Fear not. No one knows of this save the two of us. Those few who know of the location know only that they protect something else entirely, but of sufficient value to warrant.

I remain your humble servant in Christ,
Selim E. Woodworth

The third letter, dated four years later, was equally curious.

Your Grace,

I hope this finds you well. The news here is not good, I'm afraid. The threat of war grows more imminent with each passing day. If we are forced to choose between a united nation and the abomination of slavery, then you know where my loyalties and sentiment lie. I hope France is not forced to choose sides should it come down to that.

I am pleased, however, that you've found a willing subject to undertake my suggestion of a mission to the Washington Territory. I look forward to meeting Sister Marguerite and finally assuring, in perpetuity, that Sophie Clare's legacy, which we both treasure and fear, will rest safely in the hands of her order, and therefore God's. It is too important to trust to any other.

The land is officially in my name now to do with as I please. If it pleases God, then the sisters should have a portion of it on which to do God's work. I shall provide Sister Marguerite with the coordinates (46°37'36" N, 122°18'29" W) and recommend that she and her party settle and build at the site of a small spring, wherein they might find a supply of fresh water. I, myself, considered it ideally suited for a well.

Go with God, my friend. Yours in Christ,
Selim E. Woodworth
(W 103 pls, 2 lks.)

The notation at the bottom puzzled him, but he shrugged it off. After a century and a half, Gagnon's wiser self knew it was too much to hope for, yet in his heart he believed that the talisman still existed. Once it had lain near a spring. Now it might be hidden under the church, or beneath the former convent down the block. It seemed impossible to Gagnon that the sisters hadn't found and reclaimed Sophie Clare's legacy for their own.

He got out of the car and headed for the women's shelter.

* * *

The old leather-bound journal beckoned from the table where I'd left it. I opened it and deciphered more of the nun's flowery French. The story picked up with the small band of sisters arriving in New York. They stayed three days, during which time a letter from her monseigneur in Montréal caught up with Sister Marguerite. The bishop's letter was full of encouragement and support of her mission, but also contained a reminder of a meeting with someone in San Francisco. The journal noted her concerns about breaking the order's code of conduct to get away from the other sisters and meet with this man alone.

The next dozen entries consisted of Sister Marguerite's observations of shipboard life on the journey, her concerns for her fellow *religieuses*, and speculation about what they'd encounter at their final destination. She didn't mention the meeting in San Francisco until their ship was a few days from port, and again the reference was oblique. The others obviously had no knowledge of her intentions, suggesting the bishop had entrusted her with a task outside her purported mission.

The ship landed in San Francisco on November 30, nearly a month after the sisters had left New York. Sister Marguerite's entries for the first two days described life in San Francisco, a city that had grown from about 15,000 souls just before the gold rush in 1848 to more than a quarter of a million five years later. The entry for December 3, 1856, was similar, but a second short entry with the same date simply said, *"J'ai rencontré l'homme dont le monseigneur a parlé, et j'ai reçu le paquet."* She'd met her contact and received the packet.

Frowning, I turned to next entry, dated the following day. She mentioned getting a letter off to the bishop, assuring him all was well with a curious notation, *"Enfin, la peste et le sang de ma sœur sont dans un endroit sûr."* Her contingent left that day on a ship headed up the coast to the Washington Territory. I found no further references to the meeting or the packet. The rest of the journal detailed the journey and the hardships of setting up the order's new mission in Seattle.

I wondered if perhaps the packet Sister Marguerite had received was simply a donation to help the mission get started. Or maybe I was reading too much into it, and the bishop merely had wanted to pay his respects to a friend or some acquaintance in San Francisco. But why the note that the pestilence was in a safe place? And what did the reference to her sister's blood mean?

I tossed the journal on the coffee table. It bounced off a stack of old newspapers and magazines, flipped open, and teetered on the edge of the table before sliding off and landing with a thud on the small area rug covering the hardwood floor. There had to be more. Midge had worried about somehow putting Florence in a bad, or even dangerous, spot. She'd left copies of her correspondence in the journal with all the information she'd asked Florence to get for her. Somewhere in that stack were answers.

Sliding off the couch with a sigh, I moved around the table on all fours and retrieved the book. I leafed through it and turned it over in my hands, captivated by the stitching in the leather, the feel of its worn smoothness, the musty smell of its pages— finding all sorts of reasons not to examine the contents again. A slight gap had appeared between the back cover and the last page in the journal. Colorful endpapers protected the inside back cover. A raised square outline, visible just inside the perimeter of the endpaper, had puckered the edge out a tiny fraction.

Sitting back on my haunches, I inspected it more carefully. The endpaper had come unglued along one edge. I worried it with a finger until it lifted, revealing another colored endpaper below. A white page was sandwiched between the two. I worked the false endpaper loose and slowly removed the folded page inside.

Written in script, the single page appeared to be a legal document, a lease agreement between the Sweet Sisters of Mercy and someone named Woodworth. The document granted the sisters mineral rights to a parcel of land identified only as "that to which Selim E. Woodworth is entitled under an Act granting Bounty Land to certain Officers and Soldiers who have been engaged in the Military Service of the United States, Certificate No. 38010." The term of the lease was for ninety-nine years with a ninety-nine year extension. The document had been signed and witnessed on the December 3, 1856.

Sister Marguerite's packet? But what did it have to do with Midge?

17

I called in almost all my favors with contacts I still had in the communications department over at UW and had to beg. But I wangled a press pass to a political fundraiser that night for an up-and-coming US representative from the state. I spotted some notable faces in the cocktail crowd at the downtown hotel: two Mariners players with their wives, ditto for the Seahawks, a scion of one of Seattle's retailing families, several software millionaires, a sprinkling of corporate execs, a winery owner from Yakima, the mayor, and Rafe Acasa.

Rafe stood on the far side of the room among a knot of admirers, most of them women, smiling, animated, flashing a mouthful of gleaming white teeth as he talked. A few yards closer to one of the portable bars, Dan Whiting pressed flesh and held court of his own with the husbands of the women surrounding Acasa. Whiting leaned into their midst, feet planted wide, putting a hand on an arm here, clapping a shoulder there, alternately laughing heartily at a joke or speaking in conspiratorial tones so that they moved in closer to hear.

The room smelled like money. Along with whiffs of expensive perfume and cologne, the fruity scents of wine and martinis made with flavored vodka, and the savory smell of little smoked salmon canapés and chicken souvlaki on trays carried by black-vested waitstaff came the odor of cash, that odd mixture of cotton, paper, and ink that smells like silk-screened denim. The net worth of the power brokers and movers and shakers in the room probably equaled the GNP of several small third world countries combined. But money can't buy class. Some of the richest men in the room were the most crass; the poorest in ways money or its lack thereof couldn't possibly account for. I'd worn the second of my two suits; I quickly got into character.

A stocky guy nearly a foot shorter than I sauntered up and gave me a lopsided grin. "Blake, how's it hanging? What are you doing here?" He twisted his head as if working a kink out of his neck.

"Hey, Tony, just testing the waters. Seeing if any sharks still want a bite."

Antoine "Tony D." Duval was an expat Canadian who'd played minor league hockey for a team I'd represented, moving into a front office job when he retired as a player.

"Don't tell me they've got you out shilling for the man of the hour there," I joked.

He grinned. "You haven't heard. I'm running for a city council seat over on Mercer Island. I figured it was time to stop complaining and start doing something. This is good exposure."

I'd never thought of Tony D. as a politician, but he had an honest, handsome face made more approachable by a scar on his nose left by an opposing player's skate blade. And he cared. He'd taken the team office job to actually help the business, not just act as a pretty face.

"Hey, isn't one of the state reps from Mercer Island on the transportation committee down in Olympia?"

"They both are." He turned to scan the crowd. Grasping my elbow, he pointed with the other hand. "Over there. Come on, I'll introduce you."

I followed him as he wove his way toward a small group of people across the room, and waited patiently a step behind him until he took advantage of a break in conversation to make introductions. The two state reps could not have been more unalike. One was a tall, lean man, thinning hair streaked with gray, blue eyes expressive behind thick glasses; his female counterpart was short, pudgy, and packed into a crimson skirted suit that accentuated her hips in an unflattering way. He was quiet, she loud.

After exchanging pleasantries I steered the conversation around to light rail and probed their feelings about Acasa's political vulnerability if the project didn't work out as promised to the voters. They waffled.

I turned. "What about it, Tony?"

He brightened at the opening. "I don't know about Rafe, but I'd say I'll hear plenty from voters about light rail if I get the council position on Mercer Island. The East Link will eat up a couple of I-90 lanes, restricting islanders' ability to get on and off the island." He looked from one state rep to the other. "Speaking of which, I wondered if I could pick your brains for a minute about strategy."

They focused their attention on Tony, obviously pleased to be consulted. I quickly excused myself. I moved to the nearest bar and ordered a beer, gulped half of it, then mingled again. I managed to bring up Acasa's name twice more in conversation, but apparently dirt on him was scarce as dust in an Intel chip factory, or people weren't willing to gossip.

I tracked Acasa's progress occasionally. He didn't have to move far—people came to him—but he'd made a point of paying his respects to everyone who mattered. At one point, he stood in deep conversation with Whiting, nodding seriously as Whiting used a pen to tick off points on a small pad he'd pulled from an inside pocket. Acasa obviously valued his counsel. I wondered if Acasa had promised him a spot on his team somewhere—campaign director, or chief of staff down the road if Acasa ended up in a position to offer it.

Whiting clearly had ambitions. At Bellnap & Dreier, he'd honed his instincts and had quickly learned how to work the system, to cut deals and bargain for what his clients wanted. As I watched him, though, I wondered what he wanted next. I couldn't put my finger on it until movement behind him caught my eye. His associate from the office watched Acasa, too, but with a baleful expression that spoke of ugly jealousy.

And then I understood what I was seeing. Whiting looked at Acasa the same way women had all evening, with admiration and a coy turn of the lips that hid inner fantasies, but only when Acasa's focus was elsewhere. Men looked at the councilman more openly, their approval, esteem, envy, or distaste more evident. Whiting treated Acasa almost too coolly, as if holding himself tightly together so his feelings wouldn't betray him. Rafe didn't seem to notice.

Molly joined Rafe and casually wrapped her arm around his. She wore a strapless cocktail sheath in *corbeau*, the green of a raven's feathers when the light hits them just right. Small emerald-and-diamond studs glittered in her ears, the jewels accentuating the red of her hair and the pale cream of her skin. My heart swelled against my rib cage, pounding to get out. I felt my ears go hot at the sight of Rafe's fingers lightly stroking her bare shoulder while he spoke to someone else in their group. His touch, almost absentminded, bespoke an intimacy that went beyond friendship.

The first time I'd laid eyes on Molly I'd known she was the one. Jane Thompson had dragged her to a Huskies basketball game freshman year along with a group of mutual friends.

We'd all met after the game at some place in the U Village shopping mall for a bite to eat. Maybe the wobbly knees or the butterflies had clued me in. Maybe it had been the challenge she'd presented, the fact she wasn't impressed by jocks, a category I wouldn't have put myself in, anyway. Whichever it was, I knew the feeling wasn't like any I'd ever had.

I excused myself and strolled toward them, mentally repeating a mantra several times—*lokah samastah sukhino bhavantu.* May all beings everywhere be happy and free. I stood with clasped hands, waiting politely until some well-wishers took the hint and moved on. Molly eyed me warily, despite the smile I pasted on my face. I focused instead on Rafe.

"Hello, Councilman."

He nodded. "Twice in almost as many days. What a happy coincidence."

"You don't vote Democrat, Blake," Molly said. "What are you doing here?"

"Working." I flashed my press pass.

"Really?" Rafe said smoothly. "You seem more interested in me than our guest of honor."

My smile widened. "You got me, Rafe. I'm trying to figure out what you've got tied up in light rail besides a lot of time and most of your political chips."

He smiled easily. "I believe strongly in mass transit. You know that. So do you." He chuckled. "Anyway, I doubt anyone, least of all voters, considers me a one-trick pony."

I ignored the warning darts Molly's eyes shot across at me. The sight of his fingers brushing Molly's skin turned my vision red.

"It just seems odd," I said. "A friend of mine was about to file a lawsuit that might have put the brakes on your pet project. Now she's dead. Even odder is the fact that you and she shared the same law firm. Until she was viciously hacked to death, that is."

Rafe was too much the politician to let it rattle him, but Molly stepped into my line of vision, spots of color burning high on her cheeks.

"Enough, Blake," she said, keeping her voice low so as not to draw attention. "Go home."

Rafe put a hand on her arm. "It's okay, Molly. You know he hasn't been right since the firm let him go."

Something hot bloomed inside me like a flowering volcano, petals of molten bile opening and flowing into every extremity of my body. I heard a dull roaring in my ears and the hum of cocktail chatter faded away.

"*I'm* not right? I didn't have a damn thing to do with what happened, and you know it."

"All I know is money went missing," he said, "and now you're delivering newspapers."

"I *made* you, Rafe. I came up with the green strategy, the branding platform, the campaign slogan that got you into city hall."

"My hard work and talent got me my job. The voters seem to agree."

"Get your hands off my wife." I reached out and swiped his fingers off Molly's shoulder.

He jerked his hand away. "*Ex*-wife. You're pathetic."

"The only thing that's pathetic here, Councilman, is you thinking you're going to get lucky tonight with my *ex*-wife."

"Stop it!" Molly said. Heads turned. She lowered her head and her voice. "Just stop it, you two! I'm going to call security." She turned.

"Molly, don't." I swung on her. "I'm leaving." My mouth worked, looking for words. "I'm disappointed in you. I can't believe your dance card is so empty you have to stoop to going out in public with *his* sorry ass."

Her eyes suddenly gleamed with wetness, but she wore an expression that mixed pity and shame. My ears burned.

Rafe moved in close, tipping his head up to speak softly in my ear. "People told me you were a fuckup. I should have listened. Now get your head out of your ass, and your ass out of this hotel."

I clenched my fists, then tensed my shoulders and clamped my jaw shut, willing them to keep still.

As kids, a buddy and I used to play in a field on the outskirts of the midwestern town where I grew up. In the summer, wheat covered the field, growing nearly as tall as we were by August. When it reached up to our waists, we flattened trails through it and pretended we were commandos sneaking into enemy territory. A meat-packing plant stood across the highway. On hot days, the smell downwind of the plant was sickening, like rancid cheese. Every once in a while, someone from the plant would drive a tractor across the highway towing a manure spreader full of offal. To us it was an enemy tank, and whenever we spotted it, we hightailed it out of the field.

One day, for some reason, we didn't see or hear the tractor until it was nearly on top of us. We ran through a canyon of green wheat to escape, bits of bloody entrails raining down like hail smacking the tall grass. The air filled with the smell of cow shit, decomposing flesh, and the ferrous scent of blood, the same rusty smell that had come from Midge's kitchen the night she was killed. A wet chunk of butchery slapped my buddy on the cheek and slid off his chin. He pulled up short, panting for breath, eyes wide in horror, and vomited down the front of his shirt.

Now, as two hard-looking men in blazers and gray slacks entered a side door of the large room, I spun away from Molly and Rafe feeling similarly soiled, like I'd puked on myself.

* * *

With nowhere else to go, I headed up to the tent city under I-5 before work. By eleven at night most street people had bunked down somewhere, either in a shelter, an alley, or a transient community like the one under the freeway. A few of the homeless continued to wander, afraid of inertia or crime, or still aggressively working neighborhoods around nightclubs, like Belltown and Pioneer Square, panhandling for the next day's rations of booze.

Now that I lacked the accompaniment of Pastor Paul's crew, the freeway residents I encountered eyed me suspiciously. They had no homes, no money, no jobs, and most needed psychiatric care or social services the state didn't have the resources to provide. Whether prideful or primal, they'd defend their turf viciously, instinctively, like animals.

The tent Bloody Mary had shared with the man called Stitch was gone. I checked my bearings to be sure. Silhouetted against the city skyline, dark figures huddled around a trash barrel. I headed their way. They watched me surreptitiously, eyes glowing orange, reflecting the firelight.

"I'm looking for Bloody Mary," I said, stretching my hands out over the warmth emanating from the barrel. "She around?"

"Stitch threw her out," someone said.

"Where'd he go?" I said.

Against the backlight, the speaker's shoulders rose and fell. "Who knows? Packed up and left. That's all."

"Good riddance," another man said under his breath.

"You all know anything about how Mary got bloodied?" I asked.

They stood silent. One or two glanced quickly at the man who'd assumed the job of spokesman, then cast their eyes down into the barrel. The alpha of the pack never took his eyes off me. He topped six feet, with gaunt cheekbones above a dark beard. He'd pulled a blanket over his bald head. He held the blanket closed in front with one hand and waved the other hand over the fire.

"Tried to take someone's stuff," he said.

"Whoever it was didn't take kindly to that, I take it. You saw this?"

He squinted in the flickering light. "Who's asking?"

"Name's Blake. I'm a friend of Pastor Paul. You?"

"Carl." He waggled his hand at me. "No collar. Friend doesn't make you special."

"I'm just trying to help," I said. "Cops are looking to put a murder on her."

"Mary? That's bullshit, man. I seen it go down, all right. On Broadway, down near the school..." He twirled his finger. "Seattle Central. There's a backpack just sittin' there, with a bedroll strapped to it. Nobody near it. So Mary goes and picks it up. All she wants is the bedroll, you know what I'm saying? This kid comes running up, yelling at her to drop it. She's like 'finder's keepers,' so the kid hauls off and slugs her." He pointed to the bridge of his nose. "Right here. Gushed like a fountain."

"A kid, you said? Like a student?"

"Maybe." He shrugged again. "Looked more like a street kid."

"What happened next?"

"Nothin'. Kid grabbed his stuff back and walked away."

I rubbed my hands together and jammed them in my pockets. "Thanks. You all keep warm." The circle of faces went dark now that the fire had ebbed. I turned away.

Carl's voice stopped me. "Last time you was here, a man showed up right after you left."

"What did he want?"

Carl shrugged. "Don't know. Went straight for Stitch's tent. After he left, Stitch threw Mary out and moved on. Saw Stitch the next day, though, outside the liquor store. Seems like he'd come into some money."

18

While folding newspapers, I wondered how Acasa's macho posturing had sucked me in and realized *my* fragile male ego had started it. My internal DVR was stuck on play. I needed a pause button in the middle of my forehead to give me just a moment to decide whether to let the annoying commercials play or fast-forward over the crap.

I'd taken up yoga as an alternative to tae kwon do to help stretch muscles that stiffened around my artificial hip, among others. I doubted a mantra would fix the rent with Molly that my foot-in-mouth disease had caused this time. Flashes of anger like the one in the hotel burst inside me unannounced, like aerial ordnance. The insomnia—a perfect fit with the carrier job—made things worse. My system was out of whack, full of the wrong sort of humors. Nothing a little more sleep wouldn't cure. None of it was unproductive, Jeri said, as long as I channeled it and learned from it, particularly the anger.

After loading up the car, I methodically ticked off the addresses on the list as I tossed, stuffed, or placed the papers according to each customer's instructions. I drove by Midge's house on autopilot at the end of my route. Remnants of crime scene tape hung in dirty ribbons on the ground. The house looked condemned, sentenced to death to make way for something new. It reminded me of how alive Midge had been even after a century of wear and tear. I considered looking for the codicil again. Decided not to chance it.

Remembering Midge's concern for Florence, I swung by the rectory. As if I could check on the sister at that hour of the morning. She was in bed. Where would she be safer than in a house full of priests? Seeing the dark, quiet rectory made me feel better, anyway.

Charlie found me later, hunched over a cup of coffee in my customary spot. He wore civvies, indicating his shift had ended. I motioned to a chair. He hesitated, then sat.

"Buy you a cup of coffee?" I said.

He waved a hand. "I'm not staying. Just wanted to let you know we found a gutter punk yesterday morning." He paused. "Dead."

"I guessed that. Overdose?"

He shook his head, inspecting the fine grain of the plastic tabletop. "Nah, murdered."

I frowned. "I don't follow. Why are you telling me?"

"I shouldn't be here."

He turned and stared out the plate-glass window. My eyes followed and saw the two of us reflected there, along with ghostly images flickering past on the street in the darkness beyond. He rose without a word and stood next to his chair looking down at me.

"The kid was knifed," he said finally. "A little different MO than the old lady. Still, a knife, if you know what I'm saying."

Before I could think of a reply, he'd walked out.

* * *

After a couple of hours of sleep, I got hold of a patient campus switchboard operator over at the U who gave me the names of two history professors who might have answers to my questions. I actually remembered one of them from my undergraduate days at the school—Professor Bill Royer. For the hell of it, I tried his direct office line and caught him correcting papers. I told him enough about what I'd found over the phone that he sounded intrigued and suggested I drive over.

Even with classes in session, the campus was alive with students wandering the quads. A group of them hustled past me up the steps to Royer's building. I paused to let them by, and they threw one of the double doors open with a bang. Before it closed, a well-dressed man slipped out and lit a cigarette, his athletic frame radiating pent-up energy, as if poised to leap. He blew out a long stream of pale blue smoke, which I waved away.

"*Pardon*," he said, the pronunciation French.

His thin lips curled up into what would have been a sneer had his eyes not crinkled at the corners. He gave a slight bow and whisked past me.

I remembered that Royer's office was on the first floor, but so much time had passed since I'd last been there, I peered at room numbers to jog my memory as I hurried past. Spotting familiar landmarks, I crossed the hall to Royer's door and knocked, pushing it open at the same time.

"Come in," he called, looking up from a desk in front of a large window. He blinked over the tops of half-frame reading glasses. "You're Sanders?"

He'd aged, light-brown hair thinning on top, skin around his throat and jaw loose, lines in his face deeper, but he looked much as I remembered him. His bright-blue eyes crinkled at the corners under bushy eyebrows, as if he harbored a secret joke. Still thumbing his nose at university politics, he wore a plaid shirt and zippered fleece vest instead of dress shirt and tie. I would have bet money that the desk hid a pair of shorts, though it was December.

"You don't remember me. I was in one of your classes as an undergrad."

"A long time ago, apparently." His expression didn't change.

"Yes." My face grew warm. "I'm glad you were able to see me."

Awkwardly, I pulled the document hidden in Sister Marguerite's journal from my pocket and spread it out on Royer's desk. He bent to look at it. After a moment, he peered up at me.

"How did you get this?" he said.

I told him again where I'd found it, and how I'd come to have it.

"Tell me again," he said, "what's your connection to the Babcock woman?"

"I delivered her paper. We got to be friends."

"The cops think you killed her," he said. "What's your interest in this?"

I considered him for a moment, heat creeping up from under my collar. Of course, he'd know.

"I understand. You're not sure if I killed that woman or not. I didn't. I'm only interested in finding out who did."

"Save your own skin, eh?"

"You can check me out, you know. I worked in the communications department here for years. I married my college sweetheart. I can give you references."

He shook his head slowly. "People change."

"I need help," I said softly.

He swiveled the chair around and looked out the window, arms resting in his lap. I held my tongue, a hundred thoughts wheedling into my mind, then flapping away pointlessly. He remained motionless, so I turned for the door.

His voice stopped me. "You sat in the back row. Tall guy who couldn't remember dates."

"Not to save my life."

He got out of his chair and went to a bookcase covering one wall. He hooked the spine of a book with his finger, pulled it out, and brought it back to the desk, thumbing through it as he sat. The office went quiet except for the muted sounds of conversation and laughter outside as some students passed by his window.

"How much do you know about Seattle's beginnings?" he asked. "No? Okay, time for a little history lesson. Back in nineteen hundred, a fellow from Tacoma by the name of Hugh Wallace bought a hundred and sixty acres of land in Seattle. Wallace was a former US secretary of state. Smart businessman, too, it turns out. He bought the land for a hundred and ninety thousand dollars. That afternoon—the same day, mind you—he sold it to a fellow name of James Moore for two and a quarter, a nice little profit of thirty-five grand."

"James Moore. Moore Theater? Moore Hotel?"

He nodded. "Moore was a real-estate developer with big dreams. The parcel of land was—is—adjacent to Volunteer Park up on Capitol Hill. Moore wanted to plat it, sell the lots only to people who promised to put up houses that cost no less than three thousand—a lot of money at the time—and move the state capitol up from Olympia. That's how the neighborhood got its name."

I scratched my head. "What's this all got to do with this Selim Woodworth person?"

He leaned forward. "I'm getting to that part. Wallace bought the land from Woodworth's estate. Woodworth was a US Navy commodore. To encourage enlistment in the armed services during the Mexican-American War, the government issued bounty land warrants. These warrants were good for any public land, not just land in military districts. Later, to compensate everyone who had served in the military since the Revolutionary War, the government extended the warrants under Military Bounty

Land Acts in, hmm, let me think…eighteen fifty, fifty-two, and fifty-five."

He tapped the open book. "Woodworth served as a midshipman on the USS *Warren* during the war. But he didn't benefit from the MBLA until eighteen fifty-five. When he did, he got a warrant for a hundred and sixty acres—that piece of land up on Capitol Hill. At the time, it would have been nothing but forest. But here's the kicker. Woodworth never lived in Seattle. Never even saw the property, to the best of anyone's knowledge. He lived in San Francisco. Got married, had kids. Died there in eighteen seventy-one."

"You're sure it's the same piece of land?"

"Warrant three eight oh one oh," he read, "the same number here on the lease document you found. It's dated August eleventh, eighteen fifty-six."

"So, the lease covers mineral rights under the entire chunk of land?"

"It would appear so," he said. He leaned back and laced his fingers behind his head.

"I don't get it. Woodworth gives a little parcel of land he's never seen to a bunch of nuns. So, he's benevolent. But why give them the mineral rights beneath an even bigger chunk? And why would anyone buy a piece of land that big without the mineral rights attached?"

"The simple answer is—I don't know." He leaned forward again and consulted the book. "This author says the land was kept off the market until nineteen hundred due to delays in certifying that the location of the plot in the warrant was correct and that the land was unencumbered in any manner. I guess no one found that document until now." He gestured at the piece of paper still lying on the desk.

None of it made sense. But if Midge had found the lease agreement, and Joyance House had some claim to mineral rights on Capitol Hill through the Sisters of Mercy, maybe going after Sound Transit for payment for an easement hadn't been such a crazy idea. And maybe it had gotten her killed. Another thought popped into my head.

"What would Woodworth have had in common with a French-Canadian religious order?" I said. I saw him frown and stare into space for an answer.

His eyes slowly focused, and he rubbed his chin. "I'd say it's rather curious. There was a fellow here right before you showed up. French. History professor at the Sorbonne in Paris. Alain Dufours. Said he's here on vacation because he's interested in American history, particularly the Pacific Northwest."

My thoughts went to the man outside on the steps. "What did he want?"

"Just popped his head in and said he was wandering by and figured he'd introduce himself. Asked if I specialized in Seattle history."

"And?"

He shrugged. "And nothing. I don't. I specialize in Northwest history. As you can see, I know a fair amount about Seattle, and know where to look. Just an odd coincidence, I guess."

"What, French and French-Canadian? Montréal's a long way from Paris. You don't think he's on the up-and-up?"

"No reason not to think so. He seemed a bit strange—intense—but maybe that's because he's from Paris."

A smile twitched my lips. It faded quickly as my predicament wormed its way to the forefront of the phalanx of thoughts parading through my head.

"You interested?" I gestured at the lease document on his desk.

He sat up straighter. "In solving this little mystery? Of course. I think this is historically significant. But I'm swamped right now. Semester finals and all." His voice trailed off. He clenched his jaw, then swallowed and took a breath. "I'm up for department chair."

"That's it?"

"Look," he said quietly, "Midge Babcock called me a week ago. Said she had some document that would set up the women's shelter for life. She wanted me to look into it. I made some calls. Now she's dead, and all of a sudden people are showing up on my doorstep asking questions. I don't like it."

"You knew…?" I chewed on that. "Professor, please, if not for me, then do it for Midge."

He nodded. "I'll see what I can find."

* * *

Gagnon stood under a tree out of the light drizzle and took a drag from his cigarette. He threw it in the dirt and ground it under his heel. He'd seen the tall man before, with the old nun. Gagnon hadn't gotten this far, hadn't stayed alive this long, by ignoring coincidences. He waited patiently. The history professor had been little help, but maybe Gagnon hadn't asked the right questions. Or provided the right incentives. The tall man had already stayed inside the building longer than he had with Royer. "Caution," his countryman Hugo once said, "is the eldest child of wisdom." Whoever this stranger was, he obviously knew something, was involved somehow. As difficult as inaction was for Gagnon, if his patience was rewarded the tall man might give him the answers he needed.

19

Frank Shriver sat on a bench in front of a jungle gym of steel pipes shaped like a buckyball. He'd pulled the collar of his parka up, his hat down over his ears, and hunched his shoulders against the cold drizzle. Short and slight, even bundled up in the winter coat, he could have been mistaken for a big kid. The playground, a few blocks from *The Seattle Times* building, hadn't been hard to find. Shriver looked up as I approached, and scanned the street. He fidgeted, trying to keep warm, his bulging eyes darting around the playground nervously in a face leathered and wrinkled by a pack-a-day habit. I rubbed my gloved hands.

"What took you so long? You think I got all day? And what's so damn important you can't say it on the phone?"

"You couldn't have picked a nice warm coffee shop?" I slid onto the front edge of the bench, sitting on my coat to keep the dampness from seeping through my pants.

"You wanted to talk, let's talk," he said, shivering. "I don't have much time."

I studied him. Frank had worked his way up from reporter to metro editor covering local politics, science, and the military.

A good writer with the disposition of a Jack Russell terrier toying with a sock, he rooted out stories like bones in the backyard, or one of those trained pigs sniffing out truffles in the woods. A blessing and a curse, perhaps, for me.

"I want you to look into Rafe Acasa's dealings with Sound Transit," I said.

His head came up sharply. "Why?"

"Because I want to know if he has a vested interest beyond sitting on the ST board. I want to know why he's betting his entire political career on mass transit."

"No," he said quietly. "The guy's only doing his job."

"Oh, come on, Frank. Even you have to admit it's pretty strange for a guy who has ambitions to get to Olympia to hang his hat on just one issue."

He dug in his heels. "It smells like a vendetta to me. I won't do it."

The flash of heat that ran through me almost brought me to my feet. I let the red at the edges of my vision subside before I opened my mouth. I used the back of my gloved hand to wipe rain from the tip of my nose.

"Rafe Acasa has a lot to lose if there are any problems on the University Link project," I said slowly. "Voters turned down Prop One the first time. Now they've finally funded extensions, and the cost has gone up even more. And the airport run just opened. If something goes wrong on this tunnel, it could be the nail in the coffin for light rail—and Acasa's career."

He thrust his chin forward. "And you've got a grudge against him."

This time I stood and faced him. "This is nothing personal, damn it!"

"He accused you of embezzling campaign funds. You nearly went to jail. I'd call that personal."

I threw up my hands and exploded. "What the fuck is it with people in this town? You're a reporter, Frank. Get your facts straight. First off, Rafe Acasa never personally accused me of anything. He's too smart for that. His campaign manager did that. Second, I didn't go to jail because I was never indicted. And third—"

"You weren't indicted because your firm covered your ass and settled. If Dreier hadn't cut a deal with the PA's office, you'd be somebody's bitch in Walla Walla."

I bent down and stuck three fingers in his face. "*Third*, I didn't embezzle shit. Whether or not you choose to believe that is out of my control, but it's true. I lost my job, my friends, and I have to make good on the money that was stolen. For that, I get to keep my freedom. But the fact is I'm not in jail because I didn't do it."

He reached up and pushed my hand aside. "You're not in jail because you're one lucky SOB, and you've got rich friends—first at B&D, and now your ex-wife."

I tensed, thought better of it, and flexed my fingers. "I've always been square with you. Never asked you to run with something that wasn't true, never jerked you around. You don't want to give me the same courtesy then I'll just have to suck it up. But you bring Molly into it, you're crossing the line." I broke off to see if he was listening. "What is it with you, Frank? When did getting a story start interfering with finding out the truth?"

His mouth worked like a carp's before he finally got words out. "What do you mean?"

"You used to be all about finding out what really happened before writing a story. Maybe now you just want to sell newspapers."

His ears reddened and the muscles at the corners of his jaw tightened. "Fuck you. I have a job to do." He stood.

I raised my hands. "Selling newspapers is how I make my living, too. At least I don't lie."

He stepped toe to toe with me and craned his neck to look me in the eye. "If it weren't for the fact we're grown men, I'd break your nose."

I half hoped he'd try. I needed to hit something. "Sit down."

He hesitated, then lowered himself onto the bench. I did the same and leaned forward, resting my elbows on my knees, putting my thoughts in order before I spoke again.

"I don't want to fight you, Frank. From your point of view, you're right. The evidence all pointed to me." The words felt like shards of glass coming out of my mouth. "You just reported the facts at the time. I apologize."

He nodded grimly. "Apology accepted."

I should have noticed the missing funds long before the shortfall came to light. Acasa and his managers had hired Bellnap & Dreier to handle positioning on policy issues to make him more appear more well-rounded to voters, more multifaceted. We'd also handled his campaign finances and organized many of his fundraisers. Though I'd been involved in the brainstorming sessions to jump-start his career—had come up with most of the ideas, in fact—they'd put me in charge of the campaign accounts precisely because I wasn't involved in the issues or day-to-day affairs of Acasa's campaign. They gave me responsibility for the purse strings because they thought me trustworthy, an objective third party.

Only I'd been distracted. Not the sort of distraction common to people like me. No, this distraction had been a little more pervasive, unaffected by medication, threatening to tip my whole world on its axis. Nothing like a death in the family to take one's mind off nearly everything else in life. So I hadn't noticed when money donated to Acasa's campaign war chest somehow got diverted. Someone, though, had called the accounts into question, and when the dust had settled, they'd found an account opened in my name.

All told, more than fifty thousand dollars had been stolen, but only a few thousand were still in the bank account with my name on it. The rest had been withdrawn, apparently by me. The accusations and ultimate disposition of the matter by the senior partners—my summary firing and a contract with B&D to pay restitution—had seemed just at the time, appropriate scourging for whatever other sins I'd committed. My only guilt now, however, lay in the same dissembling I'd accused Frank of perpetuating. For too long now, I'd let the story outweigh the truth. And grief had overwhelmed me, taking away any interest I might have had in finding it.

"Not much gets by you," I said, "but you know how many sides there are to every story."

"More than two," he admitted.

"You know I was arrested and you know why." I held up a hand as he took a breath. "What you don't know is that the murdered woman wanted to get an injunction against Sound Transit. A long shot, but she had a case, and it might have shut down construction on the tunnel for a while until everything got sorted out."

His facial muscles moved his features to express a jaded look that came naturally to him. "This is for real?"

"Call Molly for corroboration—it's her case—but she won't give you details."

"What's the injunction for? What did the woman want?"

"Payment for an easement." I saw his look of dismissal. "Not just under one lot. She had a document that throws ownership of mineral rights on about a quarter of Capitol Hill in question. ST may be digging illegally." I let it sink in and watched as pieces clicked into place for him.

"Acasa's not capable of murder," he said.

"We're all capable of murder," I said softly. "Even me. But I know *I* didn't kill her, so that leaves me looking for people with motive."

He took a moment to respond. "Who knew about the injunction?"

"No idea. Maybe some of the people where she volunteered. Folks at Molly's firm." I paused. "Acasa's a client there."

He chewed on that thought. "Doesn't mean he knew."

"No, it doesn't. But if anyone could find out I imagine it would be you."

The world-weariness in his lined face turned to skepticism. "Just to prove you wrong, I'll look into it. I think you're sniffing up the wrong dress. But if you really think the murder's tied to Sound Transit construction, you should take a hard look at the tunnel contractor—Damien Construction."

"I thought some Japanese firm got the contract."

He craned his neck, head wagging as he scanned the park again with glittering black eyes, sniffing the air for danger.

"You're thinking of Obayashi. They dug the tunnel under Beacon Hill on the line down to the airport. Damien beat them out this time around, and people were happy to see the contract go to a local firm. Not that Damien is small potatoes. The guy's got offices around the world—close to half a billion in projects in Dubai alone. But so far I hear cost overruns on the tunnel are rampant, and the safety record on the site is terrible."

I turned it over in my head. "I'd love to have a conversation with those folks, but it would help to have something going in, a little ammunition." I saw him hesitate. "Think of the potential stories, Frank. They'll sell more papers than your standard felony B and E. Readers don't care if some old lady got robbed and killed by a crazy paper carrier, and I didn't do it, anyway. But an elderly woman who gets snuffed because she's in the way of some conglomerate…"

He sighed. "I'll see what I can find out."

* * *

The modern brick, steel, and glass public library on Capitol Hill offered all the amenities of a chain bookstore. The books didn't interest me. Free time accessing the Internet did. I combed through the Sound Transit website, reading the official releases about the agency's good works and the progress on the U Link. Construction photos had been regularly posted to a gallery, some dated only days earlier. According to the glowing reports, ST's headway on the project was on schedule and virtually trouble free.

Newspaper accounts told a somewhat different story. A couple of opinion pieces decried the overall cost of the project and argued it wasn't justified based on the estimated number of riders ST anticipated when the light-rail line was completed. Two articles noted cost overruns based on quarterly reports submitted by Damien Construction to the board, as required under their contract. One story quoted Claude Damien's assurances that the excessive costs were anomalous and he expected the tunnel to come in on budget.

There was an article on the role one of our senators had played in the passage of a recent federal spending bill that included thirty million in grant money for tunnel construction. That same senator had cozied up to Acasa at the fundraiser.

Four articles detailed accidents on the construction site. Nine construction workers had been injured so far on the project, three in the tunnel when a rail car crashed into a concrete barrier, and six others in different accidents in and around the Capitol Hill station. None of the accidents had caused a fatality, unlike one in the Beacon Hill tunnel construction back in 2007. That was small comfort, according to the press—with the higher accident rate on this project, another death was only a matter of time.

The information I found on Damien Construction and owner Claude Damien echoed what Frank had already told me.

Damien had formed the company back in the 1960s, throwing up commercial buildings and office towers. In the 1970s, when Boeing laid off tens of thousands and a billboard on the edge of town read, "Will the last person leaving Seattle please turn out the lights," the company rode out the recession by winning contracts overseas. The contracts and the projects got bigger. Damien got wealthier but kept his perspective, apparently never losing sight of his roots. He contributed to local causes, treated his employees well, and stayed married to the same woman for forty-five years—a real prince.

My Internet searching had given me little except a splitting headache. I laced my fingers behind my head, leaned back, and stretched. Time to find out how Damien got the Sound Transit bid.

20

Liz met me in the busy food court next to the big Asian market over on Sixth. She looked brighter somehow, more animated, with a lightness that suggested she'd lifted a heavy invisible yoke from her shoulders. When we got our food, she led the way to a table, her movements quick, impatient.

The long tables were full, the food court a bobbing sea of faces and kaleidoscope of moving color. Seats filled as quickly as people vacated them, the fast-turning tables reflecting the limited time diners had for lunch. We sat across from each other. I was elbow to elbow between an elderly Japanese man and a goth girl with more piercings than a trussed turkey. Liz squeezed between a Japanese woman with two small kids and Goth Girl's leather-clad boyfriend. He sported fewer metal studs, but was no less striking. Ten-inch neon-purple spikes stuck out of his head in a Mohawk-style haircut, and he wore matching eye shadow. The corners of Liz's mouth turned up before she deftly wielded chopsticks loaded with food to her lips.

"You look good," I said before I took my first bite.

She lowered her chopsticks to look at me, chewing thoughtfully. "As opposed to what?"

Mohawk glanced at me, upper lip curling in disdain, did an eye roll, and turned away.

"Of course I look good," she said. "I looked good on that bridge. Because I almost did something stupid I'm supposed to fall apart and forget how to put on lipstick? What does that mean, you look good?"

"It was supposed to be a compliment."

Liz tweezed a snow pea with the chopsticks and looked me in the eye. "Bullshit." She popped the food in her mouth and watched me color. "You're so transparent."

Goth Girl snickered. Liz flashed her a warning look.

"What do you mean?" I managed.

"You don't keep asking me to lunch because you're interested in me," she said. Mohawk nodded, smelling blood. "You're damn right I look good. But if you really thought that, really meant it, you would have made a move before this. Asked me out to dinner instead of lunch. Kissed me, maybe. Or tried to. But I'm damaged goods to you, aren't I? You think I'm nuts, too crazy to ask out on a date. My guess: you feel guilty. You probably lost someone to suicide, someone close to you. Now you're trying to make up for it by saving me."

I detected no rancor, no accusations in her voice. But her words picked at the wound where it had scabbed over, letting guilt seep out, anyway.

"Good theory. Actually, I asked you to lunch because I wanted to pump you for information about the University Link project. You want to make it dinner instead?"

She looked disappointed for a moment. So did Mohawk. He lost interest, and with a nod to Goth Girl started clearing his things from the table. Liz glanced at them, distracted, but turned her attention to me when they stood to leave.

"The light-rail project?" she asked. "You're back to that? Why? What are you after?"

I hesitated.

"You don't want to talk about it, that's fine." She waited a beat just to make sure. "Taking advantage of me isn't much better, but at least you're being honest. What do you want to know?"

"Everything. Can you tell me how contractors get to work on the project?"

She tipped her head and looked at me. "It's not my area. But I have a good idea how it works." She explained the sealed bid process Sound Transit used.

"What do you know about Damien Construction?" I said when she finished. "Why all the cost overruns?"

"I don't know about Damien, but overruns aren't uncommon on a project this big," she said. "It happens all the time."

"Who pays for that? Surely ST holds contractors to their bids."

"It depends on what causes the job to go over cost," she said. "If it's a design problem, ST has to come up with the money to fix the problem. If the contractor underbid the job, I guess it depends on the way the contract's written up, but I'd say the contractor has to eat the cost. That's the way it works with city contracts. And a lot of times, a project will go over in some areas but come in under budget on others. I'm guessing Damien's got a lot of experience on big projects. I'll be surprised if they don't bring the tunnel in on budget. I think the media made a big stink about overruns without looking at the big picture."

She paused and took another bite of food. I did the same, mulling over what she'd said. A few moments later she stopped chewing and looked at me.

"Seriously, why are you asking me all these questions, anyway?"

I hesitated to involve her any more than I already had, but she deserved to know.

"I told you my friend was killed," I said. "It might have something to do with this."

Her eyes widened. She leaned over the table conspiratorially. "With the University Link? The tunnel? You mean your friend was murdered?"

I covered her hand with mine. She stared at it but didn't pull away.

"Look," I said, "you don't have to say any more if it makes you uncomfortable. I just…I'm just looking for answers, that's all."

She rolled her eyes. "Like that's going to happen. Besides, I'm the last person you should come to for answers. Remember? If I had any would I think about what it feels like to fly?" She forced a quick smile. "Why don't you let the cops handle it?"

"They think I did it," I said.

She snatched her hand away.

"I didn't, of course." I left my hand on the table. "But I sure as hell am not going to get any help from them proving it."

Her face darkened. "You lied to me. All that crap about how much you care."

I shook my head. "It's not crap. And I didn't lie. Not once. I just figured you had enough problems. You didn't need to hear about mine. But I could really use your help."

She slumped in her chair, eyes flicking back and forth.

"Like what kind of help?" she said finally.

"Do you think someone at Damien could be skimming off the top?"

Her brows knit. "What do you mean? Like how?"

"Using inferior materials, charging a premium and pocketing the difference, maybe."

She pursed her lips. "Like I said, I don't know anything about the company, but I don't see how," she said slowly. "Not impossible I suppose, but it's tough to get bills paid through our accounting system at the city. I'm sure ST has a lot of checks and balances in place, too."

"Is there any way to find out?"

She considered it. "Maybe. It wouldn't be easy. If someone's doing that, they're probably covering their tracks pretty well. But I could look into it."

"Thanks." I took a breath and held it.

She looked at me from under her brows. "What? What else?"

"Can you find a way to get me onto the construction site?"

She paled.

"It's okay," I said hurriedly. "I don't want to get you in trouble or anything. I can find a way to get on site."

She looked at me for a moment longer, making some sort of internal calculation. "I could get you a media pass if you can figure out a way to come up with some credentials."

"Perfect." I wondered why I hadn't thought of it.

After lunch, Liz walked back to her office. I lingered on the corner outside and called Molly to ask her some of the same questions about Damien Construction. She tried to put me off but finally relented and said she'd look into it.

* * *

Molly called me back a few hours later and insisted I meet her. She wouldn't say why. When she suggested the park a few blocks from her house I knew something wasn't right. I agreed to meet her there in twenty minutes.

The playground was empty, silent, but I heard the sound of laughter in my head and pictured kids chasing each other and pumping their legs on the swings. A little towheaded boy outshone them all, buoyant and glowing with energy and enthusiasm, racing from slide to swings to monkey bars, unable to decide which delighted him most.

Molly sat on a bench, one hand in her coat pocket, the other idly toying with the button at her neck. Hatless and gloveless, the tip of her nose had turned red from the cold. She stood when she saw me. Her face lit momentarily from within and faded just as quickly, as if someone had flicked a switch on and off. I automatically moved to embrace her, but caught myself, awkwardly shoving my hands into my coat.

Turning slowly, she scanned the park, a faint smile on her lips. "You remember this place, Blake? We came here a lot, once. Our sanctuary from the world."

I followed her gaze but shut out the memories that threatened to bubble up from beneath all that silt. She saw somewhere past the playground.

"This is where we came when we first learned about his disability."

"You make it sound like it's the same as being blind or crippled," I said.

Cole found everything interesting, a trait both charming and exhausting. When he'd finally been diagnosed with ADHD, some pieces of my own life had made more sense, too. Struggles in school, the succession of jobs when Molly and I were first married, the taste of shoe leather from putting my foot in my mouth, the forgetfulness.

"You know better," she said. "Putting a label on it helped me understand some of it. Helped me understand Cole better. You, too."

I shrugged. "It didn't fix anything, sadly. Anyway, what's wrong?" I asked. "You sounded worried on the phone."

She lowered herself onto the bench and patted the space beside her. I perched on the edge of the bench and turned to face her.

"You're in trouble," she said.

I smiled, hiding my annoyance. "Tell me something I don't know. You're not still mad about the fundraiser, are you?"

She shook her head. "No, I mean real trouble, Blake. We got word the PA's office wants to up the charges against you."

I frowned. "To what?"

"Aggravated murder." She paused. "That's a capital offense."

"I *know*." I saw her wince, and I sighed.

"Sorry. There's nothing we can do, I suppose." Her expression answered for her. "What changed their minds?"

"Your friend Midge's will." She searched my face as I tried to comprehend what she'd said. Her eyes flashed and her jaw clenched. "Don't tell me you don't know anything about it."

I felt the blood drain from my face, the air suddenly cold as death on my cheeks.

"Midge named you executor of her estate, Blake. I don't know what you did to talk an old lady into putting you in charge of her will, but—"

I put a hand up. "Whoa. Stop right there. I didn't talk her into anything. I swear, I knew nothing about this. This is all a big joke, right? I'm being punked, aren't I?"

She pressed her lips together, exasperated. "This is serious. I'm truly afraid for you. The PA is talking about the death sentence."

"She joked about putting me in her will. Even wrote a codicil. Said she wanted to repay me for all I'd done. Just for being kind. I talked her *out* of it, Molly. Honest. Told her I wasn't looking for a reward or repayment. Conversation, someone to talk to, that's all I wanted. I never thought she'd go through with anything like this."

"You could have talked to me." She spoke so softly the words barely reached my ears.

"Midge really named me executor?"

"Coexecutor, along with her attorney."

"Her attorney? The firm isn't handling it?"

"No, we're not. She had someone else draw up the papers."

"Why would she ask me to recommend a lawyer if she already had one?"

She looked exasperated. "I don't know. Maybe she thought a big-name law firm would scare Sound Transit more easily than a small one." She paused. "Damn it, Blake, we're talking about your life!" She glared at me and suddenly turned away.

I tentatively put a hand on her shoulder. She'd always been tough, even through the months of agony we endured before our split. This Molly was someone new to me.

"Hey, it's okay. Everything's going to be all right."

She whirled on me. "How can you say that? The evidence all points to you, Blake. They've got your fingerprints on the murder weapon, a witness who places you at the crime scene, along with your own admission you were there, and now they've got motive. How can you possibly believe this will turn out well?"

"That motive isn't exactly compelling. Being executor only means I carry out her wishes, right?"

"There's a fee involved, according to the will. A sizable one."

"Sizable? Midge?"

"She wasn't rich, but she was comfortable, according to her attorney. She lived frugally is how he put it, and invested well. You're destitute, so the prosecutor will argue that you needed the money desperately and you're colluding with one of the beneficiaries, whoever they are."

"I didn't do it, Molly."

"Simple as that?"

"Simple as that. Plus, I have your firm defending me."

I watched her calm herself, arguing and hearing the case in her own mind. She appeared to have a hung jury on her hands.

"I'll contact her attorney, find out who's named in the will," she said. "You're the suspect, so don't go anywhere near her lawyer, you hear me?"

"Fine, but I'll have to meet with him at some point. Who is he?"

She hesitated. "George Adams. But wait until I give you the go-ahead."

I nodded. Worry still lined her face.

"Look," I said, "your guys will do their best to find a way to pick the cops' case apart. In the meantime, I'll find out what really happened. I promise."

"How?" She looked grim. "Oh, no. You're not thinking of trying to put this on Rafe Acasa, are you? Blake, if you so much as..."

"As what? Look, I don't know how involved you are with Rafe, and I don't care. But I'm not out to get him. I'm trying to find out who killed Midge Babcock. If Rafe didn't have anything to do with it, he has nothing to worry about."

"I can't believe you'd go that far to prove you're innocent. I can't believe you'd try to implicate someone like Rafe."

"What? He didn't get his licks in when I got set up for stealing his campaign funds? Give me a break. I let it go. It's over and done with. I'm not gunning for Rafe, but so help me, if he gets in my way..."

"I knew it. You're jealous."

"He's a politician, Moll, for chrissakes. About as plastic as you can get. He's not good enough for you."

"You *are* jealous."

"What did you expect, damn it?" I watched her recoil, surprise in her eyes. "I've never stopped loving you. You think I don't care?"

She stared at me, open-mouthed. "Why are you telling me this? Why now?"

"I thought you knew. I've always been in love with you."

"You walked away." Her voice sounded incredulous. "You're the one who wanted the divorce."

Despite the cold, my face now was suffused with heat. "I...I had no choice."

"You gave up on us."

My stomach churned. "No, I gave up on you, Molly. I needed you. I didn't know how to deal with everything that happened. I didn't know how to live, how to go on after..."

"I was right there. I had to deal with it, too, Blake."

I nodded quickly. "I know, I know. You've always been so tough. A rock. I never saw you cry. Not once. Not for…not for *us*, for what *we* lost."

"Of course I did. Maybe I was too proud to let you see me crumble, but I did. I couldn't help it. I cried over all of it, Blake. My loss, your loss. Losing each other."

"You were just so far away. I couldn't find my way back to you. I couldn't find a way to talk to you about any of it. And you didn't seem to care."

"How can you say that? Of course I cared. I still do." She eyed me in silence for a moment. "I don't blame you. For any of it. I never did. We all grieve differently, but you took on this mountain of guilt. I struggled, I'll admit. I still do. Maybe I was distant. Maybe I wasn't there for you, but for God's sake, you of all people should understand why. I just couldn't handle both at the same time. I'm sorry. I had to find a way to move on, but you're still dragging that mountain around."

I heard her words, but they felt hollow compared to the blinding pain I felt inside. Of course she blamed me. How could she not? I blinked back the wetness that threatened to leak from the corners of my eyes. "You don't understand."

"No, I don't. I guess that's the problem. Until you figure out how to get over all this guilt, I'm not sure you'll understand yourself." She gently laid a hand on my thigh. I felt its warmth through the layers of cloth separating our skin. Her touch had always soothed and thrilled me at the same time. "I wish you'd remember all the good times, how much joy we had in our lives back then. It might be too late for us, Blake, but don't let bitterness and remorse poison you."

My chest tightened hard as the closed hands in my lap wanted to flail against an uncaring universe. *Lokah samastah sukhino bhavantu.* The words of my yoga instructor sounded feeble, and my heart felt as clenched as my fists. I still could not talk about what had brought me to this place. Not even, it seemed, to Molly. Strange, how we keep parts of ourselves sealed off to those we love the most, the ones closest to us.

The words I'd learned years earlier in the *dojang* where Cole and I had taken tae kwon do lessons popped into my head: *Finish what you start*. They suited me, I thought.

Molly lifted her hand and raised it to my face, briefly caressing my cheek. "I really do want to believe you. But you've changed so much. I don't know what you're capable of anymore."

Once I'd wondered. Now I knew. One more thing I didn't share with Molly.

She held my gaze a moment longer and then looked out across the empty, rain-soaked playfield. "You need to be careful," she said. "If the PA refiles, he'll probably want another bail hearing. They'll issue a warrant for your arrest. I'll try to warn you, but I doubt they'll give us the consideration of letting us know in advance."

"Thanks."

Impulsively, I leaned in and gently bussed her cheek, then stood and hurried away.

21

The office closes for most people at five, and they go home. After leaving Molly, there wasn't much I could do to find out more about Damien or Rafe. So I went looking for Bloody Mary again before heading to Ballard for the night's bundle of newspapers. She either didn't want to be found, or worse, had moved on to another part of town. If Stitch had tossed her out and left, she'd have to stake out new territory somewhere.

Low-hanging clouds sandwiched the skyline, squeezing reflected light down onto the city like a thick layer of mayo. From the Ship Canal Bridge, the twinkling cityscape looked like a scene inside a snow globe. All it needed was a good shake and snow would fall. The air snaking through the half-inch crack between the car window and doorframe felt cold enough. Strings of white lights topped the Space Needle in the shape of a Christmas tree. I wondered how many of the city's homeless—huddled under viaducts and around sidewalk steam grates—had been cheered into the Christmas spirit by the festive lights, the window displays downtown, and the carols blaring from every door.

I worked my route on autopilot, my mind whirling with possibilities. One said Midge had succumbed to a random misfiring of a schizophrenic mind—Mary had freaked for whatever reason and killed her. If so, she also might have killed the gutter punk for messing with her stuff. Find her, and I might easily prove my innocence if the blood on her coat belonged to someone else. Another scenario—the one I'd suggested to Shriver—put Midge in the role of innocent victim who just happened to be in the way of a massive machine of money and power, both corporate and political. That one had too many variables, and odds stacked in favor of the men behind the machine. The man who'd visited Mary after I'd spoken to her may even have paid her to kill Midge. And there was the matter of Midge's will. No one had mentioned the codicil, so perhaps she'd never had it executed, leaving me out of it. But whoever stood to inherit might also have wanted Midge dead. The permutations made my head hurt.

* * *

Frustration filled Gagnon like an ocean swell sweeping into a blowhole, looking for the point of egress. He should have found what he was looking for already, but he still didn't have enough information. He was thrashing around in the dark, literally, a naked mole rat burrowing aimlessly in search of a prize. The women's shelter had been easy enough to break into, but the basement held nothing beyond what anyone would expect to find: a massive oil-fired boiler, water heaters, storage rooms, lots of mold and mildew and cold dampness. The church was next.

Gagnon glided down the dark street through the mist, a wraith in the shadows, and slipped into a side door of the church. Votive candles cast flickering shadows on the walls. He quickly stole down a side aisle and found the short hallway to the sacristy. Stairs led down to the crypt. Halfway down, darkness swallowed all the light from above. A small flashlight guided him the rest of the way down to a small foyer.

An open door led to a small chapel, empty and still. A few small votive candles cast a feeble glow along one wall. Gagnon explored the chapel thoroughly, examining the altar and the walls closely. They revealed nothing but age. Out in the foyer, Gagnon tried another, more modern door—locked. He stepped back, gathered himself, and kicked the door in. He stepped inside and found himself in a utility room. A furnace took up the bulk of it. He shone the light around the walls and saw nothing.

An ornately carved wooden door guarded the crypt. It, too, was locked, and Gagnon knew that trying to kick it in would simply lead to a broken foot. But if he could smash the lock, or the jamb around it, he might be able to get inside.

He swiftly climbed the stairs into the church and hurried to the altar. Assessing the candlesticks placed around the apse, he picked up a four-foot brass Paschal candleholder and hefted it in both hands. In seconds, he stood back in front of the crypt door and heaved the heavy candlestick at it. The brass clanged against the iron-ring door handle, sending a shock up through his arms. He waited several moments in silence to see if the noise had roused anyone. He aimed for the door just above the handle and smashed it again with all his might. A resounding boom echoed in the small space. Again, he waited a minute or two.

He tried a third time and examined the door while he waited in the silence. This time there was a small gap between the door and the jamb. Excited now, he smashed the door twice in quick succession. The noise was deafening, but now he was close to success. The wooden jamb was old, brittle, and the iron deadbolt had split it at last. He set the candlestick down and drove his shoulder into the door. It gave and swung inward.

Smaller than he anticipated, the crypt was only about twenty feet in depth, the center chamber only about eight feet wide, just enough to easily turn a casket. A marble floor reflected his light, but the walls were stone tiles, some of which bore inscriptions about those interred behind them. The ceiling was vaulted, limestone arches standing out in relief. Otherwise, the rectangular chamber was empty, floor and walls meeting at tight, perfectly square angles. With a grunt, he quickly turned and left, climbing the stairs soundlessly.

At the top of the stairs he turned in to the sacristy. He didn't care how carefully what he sought had been hidden; the church must have kept records if it was on church grounds. He pawed through cupboards for the books the priests kept of all the parish functions—births, baptisms, confirmations, weddings, funerals; any sacrament a priest performed was recorded, along with celebrations—feast days, birthdays, special anniversaries, and more. He only hoped the records going that far back had not been put in storage somewhere. He shone his light on one book after another. His excitement grew as he found a set with dates closer to those of the church's founding.

A sound from the nave of the church penetrated his concentration. He paused, alert to the slightest movement. He moved to the doorway and stopped. Soft, slow footfalls from the back of the church reached his ears. Someone had seen his light through the sacristy windows. He raced silently down the hall to the church and poked his head around the corner. A small, dark figure moved down the center aisle. He dropped into a crouch and eased around the corner. Creeping on all fours, he stayed in the shadows near the floor and made his way back to the transept. Cutting across to the main aisle, he circled behind the shuffling figure already halfway up the nave.

He saw her more clearly now in the flickering glow of the votives. The old nun, come to snoop. He came up behind her and clapped a hand over her mouth. She struggled and lifted her head. He saw the sudden fear in her eyes when she recognized him.

"*Où est le puits, ma sœur?*" he said. "*L'eau.* The water. Where is it?" He took his hand away.

"Who are you?" Her voice quavered. "What do you want?"

"Never mind who I am. *Le puits—l'eau*, Sister. How do I find it? You know something about *l'histoire de* Sister Marguerite, don't you? I know you do. Tell me."

"I don't know what you're talking about. What do you want?"

"*L'eau!* Water! Where is it?"

"Water? The baptismal font?"

"What did the Babcock woman want? Tell me! What was she looking for?"

Tears streamed down the old woman's face. "I don't know. She was just making trouble. Please, don't hurt me!"

"For the last time, Sister, tell me where they hid Sophie Clare's legacy!"

"I don't—"

He struck her across the face. "Where?"

When she did not answer, he gripped her throat and squeezed, the roar in his ears growing louder. Still she refused to speak. His vision went red. He lifted his hand to strike her again and realized she'd gone limp in his grasp. He stood for a moment, breathing hard, until his vision cleared. She was useless. He dragged her across the floor, down the hall to the sacristy, unclenched his fingers, and let the nun drop to the floor in a heap, unconscious.

He hurried back to the books to seek the answers she had not given him.

* * *

I cruised slowly past Joyance House after delivering all my newspapers. It was late, and I was tired, but Midge's murder was somehow connected to the former convent and the sisterhood that had founded it. Proximity to the house, I hoped, might help me sort through the possibilities. I twisted the wheel, pulled over to the curb, and stopped with a jerk. The engine died with a shudder. A security light illuminated a white cone of drizzle at the corner of the building. The house seemed quiet, its occupants all safe in bed, where I should be.

Neurons fired faster in my head than the thoughts could fully form. Images flashed against the backs of my eyes in quick, capricious cuts like a poorly edited film. The freckled top of Molly's pale, rounded shoulder...Molly in the park pushing a stroller, dappled sunlight filtering through the trees, sparking in her red hair...*did I double-bag the paper for that house on Interlaken?*... Frank Shriver on the bench at the playground, hands in his coat, hiding them the way he hid his alcoholism...the smeared blood on Midge's kitchen floor...pale indentations—footprints—in the snow...*what did I have for dinner? I'm hungry*...the rust-colored blotch on Bloody Mary's coat, black in the subterranean gloom beneath the freeway...patches of rust on the construction equipment littering the site around Capitol Hill's future light-rail station...*did I even have dinner?*...a kid running up Broadway, fear on the face he turned over his shoulder...barely concealed smugness on Acasa's face in Molly's office...*I wonder when Midge realized she'd let her killer in the house*...Liz Tracey's coat spreading out behind her like a cape as she launched herself into thin air, hoping to erase herself...the easy smile of a fair-haired youth running onto a soccer field, and his unselfconscious wave when he saw me...the same face, pale and somber, framed by satin folds the color of a cardinal's claret robes, eyes closed for eternity...*why hadn't I been able to stop—No!*

My stomach growled. I stretched, yawning widely. Up the street, the stained-glass church windows glowed faintly, lit from within. The church was usually locked this time of night. Sanctuary or not, even the church didn't leave valuables vulnerable to thieves and addicts. The glow lightened and faded. The flicker of candles, maybe. The sacristy window brightened, dimmed, brightened again. Not candles this time.

Curious, I climbed out and hunched my shoulders against the mist, striding quickly up the block and the steps to the big double wooden doors of the church, both locked. I rounded the corner of the church into a courtyard between it and the rectory. Landscaped walkways led to a small reflecting pool at its center, all now shrouded in darkness and shadow. A side door in the court-yard yielded to a sharp tug, and I eased inside. Darkness filled the cavernous nave, the gloom broken slightly by dim light from the street and the guttering candles in the alcove chapels. I crept along the wall toward the sacristy, feeling foolish. Maintenance or a jani-tor probably came in early to fix and check on things.

Muffled sounds emanated from up ahead. A yellow glow spilled out of the sacristy onto the marble floor. I edged down the hall, blood singing in my ears. The glow brightened as I drew closer to the sacristy door. Shadows flickered on the walls and floor, the empty pews standing out in relief. I poked my head far enough through the doorway to glimpse into the room. Light glimmered from a doorway at the end leading into the vestry.

I picked my way through the dark room toward the light. Halfway, I stumbled over a soft bundle on the floor. I went down on one knee, hands splayed out on the cold stone floor for bal-ance. Shielding my eyes from the flickering glow, I reached out to touch the black bundle, nearly invisible on the dark stone tiles, and felt fabric, a coat. A plastic rain bonnet tied over white hair glinted dully.

The shuffling sounds stopped. The light went still, shadows firmly in place. Slowly, I rose to full height and stepped toward the doorway. One more pace brought me within reach, and I stretched a hand out to the doorframe. A man barreled through the opening, smashing a shoulder into my midriff. I staggered backward, and clutched at him reflexively. He bulled past and turned his shoulders, rolling me off and sending me crashing to the floor. I caught a fistful of trouser leg. He viciously kicked free and sprinted for the door.

A beam of light from the other room illuminated the back of his dark windbreaker and briefly caught his profile as he swung around the corner into the dark church. I scrambled up and gave chase.

I caught sight of him again in the church. He burst through the side door without a backward glance. By the time I sprinted outside he'd vanished. I ran for the street without stopping. When I reached the corner of the church, I saw his running figure halfway up the block. I summoned up some reserve energy and kicked it up a notch, pain radiating from my knee and hip with each jarring step. He sprinted soundlessly up the sidewalk. Not even my longer stride closed the gap. After another block, I pulled up short, hands on my knees, breathing heavily as he disappeared into the night.

I hurried back to the church. He was the same man I'd seen coming out of Bill Royer's office building a day earlier, the smoking guy on the steps with the French accent. I frowned. Royer said a French professor named Dufours had visited him not long before I showed up. This had to be the same person. But what could he possibly want in a church in the middle of the night?

The dark nave felt more familiar this time, and I quickly made my way along the wall to the rectangular glow of the hallway to the sacristy. Inside, I ran and grabbed the flashlight left by the intruder and heard a moan from Sister Florence. I stooped and gently cradled her in my arms. Her eyelids fluttered. She stared up at me, confusion on her face.

"Are you all right, Sister? Are you hurt?"

She groaned, and her eyes slowly closed again. Water coated her face, and her coat was damp. A quick survey with the flashlight revealed soaked slippers and a bedraggled nightgown hanging below the hem of the coat. She'd walked from the rectory through the rain.

I gathered her up and carried her out to the car. She weighed nothing in my arms, like the broken-winged sparrow I'd once found as a kid, just bones and feathers. I laid her carefully in the backseat and drove like hell for Harborview.

22

The QFC on Broadway and Harrison was practically empty that time of morning save for a couple of goth girls buying cigarettes and a junkie swaying precariously in front of the candy rack, jonesing for something sweet. I bought flowers and a more expensive bottle of wine than I could afford for Peter and Chance for covering for me over the weekend, and drove home, exhausted after the lengthy process of getting Florence admitted at the hospital. The staff had asked me question after question, and I hadn't known the answers to the simplest, even her birth date.

The Toyota's engine burbled and knocked once or twice before finally recognizing the ignition was off. I clambered out wearily, thumbed the lock, and swung the door closed. The *click-clack* of heels on pavement brought my head up. More than halfway down the block, a figure traversed from light to shadow through the cone of a streetlight's illumination. I watched carefully as it came toward me. People still considered the neighborhood part of the Central District, an area with a reputation for crime. Gentrification had worked a slow transformation.

A carrier with a route not far from mine had his car stolen twice when he left it running in the street to deliver a paper. Customers with special requests dot every route. They don't want the paper thrown because it makes too much noise when it hits the driveway. Or they want it on the porch out of the rain. Or placed between the screen and the front door so the neighbor doesn't steal it. After hearing a few stories at the warehouse, I locked the car every time I had a special delivery just to save myself the hassle of reporting it stolen. I rarely gave a thought to my own safety. My size tends to warn people off.

The footsteps grew louder, and the outline of a woman in an evening dress with a dark fur stole and hat moved into the next cone of light. She walked with arms crossed over her chest to ward off the chill, head down watching for icy spots.

"You're out late," I called.

Her head came up sharply, and she stopped dead in her tracks. "Christ, doll, you nearly gave me a heart attack. Good morning to you, too."

"Late, late, late show?" I said.

She reached down to tug at her hose and started toward me. "Goodness, no. A slow night, actually, with the holiday and all. And I suppose the snow kept some people away. A bunch of us went to Gabe's house after the last show and drank champagne."

"You didn't walk all the way home, did you, Chance?"

"In these heels?" Her face split into a wide smile. "You have *got* to be kidding. Toji dropped me off up the street on his way home." She stopped a few feet away.

"You know all you have to do is call if you ever need a ride."

"Clothes like these will never—"

"See the inside of *that* car."

She waved dismissively at the Toyota. "Maybe when you trade it in for a Bentley, doll, but you're sweet to worry."

I smiled and took stock of the silver beaded gown and black fur stole. "Who is it tonight?"

"I think I was channeling Joan Rivers a little tonight in Oscar de la Renta," she said. "Or maybe I was channeling Frank Marino doing Joan Rivers." I must have looked quizzical. "He's a Vegas act, honey." She waved a hand. "Whatever. Well, don't just stand there. My nipples are freezing out here, and I can't wait to get this makeup off."

I stepped aside and let her precede me up the walk to a modest little house.

"Aren't you taking a chance, wearing that fur?" I asked her. "Don't you get a lot of crap from the animal rights people?"

"It's fake, honey," she said over her shoulder. "Like everything else." Her laugh was harsh.

At the front door, she stopped and faced me. The bright porch light diminished her illusion somewhat. The carefully applied makeup had been marred and smudged by a long night out partying, letting some whiskery shadow show on the edge of her jaw, and up close the hips looked too slim in the designer sheath to be female. If I hadn't known, though, she still might have fooled me. Later in the day, "she" would be Chance Reno again, one half of the gay couple that owned the house and rented out the studio in-law apartment on the lower level to me.

I held out the wine and flowers. "I was going to bring these by later, but here you are."

"What's this?" Chance took the gifts hesitantly.

"Thanks for handling my route last weekend. Peter, too."

"It was nothing. Anytime, you know that. You'll have to at least stop up later and help us drink this."

"I'll try."

"Good. See you later, then." He gave my arm a squeeze and turned to open the door.

I took the path around the house down to the apartment, let myself in, and collapsed onto the bed, falling asleep within seconds in my clothes.

* * *

I stopped by the hospital midmorning and sat with Sister Florence as she slept. When she woke, her gaze roved the room, her white, wrinkled face blank at first, then frowning with confusion until her eyes lit on my face. She blinked a few times before seeming to recognize me.

"Where am I?" she croaked.

"In the hospital. I found you unconscious in the sacristy."

She bit her lower lip and stared at the ceiling, brow furrowed in concentration. "What was I doing in church?"

"I hoped you could tell me." I smiled. "Do you remember me, Sister?"

She lowered her gaze to my face. "Midge's friend. I gave you all those papers."

I let out a breath I didn't know I was holding. "Yes. You don't remember what happened to you in the church?"

She frowned again. "I woke up. Saw a light in the church. Moving around. I couldn't sleep, so I put on my coat and went to see who it was. After that…?"

"A man attacked you," I said softly. "In the church. He was looking for something. Do you know what it might have been?"

She wagged her head and looked at me again, pale blue eyes watery and rimmed with red.

"What were *you* doing there?"

"I saw the light, too."

She nodded as if it was all the explanation she needed.

"Tell me about Midge, Sister," I said softly. "I need to know everything you told her."

Her head came up quickly, eyes narrowing as she focused on me. "Look where curiosity got her. And now you?"

"I need to know. It's the only way I'll find out why she was killed. Something you said, something you spoke of, got her started."

"I can't imagine what. We talked of all sorts of things."

"But she was curious about your order. Its history. Tell me about that."

She sighed and patted the thin hospital blanket covering her tiny frame. In halting sentences she related the convent's story. Founded in France in the late eighteenth century, the order focused on caring for the sick and indigent. In 1843, the mother-house moved to Montréal, though the house in France remained open. As I'd read in the old journal, the order sent a mission led by Sister Marguerite to the Pacific Northwest in 1856.

"One of our sisters was venerated, you know," she said, head bent with exhaustion.

"I had no idea."

"Oh, yes. Sophie Clare. Missionary in Africa. Ministered to the sick in Liberia. In the eighteen forties. Captured by slavers. Almost killed." She winced and put two fingers to her temple.

"I'm sorry, Sister," I said quickly. "Of course you're not feeling well. You must be tired."

She waved weakly. "I'm fine. Glad of the company."

She lay back against the pillows and closed her eyes. I thought she might sleep despite her assurances. I sat quietly on the edge of the chair. After a moment, her eyelids fluttered open.

"Perhaps some water," she said.

I filled a glass from a pitcher on the bedside table and held it steady while she sipped from a straw. A little color came to her cheeks. She gently pushed my hand away.

"Cannibals, those savages," she said. "Some of them. Sophie Clare saved them, anyway." She glanced around the room, blinking rapidly. "Where am I?"

"The hospital, Sister. You're safe. Getting better. Sophie Clare?" I prodded.

Her face slackened. "She saved some," she said, her eyes slowly closing. "The ones who believed." She made the sign of the cross. "With Christ's blood. The rest died."

I waited. "Who died?"

Her hand fluttered at her side like a small bird. "All of them. Slaves. Crew. Officers." She took a ragged breath. Bright spots of color burned high on her cheeks. "Oh. *That's* what he wanted. Something about Sophie Clare."

"The man who attacked you? What did he want?"

"I don't know. He rattled on about low water and someone named Dupree or Lepwee."

"He was looking for something? Something to do with Sophie Clare? Not Sister Marguerite?"

"No, no, I remember now. Something about Sister Marguerite's history, but he was looking for Sophie Clare's legacy. That's what he said."

She fell back, looking drained of energy.

My fingers drummed the armrest. "Sister? Florence?" I got to my feet and stared down at her, forking over all she'd told me, trying to discern the compost from the crap.

"Thank you, Sister," I murmured.

She gave no sign she'd heard me. At least she'd given me a place to start.

Seattle's Central Library stood only a short walk from the hospital. I found a reference librarian who steered me to a Catholic almanac and some other materials. After a fair amount of searching, an entry on Sophie Clare turned up. It tracked with the few details Florence had offered.

Slave traders had captured the missionary along with the others in her village and taken them to a ship on the African coast. The ship's captain took her aboard for luck and to help keep the slaves quiet. The ship took on more slaves a week later down the coast, crowding the hold with 383 souls, and put out to sea. Sophie Clare ministered to the frightened slaves, converting those who would listen. With no priest aboard, she administered sacraments herself, baptizing converts with seawater and offering them Communion.

A week out to sea, a terrible disease raced through the ship, first killing off most of the slaves, then spreading to the crew. In less than a fortnight, all aboard died horribly except Sophie Clare and the few slaves she'd converted. Without a crew, the slave ship drifted aimlessly until intercepted by another vessel. Sophie Clare and the few survivors were brought aboard. Fearing disease, the captain ordered the slaver burned and sunk. Eventually landing in New York, the nun made her way to Montréal.

It made one hell of a story—if it was true.

23

Reyna snatched up the ringing phone impatiently. She still had hours of work to do, and the clock on the wall said it was almost quitting time. Another late night coming up.

"Chase," she said.

"Commander, it's Jones, from NHC. We got another command signal."

"When?"

"This afternoon. The professor, Royer, who caused the last one? He called again. I logged the call and the subject matter, and—"

"What's it say?" Reyna interrupted.

"That's the weird thing. Nothing came up on screen. I answered Royer's questions—at least the ones I could. When he asked to see the deck logs of that ship again, I explained that old logs are kept at the National Archives. He said they didn't have them, so we must. They couldn't have just disappeared."

"Is there a point?"

"Yeah, well, one of my stack rats hands me a sealed envelope while I'm on the phone with Royer. An old one. You need to see this, Commander. Give me a secure fax number."

Reyna rattled off the number of a machine not far from her cubicle. "This better be good."

"Call me when you get it."

Reyna hung up, walked to the copy room, and saw the fax machine already printing out a sheet of paper. She picked it up and squinted at the ornate script of what appeared to be a letter. Jones hadn't been kidding. Marked "Top Secret," the document was dated March 1849. What the hell was going on? She picked her way through the handwriting and stiff language.

Her eyebrows rose as she read the instructions, "a matter of national security." The orders assumed that the command signal had been activated due to the failure of the previous command. *Her* failure. But more surprising than the orders were the signatories at the bottom. They included several names she recognized—two US senators, a secretary of state, and a bank president.

Reyna walked to her office and called Jones back.

"Is this a joke?" she said. "These guys are all dead. What am I supposed to do now?"

"Me? I'd file it and forget it. What about this guy Royer?"

"He checks out." Reyna paused. "Well, thanks, Jones."

She hung up, torn between an impulse to do what Jones suggested and what was right. The orders were clear. She had to kick it upstairs, and not just one or two rungs. The orders could only be carried out by the top man himself, the secretary of the navy. With a sigh, she walked the memo to Farley's office. She paused a few feet from the door, thoughts racing. She'd send it up the chain all right, but not without covering her butt. It wouldn't hurt to have Tolliver monitor Royer's phone records.

* * *

That afternoon I met a Sound Transit community relations liaison named Amy Chen just outside the south construction gate off Broadway. Liz had left a note along with the press pass, explaining the procedure and who would meet me. Chen juggled a shoulder bag, purse, and two hard hats, freeing one hand. She shook mine firmly and handed me a hard hat. Stuffing a fuzzy white hat in a pocket of her coat, she jammed the other hard hat on her head. She flashed an ID card at the security guard posted by the cyclone fence and led me through the gate. Petite and voluble, Chen kept up a steady patter of factoids interspersed with questions about me, the angle of my article, what I hoped to see. I deflected as many as I could with questions of my own, steering the conversation back to the construction project.

She walked me through the shell of the aboveground station itself, what she called the "headhouse." The south entrance to the belowground station platform actually consisted of two buildings sitting across Broadway from each other. A walkway beneath the street connected them. Passengers would be able to access the platform from a north headhouse as well, a block up at John Street. She rattled off more statistics about the construction and the eventual number of riders expected to pass through the station each day, speaking loudly over the din of machinery and men at work. I took careful notes, though they'd end up in a recycling bin soon enough. She glanced at her watch several times as we walked, growing impatience flashing across her face.

Fifteen minutes into the tour, a burly man dressed in denim, plaid shirt, fleece vest, and heavy work boots walked up to us. Relieved, Chen introduced me to John Stark, a construction supervisor with Damien. Chen said he'd take me through the rest of the tour and answer my questions. She excused herself, saying she unfortunately had unavoidable meetings to attend. She gave me her card and told me to call if I needed more information after the tour.

Stark was gruff and reserved, Chen's polar opposite. He warmed to his subject, though, as we progressed and I asked observant questions. He led the way to the main shaft, where we descended more than a hundred feet down in a cage to the wide tunnel that would eventually accommodate the station platform. It stretched out a block to the north in dim light. Behind us, twin openings yawned blackly, interior details of the tunnels quickly disappearing in the murky darkness. The sheer massiveness of the undertaking staggered the imagination. Workmen busily moving about at their assigned tasks appeared the size of ants in a colony, dwarfed by the scope and scale of the project. Stark patiently explained the construction process.

"We dug the main shaft for the station first," he said, leaning in to be heard over the construction noise. "Then we excavated the station platform. Once that was complete, we ferried the TBM in pieces into the stub tunnel under Pike Street. Hauled it in on flatbed trailers with semis. We dug the stub a couple years ago when we refurbished the old bus tunnel under downtown Seattle to accommodate the light-rail trains.

"While our crews worked on the station here, the TBM tunneled up from downtown, through the station, and kept on going north. When it finally reaches the station next to Husky Stadium, which is also under construction, it'll be disassembled. We'll lift the pieces by crane, load them on a flatbed, and drive them back downtown to dig the second tunnel. I'd offer to show it to you up close and personal. It's pretty amazing stuff. But they've really clamped down recently. Best I can do is show you the supply train coming back through the station."

"Why all the concern?" I asked.

"Safety. There've been a few accidents on site. We have to be extra careful now."

"What kind of accidents?"

"Stupid stuff, mostly," he replied readily. Then he hesitated. "Off the record?"

I nodded and put my pen away.

"People not paying attention to what they're doing," he said. "We had a train come out of the tunnel too fast and ram a concrete barrier. Turns out the kid driving wasn't trained on the equipment. His buddy let him drive. Fortunately, no one was seriously injured, but I can tell you they ended up in a world of hurt of a different sort. Would've been fired on the spot except for the union. That was the worst. Other stuff—things like slips and falls, materials falling over because they weren't stacked right—just dumb mistakes."

"Bad luck?"

"Human error," he said. "You make your own luck if you do your job right."

"No problems with poor materials or shoddy workmanship from your subs?"

His surprise looked genuine. "As a cause of accidents? No. Not in any sense, in fact. On the record, we've had more accidents on this project than the Beacon Hill tunnel a few years ago, it's true, but we've had fewer injuries per man-hour than any other major contractor that's worked on light rail for ST."

"There's been a lot of talk about cost overruns. Must be a lot of pressure to control costs."

His jaw tightened. "We've had a few overruns. But that's because we're doing the job right, not because we're skimping. And I guarantee we won't sacrifice safety to keep costs in line."

"I don't suppose cutting corners is something you'd admit if it were true or not."

He colored and flexed his fingers. "This tour's about over."

I shrugged. "If you say so. No offense. Hard questions are part of the job."

"That wasn't a question. And it wasn't hard, just rude. Let's go."

He motioned toward the main shaft, where an elevator cage waited to take us up. We rode in silence. Anger roiled off him like spray off a wave in a stormy sea. I ignored him, indifferent to who

I pissed off anymore. I needed answers. I thanked him, anyway, as I stepped out of the cage. I felt his eyes on me all the way out to the gate, but when I glanced back, he'd turned away and was talking to someone on his cell phone. I wondered who.

24

In the car I called Bill Royer and asked if he had any news. He answered with silence.

"Bad time?" I asked. "Someone in your office?"

"No-o."

"You've learned something," I surmised. "But you're not happy about it."

"Yes, I learned something," he said. "Quite a lot, actually, which goes to show us old dogs can learn new tricks. Then again, this period of American history isn't my area of expertise." He paused. "I made some calls. You've stumbled across a history mystery."

"What did you find out?"

"It's all in the archives at the Naval Historical Center. You can look it up, you know."

"And?" I steered in the direction of campus as if it might somehow prompt him.

"Let's start with Selim Woodworth, second son of Samuel Woodworth, who wrote the poem 'The Old Oaken Bucket.' Born eighteen fifteen. Left home at age nineteen and sailed out of New York on a three-year cruise. The ship was lost off the coast of Madagascar. Only Woodworth and a lone sailor survived. A native woman gave Woodworth shelter and protection until he was rescued by a whaling ship. You with me so far?"

He plowed on without waiting for an answer, as if eager to be done with me, the story coming faster now. "Woodworth made his way back to New York, joined the navy, and was appointed a midshipman in eighteen thirty-eight. He served on several ships, and in late eighteen forty-five asked for a leave of absence. A few months later he asked to join the Pacific Squadron and hitched up with a wagon train of about eighteen hundred people headed out on the Oregon Trail from Missouri."

"So that's how he ended up in San Francisco?" I said.

"Not quite. There's more." He paused. "Woodworth expected to rendezvous with the squadron at the mouth of the Columbia River. On the way, the wagon train got word that another party of travelers was stranded in the snow in the Sierra Nevada mountains—the Donner Party."

"*The* Donner Party? The ones who had to eat their dead to keep from starving?"

"Woodworth volunteered to help look for them and joined a search party. With the navy's permission, of course. There are conflicting reports about what happened next. In any event, Woodworth never played any part in actually rescuing members of the Donner Party.

"Let's see, that was January, eighteen forty-seven. In May that same year, he reported to the USS *Warren* in Monterey Bay, a sloop of war. The rest of the squadron had already sailed in the event they were needed in the war with Mexico. Woodworth asked the navy's permission to take another leave and join the squadron either in Brazil or back in the US, wherever he could catch up with it. The navy told him they would grant his request when they could spare him. Apparently, they had other plans for him. In February eighteen forty-eight, Woodworth left the *Warren* to take command of a transport ship called the *Anita*."

"Where did you get all this?" I said when he paused.

"I told you, Naval records, mostly," he said. "I originally put in a request with the Naval Historical Center when Midge Babcock pestered me about this. Particulars about Woodworth's life are sketchy, but navy records show he was attached to the Pacific Squadron and in command of the *Anita* from the time he left the *Warren* until February eighteen fifty, two years later. But there's no record of what he did during those two years. Most ships kept deck logs that tracked their movements. The *Anita*'s are gone."

He let that sink in, but it meant nothing to me. "So, what happened next?"

"Nothing." He said it with finality.

"Nothing? That's it? End of story?"

"Well, nothing that seems to pertain to the mystery of that document you found. Woodworth resigned his commission and settled in San Francisco. California had already been pushing for statehood, and Woodworth was elected to the state senate. The navy has a copy of his resignation letter, dated in October of forty-nine."

He recited the facts without enthusiasm. I heard the sound of shuffling papers, then tapping, as if he were noting something on a page with his finger.

"Right," he said. "California ratified its state constitution in November—Woodworth played a role in that—and was officially admitted to the Union the following year, September eighteen fifty. He started a business with one of his brothers. Stayed active in the Bay Area for the next decade. When the Civil War broke out, he reenlisted and served on several ships. Eventually made commodore. He went home after the war and died there in eighteen seventy-one."

"Let me get this straight. Woodworth was just an ordinary everyday citizen living in San Francisco in—when was it?—eighteen fifty-six?"

"That's right."

"And there's no connection between Woodworth and the nuns?"

"None that I could find," he said.

"So is the document legitimate or not?"

"Who knows? Do I think it's historically authentic? It certainly appears so. You could have several experts take a look to determine whether it is or not. You still have it?"

"It's safe. I put it—"

"Better I don't know," he said hurriedly. "What we don't know is if it's legitimate in a legal sense."

"Midge must have thought so, or she wouldn't have pressed for a lawsuit. But what could she have known that would make her think that?"

"It's easy enough to find out that Woodworth once owned a plot of land up on Capitol Hill," he said slowly. "It's part of Seattle history. If I'd found that lease document, I'm sure I would have come to the same conclusion, knowing the property once belonged to Woodworth."

"I still don't understand what connection Woodworth could have had to the religious order in Montréal. And how could he have known the order planned a mission up this way?"

He finally filled the silence. "There may be some clue in the order's papers. The sisters are in Bellevue, you said? You might have to go digging in the order's archives in Montréal." He sounded regretful. "I don't know how cooperative they'll be."

As if I had the time or the funds to fly off to Montréal. "So, we're back where we started."

"Not entirely. You know a lot more about Woodworth." He sounded reluctant again.

"*I* do." My voice trailed off. "Any way you can come up with something else?"

"I don't think so." He drew the words out slowly.

"What's going on?"

The silence stretched out a little longer this time. "Look, I was happy to help, make a few calls, see what I could find. In other circumstances I might make time to help solve this little mystery. But I've done what I can. You can take it from here."

"Professor?"

"Something feels a bit off here," he said impatiently. "First, the Dufours fellow. Then…"

"Then what?"

A chair creaked in the background.

"Something changed when I called the navy this time. Maybe it's my imagination, but it was like a wall went up. The fellow at NHC turned officious, cold. I pressed, saying it seemed unlikely the National Archives would have lost the logs. That they were essential to the research I was doing. He cut off the interview at that point." He paused. "Do you understand what I'm saying?"

I didn't reply.

"I'm uncomfortable pursuing this further, Blake."

"Professor, if you could—"

I heard a distant rap of something hard on wood, a low murmur, then shuffling sounds and a muffled "Yes?" as if he'd covered the mouthpiece.

He came back on the line, saying, "I have to go. Someone's here. Good luck to you."

The line went dead before I could open my mouth. Thoughts tumbled through my head as if on spin-dry. Something was hinky with the way the NHC had responded to Royer's request. And Dufours no more taught French history than I did. What had we—I—stirred up?

* * *

Gagnon snugged the pistol in a specially designed holster under his left arm. The silencer nearly reached his waist, but the windbreaker was cut to hide it. The gun snapped in place. Satisfied, he climbed out of his car and headed across campus. The church had refused to reveal its secrets. But Gagnon was convinced he was on the right trail, if only he had more information. It was time to get answers from the professor.

The hallways outside the classrooms were deserted at this time of day. Gagnon reached Royer's office without encountering a soul. He raised his hand to knock, but stopped when he heard a murmured voice behind the door. When the voice paused Gagnon heard no reply, so he tapped lightly on the door.

The voice murmured again, then said loudly, "Come in."

Gagnon stepped inside and closed the door behind him without latching it.

Royer looked startled, wary, but unafraid. "Professor Dufours. What can I do for you?"

"Ah, *monsieur*, I think, perhaps, you know more about the history of Seattle than you let on last time I was here, *non*?"

"I don't know what you're talking about."

Gagnon took a step toward the desk. "Oh, come, now. Don't be foolish. We both know I refer to the American sea captain, Woodworth. You've been inquiring into his background, *oui*?"

Royer laid his hands in his lap and sat still. "Certainly your questions made me curious. I have done some research, yes. Unfortunately, I found out very little about his connection to Seattle. From all accounts, he never set foot here."

Gagnon took another step. "I don't believe you. Not only do I think he came here, I think he hid something of great value here."

He gauged Royer's reaction and sensed confusion at first, then dawning understanding.

"I know nothing of the kind," Royer said.

"Why else would you help an old woman?"

Royer's expression turned grim. "You're obviously not a history professor. Your name probably isn't even Dufours. But I'll tell you what I know just to get you out of my office. The woman asked for my help on behalf of a religious order. Woodworth once owned the land on which the order's convent sits. Mrs. Babcock came across a document that apparently ceded the mineral rights under that land and the rest of the acreage he owned to the nuns under some sort of lease agreement."

"You've seen this document?"

"Yes, but I don't have it."

"Where is it?"

"I don't know. And that's the truth. If Woodworth ever did visit Seattle, which I doubt, and buried something of value, also doubtful, then legally it could belong to the nuns."

Gagnon gave that a moment's thought. Who did or didn't own mineral rights was of no concern to him. But it further corroborated the notion that Woodworth had secreted something of great value on his land. He pulled Woodworth's last letter from his pocket and placed it on the desk in front of Royer.

He pointed to the notation at the bottom. "What does that mean?"

Royer frowned and leaned over. "Where did you get this?"

"That's not important. I want to know what the notation means."

Royer peered at the letter. "I'm not sure. It looks like a surveyor's notes. To measure distance."

"Who else have you told about this?" Gagnon said.

"About what? There's nothing to tell."

Gagnon pulled out the pistol and aimed it at Royer's chest. "Who else?"

"Are you insane? I teach history for God's sake! I don't know who you are, but I've told you everything I know."

"The tall man, perhaps. He seems to be in the middle of this. I saw him here the other day."

"He's a friend of the Babcock woman. He just wanted to know if I was helping her out. He doesn't know anything, either. Put that gun away, please!"

"Of course, *monsieur.*"

Gagnon raised the tip of the silencer a hair and shot him in the forehead.

* * *

I redialed Royer's number, then realized what I'd heard over the phone. An accented voice at Royer's door. *Dufours?* Of course he'd go back to see Royer after he'd seen me in the church.

I pressed my foot down, breaking into a cold sweat. Royer was in danger. Dufours had nearly killed Florence to get what he wanted. Already within blocks of the center of campus, I maneuvered the car through narrow streets as close as I could and parked in the first open space I found. Thoughts tumbled through my head as I ran over to Royer's building. Like why the government had given Woodworth land in Seattle for his military service if he lived in San Francisco. So he could hide something, I realized...something that Dufours wanted badly. Something the nuns had been charged with protecting?

Darkness had descended long before. The corridors of Smith Hall were quiet, students and staff either at dinner or gone for the day, the lights dimmed.

A pronounced hush hung over the hallways. Dampness on one of the soles of my athletic shoes caused it to squeak on the tile floor. The sound echoed loudly in the empty corridor, slowly fading as the shoe dried. I padded silently the rest of the way to Royer's office, suddenly aware of my heart beating against my ribs. A narrow ribbon of light spilled into the hall through Royer's open doorway. I hesitated, holding my breath, waiting. A shadow—something—caught my attention. I stopped and cocked my head to listen. *Nothing.* Not even the creak of Royer's chair, rustling paper, or the scratching of a pen.

I touched the door with my fingertips and gently pushed. The corner of Royer's desk appeared in view, then the lamp, then Royer himself, seated behind the desk, head tipped against the high-backed chair, staring wide-eyed at the ceiling. A wet trail of blood, black in the dim light, trailed from a jagged white-edged keyhole the size of a nickel in the middle of his forehead. Minutes seemed to pass, but the images rushed in and burned themselves into my brain in nanoseconds. I felt more than saw the barest flicker of movement reflected in the window.

Part of my brain screamed at me to get the hell out of there, but instinct took over, putting me in a zone just as it had when I was on the basketball court. I advanced, using the tension in my legs to spring through the doorway, throwing all my weight into the door as I bolted into the room. *Focus on survival. Do the unexpected.* A shadow by the bookcase, darker than the rest, moved, spinning toward me. *Have confidence in your training.* I took one stride, pivoted, took a second onto a chair, and a third up onto the desk. *Expect to be hurt.* A fourth step planted my foot on the edge of the desk. Something twitched at my sleeve. Reflected in the window, a tongue of flame reached for me from behind. *Direct your fear into rage and action.* Adrenaline rushed through me. I exploded, launching myself over the professor's three-eyed face, and crashed through the window behind him, arms over my head. Bushes beneath the window barely broke my fall. I tucked my shoulder and hit the ground hard, rolling to dissipate the impact.

Scrabbling to my feet, I ran, raindrops pelting my face, pain radiating from my shoulder. A pair of startled students on the path stopped and stared. Shouts behind me turned their heads.

Over my shoulder a man waved his arms wildly, silhouetted in the broken window.

"Stop that man!" he yelled, French accent more obvious than in normal conversation. "He is a murderer!"

The students' heads swiveled from a crazy man in the window to another crazy man running a zigzag pattern across the quad as fast as his legs would carry him. The Gallic profile against the dim office light and the French accent gave away the real killer— Alain Dufours. But the students hadn't seen the silenced pistol that had spit lead at me. One pulled out a cell phone while the other came after me. I darted between a pair of buildings into the next quad and put on a burst of speed, ignoring the pain in my knee. By the time I'd crossed a third quadrangle, my pursuer had dropped farther behind. I risked a backward glance as I crossed the street. He'd stopped running. I took no chances, jogging the rest of the way to the car.

25

What the hell happened?

I drove in a daze, heart still hammering in my chest, staying on side streets and never lingering anywhere for long. Images and half-baked thoughts flashed through my head in rapid-fire succession. I'd lost my focus, and it felt like I had on a hat a size too small, sure signs that I'd missed a dose of meds. I shook myself like a retriever coming out of a duck pond. Lethargic wiper blades slapped hypnotically at tiny raindrops pelting the windshield.

I concentrated. Dufours killed Royer. *But why?* After snooping in a church in the middle of the night, attacking Sister Florence. The only common thread tying the two events together were the papers Florence had given me. Dufours…could he be French Canadian, not French? Know something about the sisters' Montréal headquarters?

Jesus! Royer was dead!

As I tried to control my racing thoughts, I ended up driving on the route I usually took to my first paper delivery. I wound down the slope toward the one-lane bridge where Liz Tracey had tried to fly. Swinging the wheel impulsively, I pulled over. I climbed out and walked to the middle of the bridge. Empty without a line of cars waiting in anticipation to see what an anguished woman would do, the bridge rose like something from the minds of the Brothers Grimm, conjured out of forest and fog. The four-globed light posts stood like silent sentinels. The treetops in the Arboretum stood out clearly, a wood of enchantment replete with gnomes, elves, fairies, witches, and other magical beasts. Their spells moved my feet to the abutment overhanging the avenue below.

I peered over the edge. A lone car passed underneath, winding down the hill. I climbed onto the rail and stood there, motionless. A breath of cold air shivered past my cheek. I swiped at a runny nose with the back of my hand and wondered what had gone through Liz's mind. If she'd wanted the air to pick her up and carry her off this precipice. If she'd really thought, for the brief instant before gravity took hold, it would feel like flying.

Only those who welcome death aren't afraid of it. Standing atop that stone wall, the earth falling away down the hill beneath me, indigo sky stretching out to infinity, only two reasons to embrace death came to mind: belief, complete faith, in a better place beyond; or pain so consuming that death becomes a viable way to end it.

My gaze fell to the pavement below. The black asphalt didn't look very far away. Pain was an old friend, as familiar and constant as daybreak. Who doesn't know both hurt and heartache at some time in their lives? They colored my days, sometimes with delicate brushstrokes of pallid watercolor, and with buckets of black tar on others. But I still couldn't imagine what it would take to make me step into space.

I hopped back down onto the pavement and shambled back to the car. If I ever reached a point when life became intolerable I'd rather eat the barrel of a gun.

Then again, if I were intent on destroying myself, I could simply let Dufours or the police find me.

It would take a little time for the cops investigating to connect me to the shooting. I rummaged through the glove compartment for the prescription bottle of pills, swallowed a dose, and headed for the warehouse to sort papers and think.

* * *

After running my route, I stopped at the club where Chance worked. Chance tended bar a few nights a week and performed on weekends in one-hour revues, two shows a night. The shows featured a number of drag queens lip-synching to their favorite songs. Some were good, some bad but campy fun. Chance was a true female impersonator, a class act.

When he was free, I gave him a quick recap of what had happened and told him I needed a place to crash for a few days. Not long before, I wouldn't have thought twice about calling on friends in high places—who lived in wealthy enclaves like Medina or Mercer Island—and asking if I could borrow a guesthouse. Or whipping out the AmEx Platinum card and booking a decent hotel room. Those "friends" preferred fair weather, and my now environmentally friendly wallet no longer contained much plastic. I'd seen to that in the divorce, insisted Molly get everything that wasn't already hers. Her attorney hadn't objected.

He told me not to worry and headed for the back office where Toji, one of the managers, counted the night's receipts. A few minutes later Chance strutted back across the dance floor, hips swiveling in time to a hip-hop beat that rippled the soda in my glass.

"It's all set, doll," he said, slipping back onto the stool and handing me a key. "Toji said you can stay as long as you need."

"Thanks." I put a hand on his shoulder. "But you have to promise me you and Peter will be careful. I don't know what the hell's going on, but I may be putting you in danger."

"Life's a bitch." He shrugged. "It's nothing we're not used to."

I quickly looked away.

* * *

He sat in his car on the street outside Sanders's apartment and stewed. He should have been ecstatic. Their haul for the night had been excellent, far more than they'd gotten out any previous night. And there was so much more to be had, such easy pickings. But Sanders was getting too close. He'd even visited the construction site.

Where the hell were the cops when you needed them? How long did it take them to match some fingerprints on a bloody knife, for fuck's sake? Sanders should be back in jail. The more he thought about it, the more incensed he became.

He picked up the crowbar from the seat next to him and got out of the car. With grim determination, he walked around the corner of the house and down the slope to the door of the in-law apartment on the lower level. Taking a quick look around, he forced the tip of the crowbar between the door and the jamb. With a sharp tug and a grunt of effort, he splintered the door and shoved it open with a shoulder. He turned on the lights. No one could see in back here, and he knew Sanders wouldn't be home for hours because of his job.

He found a knife in the kitchen with a sharp blade and good heft and methodically set about slashing curtains and ripping open cushions. He opened drawers and dumped their contents on the floor. The destructive work slowly calmed his nerves and filled him with satisfaction.

26

First thing the next day, after a restless few hours of sleep at Toji's, I went out and bought a throwaway cell phone. No sense making it too easy for the wrong people to find me. I used it to check my other cell phone's voice mail. Two messages waited in my in-box—one from a Colin Beardsley and one from Charlie. Beardsley's cultured tones threw me, and it took me a moment to place his name—Midge's friend from the museum. I called him immediately, and he asked if I had time to meet him at his office. I told him to expect me in an hour. I saved the other return call for later. I didn't much feel like talking to Charlie, given whose side he'd taken in all this.

I snuck back to my apartment like a teenager coming home after curfew. I did a turn around the block in the car scouting for loiterers, heads ducking out of sight in parked cars, low clouds of exhaust drifting in the cold air from cars at the curb. I drove several blocks away, parked for fifteen minutes, then came back and did it again from the other direction. An old man out walking a rail-thin dog tugged on the leash as the dog whined and strained in the opposite direction. A homeless person headed toward Madison pushing a shopping cart overflowing with boxes and torn trash bags filled with plunder from raids on dumpsters. I parked two blocks away and came in through the alley just in case, a knot in my stomach tight as a fist. No one jumped out of the bushes. The sight of my apartment door yawning widely, however, sent my pulse racing. Scanning the area, I approached the door cautiously.

The apartment was trashed. I stood inside the open door and surveyed the mess, a ball of lead in my gut growing more palpable by the second. I carefully fingered the doorframe near the latch where it had splintered. Upended furniture, overturned drawers, slashed cushions, and shredded bedclothes littered the floor. I didn't have many material things—one of the benefits of downsizing after the divorce—but the detritus cluttering the small space looked like the belongings of a small village.

I moved to the center of the room and slowly rotated, taking it in by degrees, words spray-painted on one wall stopping me cold—"*Don't fuck with me!*"

"Blake?" The voice behind me sounded tentative. "Are you all right?"

Chance stood in the doorway dressed in sweats, flip-flops on his feet. Peter's face peered in over his shoulder. I motioned them in.

"I'm fine," I said. "Pissed, but fine. What about you two?"

"Worried," Peter said, surveying the damage.

Chance dismissed him with a wave. "We're fine. Peter heard banging down here late last night before I got home but didn't say anything until this morning. I told him you were at Toji's last night, so we came down to see what happened."

"I'm glad you didn't come down when you heard the ruckus," I said to Peter. He gave Chance a silent and uncharacteristic *nyah-nyah* behind his back. "You might have been hurt."

Peter pointed to the wall. "That's not nice. Anyone we know?"

"I'm not sure it's anyone *I* know," I said, "but someone's really ticked off."

The message was personal, but I didn't have a clue who sent it. Dufours, maybe. Or Midge's killer, in which case I'd stirred up a hornets' nest. Which must mean I was on the right track. Were they one and the same?

"We should call the police," Peter said.

"Not much they can do. It could have been anyone. A pissed-off newspaper customer, even," I lied. "Promise you'll be careful until this blows over."

"Blake," Chance said gently, a trace of exasperation on his face. "This is us you're talking to. What's going on?"

"If I knew, this wouldn't have happened. Just promise me, okay?"

I turned away and looked for a place to start attacking the mess. I wanted to hit things, to feel the solid, reassuring connection of some part of my physical being with the world around me, to experience the jolt of resistance up my arm or leg. Pain replacing pain. Hitting *people*, of course, would have been more satisfying than striking inanimate objects. More feedback, clearer results. It caused pain or it didn't.

My limbs twitched, hungering to lash out. I drew air in through my nostrils, filling my lungs, and slowly expelled it through my mouth. Closing my eyes, I repeated the breathing technique several times.

"Can we help, doll?"

"I'll take care of it." I looked around again. "You know what? Go ahead and report this. Tell the cops what you heard. Maybe they'll give me a break and see I'm a victim here, too."

I grabbed a prescription bottle from a kitchen cupboard, picked a few articles of clothing out of the ruins, and walked out.

* * *

The Maritime Historical Society occupied space in a museum building at the edge of a park across the cut from Husky Stadium. I got directions to the offices from a docent. Beardsley met me in the reception area. A small man with a Vandyke neatly trimmed to a sharp point, Beardsley dressed the part in a tailored tweed houndstooth jacket and creased gray wool slacks. He shook my hand with a short bow and motioned me to follow him back to a small office.

"I've been looking forward to meeting you," he said when we were settled. "Midge Babcock mentioned your many kindnesses to her. My condolences."

"I'm at a disadvantage. She never mentioned you."

He waved it aside. "No matter. She was a wonderful woman, and a dear patron. She'll be sorely missed." He paused and looked discomfited when I waited him out. "To business, then. I understand you've been named coexecutor of Mrs. Babcock's estate. It may seem indelicate to broach this so early after her unfortunate death, but I wondered if you'd had a chance yet to inventory the contents of her home."

"No."

He blinked. "Have you, ah, determined what's to become of her belongings?"

I pursed my lips. "You're not concerned who killed her?"

He brushed his fingers on his desk blotter and looked at me levelly. His calm made me wonder for a moment if I should share the same apprehension about him.

"What concerns me," he said, "is the proper disposition of her estate, particularly items of historical interest she intended for the society and the museum."

"And those would be?"

His nostrils flared and he straightened. "My god, man, do you have any idea what she has in that little shack? Original maritime paintings by Buttersworth, Bradford, Gifford. Instruments from the most famous ships that ever sailed. Bits of nautical arcana that are positively priceless. They shouldn't be sold off. They deserve to be preserved, exhibited, cared for, and shared by those who appreciate that sort of thing. Not stowed away in some private collector's den."

"I haven't talked to her attorney, yet. Hopefully the will stipulates this?"

"We had an agreement," he said, raising his hands helplessly.

I shook my head. "I'll let you know when I've had a chance to review the will with Midge's lawyer. In the meantime, perhaps you can help me."

He glanced down to hide his sudden eagerness and inclined his head. "If I can."

"Do you know anything about Selim Woodworth? US naval officer whose land up on Capitol Hill was sold to James Moore back in nineteen oh five?"

He nodded. "I know of him, yes. What about him?"

"I'm trying to find a connection between Woodworth and a French women's religious order that moved to Montréal in the eighteen forties."

"A nunnery?" He frowned. "You mean, how he might have come into contact with them?" He shrugged and shook his head.

"Woodworth served on several ships before he came west. Perhaps on one of them…"

Shifting his elbow to the armrest of the chair, Beardsley propped his chin on his palm and tapped his mustache with a finger. He swiveled to face a computer screen and keyboard, typed in some words, and watched the screen change.

"Ah, yes," he said after a moment. "Easy enough to find things online these days. Woodworth served on the *Ohio* in the Mediterranean as a midshipman and visited Italy before being ordered to report to the *Falmouth* being fitted out in New York. Nothing suggests he went to France."

"And after that?"

He turned to read the screen for a moment. "He sailed with the *Jamestown* off the coast of Africa, and the *Truxton* after that, intercepting slave trade ships."

My mind whirled. "There's a story about one of the nuns," I said. "Sophie Clare. A story that she worked a miracle aboard a slaver, saving some of the slaves from a deadly disease. The rest died, including the crew."

He stroked his beard with a thumb and forefinger. "The *Truxton*. I've heard some of the legends about ghost ships. The *Truxton*'s encounter with that slaver was one such story."

"Then it's possible Woodworth and this nun could have crossed paths."

He nodded. "Certainly. The *Truxton* intercepted several slave ships. If she was aboard one, the *Truxton* may have given her transport to its next port of call."

"Thank you, sir." I got to my feet. "I'll be in touch."

"That's all?" He looked surprised.

"For now." I tried to hide my impatience to leave. "Thanks for your help."

27

I sat in the car outside the maritime museum and thought it through. I hadn't put much stock in Sister Florence's story about Sophie Clare, but Beardsley's confirmation lent it credence. As far-fetched as it seemed, Dufours's interest in the convent and whatever Woodworth had hidden suddenly made sense. Sister Margeurite's journal had referred to *la peste*. Was that what Dufours was after? Was it even possible?

I dialed Molly's number.

"Hey, it's me," I said. "Have you talked to Jane recently?"

Molly and Jane Thompson had been friends since our UW days. Jane had been at the U ever since, first in med school, then internship and residency at UW Medical Center, and recently as a research professor of epidemiology. We hadn't spoken since Molly and I split, no surprise.

"No, why? Afraid you're coming down with something?"

I heard the gentle mockery in her voice. "Just curious. Wondered if she was still on that CDC task force. Remember that case of food-borne illness I worked on?"

A restaurant in town had come to Bellnap & Dreier after some of its patrons had gotten sick. I'd been on the team that had quickly thrown together a crisis communications plan to help deflect the bad press. The health department had traced the source of the illnesses to contaminated beef, prompting a recall by the processor and preventing a wider outbreak. But not before several dozen people ended up hospitalized and one person died.

"She helped coordinate the response with the CDC," Molly said. "I remember."

"You think she's talking to me yet?"

"Why? What's going on?"

"No big deal. I just had some questions I thought were up her alley."

"Give her a try." She paused. I didn't say anything. "She can't hold a grudge forever. Call her. Got to go, sweetie. Bye."

Screwing up the courage to face Jane's displeasure at hearing from me, I called her office. She wasn't in. I didn't leave a message.

* * *

"You're not going to like this," Tolliver said.

Reyna looked up from her desk. "What've you got?"

Tolliver tugged on her neatly braided hair. "Police report came in from Seattle. The SSBI subject—Royer—was shot and killed last night in his office. SPD says it looks like a hit."

"Tell me they got the shooter."

Tolliver shook her head. "Eyewitnesses report two men at the scene. A tall man fleeing, and a man with a French accent in Royer's office. Both got away before campus police arrived."

"Chase!" Farley called from his office door. "You're with me."

"Yes, sir!"

As Reyna squeezed out of her cubicle, Tolliver rolled her eyes and mouthed, "Good luck."

"Stay on those phone records," Reyna said as she brushed past. "I want to know who Royer talked to in the last twenty-four hours."

Reyna caught up to Farley halfway down the hall but had to walk briskly to keep pace.

"Command performance," he said before she had a chance to ask. "The brass want to see us."

She kept her questions to herself as she followed him to a large conference room on another floor. She stopped abruptly just inside the door, then went to find a seat when she realized people were staring. She recognized most of the faces though she'd never met several of them. Farley hadn't been kidding. There was enough brass in the room to form a marching band, from Admiral Miller, the CNO—Chief of Naval Operations— to both the deputy director and director of ONI, or COMONI, Captain Hinson. Even Secretary of the Navy Treadwell was present, so whatever this was about, it was too important to delegate.

Treadwell spoke first. "Commander Chase, I understand you're the one who kicked this can of worms upstairs."

Her face grew warm as she saw the men around the table smile. "Yes, sir."

"That's not a complaint," he reassured her. "You just followed protocol. Any idea what this is about?"

"No, sir."

Treadwell gestured at the COMONI. "Captain Hinson?"

"Interesting bit of history here," Hinson said, holding up a thick file. "The command signal you bumped up had a code that uncovered the *Anita*'s deck logs. The short version: Woodworth spent two years on a top-secret mission. We think someone found out somehow."

"How did that mission stay secret all this time?" Reyna said. "Surely, the need for the command signals would have passed at some point."

Hinson glanced at Treadwell.

"From what we can tell," Treadwell said, "Woodworth's mission wasn't exactly official. He acted at the behest of men very high up in our government, patriots all. But it wasn't sanctioned."

"What?" Reyna's eyes narrowed. "You mean like some nineteenth-century Iran-Contra affair?"

"Something like that," Hinson said. He slid the file across the table. "Read the logs. Get very familiar with what's in that file. Commander, there's a lot at stake here."

"I don't understand, sir," she said. "What do you want me to do?"

Miller, the CNO, spoke up. "It looks like Woodworth hid something, something of tremendous value. We think someone's after it."

"What has your SSBI turned up on Royer?" Hinson said.

Reyna shook her head. "It's not Royer. He was murdered last night."

"Then this just took on new urgency, gentlemen," Treadwell said.

Hinson looked at Reyna. "Get out there. Find out what's going on. Locate whatever Woodworth concealed."

"You really think it's there after a hundred and fifty years?"

"We have no reason not to believe it," Treadwell said.

"Like I said, read the logs," Hinson said. "You're on a plane in three hours."

"Yes, sir." Reyna saluted and turned for the door.

"Oh, and, Commander," Hinson said, "you report directly to me on this."

Reyna nodded and walked out, nearly running into Tolliver in the hall. Startled, she backpedaled and saw the excitement on Tolliver's face.

"What is it?" Reyna said.

"You're not going to believe this." Tolliver handed Reyna a single sheet of paper.

Reyna scanned the list of phone numbers and names, immediately picking out the one that Tolliver had highlighted—Blake Sanders. She glanced up and down the empty hallway.

"Have you got anything on this guy yet, Janet?" she said in a low voice.

"Some. Back in my office."

"I want it all, whatever you can dig up. You've got one hour before I leave to catch a plane."

* * *

I showed up for my bundle of newspapers at the warehouse. The local section of Friday's paper had carried Royer's murder on the front page. When I checked Saturday's, the story was essentially the same but shorter, relegated to an inside page. I didn't expect anyone in this bright and public space to confront me, but I regularly scanned the exits just the same. I loaded my assembled papers into the car warily, paying more attention than usual to the other carriers.

Halfway through my route, headlights fell in behind me on Madison, following at a respectful distance. When they dogged me onto Twenty-Sixth like a wedding attendant carrying a bridal train, I sat up straighter and tried to get a better look in the rearview. The vehicle passed under a streetlight, light bar on top of the car popping out in relief. Patrol cops usually knew the carriers on their beats. We drove as erratically as drunks, but didn't get pulled over as long as cops recognized us. When the Toyota's interior alternately lit up red and blue, I worried about more than the possibility one of my taillights was out.

I slowed and pulled over, thinking furiously, trying to recall if I'd touched anything in Bill Royer's office. Witnesses might be able to put me on campus, maybe even identify me as the madman that dived through a window. But there was no hard evidence in Royer's office to link me to his murder.

The cop's searchlight lanced through my back window, pinning me in place. I rolled down the window, cold air swatting me alert. Putting my hands on the steering wheel where the cop could see them, I waited, heart hammering in my throat. Another beam of light angled through the side window, blinding me in the crossfire.

"Get out of the car, asshole," said a voice behind the light.

I shielded my eyes with a forearm and squinted at the flashlight pointed at my face.

"Charlie?"

"Don't keep me standing out here, for shit's sake. Get out."

The beam from the flashlight swung down and away. I heard the receding sound of footsteps crunching loose pebbles on the pavement as the red blur in my vision faded. I climbed out, shambled around the back of the car, and eased into the passenger seat of the cruiser. Charlie leaned against the door and stared out the windshield, legs splayed, wrist draped over the top of the steering wheel, finger idly tapping the dash.

"You're a dickhead, you know that?" he said. He looked pained, as if constipated. His finger continued to drum a syncopated rhythm. "You don't return calls. I don't suppose you want to get anything off your chest, maybe tell me where you were Tuesday."

"Tuesday? Gee, I don't know. Here and there." I shrugged. "The usual places."

He looked at me and sighed.

"Wait. Tuesday? You're not trying to put that gutter punk's murder on me, are you? Give me a break. If Donovan or Hiragawa thought I had anything to do with it I'd be in jail and CSI would be taking my place apart looking for evidence. Oh, wait, some asshole already tossed it."

He banged a hand on the steering wheel and peered at me through narrowed eyes. "I'm trying to do you a favor here. If I wanted to hassle you, you'd be spread-eagle on the hood of that piece of shit answering someone else's questions for the next few hours. I've been out looking for you the last two nights to give you a heads-up. You're a person of interest in the UW murder. And don't tell me you don't know anything about it. You deliver newspapers. I assume you read them, too."

"*I'm* a person of interest?" I glared at him. He didn't flinch. "How much interest?"

Blood drained from his face, and something else, too, hollowing his cheeks and accentuating the fatigue that darkened the skin around his eyes. I still remembered his face at twenty. He looked the same, creases a little deeper, hair salted at the temples, but the same. Some guys from our class had really aged. When I looked at Charlie—or my own reflection in the mirror—I saw the same kid I knew back then. A few more miles on the odometer, a little more experience in his eyes. Now that experience was telling him something I'd rather he didn't hear.

"You were there," he said, voice holding a note of disbelief. He raised a hand. "I don't want to know. Witnesses place a really tall dude at the scene." He emulated the voice of a stoner, or a student, when he said it. "It didn't take long for Donovan to make the connection."

I looked at him sideways. "Why aren't you taking me in?"

He sighed again. "Let's say I'm working off my debt." He paused, color rising in his cheeks again. "Look, it's not like there's an APB out on you, or a warrant even. They just want to talk."

"And I'd have to keep my mouth shut or lie. It's better I don't have to make the choice, don't you think? I don't have much credit with those two."

"If you know something, you're better off coming clean."

I looked out the side window, saw my ghost reflected there, and turned back, less afraid of flesh and blood. Even if I wasn't sure whose side he was on.

"I don't *know* anything," I said.

His eyes glittered and he chewed on the inside of his lower lip. "Jesus Christ," he said in a mutter. "You saw it go down. You saw who did it."

My hands clenched reflexively, and my skin felt too tight. Charlie was the one who'd been quick with his fists back in the day. Too quick. The smallest hint of a slight—a knock against the Huskies, a derogatory remark about a friend, an insult to the honor of the frat house—and Charlie was up in the person's face, ready for a physical challenge. I remembered a lot of scuffles in off-campus bars late at night. Whether fueled by alcohol, a warped sense of honor, or some sort of complex, Charlie was the first to throw a punch without fear of the consequences. He seemed impervious to pain, or just didn't care, often taking worse lickings than those he meted out, especially when he bit off more than a mouthful—say three or four guys at once.

I remembered, too, the sickening sound of flesh smacking flesh, bones popping, and drops of blood spattering the walls and floor of Rick Tobin's dorm room when I burst in that night senior year, breathless from running across campus. Too late. Ten minutes earlier, Charlie's sister Sarah, a freshman, had staggered through the front door of the frat house sobbing hysterically, clothes askew, a twig and a couple of leaves sticking out of her long tousled hair, knees of her jeans stained with mud. Still too new on campus to confide in untested girlfriends, she'd turned to Charlie. A group of us brought her inside, bundled her up in a blanket, sat her on a couch in front of the fire, fixed her a mug of hot chocolate with a stiff shot of brandy. While we were busy trying to feel useful, Charlie calmed Sarah down enough to get a few details of what had happened to get her so worked up. That was all he needed.

It took another moment or two to learn why Charlie bolted out of the house like a shot. Bob Miller said we should call the campus cops. Molly's best friend Jane, a pre-med student and

Bob's girlfriend at the time, wanted to take Sarah to the hospital. A few other suggestions were tossed into the air like juggler's balls. All of them horrified Sarah even more, shame painting her crimson face with tears. Charlie had obviously gone to defend Sarah's honor the old-fashioned way. I outshouted everyone, hushing them all, and made them promise not to call anyone until I got Charlie back. Molly gripped my arm to keep me from going, so hard it hurt, but saw something in my eyes that made her nod and loosen her grasp.

Charlie'd had less than two minutes' head start, but it had been enough. I remembered the scent of blood assailing me as I arrived and quickly took stock of the scene, feeling the primal thuds of Charlie's fists landing down deep, reverberating like a bass drum. Remembered rushing across the room and wrapping Charlie up in a choke hold before he could hit Rick again. The strength it took to pull him off, even with two of us when Mitch Evans finally caught up to me. Charlie's expression, devoid of anything human, contorted by rage into a grotesque mask. The sight of Tobin's puffy, formless face streaked with blood, saliva, and snot twisting my stomach.

We hustled Charlie out of there and back to the house. On the way, trembling on the adrenaline rush like a crackhead, I dragged Charlie into the shadows and spewed vitriol at him. I called him a pussy and a faggot and defamed his mother, shuddering inside with the utterance of each epithet. I remembered how much it hurt the first time Charlie slugged me, the salty taste of blood running from a split lip. I remembered the second blow hurting less, feeling almost comforted by the punishment for what I'd said to my best friend, then not feeling the next few at all before I got my arms up in front of my face and Mitch forced his way between us, frantically yelling at Charlie to stop.

When Charlie stepped back, eyes still bright with anger, I mumbled at the two of them to get Charlie's hands into a bucket of ice water right away. And I made Mitch swear he hadn't been to Tobin's residence hall that night, made him swear that all he'd seen was Charlie and me get into a fight outside the frat house. As I talked, Charlie's anger ebbed just enough to give understanding a little room to creep into his expression. He turned and walked away without a word, tightness in his shoulders radiating his fury and frustration like a heat lamp. Mitch went inside, an obedient mutt eager to please. I straggled in the back door of the house several minutes later, gathering shreds of my dignity around me like a skinny-dipper whose clothes had been stolen.

Molly winced when she saw my face but said nothing, simply went and got ice and a wet towel to clean me up. Her silence and the disappointment on her face as the others wheedled sketchy details out of Mitch hurt more than Charlie's fists. She met my eyes for only a moment, as if giving me one chance to come clean and redeem myself, one shot at an alternate version of the story that fit better with the person she thought she'd come to know. But I'd put the lie in motion, so I said nothing.

Rick Tobin was in pretty bad shape. He spent a couple of weeks in the hospital and sucked food through a straw for several months, his jaw wired shut, broken in three places, his cheekbone shattered. I went to visit him once, a week after the beating, just to remind him that a hospital bed was better than prison. He was high on a morphine drip for the pain, but his eyes said the words registered loud and clear.

I looked at Charlie now, face jaundiced by the cruiser's yellowed dome light, and wondered when we'd switched temperaments.

He shook his head. "What the fuck are you mixed up in?" he asked.

"I wish I knew, Charlie," I said softly. "I really do."

He stared at me. "Get out. Before I change my mind about taking you in."

* * *

Gagnon stood outside the house, watching. The woman had come home late, a little tipsy, fumbling with her keys in the lock at the side door. He could have easily overpowered her then, forced his way in. But he'd waited, watched as she keyed in a code on the alarm pad next to the door. She'd thrown her keys on the kitchen counter and had gone straight upstairs. She'd turned the lights off soon after, but Gagnon had waited an hour until he was sure she was deeply asleep.

Now he walked unhurriedly up the walk to the front porch as if he owned the place. He traced the woman's steps around to the side door. He pulled the set of picks from his pocket and knelt in front of the door. Slowly, carefully, he set the pins and tried the handle. He eased the door open and slipped inside.

The professor had said the notation at the bottom of Woodworth's letter was a surveyor's note. He'd looked up how nineteenth-century surveyors had measured and platted boundaries and had found out exactly what he'd needed to know. If the nuns had founded the mission and built the church on the site Woodworth had recommended, then the surveyor's note led straight to this house. The question was whether Woodworth had added the note to direct the reader to the correct site or to throw people off the scent. Only one way to find out.

Gagnon moved farther into the darkened house, padding silently through the downstairs rooms until he found a door that opened to the cellar stairs. He switched on his torch and descended.

He searched every square inch of the basement. When he finished, he searched again, walls, floors, every crack and crevice. He found no sign of a subbasement or a tunnel. He shouldn't have been surprised. The house had been built fifty years after Woodworth had hidden the talisman. But somehow he had hoped beyond hope that Woodworth had made a proviso of some sort. Gagnon had already searched the grounds—no sign of a well or burial marker. Nothing to guide him to the spot he so desperately wanted to find.

He started up the stairs but stopped at the sound of a bump overhead. He held his breath and listened. There it was again, the regular thump of footsteps, muted as if made by bare feet. He glided up the remaining stairs and eased the door open an inch. Pressing his eye to the crack, he saw the woman down the hallway. Her back was turned and she took a hesitant step. He pushed the door another inch and the hinge squeaked.

Before the woman even turned toward the sound, he bounded through the door and pulled his gun. She didn't even have time to scream before he was on top of her, slashing the silencer across her face. Her head whipped around, but she stubbornly refused to go down. She turned toward him, blood streaming from her face, tears in her eyes, straining to see her attacker in the dark. He pulled his arm back and punched her in the face as hard as he could. Her head bounced against the wall with a resounding smack, and she collapsed like an empty sack.

He'd wasted too much time already. Despite the risk, he would have to come back during the day when she was at work and search in the light. The police might increase patrols past the house to appease her when she reported this. But they'd never really consider anyone bold enough to break in again soon after. They wouldn't be that vigilant, especially during the day. He hurried out the side door, checked the street for passersby, and vanished into the night.

28

Humans aren't nocturnal creatures. Our circadian rhythms are governed by light and darkness. The human body is programmed to sleep when it's dark. During the day, light blocks the brain's production of melatonin, the hormone that makes us naturally drowsy. More than three million people across the country kept me company on the night shift, all of us subjecting ourselves to the hazards of working unconventional hours, among them higher rates of cancer, ulcers, heart disorders, colds, flu, and substance abuse. The sleep deprivation most of us experience leads to poor coordination, anxiety, depression, and short-term memory loss. We're five times more likely to make serious mistakes on the job, and 20 percent more likely to have serious accidents. And the worst hours, no matter how long someone's been working graveyard, are between four and six in the morning. Rational thoughts are damn near impossible at four or five in the morning. I had at least one: keep moving.

Everything came back to Midge. Last paper delivered, I drove aimlessly, thoughts tossing like a restless sea as I tried to make sense of all that had happened. The rush of events had barely given me time to consider Midge's last request. *Why did she make me executor? Why not let her lawyer handle it?* She hadn't just found another way to leave me something instead of naming me in her will. For some reason, she hadn't trusted the people at Joyance House. Why else would she contact Molly's firm without Nylund knowing? I needed to talk to Bloody Mary again and press her about what she knew. Something had been going on at Joyance House, and I had a feeling that Mary's expulsion from the house had been connected. She knew more than she'd told me at the homeless camp.

Alone in the darkness, my eyes suddenly teared, and I wondered at the unlikely friendship that must have meant more to Midge than I ever imagined. Through the blur, headlights suddenly stabbed me from behind. Quickly swiping my face with a sleeve, I checked the mirrors and saw a car rapidly closing in on me. It pulled to within a car length behind my bumper and turned on its high beams. I squinted against the glare, checked the mirror to see it drop back another few yards and keep pace. No light bar, so not SPD. A drunk, no doubt.

I took the next right to get out of the way. When the headlights followed me, sweat dripped down my sides. With a hurried glance to get my bearings, I gave the Toyota some gas and headed west down the hill. The car in the rearview stayed with me. At the last minute, I swung the wheel hard and drifted around a corner on the wet pavement, tires squealing. I gunned it up the block, tapped the brakes, and took a left, ignoring stop signs and hoping to gain some lead as the street jogged right, left, and right again down the hill toward the lights of downtown. I floored it when the street straightened out.

The little Toyota leaped down the hill, the headlights falling a little farther behind, and I rocketed around a curve onto an arterial doing close to sixty. On an impulse, I braked, took a quick right at the next corner, and doused my lights as I accelerated up a side street. Headlights flashed past the corner behind me, and the street plunged into darkness. Dark houses sped by on either side as I raced on, skin tingling. My excitement was short-lived. Halfway up the long block, the car's interior brightened as headlights reappeared in the mirror. They were moving fast. The steering wheel felt slippery under my wet fingers. Breath rasped hoarsely in my throat.

Taking the next left, I angled back up the hill, trying to lose the tail. The little car strained, engine revving past the red line, and gained speed as the street straightened due east. My thoughts raced as fast as the engine. *Who the hell was after me? Dufours? The person who scrawled on my wall? Why?*

After racing past two more intersections, headlights popped into view again down the hill behind me. Two blocks farther and they'd started gaining on me again. The street jogged right, then left again as it approached the crest of Capitol Hill, merci-fully obscuring the lights from view for a few moments. Through the bare trees on the left, the dark bulk of the water tower in Volunteer Park loomed up ahead.

At the next cross street, a car's bumper flashed silver as it nosed into the intersection, the driver oblivious to the onrushing Toyota. My lights were still off! I laid on the horn and swerved into the other lane to avoid a collision. I caught a glimpse of the driver's terrified face through the glass as his car nose-dived to a stop, saw him press himself back into the seat as if mak-ing more space for the Toyota to blow by. With a shriek of rub-ber, the Toyota slid over and missed his bumper by inches. In the rearview, the car sat unmoving in the street, the driver sil-houetted in the passenger window by headlights coming up the hill. With luck he'd slow my pursuer down, too. Blood pounding in my ears; I downshifted, spun the wheel left, and roared into Volunteer Park, circling around the water tower.

A hundred yards down the tree-lined boulevard, past the museum, the headlights reappeared again, sweeping onto the pavement beneath the tower far behind me. The statue standing in the circle fronting the conservatory rose out of the darkness ahead. I downshifted and cut in front of it, tires groaning as the car skidded into the turn. The rear end broke loose, and I struggled to keep control, turning into the skid and stomping on the gas. The little car fishtailed, then straightened and shot forward. Fifty yards down the road I leaned into a curve, willing the old beater to go faster. The narrow road curved right, then left and right again.

With a sudden bang like a cannon shot followed by loud thumping, the car pulled sharply to the right, jumped the curb, and skidded in the wet grass. I slammed on the brakes, jumping out of the car as it swung in a half circle and jerked to a stop. Chunks of black rubber shadowed the gray asphalt in the darkness, the shredded remains of one of the front tires. Lights from the city below painted the low, overcast December sky a sickly salmon against an indigo background. As I sprinted across the road, twin beams of light clawed their way through the blackness, grasping for me as the pursuing car rounded the curve up the hill.

I spotted a trail through the undergrowth and scrabbled up the steep slope, feet slipping on the muddy path. Behind me a car engine snarled, and the pavement below reflected the glare of headlights. A squeal of brakes and tires suddenly replaced the sound of the engine. Over my shoulder I caught a quick glimpse of the car pulling to a stop in the middle of the road. A charge of adrenaline hit me like a high-pressure front, clearing my night vision and pushing me up the slope with gale force.

Across the sudden silence came the sound of a car door opening, and two soft *thuts* almost simultaneously. The soggy earth on the slope a yard to my left erupted in a small geyser of mud. Between footsteps came another *thu-thut*, and bark from a tree on my right exploded, bits of wood hitting me in the face. *Shots? Fuck!* Dufours. It had to be.

In two steps I reached the top, coming out on a paved walkway just below the park's big reservoir, lighted by lampposts every fifty feet. Ignoring the stabbing pain in my knee, I sprinted up the path toward the art museum. The artificial hip wasn't built for the pounding, but I had no time to worry about it. A metal trash can by the path ahead of me jumped suddenly with a loud *whang*. I cut left, away from the light, putting the trunk of a large tree between me and the path, and raced across open grass toward the boulevard fronting the museum.

The space between my shoulder blades widened, a neon sign between them blinking: "Shoot Me." Less than fifty yards now to the road. No sounds registered over my own labored breathing. Dufours must be concentrating on getting closer before wasting more bullets. I feinted left and right a couple of times, just in case.

Bursting through the trees lining the road halfway between the museum and the statue, I sprinted across the pavement, breathing now ragged from the strain, heart pumping in triple time. I couldn't keep up the pace much longer, but the shuttered museum offered no safe harbor. My best chance of losing him was back on city streets. Another seventy yards of open grass separated me from the shelter of the closest trees on the east side of the park. I bent my head and aimed for them, listening intently for the sound of pursuit.

The growl of a car engine wormed its way into my consciousness instead. Headlights reflected off the glass of the conservatory at the end of the boulevard. Tires squealed on the pavement behind me, jerking my head around. A car screeched to a stop on the boulevard, and a dark form leaned over the front seat and flung the passenger door open.

"Get in!" a voice shouted. A woman's voice.

There was a crackling sound like ice breaking on the surface of a pond, and a shower of glinting silver sparks rained on the dark figure bent over the car seat.

"Sanders! Get in *now!*"

The sound of my name clinched my decision. I backtracked to the car in just a few strides and threw myself in the passenger seat. The car was already moving before I turned to look for the door handle. I slammed it shut and twisted in the seat. Through the window over the driver's left shoulder, I saw a dark figure run toward us, stop, and raise both arms.

"Down!" I yelled, leaning forward, head down by my knees.

The car rocked from side to side as she yanked the wheel. The engine revved and tires smoked as they sought a purchase on the wet pavement. She eased off the gas and the car spurted ahead. I craned my head to look behind us. Black against the trees, the gunman was running back the way he'd come, back toward his car. She cranked the wheel to the right, and I jammed an arm up against the roof to keep from falling against her. "Wrong Way" and "Do Not Enter" signs flashed by on the right.

"Shit! This is one way!" I yelled.

She ignored me, barreling down the road to the park entrance. With barely a tap on the brakes, she shot into the intersection and turned left onto an arterial leading north. Columns of mist whorled up like ghosts from the cemetery on the left as we sped past. I twisted in the seat, saw no sign of pursuit.

29

Gagnon stared after the woman's car, rage shaking him like a sock in the mouth of a terrier. He caught his breath and tamped down his anger. Emotion led to mistakes. He couldn't afford to make mistakes. The woman was new in all this. A pro, maybe, given the way she'd swooped in, put her car between him and his quarry. A good driver, too. Pro or not, she'd given him something he hadn't had a few minutes ago—the man's name. Sanders. That should make his job easier. Since little had gone right since he'd arrived in this loutish and barbaric country, something easy for once was welcome.

He walked quickly back to his car. The man's Toyota sat on the shoulder where he'd abandoned it. Gagnon circled to the passenger door, got in, and rifled through the glove compartment. He found the registration in moments and committed the name and address to memory. He glanced around the interior and got out. He had what he needed.

* * *

She stared out the windshield, lower lip caught between her teeth in concentration, focused on driving. From time to time she checked the mirrors, no urgency or concern reflected in her actions. Instead, she looked almost relaxed, radiating a calm that slowed the thudding in my chest. Maybe she was accustomed to being shot at. The car moved at a good clip, but the glowing needle on the speedometer hovered between only five to ten above the limit, not enough to attract SPD's interest if we passed a patrol car.

I caught fleeting glimpses of her features each time we passed a streetlight, her face winking on and off like a construction flasher. Straight, delicate nose, full lips, large dark pools for eyes reflecting the dim light from the instrument panel. Her dark hair fell in a curve that hid half her face, spilling over the upturned collar of her coat an inch or so. She reached up and tucked a strand of hair behind a perfectly rounded ear and leaned forward to switch on a small GPS device mounted on the dash with a suction cup. The screen popped to life, casting a bluish glow on her features.

A low whistle like someone blowing across the top of a beer bottle emanated from the jagged hole in the window next to her head. In the background came the muffled, steady hum of the engine. She worked her way down the hill, toward the Ship Canal. The relative silence slowly sucked the air out of the car, the vacuum waiting for one of us to fill it.

I caved first. "Where are we going?"

She glanced at the GPS and back out the windshield.

"Somewhere safe."

I contented myself with that for a moment. After all, she had in all probability saved my life. I closed my eyes and slowed my breathing, silently repeating a mantra. When I opened them, the car was midspan on the University Bridge. She turned off at the first opportunity and worked her way through the U District on side streets.

"How do you know my name?" I asked after a few minutes.

She didn't look at me. "I know everything about you."

I frowned. "What do you mean, everything?"

Her shoulders rose and fell as she checked the mirror. "Where do you want me to start? You were born in Centralia, Illinois, son of Doug and Helen Sanders. You have an older sister, Christine. You haven't seen her in twenty years. Your father died when you were seventeen—heart attack. He was one of six kids, and his father—your grandfather—was killed in the Centralia coal mine explosion of nineteen forty-seven. Your mom's in a nursing home. You probably feel guilty that you don't visit more often."

I stared at her, mouth hanging open. "How...?"

She continued before I could finish the thought. "You played basketball for the Centralia High School Orphans, the winning-est high-school team in the country. Guard, right? Pretty good, too. Good enough to get a scholarship here at UW." She paused to look out the window at the campus buildings passing by. "But you lost your scholarship when your left knee and hip deterio-rated so badly from chronic osteomyelitis you had to get an arti-ficial hip at age twenty."

"Who the fuck *are* you?"

"You met Margaret Catherine McHugh your freshman year of college and married her immediately after graduation. You had a son early the following year, which may have had some-thing to do with why you married so soon out of college."

"Hey! I married Molly because—"

She waved a hand, cutting me off. "None of my business. Want me to go on?" She didn't wait for a reply. "After a succes-sion of short-lived menial jobs, you finally landed a position in the UW athletics department in communications, and supported Margaret—Molly—while she got her law degree. Then you moved up to the university's office of news and information. You spent four years there before going into public affairs with Bellnap & Dreier. After seven years there, your career blew up about twelve, fourteen months ago when you were accused of stealing campaign funds from one of the firm's clients. That about sum things up?"

I cringed at the sound of my own CV inventoried in just a few short sentences, a life reduced to a small litany of minor milestones and major failures.

Then she looked directly at me for the first time. The full-on sight of her face was somehow more disquieting than how much she knew about my personal history or how she'd learned it. I considered Molly beautiful, but Molly's classically Irish nose—a tad crooked, and pointed at the end—wide mouth, and slightly thin lips gave her face character, individuality. This woman's features were flawlessly sculpted and perfectly symmetrical, from square jaw and elegant nose to pouty lips, so exquisite that she was almost painful to look at, like a breathtaking sunrise that hurts the eyes with its bright luminosity.

Turning away, I watched the campus buildings give way first to retail stores then apartment buildings and houses up in Laurelhurst. We passed Magnuson Park, formerly the old Sand Point Naval Air Station, and wound around the golf course into a quiet, hilly neighborhood somewhere north of there. Large houses sat on lots separated from neighbors by old-growth trees and well-manicured shrubbery.

She pulled into the drive of a darkened house far up the hillside, pushed a remote on the visor that opened one of the garage bays, and drove the small car into the dark, empty space. She parked, shut off the engine, and climbed out briskly. I got out more slowly, torn between curiosity and caution. At the door leading into the house, she tapped her foot. I followed her into a dark room. She flipped a wall switch, bathing a modern kitchen in light, making me blink. Dark wood cabinets and counters covered in warm gray granite with black flecks softened the sterile appliances, all in matching black and stainless. In addition to the recessed lights in the ceiling, lamps with glass shades hung over an island in the center of the kitchen.

"Sit down." She gestured toward an oak table in a nook off on one side.

She stripped off her black pea coat and tossed it over the back of a chair, then rummaged through the cupboards, finding a canister of coffee, filters, and mugs. The house wasn't hers.

"Who are you?" I watched her set up the coffee brewer with deft, precise movements.

Her hair lightly painted the neck of her white turtleneck as she shook her head. "I need to know what happened back there first," she said, turning to face me.

"How the hell should I know?" I slouched in the chair.

She put a hand on her hip, drawing attention to long legs packed in low-slung, tight-fitting black jeans. "Who was chasing you?"

"I don't know."

"You have no idea?"

She appraised me with a challenging stare. Her looks alone would intimidate most men. But behind the eyes I saw a calculating intellect, and she'd already proved cool under fire. She wasn't a cop, but she wasn't any ordinary civilian, either. *Military? No uniform. Government, maybe? Agent of some sort, perhaps, FBI or CIA. Why?* Her questioning eyes wanted to know how smart I was, if I were smart enough to trust her. I had no reason not to—yet. I shivered.

"Hard to tell in the dark, but since I'm not used to having people take potshots at me with a silenced pistol, I'll venture a guess," I said. "Alain Dufours."

She frowned. "Who's he?"

I shrugged. "You don't know? French. Supposedly a history professor at the Sorbonne."

"Why was he trying to kill you?" She eased into the seat next to mine and set an empty mug in front of me.

I told her what had happened in Royer's office.

"Why would this man want a UW professor dead?" she said when I finished.

"I'm not sure," I said.

"Maybe you better start at the beginning. You need to tell me why you went to see Royer."

It was my turn to assess her. "Look, I appreciate what you did back there. You took a big risk. But why are you so interested in all this?"

"For the time being, let's just say it's my job to be interested."

"How do I know you're not working with Dufours?"

"You don't. But it looked to me like he was trying to kill you. If I were working with him, you'd be dead."

She retrieved the coffeepot while I considered her. Like I said, rational thought is tough at five in the morning with no sleep. I told her the whole story, as much of it as I knew, starting with Midge's murder. I left out my conversation with Beardsley or any reference to *la peste*, since I hadn't had a chance to talk to Jane yet. The idea still sounded crazy to me. No sense giving this woman a reason to think I was some nutcase. She listened thoughtfully, interrupting a few times for clarification, stopping me when some thought had taken me too far off track on some side spur. When I finished, she nodded and leaned back, chewing on her lower lip again, arms folded. After a few moments, she refilled her coffee mug and held out the decanter.

"Want some?"

I shook my head no.

"Excuse me a minute," she said.

She got up and replaced the pot, took a cell phone out of her pocket, and made a call.

"Yes, sir," she said into the phone, making no effort to keep her end of the conversation private. "No, sir... He's with me, sir, at the safe house... There were complications... A tail, sir... No, sir, termination..."

She watched me with an absent stare while she listened for several moments.

"Yes, sir," she said suddenly. "I need information on a subject. Alain Dufours. History professor at the Sorbonne." She spelled the name and relayed the physical description I'd given her then fell silent again for a moment. "Very cooperative," she said. "I think so, sir. I have your blessing...? Good... Thank you, sir."

When she came back to the table, she seemed to have come to some sort of decision. She leaned forward, forearms resting on the table.

"How much did Royer tell you about Woodworth's naval career?"

I felt my brow furrow. "As much as he knew, I suppose. He told me he'd gotten it from records in the naval archives. Why?"

She nodded. "A lot of people in my position would stonewall you, Mr. Sanders. Give you a long lecture about national security or some other bullshit. Pat you on the head and send you home. After what happened tonight, you deserve more than that. So, I'll tell you what I can.

"My name is Reyna Chase, Lieutenant Commander, US Navy. I'm head of an information analysis team with the Office of Naval Intelligence. A week ago, Professor Royer placed phone calls to the National Archives and the Naval Historical Center looking for information about Selim Woodworth. The calls and the nature of his questions triggered a command signal in my department that's lain dormant for more than a hundred and fifty years."

"The missing deck logs," I said.

Her eyebrows rose. She nodded. "We followed procedure and alerted our superiors. Beyond the curious nature of how old the signal was—it predates the formation of ONI itself by more than three decades—I passed the alert on up the chain. When Royer was subsequently murdered, I got called into a meeting with my immediate boss, two navy flag officers, the CNO—sorry, Chief of Naval Operations."

"As in one of the Joint Chiefs?" Under the table, I dug my fingers into my thigh to see if I was awake or dreaming.

She nodded. "The big brass, including the secretary of the navy. Normally, the command signal triggered by Royer's phone calls would have been handled through a routine investigation. His murder put a big priority on it. We think the two are connected. Which is why you heard me asking for background on the Frenchman."

"That was your boss?" I glanced at the cell phone she'd laid on the table.

She nodded and looked at me intently for a moment, as if trying to read me. "Only six people know what I'm about to tell you, Mr. Sanders. After the briefing, I got on the first plane out of DC to assess the situation here. I've been here for less than a day. My boss said to go with my gut. My gut says you're the key to this."

"Key to what?" I couldn't keep exasperation out of my voice.

"To what's been happening. You know something you're not aware of, or you're a catalyst." She shrugged. "In any event, I think we can use you, if you're willing to help."

"Help you do what? You keep talking national security and secret intelligence shit. You're eating into my sleeping time."

The corners of her mouth turned up in a faint smile. "This intelligence shit is a chance for you to help your country."

"How did you find me, anyway? And how do you know so much about me?"

"We did a routine background check on Royer when his call triggered the command signal. Phone records showed a lot of calls from Midge Babcock. When she was murdered, your name came up as a suspect. I ran your background, too. When Royer was killed and your name showed up on his phone log, I could tell you were in this up to your neck. So, what do you say?"

"Look, all I want is to find out who murdered Midge Babcock and stay out of jail."

She gave it some thought. "Fair enough. I think we can help each other. We probably have some traction with the locals. If we can figure out what's going on, I'll put in a word for you."

"That's it? You'll vouch for me and all my problems will disappear? You going to make the evidence disappear, too?"

She didn't answer; eyes the color of bloodstone leveled at me coolly.

"You don't seem to have a problem with the fact that I'm up on murder charges," I said. "Why is that?"

She hadn't blinked. "We did our homework. We don't think you murdered anyone."

"Does that mean you believe me? Or you just don't think I'm capable of killing someone?"

Her face remained impassive, as if she were waiting to see if I was through. "You're right—your friend's death and Royer's death both have something to do with Selim Woodworth."

"This is nuts." I pushed away from the table.

She held up a hand, her expression unchanged. "Hang on. Hear me out, then decide."

I paused. "And if I still think you're crazy?"

"You walk out. I'll drop you off wherever you want."

"Just like that? Without even telling the cops?"

She shrugged. "They're not my problem."

I crossed my arms and leaned back.

She took a sip of her coffee. "Royer told you that Woodworth volunteered to go look for the Donner Party. That's all in his official records. When we got the second command signal, the NHC had instructions to send over sealed documents, documents that aren't part of the records."

"The lost logs," I said.

"Those, along with secret files that haven't been opened since before the Civil War." She raised an eyebrow.

"I'm suitably impressed."

"I just want to make sure you understand the importance of this." She paused. "Something's going on that no one, not even people with the highest clearance—at ONI, at least—knew anything about. We're all starting from scratch here."

She seemed to be waiting for validation, so I gave her a grudging nod.

She went on. "Woodworth never found the Donners."

"I knew that."

Again, she looked at me like someone exercising patience with a toddler. "He led a small retinue of men into the mountains and got lost," she went on. "The men turned back, but Woodworth pressed on, wandering for days in the same conditions that had trapped the Donners.

"Somewhere in the mountains, about halfway between Sacramento and the spot where the Donner Party was eventually found—near what's now Truckee—Woodworth stumbled into a streambed littered with gold nuggets. A huge placer deposit. He made camp, explored the area for three days, and realized he'd discovered a major vein. Keep in mind this was a year before gold was discovered at Sutter's Mill. You know, the start of the California Gold Rush? Woodworth could have kept the discovery to himself, could have taken what he could carry and walked away a rich man. He didn't. He was a loyal navy man, and when he made his way back to civilization he reported his findings to a superior he trusted."

I shook my head. "What an idiot."

She actually smiled. I relaxed a little. It couldn't hurt to indulge her little fantasy. For a while, at least.

"Maybe he was. A lot of men would have taken the easy way. Apparently Woodworth was motivated by his conscience, not just money." She tilted her head. "What do you know about the period leading up to the Civil War?"

"Not a lot. I hated history. Why?"

"A lot of the politics for decades before the war revolved around the issue of slavery and states' rights. The way I understand it, when James Polk was president the agreements he negotiated with Mexico for Texas and California, and with Great Britain for the Washington Territory, made a lot of people nervous. All that territory came with conditions about where slavery would and wouldn't be allowed. People thought Polk's actions might goad Southern states into thoughts of secession. No one wanted that. Not only would it break up the Union, but also it might lead to civil war. And eventually, it did.

"But at the time, the fear was so strong that a group of powerful northerners in Washington formed a secret coalition. The group crossed political lines. Some were businessmen, some were bankers, and there were a couple of US senators in the group, too. Maybe the most influential member was Daniel Webster."

"Wasn't Webster an abolitionist?"

"Yes," she said patiently, "but above all, Webster wanted to preserve the Union, so he looked for compromises wherever he could. It's one of the reasons he was considered such a great statesman. He gave up a shot at the vice presidency to stay in the Senate and help push through the Compromise of Eighteen Fifty."

"All right. So what's the point?"

"Just setting the stage for you. These men were fiercely intent on preserving the Union. Maybe even desperate. So, shortly after Woodworth's discovery the navy entrusted him with a secret mission—mine the gold and hide it."

"Why? Why not just claim it for the government?"

"The coalition intended to stockpile the gold in the event of civil war. But they didn't want to tip their hand to anyone in the South and let them know how nervous they were about even the hint of war. The coalition funded the mission, not the navy or the government."

"The group had the US Navy in its pocket?"

"Not in that sense, no." She paused, her face earnest. "These men were all patriots, trying to prevent the nation from tearing itself apart—and failing that, to win any eventual conflict."

"I'll take your word for it. So, what happened to the gold?"

She smiled again. It made her more accessible somehow, more human. "I'm getting to that part. Woodworth went to Monterey Bay and reported for duty aboard an old warship called the *Warren*. It had been turned into a stores ship for the growing navy presence around San Francisco. He sent all but a skeleton crew of trusted, handpicked officers and sailors ashore. Then he and his crew recruited or induced nearly a hundred Chinese immigrants to accompany them up the American River and overland to the spot where he'd discovered the gold."

"Induced?"

She saw the skepticism on my face. "There's no evidence they were conscripted against their will, but the Chinese didn't start immigrating to the West Coast in big numbers until a few years later. It's a pretty sure bet that only a very small handful spoke any English, so most of them probably had no idea what was in store for them. But the documents we have indicate they were free to leave at any time.

"In any event, the work party spent the next year excavating and mining the site. Woodworth eventually took command of the transport ship *Anita*, loaded all the gold and the work party on board, and sailed north up the coast."

"To Seattle," I said, the picture starting to coalesce in my mind.

"To Puget Sound, anyway," she said quickly. "Seattle hadn't officially been settled yet."

"You think he buried the gold here somewhere."

"We don't think. The documents unearthed by the command signal say he did."

"But you don't know for certain." I saw her hesitate. "And you have no idea where."

"We think we do now," she said.

"Of course." A light went on in my head. "The Military Bounty Land Act grant. When the government finally gave him land for his military service, Woodworth must have arranged to make it here in Seattle, where he buried the gold."

"That's what we think. Some of the *Anita*'s deck logs really are gone. Maybe destroyed on purpose to keep the mission secret."

Half-baked thoughts tumbled around in my head like socks in a hot dryer. I snagged a few and tried to focus. "It still doesn't explain what Dufours is up to. Why kill the professor?"

She shrugged. "Maybe Royer told him something. Or let something slip." She looked pensive. "It's obvious Dufours wants to eliminate you because you're a witness. But he's after something else. The lease agreement your friend discovered, maybe. You realize what that piece of paper means?"

I sat up straighter. "The nuns had a claim on the gold. Still do." I thought about it. "How much gold was there?"

"Woodworth's communiqués indicate the work party extracted and moved about fourteen tons of nuggets and extremely high-yield ore worth about three million." She paused. "In today's dollars that much gold would be worth nearly two hundred million, give or take a few."

"Holy shit!" The number boggled the mind. "I wonder if Midge had a clue."

Reyna shook her head. "The old lady? Maybe. I doubt it. But from what you've told me, she still knew that lease document was worth money because of the light-rail tunnel."

I gulped some coffee and made a face—it was cold. I pushed the mug away. "How the hell could the government forget about that much gold?"

She picked up both mugs and took them to the sink.

"Well, remember," she said, "it wasn't the government per se. It was this coalition. And the coalition wanted it kept secret from southerners in the government, so they buried all evidence the mission ever took place. By the time the Civil War actually started, every member of the coalition except Woodworth was long dead."

"I can't believe no one ever talked. What about the work party? The crew? What happened to them? Burial at sea?"

"From what we can tell, the crew was well paid to keep their mouths shut. Only the Chinese who buried the gold knew its location, but they had no idea where they were. They could have been in Timbuktu for all they knew. And almost none of them could speak English, anyway."

Neither of us spoke for a moment. I tried to digest what she was telling me, head whirling as if in some surreal dream from which I'd wake any minute.

"What about Woodworth?" I said. "Why didn't he ever come back for the gold?"

She shrugged. "Who knows? He was successful enough in business and politics, and we know he was a patriot until the day he died. I guess he didn't think it was his to claim. The North had enough gold to fund the war when the shooting eventually started, anyway."

Maybe the late hour and months of too little sleep had short-circuited the wiring in my brain. Maybe after the events of the past two weeks my definition of normal had shifted somewhere closer to that of a Disney character's. As improbable and fantastic as her story sounded, it made an odd kind of sense. Exhaustion broke over me, along with a strong temptation to just roll with it, take her at face value. But some things still didn't fit.

A loud snap from somewhere outside startled us both. My head jerked toward the window, still opaque in the dark of early morning. Reyna, if that was her real name, put a finger to her lips, eased out of her chair, and slipped on her dark coat, pulling the collar up to cover the white turtleneck. She reached into a pocket and pulled out a black semiautomatic pistol.

"Stay here," she said in a whisper as she headed for the door.

30

Heart hammering in my chest, I got up and moved silently into the kitchen to look for a knife, a meat tenderizer, another pistol, something. *Christ, what have I gotten myself into?* A chef's knife nestled in a utensil organizer in one of the drawers. The faux-wood handle molded itself into my palm, giving me a very small sense of comfort. I stepped away from the counter, found the wall switch, and killed the lights. The windows turned charcoal, revealing streetlamps that dotted the hill below and the broad expanse of black lake water separating them from the lights marching up Big Finn Hill in the distance.

I crept back to the glassed French doors leading off the breakfast nook. Listening intently, I craned for glances into the backyard without exposing myself. Branches silhouetted against the sky waved gently in the breeze, the only visible movement. Every creak in the house—the refrigerator rumbling to life, the tick of a heating vent—echoed in the silence, stopping my heart for a fraction of an instant until it passed muster. Shadows slunk out of the corners only to jump back into position when my eyes jerked toward them. Branches undulating in the dim light threw shadows around the room as if they were wrestling each other.

She'd been gone too long. *Breathe.* My eyes darted around the room, back outside, peering, searching. My nerves jumped with each shift in the shadows. The hand holding the kitchen knife trembled like the leaves fluttering outside. Seconds oozed past, sap from a cold tree. Time lost its meaning. The days of the past week had collapsed into minutes, and now the seconds expanded into hours as if a huge sun had caved in on itself, forming a black hole, then exploded into a supernova, everything rushing, rushing. I closed my eyes. The inside of my lids turned red as a beam of light abruptly slashed up at my face from the doorway. I threw up an arm as a shield.

"Jesus!" Reyna said, hitting the light switch. "Put that knife away. You'll hurt yourself." She walked to the table, shedding her coat, and sat down.

"There's no one out there," she went on. "Probably just a branch breaking in the wind. Or an animal. Maybe a cat or a raccoon."

"Are you sure? No way Dufours could have followed us?"

"I don't see how."

I slid the knife back into the drawer, turning so she wouldn't see my hand still shaking. "Sorry. My nerves are fried. I've never been shot at. Have you?"

"I think it's safe here, if you want to crash for a while," she said, changing the subject.

I joined her at the table. "Why do you think Woodworth assigned mineral rights to the religious order? Change of heart? Or did he change sides?"

"I don't know." She stared out at the blackness for a moment. "I don't think he turned. He served faithfully during the Civil War, according to his records. Maybe he didn't trust his secret to the navy after all the members of the coalition died. A lot of navy men were pro slavery before the war, all the way up to the secretary of the navy. Maybe he was just hedging his bets. When did you say he met with the nun in San Francisco?"

"Eighteen fifty-six."

She pressed her lips together. "That would fit. Maybe he was just trying to make sure whoever came across records of the coalition's mission didn't get greedy and try to make off with the gold."

"The property was his by then. Why give away his claim to the gold? Wouldn't it have been just as safe in his hands as the hands of a few nuns? Safer, even?"

"I can't answer that, sorry." She shrugged. "Maybe he was creating some kind of leverage. Covering his ass if things went south. Look, I'm here to find out if the gold is still there, who knows about it, and why the sudden interest. Obviously, Royer's death and your involvement complicate things a bit. But you seem to be coming at this, too, from a different direction. I still think we can help each other, Mr. Sanders."

"How? And stop calling me Mr. Sanders. You know so damn much about me you might as well call me Blake."

Her head inclined slightly. "Blake, then. Where's the document you showed Royer?"

The question took me unaware, a sucker punch from my blind side. I looked for signs of prevarication. Her eyes gave away nothing. But it was a mistake, the first she'd made from what I could tell. She'd played it straight, gained my trust, hadn't even offered the barest hint of feminine wiles though she couldn't be blind to the effect she had on men. Now I was no longer sure of her intent.

"It's safe," I said.

Sister Marguerite's journal sat tucked away in a locker at the Greyhound bus station. The locker key was taped to the inside of the grille of the Toyota, next to a spare ignition key I kept in case I locked myself out when delivering papers.

Her gaze sized up whether the subject was worth pursuing. "Good. We don't know what this Dufours character is after, but he may know about the document. He's French? Maybe French Canadian for all we know. You said the religious order was from Montréal, right?" She waited for my nod. "I'll see what I can find out about him as soon as the folks in Washington have had a chance to run him through the computer."

Something sat below my sternum like a bad case of indigestion. I didn't see how Midge could have known about the gold. And though she obviously regarded the women's shelter highly enough to donate her time and perhaps her estate, she wasn't about money. Not from what I knew about her. She'd been a caring sort—Gray Lady and nurse. She hadn't asked Molly's firm to file suit to get easement money out of Sound Transit. She'd wanted an injunction, to stop the digging. Because of what was buried beneath the city. And if not the gold...it had to be *la peste*...but I still couldn't figure out what Dufours was really after.

Reyna glanced at a slim watch on her wrist. "Nearly seven here. That's ten, DC time. I'll give it another hour or so and check in."

I kept my half-baked thoughts to myself. "So what do you want me to do?"

"Get some rest." She pushed away from the table. "You can stay here for a few days. At least until I figure out what's going on, if you want. I can bring in some food."

"I can't do that."

"Why not? I'm offering you a safe haven, courtesy of the US government." She tipped her head. "It's a big house. I don't bite. Separate bedrooms, if that's what you're worried about."

She looked mildly amused.

"It's not that," I said quickly. To my surprise, a shadow of something crossed her face. *Disappointment?* Before I could think better of it, I leaned in. Her eyes widened, but she didn't pull away. Somehow unable to stop, I kissed her lightly, brushing my lips against hers, lingering for just an instant. My body jerked back as if jolted by a live power line, lips seared with heat from the quick contact.

"I'm sorry. I shouldn't have done that."

She tipped her head, her expression reflecting only curiosity. But her honey-colored skin was now tinged a pale salmon.

I hesitated. "You're not angry?"

"It's a natural reaction. You came close to death; you want to reaffirm you're alive. Touch someone. Make contact." She stopped for a breath. "I would have been surprised if you hadn't tried anything. As it is, you've been pretty calm under the circumstances."

My chagrin must have shown. She put a hand on my arm. The heat from her fingers seeped into my skin. I stifled a groan, abruptly conscious of how long it had been since I'd held a woman.

"Hey, it's okay," she said. "In answer to your earlier question, yes, I've been under fire. First time it happened, I wanted to screw the nearest airman right afterwards. It passes." She didn't elaborate further.

I frowned, unsure if I wanted the feeling to pass or not.

"I've got obligations," I said finally. "I can't afford to lose my job. Either one of them. That's why I can't stay here."

She pulled her hand away. "Of course."

"I'll crash here for a few hours, but I have to go back. Figure out what's going on."

I had the sense that, despite her assistance and apparent openness, Reyna wasn't telling me everything. If her loyalties were ever tested, I doubted they'd come down on my side. Something told me I'd be smart to get some hard information to trade.

"I can't protect you out there, you know."

I shrugged. The idea of her slight frame shielding my bulk from harm turned the corners of my scowl up in grudging amusement.

"What?" Her eyes widened.

"Nothing." I let my gaze fall to the table and rubbed my face, wiping the grin away. "Dufours didn't kill Midge Babcock."

The change in subject took her by surprise. "How do you know?"

"It doesn't fit. This guy's a pro. Don't you think? The silencer. The way he killed Royer. He came after me with the same gun. Midge was killed with a knife." The memory turned my empty stomach. "I've never seen so much blood. Whoever did that was in a rage."

"Or making it look that way," she said.

I ran a hand across my mouth again. "Maybe."

Her eyes flicked over my face and she nodded. "You should get some sleep. Bedrooms are down the hall. Take your pick." She stood. "Look, I can't stop you if you want to put yourself back out on the street, but this guy Dufours knows your car now. He may even have a line on where you work already. The least you can do is take my car in the morning. It's a rental, so no big deal. You can return it in a day or two."

"What about my car?"

"I'll take care of it. Make sure the cops don't tow it. Got the keys?"

"What will you do for wheels?" I said, exchanging with her.

"Don't worry about it. I'm resourceful. Is there a way I can reach you?"

"I bought a disposable cell phone." I saw her eyebrows go up a notch as I gave her the number. She didn't bother writing it down, apparently committing it to memory. "What if I need to get in touch with you?"

She hesitated. "Call this number." She rattled it off twice to make sure I got it. "I'll get a page and call you back when I can."

I pushed away from the table wearily. The gray outside the windows had turned several shades lighter, signaling the coming arrival of another day of Seattle sunshine, that bleak *drip, drip* that endears some and drives others mad. She watched me slouch toward the hallway leading to the bedrooms. Before the dark tunnel swallowed me, I had one last thought. I stopped and turned.

"How did you find me?"

She smiled. "I put a tracking device on your car at the warehouse. You started driving like a bat out of hell. I figured you were in trouble."

* * *

Life, someone said, isn't about what happens; it's about what we do when something happens. A relatively new concept to me. I tried to live by it. Like anything, it took practice.

My watch said it was well past noon when I opened my eyes and rubbed the grit from them with a thumb and forefinger. I swung my legs over the side of the bed and padded silently through the house. There was no sign of Reyna, no sign that she'd ever been in the house. The bedclothes in the other bedrooms were undisturbed, the cushions on couches and chairs unblemished, not even dented. The kitchen was spotless, coffee mugs washed and put away, trash emptied. I retrieved my shoes from the room where I'd slept, smoothed the wrinkles from the bedspread, and left.

I kept telling myself that all I wanted was to be left alone. Left to myself to share lattés with my ghosts. But if that was true, why had I confided in an old lady, looked forward to our conversations like a poor man looked forward to payday? Why had I bothered trying to save Liz Tracey from spattering her brains on pavement? Why did I miss Molly so damn much? Why did I bother trying so hard to stay out of jail? Why had I kissed a naval intelligence officer in the dead of night? A way of proving my own existence? Making a difference?

I thought I'd been through every stage of grief the shrinks had come up with. Denial, bargaining, depression, shock, guilt, anger—especially anger. There was one stage, though, I hadn't managed to get through, hadn't yet mastered.

The lights were on in the office building by Green Lake. Someone always manned the suicide hotline. And suicide survivors—the family and friends of those who take their lives—are a little like alcoholics. Time heals, but anniversaries, familiar places, songs, memories, anything really, can trigger a crisis of faith, a relapse into crippling depression or just plain sadness. Jeri had set a regular time for daily support meetings for anyone who wanted to attend, and people could drop by anytime just to chat if hotline volunteers were available. I arrived in time for a regular meeting.

Toward the end of the hour, Jeri turned to me. "You've been pretty low-key today, Blake. Anything you want to share?"

A giant hand squeezed my chest, making it hard to breathe. *Now or never.*

"No." I pushed away from the table. "Thanks."

"What are you going to do?" Jeri said, unable to keep concern and fear out of her voice.

"I don't know," I said. "But this time I'm not going to sit on my ass and let them take my life away from me."

I turned and walked out, through the door to the street, into the raw December air.

* * *

I drove back to Toji's to get a change of clothes. Toji sat on the floor in the darkened living room, wan gray light filtering through the window. He looked up silently when I entered, his face an unreadable mask. He lowered his eyes. I followed his gaze to the head cradled in his lap. Chance, curled in a fetal position, his back to me. Toji stroked his hair.

"Sorry," I said, backpedaling from the intimacy I'd clumsily disrupted.

"Who's that?" Chance mumbled. He rolled his shoulders and turned his head toward the sound of my voice. "Blake?"

One side of his face had swollen to the size of a cantaloupe, a fist-sized circle on his cheek and jaw painted the color of eggplant. He stared at me with one eye, a puffy black slit the only indication of his other. Engorged lips deformed one side of his mouth, the lower one scabbed black with dried blood.

"Jesus, Chance, what happened? Did someone come after you and Peter? Is Peter all right?" I thought of the warning scrawled on the wall in my apartment.

Chance worked his mouth open, tried to wet his lips. Toji leaned over and shushed him.

"Don't try to talk, baby," he murmured, smoothing the hair out of Chance's eyes. He looked up. "Peter's fine. He's at work."

"What happened?"

Toji's shoulders moved slightly. "Lover's spat."

"No." I looked at Chance's ruined face. "Peter couldn't have done this to you."

"It happened down at the club, doll," Toji said. "Peter wasn't there."

My shoulders sagged as the tension drained away. "Then who...?"

He shrugged. "Some asshole at the club. Just went ber*serk*. Took three guys to get him off."

"Didn't like the Vera Wang, I guess," Chance said, the words distorted.

I wiped my mouth. "My God! Out of the blue? What the hell is wrong with people? I'm so sorry, Chance. Are you all right?"

He nodded and sighed. Reached up and touched Toji's cheek.

Toji looked me up and down, a corner of his mouth turned up sardonically. "Where did you find this big, strapping man, Chance? He's so delightfully clueless." He gave me a wink.

"Don't mind Toji," Chance mumbled. "Just being protective."

Toji hadn't taken his eyes off me. "Isn't your kid gay?"

"Toji!" Chance scolded.

"Gay, straight," I said, "what difference does it make? I could care less. We're all people."

Toji's expression turned wistful. "Gee, I wish *my* dad had been that understanding." His eyes hardened into black marbles. "Get real. This crap happens all the time. No one does anything to stop it. Not the cops. Not politicians. You of all people should know better. They're *hate* crimes. Lucky Chance wasn't killed."

"That's enough, Toj," Chance said gently. "He's not the enemy."

Toji looked into his face and rocked him gently. I silently backed out of the room, ears ringing, and slunk off to find clean clothes.

31

My conversation with Reyna from the night before convinced me more than ever that Dufours was after something other than the gold Reyna thought was buried. Sister Marguerite's journal had said *la peste* was safe.

I dialed a once-familiar number when I got in the car and was surprised to get a live voice.

"Jane? Blake."

The silence made me think she'd cut me off. Then, "I'm not talking to you."

"Wait! Please, Jane. I didn't call about Molly. I know how you feel about me."

More silence. Finally, "I'm busy. What do you want?"

"I need your expertise. I'm doing some research on a story I came across about a nun who supposedly performed a miracle back in the mid-eighteen hundreds. There's a legend that she saved some slaves from an outbreak of some sort of shipboard disease. I found a journal that suggests a sample of this disease may still exist. Is that even possible?" I waited. "Jane?"

"I'm here." She paused. "Possible? I suppose. But not likely."
The condescension in her voice sounded more like the Jane I
knew, although she also sounded slightly uncertain, not at all
like her cocksure walking-medical-text self.

I thought about how to frame the question another way.
"Could anyone get sick by being exposed to something that's
been buried for a long time?"

"Depends on what it is. If it's a bacterium, it could only survive in the right conditions. Buried underground? No, not if it's
been any length of time."

"Doesn't bacteria survive in hostile environments? Places like
Antarctica and around steam vents at the bottom of the ocean?"

"Evolution. They evolved in those conditions."

"What about a virus?"

"Generally needs a living host to survive. Not likely to last
long buried underground. The only thing that could is a spore,
like anthrax. We can handle that, too. What kind of disease are
we talking about?"

"I'm not sure. From what I've heard, it may have been some
sort of plague."

"Black Death? That's caused by *Y pestis*, a bacterium."

"Which doesn't live long, underground or not, except under
the right conditions."

"Right."

"Is there another disease with similar symptoms—?"

"Anthrax. Not likely your nun saved people without antibiot-
ics. Which nobody knew about back then. We have them now. I
told you, anthrax doesn't worry us too much. Look, unless there's
anything else, I've got an appointment waiting."

"No, that's okay. Thanks, Jane."

I hung up and digested the bad news. There had to be a reason Dufours wanted what the sisters had hidden. Something
nagged at the back of my brain. Something I'd forgotten to ask
Jane. It scuttled out of sight.

I checked voice mail—another call from Charlie. I sighed and dialed his cell number.

"Yeah," he said.

"You up?"

"Barely. Who's this?" His voice was hoarse. I'd woken him.

"Blake. You called."

"Sorry. Didn't recognize the number."

"Since our chat the other night, I figured it was safer to use a burner."

He grunted. "Look, you probably heard already."

"Heard what?"

The line was silent too long. "I figured she'd call you. Guess not."

"Who'd call? Shit, Charlie, spit it out."

"Look, I called to let you know SPD responded to a call at Molly's last night. B and E."

An unseen fist slammed into my stomach. "Is she okay?"

"Yeah, yeah. Well, not exactly. She went to Virginia Mason, but they may have cut her loose and sent her home by now. It wasn't *too* bad."

"What happened?"

"Like I said, looks like a burglary gone bad. She surprised whoever it was and got banged around pretty good before the creep got away."

"Thanks, Charlie." I hung up before he could reply and headed for the hospital.

Molly stood arguing toe-to-toe with an aide when I arrived at her room. She wore nylon jogging pants and a sweatshirt, the clothes she must have worn when she was admitted.

"I'm leaving," Molly said, going around the big woman in blue scrubs.

The woman sidestepped, blocking her path. "No, you ain't. Not without sittin' in this chair." She patted a wheelchair.

Molly caught sight of me over the aide's massive sloped shoulder. A black-and-purple bruise circled a puffy eye, and a hairy caterpillar of stitches crawled across the opposite cheek.

"Blake!" she said. "Thank God. Help me out here."

The aide turned and glared at me.

My gaze wavered between the two. "Did the doctors give you an okay to go home?"

Molly's nod was impatient, her head a little loose on her shoulders. "Of course. I'm a lawyer, remember?"

"Get in the chair, Molly. I'll give you a ride home."

She settled heavily in the chair. The aide reluctantly threw me a look of gratitude and deftly wheeled Molly out of the room. I trailed out after them.

The aide washed her hands of us at the hospital entrance. I helped Molly out of the chair and supported her weight across the street to the parking garage. In the car, Molly took in the interior, head looping like she was balancing an inverted bowling pin on her shoulders.

"Vicodin?" I said.

She looked at me and grinned. "Percocet."

"Strong stuff, Moll. Sure you don't want to spend another night here? See how you do?"

Her face disappeared behind a curtain of red hair. "Nope."

"What about staying with friends? Somebody who can look after you?"

"Take me home, Blake." She glanced around again. "You got a new car."

"It's a rental. Toyota's in the shop," I lied.

She leaned toward me, peering past my chest, wrinkling her nose as she squinted at the large square of duct tape Reyna had thoughtfully pasted over the hole in the window. "Crappy rental agency," she said.

"Street punks. Probably looking to boost the radio and got scared off."

I glanced at her. For an instant I saw not just the woman I'd loved for half a lifetime, but the face of the son we'd raised together reflected in her features—in the strong nose and chin, in the depth of the blue eyes, like clear water over a Caribbean reef—and my heart puddled in my chest. She turned and stared out the window silently, watching the buildings slide past, a blur of grays and browns. We drove the rest of the way without speaking.

Margaret Catherine McHugh descended on her mother's side from one of the original "Mercer Girls"—the women Asa Mercer imported from New England in 1864 to provide Seattle men with wives—and a self-made Irish immigrant on her father's. The McHugh family had lived on Capitol Hill since the early days of its development. The house—mansion, really—would have gone to Molly, anyway, when her parents died, but Tom McHugh was a shrewd businessman. He'd retired, and he and his wife, Elizabeth, had been spending most of their time in Arizona. When Molly and I split up, he sold Molly the family home and moved to Arizona permanently. The little house Molly and I had purchased in the Ravenna neighborhood a few years after Cole was born went to her in the divorce, and the price it fetched when she sold it made a nice down payment on the old homestead.

I parked the car in the drive on the side of the house and circled around the front bumper to open Molly's door. She took my hand and got out unsteadily. I wrapped her arm inside mine and walked her up the steps. Designed in Renaissance Revival style with steeply gabled roofs, towering chimneys, and classic and gothic touches, the brick home was both daunting and comfortingly familiar. I'd eaten a lot of meals with the family in the dining room, working hard for acceptance as an outsider, first as "the boyfriend," later as "the guy who got Molly pregnant and delayed if not derailed her brilliant career," and finally as "son-in-law." The last honor only a little less dubious than the others.

I'd argued sports and politics with Tom in the cramped den tucked behind the stairway to the upper floors. My memory climbed the stairs inside. I'd made love to Molly in at least three of the six bedrooms.

Molly led me around the corner of the veranda and unlocked the side door. I followed her into the warm interior and turned on some lights while she fiddled with an alarm panel.

"Are you sure you'll be all right?" I steered her to the kitchen to make some tea. "I could stay, you know."

She waved a hand feebly. "It's not a problem. I'll be fine. Really."

"You're not afraid to stay here alone?" I sat her down on a stool and refreshed my memory, remembering where to find tea bags and cups.

"No. I'm just so damned angry. At myself for forgetting to turn on the alarm last night. And that asshole who broke in. He *hit* me, damn it!"

"He could have killed you, Moll. Lucky he didn't have a gun."

"He did! That's what he hit me with!" She pointed to the stitches over her cheekbone. "I barely saw it coming, but I caught a good enough glimpse. Definitely a gun."

Wordlessly, I stepped to the side of her stool and wrapped my arms around her. She pressed her face into me and gave a shuddery sigh. She smelled like antiseptic and herbal shampoo and my mind suddenly flooded with memories of her in the delivery room. The pain, exhaustion, and brief flashes of fear on her sweat-soaked face, transformed when she heard Cole's first cry and held him in her arms to an expression so rapturous, so pure, it shone like an angel's. With all the images came a swirling whirlpool of feelings for the woman I'd loved and lost. For an instant, Reyna's face flashed in my mind, and I felt something gnawing my insides. I brushed it away.

"I don't think I could bear to lose you, too," I said.

Molly pulled away and looked at me.

"You know what I mean."

She bit her lip and nodded.

"Anyway," I said, stepping over to the counter, "I'm glad you're safe. Did the guy take anything?" I dropped a tea bag into a cup and filled it from the special hot water tap at the sink.

Molly frowned. "That's what's so weird. I woke up sometime around two. I don't know why. I don't think it was a noise. The house was quiet. The usual city sounds. You know. Anyway, I remembered the alarm and came downstairs. Things have been so busy at work I was dead-dog tired, and a few of us went out last night for a glass of wine before going home. I just plain forgot when I went to bed.

"I got down here, and this shape, this shadow comes up through the basement door. I didn't have time to react, Blake, I swear to God. Without so much as a word, the guy took a step toward me and hit me with the gun. I stayed on my feet and tried to get a look at him. I was so angry, I wanted to make sure I could ID him in a lineup later. But he punched me." She put her fingertips up to the bruise below her eye and winced at her own gentle touch. "Knocked me out cold. I don't know how long. A few minutes? By the time I came to and called nine one one, he was long gone."

"You didn't get a good look at him?"

She shook her head. "Too dark."

"How'd he get in?"

"Charlie said it looked like someone picked the lock on the back door."

"Picked? And you're sure the guy was coming up from the basement?"

Going to the trouble of picking the lock instead of jimmying open a door or window made sense only if a burglar was after high-end jewelry, contents of a safe. The basement held nothing of value that I could recall.

"Yes, I'm sure." Molly looked tired. She took a listless sip of her tea and pushed it away. "I just feel like going to bed."

"Are you sure you don't want me to stay?"

She didn't answer right away. "I think you better not."

I thought of telling her what I'd almost admitted at the group meeting that afternoon. Instead, I kissed the top of her head and left.

Sitting in the dark car in Molly's drive, I checked voice mail. There was a message from Frank Shriver. I called him back.

"Jesus, took you long enough," he said.

"I've been busy."

"I got nothing on Acasa."

"You sure?"

He heard my disappointment. "Keep your pants on. I *did* find something on Damien. Seems he has a soft spot for family. He brought his brother Leonard on board several of his big projects in Dubai and Abu Dhabi as a subcontractor. They don't care as much about nepotism over there as folks here do, but brother Lenny's a fuckup. On two of the projects, either Lenny's company or a company *he* subcontracted with screwed up big time and Damien Construction—meaning big brother Claude—ate millions in costs to straighten it out."

"How did you find out?"

"I told you, Leonard's a screwup. He's an alcoholic. He's got lots of drinking buddies. Buy a man enough rounds and eventually he'll tell you his life story."

"Did Claude give him a piece of the tunnel contract?"

"Don't know. But if you check ownership of all the companies with Sound Transit contracts, his name might pop up. If not, get me the list and I'll see if any stand out."

"I can get someone on it tomorrow. You want to know what I find out?"

"I'd do it myself, but I'm on deadline. Of course I want to know."

"That sounds like the old Frank. I'll be in touch."

"Sanders!"

I brought the phone back up to my ear. "Yeah?"

"You're not in the clear yet." He broke the connection.

I didn't need reminding. I climbed out of the car and went back inside to talk to Molly. She nearly exploded when I told her what I wanted, angry that I was still investigating instead of letting my defense team take over. I reminded her that identifying another suspect with motive for wanting Midge silenced would give them something to work with.

She told me she'd pull the list in the morning.

* * *

I took a chance that Dufours didn't know enough about me yet to track me to the warehouse. I couldn't afford to give up my route, but I might have to ask Chance to fill in for me for a few nights soon if he was feeling up to it. When Liz Tracey stepped out of the shadows next to the loading dock, I clutched my chest.

"Jesus, Liz! What the hell are you doing here?"

"Where have you been?" Her accusatory stare set my face aflame. "You're all over me to help you get information on Sound Transit and suddenly I don't hear from you."

"Sorry. I've been a little busy."

"What a crock of shit." Her voice rose. "I never should have believed you. You're like all the rest."

She swung from down low and slapped me with a gloved hand. Stepping back, she put a hand to her mouth and sobbed. Big tears rolled down her cheeks.

I blinked rapidly. "What the hell was that for?"

"I checked up on you." She choked out the words. "That suicide prevention group? Your son *killed* himself! You're using me because you feel *guilty*. I trusted you. You're such a shithead."

"Liz, I'm sorry." My ears burned. "Believe me, I didn't do it just for me. I…I should have told you. About Cole. I don't know why I didn't."

"You don't really give a shit about me, do you?"

"I *do* care about you. I just have a lot on my mind right now."

She threw her arms around my neck, stretching up on her toes, weight pulling me down, and kissed me. Too stunned to move, I felt her lips soften and heat radiate off her like a sunlamp.

She let go suddenly and pushed me away. "You can't just pretend to be a part of people's lives." Tears filled her eyes. "If you only want my help to stay out of jail, then at least thank me. If you want to sleep with me then do something about it. If you want to be my friend, then act like one. Either I mean something to you or get the hell out of my life."

She put a small hand in the center of my chest and gave me another shove.

"All right! Stop. I admit it. All of the above. Jesus, Liz. Yes, I feel guilty about my son. Yes, I wanted to save you. Yes, I've had thoughts about getting you into bed. Which would be a terrible idea for both of us right now, and probably forever. And yes, you're in a position to help me. But damn it, I *like* you. I didn't think I would. I'm afraid of people who think about jumping off bridges. It means they might not be here tomorrow. You want me to be part of your life? First, I have to believe you'll be part of mine. So, maybe I'm not very good at this friendship thing. Give me a chance."

She looked at me from under a strand of dark hair. "Where were you?" she said quietly.

"This thing at Sound Transit, it's worse than I thought. Dangerous. People have gotten killed."

Her face soured. "You don't have to be so bitchy."

I sighed. Rubbed my cheek. "How are you doing, Liz?"

"Crappy." She dropped her gaze to the pavement, then glared at me with a mixture of defiance and sullenness. "Thanks for asking."

I studied her for a moment. "How are you feeling?"

She straightened and tossed her head. "How am I *feeling*? Lonely. Sad. Frustrated." Her face screwed up in thought. "Bored. *Used*."

"Do you have any plans to harm yourself?" I asked calmly.

I told myself that I hadn't seen the signs when it came to Cole's intent to kill himself. But I had seen the depth of his depression, the sadness in his eyes, the hopelessness. In spite of us, our support, Cole had slipped into a dark place where Molly and I couldn't reach him, where light was distorted and bent by gravity so enormous it disappeared altogether. And he was a young adult, responsible for his own decisions.

We'd encouraged him to get counseling, gone so far as to interview a couple of therapists who we thought might be able to help. Yet all the while I'd kept telling myself, telling Molly, it was just young love, that first broken heart that would heal given enough time. The signs had been there. I'd simply chosen to ignore them, and hadn't asked the right questions. Even if I had, Cole still may have made the same decision. Maybe not then, but eventually. I couldn't live Liz Tracey's life or choose her death any more than I could have Cole's.

Liz reddened, but tossed her head again, feigning annoyance now. "No, I don't have any plans to harm myself."

I stared at her. "I'll be honest. I gave you something to do to make you feel needed, and because you were attracted to the intrigue, the potential danger of helping me. I did you a favor, gave you a distraction. Something to keep you from thinking about all the things in your life that suck. But things have gotten complicated. Hanging around me isn't good for your health."

Her shoulders hunched, head tipping toward the dark pavement. She looked at me from under her dark bangs like a six-year-old scolded for not minding her manners.

"Jesus, Liz," I said. "I'm trying to keep you safe."

She sucked air in softly through her teeth. "Okay," she said at last. "Be in touch. And good luck." She headed for the parking lot.

"Liz?"

She turned.

"Thank you."

After I assembled my papers and loaded the car, I mixed up the route I usually took and kept one eye on my rearview mirror. The combination of paranoia and sleep deprivation made me skittish as a flea-bit cat. I couldn't remember the last time I'd been that grateful to finish deliveries in one piece.

After three hours of shut-eye at Toji's, first thing Sunday morning I called my old PR colleague Nick McIver at home. Once again, he wasn't happy to hear from me. I gave him the disposable cell number and told him to call me back when he could talk freely. He didn't make any promises.

I thought about what Shriver had told me about not finding any dirt on Acasa. Rafe Acasa grew up in the Yakima Valley, the son of migrant farm workers fortunate enough to find steady work. Real jobs enabled his parents to stop moving up and down the West Coast in search of crops to harvest. Jobs got them green cards before the anti-immigration sentiment grew so strident that businesses were afraid to hire anyone with a Hispanic accent. Jobs gave them enough money to open a *taquería* and provide for a growing family.

Rafe was a small-town boy who had made good. I knew what made Acasa tick. We weren't all that different, other than the fact that his family spoke a second language at home. I understood what had driven Rafe to leave his family behind when he'd had a chance to attend Central Washington in Ellensburg. He'd heeded the call to "Go West, young man," moving from there to law school at Seattle University, each move bringing him a step closer to success. But Rafe thrived on something that made me uncomfortable—power. I hadn't made up my mind about Rafe. Either he'd do anything to get it, or he was as squeaky clean as his reputation.

I drove over to Molly's in the late morning, before lunch. She'd managed to cover some of the bruising with makeup but couldn't hide the puffiness and the bandage covering her stitches.

The sight made me wince. As promised, she'd managed to get a copy of the list of contractors from a contact at Sound Transit. Her fingers grasped it tightly as I started to take it from her.

"You're using me," she said.

First Liz, now Molly. Touchy.

"Yes."

Her eyes widened momentarily, too surprised to reflect hurt.

"Christ, Molly, this is my life we're talking about. You'd do the same thing."

She let go of the list. "You're right."

* * *

I took the list to the library and spent a tedious two hours cross-referencing the contractor license numbers of all the companies on the list and their owners with the state's website. Leonard Damien's name didn't appear anywhere. I jotted down a quick cover note and faxed a copy of the list with my notes to Frank Shriver, using a couple of dimes and the library's fax machine. I left him a voice mail to be sure he got it.

The vibration of the cell phone in my pocket took me by surprise. I carried it outside to answer it to avoid the evil eye of the librarians.

"What do you want, Blake?" McIver's voice held a worried note. "I can't talk long."

"Who had access to the campaign account, Nick?"

I thought I'd lost him for a moment.

"Acasa's? When you were still here? That's ancient history. Why are you asking now?"

"It's important. Come on, Nick. It's not that tough a question."

"Shit, I don't know. You're the only one I recall. In-house, that is. When Rafe's campaign manager hired someone to handle the finances after you left—who was it? Candace Wilder?—she was added to the account."

"You're sure? No one else at the firm?"

"You should know. Everything had to go through you for approval. You don't remember?"

"Those were rough times. There's a lot I don't remember." I thought for a moment. "I need to see the files, Nick. I need to see what I approved. What I did."

"Christ, I can't do that! You don't know what you're asking." The worried tone bordered on fear, now. "Those have been locked up since you got busted. No way I can get them for you."

"Help me out here. Please." He went silent again. "Nick?"

"I've got to get back to the family. It's Sunday."

"Nick?"

"Sorry, buddy. Can't help you. Don't call me again, Blake."

32

Damien Construction took up the top four floors of a newer midrise office building down near Qwest Field. The space looked more emblematic of a high-end architectural or legal firm, and the décor whispered "money" in a conservative, understated way. I could smell it—the rich, musty, dry scents of mahogany and raw silk mingled with tobacco, like opening a humidor of fresh Cuban cigars.

A pretty blonde wearing a bored expression thumbed the pages of a fashion magazine behind a sleek reception desk. She forced a smile as I approached her. "Can I help you?" The treacly voice matched the fake smile.

Shriver had given me what I needed. I just had to figure out a way to make it pay off. I looked at the nameplate on her desk.

"Yes, Jennifer. Claude Damien, please."

"Your name?"

"Blake Sanders."

She moved an empty water bottle and slid the magazine to one side to consult a desk calendar, frowning. Pulling a keyboard shelf toward her lap, she typed something and peered at a flat-screen monitor.

"I'm sorry, I don't see your appointment with Mr. Damien."

I gave her an aw-shucks grin. "He must have forgotten. He is in, right?" Her head bobbed up and down earnestly. "I'll wait. I only need to speak with him for a few minutes. Maybe I can ride down on the elevator with him when he leaves if he's too busy now."

A corner of her mouth turned down for an instant, but she quickly buried her nose back in the magazine. She pointedly ignored me for a good fifteen minutes before curiosity brought her head up to check on me. I offered a patient smile. Ten minutes later, she glanced at her watch, annoyance crabbing her mouth. The fidgeting escalated. She picked up the phone with a huff of breath, held the receiver to her ear for a moment, and set it down with a bang.

She stood. "Um, 'scuse me. If anyone asks, I'm going to the ladies' room."

"Sure. No problem."

She swished down a hallway past the elevators in a hurry. I slipped through the door before she changed her mind. A long hall passed cubicles on the left and offices on the right. A woman wearing half-frame cheaters and lacquered black hair that fit like a helmet commandeered a desk outside a door at the end.

She looked over her glasses. "Can I help you?" Her disdain turned to alarm when she saw me make no attempt to slow or stop. "You can't go in there, sir."

I pushed through the door, closed it in her face, and twisted the lock. The man standing behind the traditional mahogany desk held a finger in the air, stopping me midway across a large, richly patterned Persian rug, and continued speaking into a phone. Steel-gray hair curled tightly against the man's skull, cutting a straight line across his forehead over a broad face.

Eyes like arctic ice floes gleamed against a ruddy complexion. A perse V-neck sweater complemented a blue dress shirt and dark slacks, making him look more like a construction foreman dressed for a night out than CEO of an international contracting firm. Thick arms hung from wide shoulders, a wrestler's muscular build that suggested he hadn't always pushed pencils behind a desk.

He cradled the receiver and raised his eyes. "What do you need?"

"You've got a problem."

His forehead wrinkled. "There's always a problem somewhere. Which one?"

"Kliewet Construction." I saw a flicker of recognition in his eyes. I had his attention.

A scrape of metal sounded behind me as the bolt in the door slid back. I glanced over my shoulder to see the guard dog shoulder the door open, key in one hand, glaring at me like I'd stolen a bone from her bowl.

"I'm very sorry, Mr. Damien," she said. "He walked right past me."

Damien waved, dispassionate gaze fixed on me. "It's okay, Bev. I'll just be a moment."

She hesitated, unused to being called off, but backed out and closed the door, mouth set in a grim line.

"Who are you?" Damien said.

"Blake Sanders."

"I know you." He considered me, rubbing his chin, and his expression lightened. "Wait—I've got it. You played ball, right? At UW. Two seasons. My kid went there same time as you. I watched you play." His eyes narrowed. "I heard you ran into a little trouble recently. Bad trouble. What do you want?"

"The truth."

He looked through me, contemplating something far away. His eyes slowly focused on me.

"You made a mistake coming here." He turned away dismissively.

"You're hiding something. I want to know what."

He twisted. "You're wasting my time. We're all hiding something. They say you hid money that belonged to someone else—a city councilman. True or not, you've been hiding ever since. Am I right?" He paused and watched his comment hit home. "*I've* got a problem? Be more specific or get out."

I took a breath and let it spill out in a rush. "Kliewet is the name of your sister-in-law's cousin. Your sister-in-law—Lenny's wife—is listed as an officer of the company. The company's held in trust with Lenny's wife as a named trustee. It's not tough to connect the dots. Lenny didn't want his company to bid the job because he figured Sound Transit would call it nepotism. You helped him get a contract with ST on the University Link. The problem is he fucked up just like he did in Dubai and Abu Dhabi. This time, it looks like he skimped on materials so he could skim money off the top. A couple hundred thousand. Who knows? Maybe more. Only his screwups are causing accidents on the site. A bunch of them."

The muscles along his jaw bunched. A vein pulsed in his temple.

"It's a safe work site," he said.

"How long do you think it'll take before ST's oversight committee figures it out?"

Suddenly his face went slack as if a wire stringing up the muscles under the skin had been cut. Weariness washed over him, and his pallor went gray. He sagged against the desk and wiped his face with a big paw, looking at me as if haunted by old ghosts.

"You have a brother? No? Kids?"

"I had a son," I said.

It slowed him, but he went on with a look of acknowledgement. "Then I guess maybe you know what it's like. My brother's a…" He clamped his jaw, refusing to complete the thought. "Lenny's not a bad person. He just never grew up. I don't know. It's like his wiring's messed up or something. He's not like you and me. Never has been. And frankly, it's none of your damn business, but I'm tired, you know?

"I'm getting too old for this. My wife wants me to retire. Sit on a beach in Hawaii or Costa Rica instead of slowly eroding, rotting in this pissing rain." He gestured out the window, speckled with water. "My competitors circle like vultures, waiting for me to make a mistake. Eat their young given half the chance, I swear. I want out someday. But I've got no one who can step up and take over."

"No kids?" My eyebrows rose.

"My son?" He snorted. "He makes more in a day on Wall Street than I can in a year in this business. He laughs at what I do for a living. I build things, I tell him. They'll be here when I'm gone. What does he do? Sells derivatives and hedge funds—air. My daughter's waiting for me to roll over so she can inherit. Sure as hell isn't anyone in this office I'd want to see in this chair."

He didn't sound bitter. Just resigned. He looked out the window for a moment. My fingers twitched. I barely breathed. Just when I was sure I'd lost him, he faced me.

"Sure, Lenny owns Kliewet Construction," he said.

"And the Sound Transit contract?"

"Got it all on his own. I had nothing to do with it. He went through the bid system like any other contractor, same way we did."

"You didn't pull any strings?"

His nostrils flared, whitened. "You're not listening. There's no way I can. No one I could buy even if I wanted to. Too many people involved. No way you could pay them all off."

"Not like you didn't think about it."

He shook his head. "Never have. Despite the talk. Did I underbid some jobs to get the work? Damn straight. I worked hard to build this company, and I'm not going to roll over for anybody. It's a rough business. But I've never taken a kickback, never offered one. I can play rough, but I don't play dirty. You know what I'm saying? You've been there. On the court."

I pursed my lips. "So what happened?"

He drew a breath, blew it out. "Lenny got the specs wrong. That's all. He wasn't trying to run a scam. He just fucked up. Again." He raised his hands and let them fall on his thighs. "You understand? There was no kickback scheme. He made a mistake. As usual, I tried to clean up after him. I had my guys fix it and hoped it would go away."

"Just like that."

His shoulders rose and fell. "He's my brother. What can I say? I don't expect you to believe me, but I love the guy. I try to look out for him. He needs the work. Two kids in college by his second wife, poor bastard, and still paying alimony to the first wife." He shook his head and his face grew stony. "Look, I don't know what you want, but I'm not paying any hush money. Go to the oversight committee if you have to. I'll take my lumps for covering Lenny's ass, and if Lenny loses the contract, so be it. It's about time he stood up like a man."

"I don't want your money."

His surprise was palpable. The color came back to his face. "Then what are you here for?"

I weighed how much to tell him. "I'm getting jammed up for murder. I'm pretty sure it has something to do with the tunnel you're digging." I shrugged. "I'm just seeing who has the most to lose if the project goes belly up."

"That old lady in the news? You think *I* killed her?" He scratched his head and laughed. "I'm sorry, son. I'm not trying to be rude, here. I'm just relieved, that's all. As far as I'm concerned, I don't have a damn thing to lose on the tunnel. I've got a contract. I get paid for the work I do. A bonus if I finish ahead of schedule. A penalty if I don't. But if ST pulls the plug, I'm not out anything except the aggravation. Tell the truth, I wish I hadn't bid the job. Ego, that's all it was."

I considered him silently, a thousand what-ifs spinning through my head. I lassoed one and roped it in.

"Maybe Lenny bought off someone on the board to get the job," I said. "Someone with pull. Like Rafe Acasa."

Damien's face went blank, then slowly contorted as if he'd bit into something sour. "Just when I was beginning to think you're okay you go and say something stupid. You weren't listening, son. Nobody gets around the bid system. It just isn't worth the aggravation. Lord knows Lenny's not smart enough. Or rich enough." His words were painted with disdain, whether for me or his brother I couldn't tell. "Oh, and Acasa? I don't think you'll find a bigger boy scout. I don't know where you got the idea he can be bought."

He stopped talking, walked around his desk, and sat down. Donning a pair of reading glasses, he pulled some drawings to the edge of the desk. After a moment, he glanced up as if suddenly remembering I still stood there.

"I think you got your answer," he said. "Sorry I couldn't be of help." He lowered his head to the problem on his desk.

* * *

A man without a home, I kept moving, avoiding my usual haunts. Even in the rental car I felt conspicuous, vulnerable, fearful that Dufours would find me somehow. The cops I could handle. A jail cell might even be safer. But Dufours was an unknown quantity, a loose cannon.

I didn't know whether to believe Damien or not, but I had little choice except to push forward, keep asking questions, and try not to get my head blown off. There was stupid, and then there was *really* stupid. I called Frank Shriver and asked him to track down a list of Acasa's campaign contributors. I told him to look for Lenny Damien's name or those of anyone close to him. Maybe Lenny screwed up like Damien said. Or maybe he was dumb like a fox.

Shortly after seven thirty, I parked across the street from the loading dock behind the loft building that housed Bellnap & Dreier. Like clockwork, a battered white pickup truck pulled up and backed into an empty space at the dock a few minutes before eight. The doors of the truck swung open and a middle-aged couple got out. The man pulled some things out of the back of the truck and they both went inside. I took a dose of meds to help stay focused and waited another few minutes. Then I climbed out, checked for traffic, and crossed the street, hunching my shoulders against the drizzle.

Yuri and his wife Sofiya didn't need to clean offices anymore. The pair started out cleaning houses after immigrating to the States from Russia, and reinvested their hard work and money in the business, hiring new immigrants from their homeland. The business grew. Yuri now spent most of his time managing the janitorial crews and calling on clients. Sofiya had taken some of their savings and opened a *piroshki* stand in one of the shopping malls on the Eastside.

I reached over the side of the truck bed and rummaged through a pile, pulling out a pair of white coveralls. In a dark corner of the loading dock I stripped off my coat and slipped the coveralls on over my clothes. They hung an inch or two short at the wrists and ankles, but they'd do. Soundlessly, I pulled a base-ball cap from the back pocket, yanked it down low over my eyes, and went into the building.

Down the hallway toward the service elevator, I kept my gaze on the floor, hiding my face from the security camera. I slouched in a corner of the elevator, trying to lose a few inches, and rode up to the Bellnap & Dreier offices with my heart up in my throat. The doors opened and I strode out as if I belonged there. I knew Yuri and Sofiya worked their way from lower floors up to give the

B&D offices time to empty out. I had to get in and out before they reached this floor.

I headed for a janitorial closet, helped myself to some cleaning supplies, and waited inside with the door cracked, my eyes on the glass office entrance door down the hall. When a couple of young women in coats appeared in the reception area, I stepped out of the closet, closed the door, and strode down the hall just as they came through the glass door. I held it open for them and slipped through after they passed, laughing between themselves, paying me no attention.

I made my way through the warren of offices to McIver's door. Stepping inside, I looked around and headed straight for the desk. If Nick wouldn't help me, I'd just help myself. He'd always kept a set of keys in the top drawer. I stepped around the desk and pulled the drawer open. Nothing. I yanked open a side drawer and pawed through the contents. I searched the second drawer even faster. Hanging file folders filled the bottom drawer. I'd hit a dead end. On an impulse, I pulled some of the files out of the drawer and peered in. A metallic glint against the bare wood bottom reflected the light. I felt blood pulse in my neck as I reached in and pulled out a ring with three keys.

Pausing at the door to breathe, I glanced out into the hall and quickly jerked my head back. Someone was coming. I backed into the office, pulled a cleaning rag from the hip pocket of the coveralls, and tugged the cap down lower. I stepped to the bookcase, turned my back to the door, and dusted. A shadow passed over the bookcase as someone stopped in the doorway.

"Hey, man, what are you doing in here?" a voice said. I didn't recognize it.

"*Yo no hablo inglés*," I mumbled.

"You don't speak—?"

I kept my eyes on the floor and raised my hands, showing him the cleaning rag and spray bottle.

"Oh, cleaning crew. Well, in that case, we need some toilet paper in the men's john. Christ, what am I talking to you for? I can't believe this."

The shadow darkened. "What's up, man?" a second voice said.

"I gotta find the janitor," the first voice said. "This wetback doesn't speak the language." The room brightened and the voice faded as they moved away. "You see the size of that dude? Biggest damn Mexican I've ever seen."

I waited another minute, then stole to the doorway and checked the hall. Empty. I went back to the desk, pulled out the wastebasket, and dumped the contents into a trash bag. I haphazardly cleaned two more offices before impatience overtook me. I made my way to the file room and slid one of the keys into the door lock. It turned easily. I slipped inside and shut the door. Banks of filing cabinets lined the walls and a row of cabinets set back-to-back formed an island in the center. I started with "A" and quickly found files for Acasa's campaign. All were recent, however, filed within the past year. I frowned, wondering if Nick could have been wrong. The firm regularly put older files in off-site storage to maintain space for active clients and current event files. The stuff I wanted was more than a year old. They could have been purged.

McIver had said they were here. For the hell of it, I tried drawers labeled "S," but my name didn't appear on any tabs. I forced myself to think. And then I had it. The files I wanted were accounting files. They were kept separately from the general files. I circled the island and found the bank of drawers holding files from the accounting department.

Files for Acasa's campaign stretched back more than a year, all neatly organized by month. I pulled folders for the three months before the ugly rumors surfaced that someone was diverting funds from the campaign war chest and suspicion quickly focused on the only person in the firm with access to the account. Acid in my gut slowly roiled. Swallowing hard, I slid the folders in with the trash, lightly stepped to the door, and opened it a crack. All clear, but I wasn't home yet.

I slipped out the door, locked it, and took the trash bag to the copy room next door. I pulled a file out of the trash bag, loaded the contents into the sheet feeder, and pushed the start button. The machine noisily pumped out sheets of paper, disturbing the relative peace of the nearly empty office. I quickly grabbed up the trash bag and hurried out, ducking into the small lunchroom across the hall. Whipping out the spray bottle and a rag, I busied myself wiping down counters and tables, nervously keeping an eye on the copy room, hoping the sound wouldn't attract attention. The copier finally stopped.

Checking both ways, I stole across the hallway and started the copier on the contents of the second file. By the time the machine finished churning out copies of the third file, the kitchenette sparkled. A second trash bag half-filled from the refrigerator with old containers of food sprouting green hair and black spots squatted on the spotless floor like a white polyethylene toad. I gathered up the cleaning rags, carried both trash bags to the copy room, loaded all the copies and the original files in a clean trash bag, and moved next door to the file room.

Listening intently, I let myself in and quickly replaced the file folders. As I locked the door on my way out, I glimpsed a shadow moving across the wall at the end of the hallway. Slipping the key ring in my pocket, I stooped and picked up trash bags in both hands, lowered my head and started walking as a well-dressed man in his twenties rounded the corner. I kept my gaze down at the floor as we approached each other, obscuring my face with the cap's visor. He passed me without a word.

I took the keys back to Nick's office and put them back. The trash went with me to the service elevator, and I left it on the loading dock on my way out. I stripped off the coveralls, balled them up, and threw them in the back of Yuri's truck. As I bent down to pick up the trash bag containing the file copies, a voice rang out behind me.

"You! Hey, you!"

I leaped off the loading dock and broke into a run.

33

Reyna Chase stood in the warehouse doorway, hands in her pockets, framed in the bright floodlights spilling on the dock. I watched her ignore the stares of the men filing in, her eyes scanning faces and quickly moving on. Even the heads of a few women turned as they passed by, their inquisitive expressions mixed with envy. The arrows of prurience, jealousy, and distrust launched in their glances bounced off and lay inert at her feet. I wondered how much that armor cost her emotionally. Her gaze fastened on me as I emerged from the shadows of the parking lot, and she shifted her weight onto one leg as if standing down from attention.

I climbed the steps to the dock and headed straight toward my assembly station, not bothering to acknowledge her. A frown darkened her face as I passed. She swung in behind me and hustled to catch up, doing a little skip every other step to stay alongside.

"We need to talk," she said.

"I'm working. Can it wait?" I didn't look at her.

"I don't think so. I've got information about Dufours."

I changed direction, angling toward the district advisor standing on one side of the warehouse with route list changes. She caught up a step later, and the advisor's eyes took a walk from her head to her boot-clad toes while he thumbed through the stack of lists. He handed me my vacation notices and route-changes with a grin.

"Got a helper today, Blake?" he said as I turned away.

"Right. I'm training her to sub for me," I said over my shoulder. My sarcasm only broadened his smile.

"Are you sure this can't wait until morning?" I wheeled a cart around and pushed it toward my table. I felt her eyes on my face.

"You're angry," she said. "Because I didn't sleep with you?"

My head whirled toward her. "No." I felt heat rise into my face as I glanced around.

"You are." She grasped my arm and pulled me to a stop.

"I'm not angry."

Her eyes searched my face. I looked away and pushed the cart up the aisle.

"What?" She caught up. "I hurt your feelings?"

I parked the cart and hefted a bound stack of newsprint in each hand onto the table.

"You didn't hurt my feelings," I said as I arranged newspaper sections on the table. "I'm embarrassed, that's all."

"Because of a kiss?"

I stopped and faced her. "I never should have done that. It wasn't right. Hell, for all I know you're married with three kids."

"It's no big deal. I told you I would have been surprised if you hadn't tried."

"You have a pretty high opinion of yourself."

Sparks of irritation flashed across her face. "What, I'm so unattractive you're embarrassed you kissed me?"

"No. God, no. I…it's…" I rubbed my palms on my thighs and looked away. "Since my wife—my ex-wife and I—split up, I…"

"You haven't kissed anyone?"

I shrugged. "Haven't even been on a date." And now I'd shared a liplock with two women in as many days.

"That's it?"

I nodded. "Like you said, chalk it up to the adrenaline, I guess. And since it didn't mean anything to you, anyway, we're good."

She shifted her gaze to the table and silently watched me assemble newspapers.

"You still love her," she said finally. "How long were you married?"

"Twenty years."

"What happened?"

I paused to face her. I didn't detect anything on her face except interest that seemed genuine. "Our son killed himself. We couldn't seem to find our way back to each other after that."

"I'm sorry."

"You mentioned Dufours?" I said.

Her head jerked up as if her thoughts had been far away. "Alain Dufours is dead."

My stomach hit the cement floor like a falling brick. "I don't understand."

"There *was* a history professor at the Sorbonne named Alain Dufours. Problem is, he was killed in an accident in the Paris metro a week ago. Fell in front of a train."

"Then who's this guy calling himself Dufours?"

She didn't answer right away. I finished up the last of the papers and started loading them on the cart. Reyna slipped off the table to help.

"Look, I'm sorry, but I have to get going," I said. "I can't afford to lose this job." I still didn't know if I should trust her, let alone trust myself with her. She had me at a huge disadvantage, and I knew nothing about her. But I had few options. "You're welcome to ride along if you want. Finish the story in the car. But it'll be a long night."

She shrugged. "I don't mind. It's important. I think you better hear all of it."

I nodded. She shouldered her bag. We made our way out to the car and loaded the papers in the backseat. She offered to help. I showed her how to fold papers and stuff them in plastic bags. We'd actually gotten a break from the incessant rain, and forecasters predicted a dry night, but some of my customers expected the plastic sleeve, rain or shine.

"Who is this guy?" I said when were on the road.

Reyna shifted in her seat to get a better look at me. "We fed the description you gave us into our databases—ONI, CIA, FBI, Interpol, the works. We think the guy you saw, the guy who's trying to eliminate you, is a French intelligence agent named Aubrey Gagnon."

"Like French CIA or something? An agent of the French government is trying to kill me?"

"Calm down. I know how it sounds. I should have qualified that. Gagnon *was* an agent with the Directorate for Defense Protection and Security—*Direction de la Protection et de la Sécurité de la Défense*. DPSD, responsible for military counterintelligence and security. Back in the mid-nineties, the agency went through a major shake-up trying to modernize. About five years ago, DPSD got concerned about the impact of the far right in military barracks and the growth of traditional, ultraconservative Catholic circles among officers.

"Gagnon apparently was a right-wing sympathizer. He disappeared a month ago, and DPSD considers him a rogue agent. We believe he arranged Dufours's accident and assumed the man's identity to get out of the country and establish a cover over here."

"And he wants the gold Woodworth buried? He's willing to kill for that?"

She shrugged. "Two hundred million reasons to kill."

Thoughts raced through my head like protons in a supercollider. Reyna Chase had dropped out of the sky like some angel and saved my life. I desperately wanted to take her at face value, but I realized that I had no proof she was who she said was. I'd even assumed she'd been talking to her boss the other night on the phone. If Dufours wasn't Dufours…

"You expect me to believe this?" I said. "Some right-wing nutcase from France is trying to get his hands on gold Woodworth buried for the US Navy a hundred and fifty years ago?"

I glanced over and saw her head bob. I jammed my foot on the brake and pulled over.

I turned on her. "You must think I'm a complete idiot. A babe in the woods. So what's the real deal? You're after the gold? You ask me to do my civic duty and protect my country by getting me to help you find it so you can cash in?"

She looked at me calmly. "Are you finished?"

"Hell, no, I'm not finished. How do I even know you are who you say you are? Maybe you're working with Dufours, or Gagnon or whatever his name is, after all. You and Dufours are in this together. Good cop, bad cop. You're asking me to take a lot on faith, lady."

She dug in a pocket and handed me a plastic ID card. I turned on a map light and peered at the photo and official seal. I glanced at her, comparing her likeness. She held out her cell phone.

"Call information in Maryland," she said. "Area code is three oh one. Ask for the main number for the Office of Naval Intelligence. Call it and ask for the COMONI. When you reach him, tell him to put the chief of naval operations on the phone. The big boss."

She pushed the phone toward me. "Go on."

I hesitated.

She looked at her watch. "Early there, but he'll be in by now. We're in crisis mode. He'll be in the captain's office."

I took the phone and dialed, wrote down the number the operator gave me, and punched it in. A pleasant but automated voice answered after four rings and told me I'd reached the ONI.

The switchboard was closed, but I was offered options that let me connect to the COMONI's extension. I listened to it ring, filled with trepidation and curiosity.

A businesslike voice answered, "Hinson."

"I'd like to speak with the CNO, please," I said, flicking a glance at Reyna. She sat with her arms folded across her chest.

"One moment," the voice said.

Muffled sounds came over the line as if someone had covered the receiver instead of putting me on hold.

A deeper voice came on. "Miller, here. Who is this, please?"

"*Admiral* Miller?" I grasped for words.

"Yes. Please identify yourself." His voice was calm, polite.

"Bear with me, sir," I said, trying to buy time while I thought it through. "I'm in a really awkward position here. I need to know your position and responsibilities there."

He didn't hesitate. "I'm Chief of Naval Operations. In broad terms, I'm responsible to the Secretary of the Navy for the command, utilization of resources, and operating efficiency of all US Navy operations. Will that do?"

He didn't treat me like a crank caller and simply hang up. His willing exchange and lack of concern sent red flags waving wildly in my head. A four-star admiral in charge of naval operations and intelligence wouldn't say "boo" to a sailor, let alone a civilian, unless he had *bona fides*. *Caller ID!* I held Reyna's phone to my ear. Hinson, her boss, would have recognized the number that popped up when the call came in.

"What assurances can you give me that you are who you say you are?" I said, staring at Reyna while I spoke.

"I guess you'll have to trust me," he said.

"I suspect you already know who I am, sir," I said.

"We assumed when your call came in either someone had compromised Lieutenant Commander Chase or you're with her now. You didn't immediately make demands, so I presume she told you to call."

"I guess there's no point in continuing this conversation, then. Do you or Captain Hinson want to speak with her?"

"In a moment. Please listen carefully to what I'm about to say. I'm the highest-ranking officer in the US Navy. I can give orders to nearly half a million Americans and expect them to carry them out without question. I can't tell *you* to do a thing. But I am asking you. If you can help Commander Chase in any way, you'll have my personal gratitude." He took a breath. "You can put her on now."

I handed Reyna the phone. She put it to a delicate ear.

"Yes, sir...? I think so, sir... It took long enough, but yes, smart enough to ask... I think so... Thank you, sir."

I put the car in gear and pulled away as she tucked the phone in her pocket.

"Don't say it," I told her through gritted teeth.

When the silence lasted several minutes, I finally mustered the courage to look at her. She stared straight ahead, her expression blank.

"Hey, look, I'm sorry if I pissed you off back there, but—"

"I would have done the same thing," she said. "Sooner."

Another pause turned pregnant. I took a deep breath, expelled it, and mentally donned scrubs and gloves to enter the delivery room.

"Okay," I said, "let's say I believe you. How did Dufours—Gagnon—learn about Woodworth and the gold?"

"We don't know," she said softly. "I know this is a lot to take in. Most people are pretty insulated from this kind of thing. I tend to take it for granted. Every day, I see hundreds of pieces of information from around the world that have something to do with terrorism and war, or threats of one sort or another—assassinations, suicide bombings, skirmishes, battles fought every day. It gets old. I forget that ordinary citizens know only what they're exposed to on the news."

She fell silent for a few minutes. We crossed the University Bridge. I stayed close to the water, intending to drive up through the Arboretum.

"We think Gagnon intercepted a signal intended for DPSD or another French intelligence agency," she said suddenly. "A signal like we got when Royer started asking questions."

"How? Why would someone alert the French?"

"Why did Woodworth give that lease agreement to the nuns? We don't know, but it looks like he was covering himself. And the religious order, don't forget, was from Montréal, with ties to France. It's the only thing we can come up with. Woodworth somehow set up another command signal to alert the French only if it looked like someone was making an attempt to retrieve the gold. He didn't trust his handlers, maybe, or whoever filled the vacuum when Webster and the other coalition members died. He set up checks and balances, just in case."

"But what triggered it? Royer called you guys—the good guys—not the French."

"My guess? Your friend Midge. She stirred the pot when she started looking into all the old records at the convent. I bet if we check phone records where she worked—Joyance House?—we'll find calls to Montréal. Someone there just passed on the information that she called."

"Setting the wheels in motion," I said.

I considered what she'd told me. Logically, it made sense. But logic in an ADD brain works differently. Laterally, or randomly, not linearly. Pieces suddenly clicked into place.

"Gagnon's not after the gold," I said. "He's after something worse. Much worse."

"What are you talking about?"

"He's after a bioweapon, something that could cause a world-wide plague. A pandemic."

"Are you out of your mind?"

I took a deep breath, told her about the journal, the story Florence had told me about Sophie Clare, and my conversation with Jane. It was the only possible connection Woodworth might have had to the religious order, the only reason it made sense for him to execute the lease agreement.

She laughed. "And you thought *I* was spinning a conspiracy theory."

I glanced at her and saw her still smiling. The smile faded when she saw my face.

"You didn't know Midge, Reyna. She didn't know anything about the gold. No one did. She read the journal. She saw the notation about *la peste*. She knew the history of the order, Sophie Clare's story. She wouldn't have done what she did for money. She did it to keep the world safe from whatever Woodworth buried with the gold."

"What are you talking about?"

I told her about my conversation with Beardsley, his contention that the ghost ship legend could be true, at least the logistics of it. "Why's it so hard to believe that Woodworth and Sophie Clare met aboard the *Truxton*?"

"And what? Woodworth carved a chunk of tissue sample from a dead slave? Kept it? Smuggled it into the country and carried it with him across a continent before finally burying it along with a couple of tons of gold ore?"

"Why not?"

She shook her head. "You've been watching too many movies, Blake. Science and medicine weren't that advanced back then. Doctors didn't know yet that diseases were caused by bacteria and viruses. Pasteur didn't come up with the germ theory until eighteen sixty-two. And the first practical microscope wasn't built until the eighteen seventies. More likely Woodworth would have been among those urging his captain to burn the slave ship to the waterline."

"Maybe Woodworth was ahead of his time. Maybe he saw the potential for a weapon someday. If he feared civil war as much as you say he did."

"Biological warfare?" She looked away for a moment. "I don't know. We've had analysts practically turning NHC and the National Archives upside down looking for information on Woodworth—letters, naval logs, anything. Nothing we've found suggests he had a bioweapon."

I brought the argument around full circle. "Then what's Gagnon after? You've got no indication Woodworth was playing his own government against the French. Sounds to me more likely the nuns' monsignor in Montréal saw an opportunity for the Church to score points with the French and told them about the order's mission without Woodworth's knowledge."

She said nothing. I finally reached over and took a paper off her lap.

"Better keep stuffing," I said. "We're close to the first stop."

She turned and got more papers from the backseat and went to work. We drove out of the Arboretum and headed up out of the valley toward Capitol Hill.

I finally broke the silence. "Any ideas where Woodworth hid the gold?"

34

Reyna reached for the black pack at her feet.

"You already know the records we found in the archives contained coded communiqués from Woodworth to his contacts back in DC," she said. "After Woodworth returned to Monterey with the *Anita*, he sent one last communiqué along with a letter of resignation to the secretary of the navy. The communiqué contained what we think are map coordinates."

"You really think these coordinates are for real?"

"It's a long shot," she said. "I can show you where they are. I haven't been able to bring in a crew yet to see what we're dealing with here, but I've been to the site."

"How accurate are these coordinates? I mean, you really pinpointed the location?" Tatty yellowed parchment with *Here there be dragons* inked in the legend came to mind.

"We can definitely mark the spot on the map, but as far as accuracy…" She let the thought hang for a moment. "Woodworth was a sailor, a ship's captain. He knew how to navigate and no doubt had a good compass, a sextant, and ship's chronometer. Those might have gotten him to within a nautical mile of any given spot in the world. After that, to get more accurate, he would have had to use surveying equipment. With the right equipment, his coordinates might be accurate to within about ten feet."

I double-parked, got out, and left the engine running while I walked a paper onto the front stoop of a house. The concept of buried treasure intrigued me, and wasn't without attractions. I reined in my impulsivity.

"Here's the deal," I said, climbing into the car. "We guarantee delivery by five thirty in the morning. If I go chasing this rainbow of yours, you help me make up lost time and get these papers out."

She grinned. "You're on." She pulled a handheld GPS device out of her bag of tricks and powered it on. "But I get a percentage of your tips."

After a moment, she said, "Take a left up here."

I did as she said and headed up the hill on Mercer. Several blocks farther she put a hand on my arm.

"Slow down. Okay, take a right at the next corner and go slow. We're close."

I made the turn and stared out the windshield as the car coasted up the block.

"Do you have any idea where we are?" I glanced over and saw the reply on her face. I extended my arm in front of her and pointed at the building on the next corner. "That's Joyance House."

She consulted the small screen in her hand. "Keep going."

I drove past the former convent, through the intersection, and cruised slowly up the next block. I pulled over to the curb just as Reyna opened her mouth to tell me to stop.

"You knew this was it?" she said.

I gave a nod at the church up ahead on our right. "Gagnon was here looking for something the night before he killed Royer. He put Sister Florence in the hospital. She lives in the rectory, helps keep house for the priests. She still volunteers at Joyance House—it used to be her home."

Reyna turned to look out the window. "Of course. Either Gagnon's following the connections between the nuns and the Church, or he has the coordinates, too. Maybe both."

"It didn't look like Gagnon found anything in the church when I saw him, but it's hard to tell," I said. "You want to look around?"

She shook her head. "It'll keep. I'll come back during the day. Get the priest to cooperate and give me a look around."

I considered her and shrugged. "That's it?"

She shifted in her seat. "That's all we've got. The deck logs contained the same coordinates. There were some notations scratched in the margin, but they don't make much sense."

"Like what?"

She held out her notebook. "This is it, near as we could make out from the handwriting." I squinted at it in the dim light coming through the windshield. She'd written, "W. 103 pls, 2 lks."

"What does that mean?"

"We haven't figured it out." She hunched her shoulders. "Doesn't matter. This is the place."

"I don't get it," I said after a long silence. "How could the gold be here after all this time?" My eyes swept the neighboring houses, the buildings that cascaded down the hill in all directions, city spreading out for miles. "All this development. A century of digging up streets and putting up buildings. You'd think someone would have discovered it."

"Fourteen tons? We would have heard about it. It'd be written up in history books."

"So maybe it was never here to begin with." She didn't look convinced. "Okay, then, what next? Any thoughts about where to start?"

She stared at the church for a minute. "I've already checked with the naval station up in Everett and the yard over in Bremerton to see what kind of metal detecting gear I can get my hands on. I'm guessing Woodworth buried it so deep metal detectors won't do us much good. We'll likely have to use ground-penetrating radar. I know we've got lots of sonar gear around over in Bremerton and on the sub base, but I'm still trying to locate some GPR."

"You'll need to get permission, right?" I jerked my head toward the church.

"Of course." She shrugged. "I don't see a problem. We're talking national security here."

The gold, if it existed, was the government's problem. Reyna hadn't given much credence to my supposition that Woodworth might have buried something else along with the gold, something with the potential to wreak havoc and cost untold numbers of lives. And I was still left with the question of who'd wanted to silence Midge. But that wasn't Reyna's problem.

We finished my route, and I drove Reyna back to the warehouse and parked next to a new rental she indicated was hers. She'd traded up. She reached for the door handle and paused.

"Your car's fixed, by the way," she said, handing me a card. "You can pick it up anytime."

I glanced at it and saw the name of a garage not far from my apartment. "Don't you think it might be prudent for me to keep the rental a few more days? If Uncle Sam doesn't mind picking up the tab, that is."

"I suppose," she replied. "It's probably a smart idea."

"What about Gagnon?"

"We'll get him." She sounded more confident than I felt. "We've got a lot of operatives looking for him."

"And in the meantime?"

"Lay low. You need to be careful. Gagnon's ruthless." She opened the door and swung a foot out. "I'll be in touch."

She leaned toward the opening, then changed her mind and suddenly turned, stretching across the center console. She put a hand on the back of my neck and kissed me on the mouth. Her lips lingered, melting me to the seat. She broke contact, slid her hand to my cheek, and lightly brushed her thumb across my lips.

"See you, civvy." She climbed out. The door swung shut before I got my breath back.

I sat there a long time in the dark. Finally, my brain rebooted. An idea grabbed hold, pulled me out of the car by the scruff of the neck, and propelled me into the warehouse. I found my boss, Terry, in his brightly lit office, still working, along with the area supervisors. He looked up from his desk when I poked my head through the doorway.

"Something I can help you with?" he said, an easygoing smile on his face.

"You're connected to the Internet, right?" I motioned to his computer monitor.

"Sure. What do you need?"

"Could you look up something for me really quick?"

He nodded. I told him what I was looking for, and he turned to the keyboard.

"Come take a look," he said after a moment or two. He pushed back from the screen, giving me room to lean over the desk and read the information. "That what you're looking for?"

I digested the words on the screen. "Yeah, that'll do. Thanks, Terry."

Pulse quickening, I hustled out to the lot, got in the car, and drove back to the church up on Capitol Hill. Wedging the car in the same spot Reyna and I had vacated an hour before, I turned on the dome light, found a piece of scrap paper and a pencil in the glove compartment, and did some quick calculations. Reyna said that Woodworth would have needed surveying equipment to pinpoint an accurate location. According to Terry's Internet search, surveyors back then used sixteen-and-a-half-foot chains to measure distances. Each chain, called a pole, comprised one hundred links. By my calculations, "103 poles, 2 links" meant about 1,700 feet. I frowned. ONI's analysts should have figured it out.

I put the car in gear, made a left at the corner, and headed west. I cleared the trip odometer and kept an eye on the bright LED numbers as they slowly ticked off tenths of a mile. When I'd driven a few blocks, familiar landmarks sent a chill up my spine. I didn't need to look at the odometer any more. I drove another block and turned the corner, pulling into the first empty spot at the curb. Ignoring the hydrant, I shut off the ignition. I twisted in my seat and peered out into the darkness at the big house on the corner beyond my reflection in the glass.

"Molly's house," I said to the empty car.

Memories swirled through my head, leaves blown on an autumn wind. I watched the images float past, reached out and caught one—little Cole laughing on the way down a slide in the park—and let it flutter away. I caught another—Molly this time, red tresses aflame in the sunlight, smile as broad as Puget Sound in the distance, sparkling like diamonds. Another rushed at me, nearly slapping me in the face, making my breath catch. The break-in—*Gagnon*.

It fit. Molly hadn't gotten a good look at the guy, but said he was coming up from the basement when she almost ran into him in the dark. She said he had a gun. He knocked her around some and took off. Not your garden-variety burglar.

I caught the barest whiff of a clean floral perfume in the car. The one that softened the hard edges of Reyna's military bearing. Her attractiveness was distracting. I imagined her striking features both helped and hindered her career. She probably had to work twice as hard to get anyone to take her seriously, but I had a feeling she'd learned how to take advantage of how often people underestimated her. I had a hard time imagining her using the gun she'd wielded so comfortably a few nights earlier, but that sort of reaction probably gave her a leg up in her line of work.

A small thrill ran through me, tinged with something hot and prickly, something hungry. My heart beat a little faster knowing Molly slept only yards away. I wondered if my thoughts made me disloyal, a bad person.

I shivered and tugged on the zipper of my coat, pretending the chill I felt was the cold air seeping into the car. The ring of the phone in my coat startled me. I fumbled it out and opened it.

"We need to talk."

"Charlie?" He didn't reply. "What's going on? Charlie?"

"There's some shit going down at the house. I can't talk about it over the phone. We need to meet." There was an edge in his voice, something I'd never heard before.

I weighed the options. I wouldn't get more out of him over the phone. He was in trouble, or I was. Either way, I couldn't put it off. "The usual place?"

"Yeah, that'll do. How soon can you get there?"

"Give me fifteen minutes." I could drive the distance in five and give myself time to scope things out.

Traffic heading south on Broadway was light. The world pauses during the hour or so between night and day. Circadian rhythms lower our body temperatures and lull us into complacency if not sleep. Armies plan predawn raids knowing their enemies will be tired, vulnerable, the streets clear of people. Despite the lights, Broadway resembled a ghost town, the occasional car drifting down the street like sagebrush.

I passed an SPD cruiser parked at the curb near the place where I usually stopped for coffee. Another rolled slowly up the street in the opposite direction. Uneasy tension spread through me. I forced my fingers to relax their grip on the steering wheel. Without slowing, I drove by the restaurant, spotting another cruiser parked in the lot. I continued a few blocks down and circled back to get a look at the rear of the parking lot from another angle. Behind the restaurant, parked nose out, another patrol car.

My blood ran ice cold. Fighting an urge to run the light at the corner as it turned yellow, I stopped and kept my eyes straight ahead. Already on overload, my tired brain tried to process the jumbled thoughts that streamed through my head. When the light changed, I accelerated slowly. The cops would be looking for the Toyota, but anything suspicious would arouse their interest.

My pulse didn't slow until I was well away from the hill, driving north. I finally pulled over to use my cell, afraid of getting stopped if a patrol saw me on it while driving.

"What the fuck's going on, Charlie?" I said when he answered.

"Where are you?" he said.

"You son of a bitch!" I slammed a fist against the steering wheel. "You set me up!"

"Tell me where you are, Blake. We'll make this right."

"No fucking way! I don't know what's going on, but get clear of your buddies. I'll talk to you, Charlie, but only you. I'll call you back in ten minutes." I broke the connection, anger seething through me like coiled snakes.

I put more distance between me and Charlie's welcoming committee, rubbing the grit from my eyes, exhaustion and adrenaline alternately rolling over me in waves. Getting on the freeway, I continued north, ticking off the minutes. Just before the allotted time, I switched the cell to speakerphone and dialed Charlie's number, leaving my hands free.

"You gotta come in," Charlie said without preamble. "You're going to have every cop in four counties looking for you in about five minutes."

"What's happening, Charlie? Why set me up? Why the trap?"

"Last chance, Blake. I'm asking you, just give it up."

"Donovan and Hiragawa...something happened. What changed their minds?"

His voice turned hard. "They took partials off the knife that killed the gutter punk, asshole. The prints match yours."

Stunned speechless, I gripped the wheel and kept my eyes on the wide ribbon of concrete sliding under the car like an out-of-control conveyor belt.

"You hear me?" Charlie said. "They've got you dead to rights. That makes two. This is it for me. I should've trusted my gut a long time ago, asshole. You're bad news."

"You bastard! You wouldn't be with SPD, hell, you wouldn't be a cop if it weren't for me."

"Don't give me that shit! You would have done the same thing if it'd been your sister. And it's old news."

"I never held it over you, either. Not once, all these years. Not till I needed a little help."

"I'm done. No more favors."

"Fuck you, Charlie." I snapped the phone shut.

Charlie'd probably had techies trying to triangulate my location while we were on the phone. Fine with me. I took the next exit and looked for the nearest strip mall. When I found one, I dumped the cell phone into a trash bin and got back on the freeway, heading south this time.

It wasn't possible. I hadn't known anything about the gutter punk, hadn't been anywhere near the spot he'd been found, didn't own a knife I could have left my prints on...*the knife on the street.* The one I'd picked up, wrapped in newspaper, and dumped in the trash. Someone had found it. Used it to kill a homeless kid a few days later. It didn't add up. Unless someone had seen me trash the street punk's knife. Someone who'd been following me. Someone who had trashed my apartment and scrawled a warning on the wall.

Someone wanted me to go down for murder, maybe two of them.

35

The motel down near Sea-Tac was cheap, but the lobby looked clean. I paid with cash from the tip envelopes I'd picked up on my route. Most people with a newspaper subscription didn't bother with tips anymore, but the few who remembered at the holidays were a godsend. The desk clerk wanted a credit-card impression or a big cash deposit. I let him run a copy of a debit card. He wouldn't submit it unless I bolted, so no one would trace me that way. I parked in the back of the lot near the room, let myself in, and crashed, falling into a restless sleep.

I woke sometime after noon. Armed with a cup of bad motel coffee left over from the morning "courtesy" pot, I went out to the car and drove to a nearby strip mall to buy a new cell phone. Tempted to buy a decent cup of coffee, too, I stuffed what was left of my dwindling funds back in my pocket. The *Times* wouldn't cut checks for the pay period that had just ended until Friday.

Back at the motel, I retrieved the trash bag of files I'd copied the night before from the trunk. It seemed like days ago already. I wanted to follow up on Reyna's buried treasure theory and explore Molly's basement and grounds. But she would have been informed by now that SPD wanted to question me, or arrest me, for the homeless kid's murder. No doubt SPD had issued a BOLO—be on the lookout—with my name on it, too. I had to keep my head down. As unappetizing as the thought was, going through the files was better than sitting around and doing nothing.

I dumped the files on the bed. After organizing them in piles I read through them one by one. The purchase orders and invoices related a small slice of local political history—Rafe Acasa's strategy to get to the governor's office, grand plans to support key political causes that would maneuver him into positions he could leverage. Do enough favors on the way up, and the chits become more valuable later. Rafe had forgotten, though, who'd put him on the city council.

The financial trail documented all the fundraisers, the strategizing, the white papers, the issues programs the firm had initiated on Acasa's behalf. I was supposed to have been the objective third party, reining in budgets, keeping an eye on suppliers, and banking donations from contributors. The pieces of paper reminded me of what I'd done toward the end of my career, for the firm, for Acasa, before life around me had spiraled out of control.

Nothing seemed out of the ordinary on the first pass, but I sensed a pattern. Starting in again from the beginning, this time I pulled out anything that appeared unfamiliar—events, suppliers I didn't remember. When the files were divided into two stacks, I combed through the POs and invoices I didn't recognize. All of them were properly approved and initialed. By me.

I leaned against the wall at the head of the bed and racked my brain, trying to remember something from those days besides the pain, the bleakness and desperation, the pit inside me that Cole's suicide had hollowed out like an ulcer. Whiting had picked up a lot of the slack, covered for me when depression had made it nearly impossible for me to function. Whiting, in fact, had handled a lot of the accounting chores for the client as my situation at home had worsened. He'd gone over many of the invoices during my absences, physical and mental, approving them as appropriate. But no invoice had been paid without my initials. And if I had approved them personally, I initialed them only if Whiting signed off first.

I looked at the invoices more carefully, wondering if Whiting could have forged my initials. But why would he set me up? He was on a fast track at the firm. I hadn't stood in his way. The papers in my hand crumpled as my fist clenched without my permission. *Why can't I remember?*

I stared at the pile on the bed, trying to make sense of it all. Pulling an invoice from a supplier I didn't recognize, I studied the phone number for a minute before dialing. The phone screeched in my ear and a voice told me the number was "disconnected or no longer in service." Trying a second number, I got the same message. Two bad numbers in a row. Competition's tough; suppliers go out of business. But we'd vetted them carefully when I'd been with the firm.

A woman's voice answered at the third number. "Three-Sixty Vision."

I hung up quickly and tried a fourth number. Disconnected. I sat back and thought.

The closest address was just on the other side of the airport in Burien, close by. I drove up to a strip-mall storefront and double-checked the address. The name on the sign, a franchise pack-and-ship company, didn't match. The supplier listed on the invoice might have gone out of business after all, replaced by a new store.

I found an empty parking spot and went in. As expected, the small space contained three copy machines, workspace for self-serve customers, and a wall rack merchandising packing materials and office supplies. An older woman and a teenage kid stood listlessly behind the counter. Both wore black polo shirts with a company logo printed over the breast pocket. I stopped halfway to the counter and made one slow rotation, taking it all in.

"Help you?" the woman said.

"You rent these boxes by the month?" I pointed to a bank of mailboxes along one wall.

The woman nodded. "By the week, if you want. You interested?"

"I might be. Thanks."

I walked back out to the car. The invoice listed a suite number after the street address. Suite number, mailbox number... same thing? On a hunch, I skipped the other addresses and drove straight to the one for the company with the working phone number. Another pack-and-ship store in another strip of storefronts, this time up near Northgate Mall. I went in and asked the girl behind the counter when they usually delivered mail. She gave me a window of time around midmorning. I thanked her and left, noting the location of the number in the bank of boxes.

I called the Three-Sixty Vision number back. The same woman answered.

"Hi there," I said, voice full of smiles. "I've got an old invoice here from your firm, and I don't think it's been paid yet. Kind of embarrassing. Is there any way to check?"

"Gee, I don't know. I'm not sure I can find it here."

"Is there someone in your accounting department, maybe?"

"We're pretty small. Um, we don't really have an accounting department. Uh, how much is the invoice for?"

"Not that much." I thought of a tempting figure. Too much wouldn't sound believable. Too little and I'd lose her. "Around twenty-five hundred." It was enough to get her attention.

"I don't suppose you could just pay it, huh? You know, just in case? I mean, if it's been overdue that long."

"I'm sure it was our mistake. We'll get a check in the mail to you today. It'll go out this afternoon, so you should have it by tomorrow."

"That's great! Thank you so much."

"I'm really sorry about this. I can't tell you how embarrassed we are. We always pay suppliers on time. Hope you won't hold it against us."

"Of course not."

"Great. Thanks again, and you take care."

I hung up before she could ask any questions, but I didn't expect any. She might wonder about the timing, but I counted on human nature. She'd be at the mailbox when the mail came in.

I called Chance and asked him if he felt well enough to take my route for a couple of nights, offering to let him keep whatever tip money he collected. He said the swelling had gone down enough that he could hide the worst with makeup and that he wanted to get out of the house. He told me Donovan and Hiragawa had come by the house looking for me and had asked him and Peter to call if I got in touch.

"Not to worry, doll," he said. "We won't breathe a word."

I did worry, though, as I worked my way back down through the city, running into the usual gridlock on I-5 over the Ship Canal Bridge. The net was tightening. I hadn't eaten for nearly twenty-four hours. My stomach complained loudly at the mistreatment. I ignored it. I considered calling the number Reyna had left me and telling her about Molly's house, but I thought better of it. She hadn't exactly sounded enthused about my theory concerning Gagnon's involvement. I wanted something more concrete before I talked with her again.

Impulsively, I checked voice mail. There was one message, from Pastor Paul. Curious, I retrieved it. An icy chill spread through me as it played.

"Blake, Paul here. Thought you'd want to know. Oh, god, how do I put this…Mary was killed last night. Her, um, partner I guess you'd say—Stitch? He beat her to death. Said he was better off in jail where he could get a warm bed and free meals. I'm…

we're all sorry to hear it, as I'm sure you are, too. Call me when you can."

I shook my head at the senseless tragedy. Whatever Mary may have known about Midge and Joyance House, it didn't matter now.

36

I bought some food and a disposable razor in a convenience store on the way back to the motel and holed up for the night. Sitting on the stained sheets of the hard motel bed with C-store junk food for dinner, my plight seemed desperate. With Mary dead and every cop in the city looking for me, I had to come at this from a different direction. Find what had set off this chain of events, and I might find the person responsible for Midge's murder. I was sure of only one person who was after whatever Woodworth had buried—Gagnon. And he'd tried to get information out of Sister Florence. "Lepwee" and "low water," he'd said. Or "*le puits*" and "*l'eau*"? French for "well" and "water."

Early the next morning, I called the hospital. Florence had been discharged and sent home. I made my way back into the city and parked a block away from the church. I skipped down the alley up to the church rectory. Lines on the wet pavement in the parking lot behind the school demarcated four-square and basketball courts, the urban version of a playground, the lot empty and barren this time of day. Two church vans sat parked on the far side midway between the rectory and the church. I angled through the courtyard to the side door and rang the bell.

A heavyset middle-aged woman answered after I pushed the bell a second time. She assessed me with a suspicious eye that roved from head to toe and back.

"I'm looking for Sister Florence," I said. "Is she in?"

"And you would be?" She sniffed.

"A friend. My name is Blake Sanders. I came to see how she's doing."

She wasn't impressed. "She's resting is how she's doing."

"May I see her?" I prodded.

Reluctantly, she stepped away from the door. "I'll tell her you're here."

I stamped my feet in the cold on the stoop and blew into my cupped hands before stuffing them deep into my pockets. Five minutes passed before the woman returned and cracked the door again.

"She wants to see you," the woman said. "Follow me."

She swung the door open far enough to let me squeeze in and shut it behind me. Waddling ahead of me, she led me to a sitting room in the front of the house. Florence was seated in a chintz armchair, a shawl wrapped around her shoulders, holding a cup of tea in her lap.

"There you are," she said brightly. Her eyes sparkled, but she looked older, diminished somehow since the day she'd spoken to me in the street. The high ruffled collar on her blouse under the buttoned-up sweater couldn't quite hide the fingers of dark bruising creeping up her neck where her assailant had choked her unconscious. A bandage still covered a spot high on her forehead where she'd hit her head on the stone floor, and her cheek was purpled and swollen.

Florence noticed the housekeeper lingering near the door. "Thank you, Martha," she said. Her voice held a hint of a bite.

The other woman straightened and backed out of the room.

Florence turned to me with smiling eyes. "She's old-fashioned. Thinks of us as wicked witches in black habits with rulers for wands. I like to put the fear of God in her once in a while. I think He understands."

I didn't try to hide my grin. "How are you, Sister?"

"Quite well, thanks to you."

I waved away her gratitude, suddenly warm. "I'm just glad you're recovering and safe."

"Seems you've poked a hornet's nest, young man."

"I think our friend Midge did that," I said, "but I guess I haven't calmed things down any. I'm sorry you got caught up in this."

She lifted the saucer and raised the teacup to her lips. Her frail hands trembled, fluttering like small birds. She took a sip and quickly lowered the cup to her lap again.

"You're making progress finding out what this is, I imagine."

I nodded. "Midge's crusade wasn't just nonsense. She was trying to prevent something terrible from happening, and discovered something that could be of great value to the order."

Her eyes brimmed. "I shouldn't have doubted her. What can I do?"

"I need to check your memory, Sister. Your order may have been called on a long time ago to protect something buried somewhere near here. We're looking for a deep shaft of some sort. Was there ever a well on the convent grounds?"

"A well? To draw water?" Her surprise turned to concentration. "There were a number of springs, of course, on the hill. And by the time the convent was built, Capitol Hill was well developed and had city water lines." She paused, deep in thought. "There was a well here. Not at the convent, though. Here at the church. Right outside in the courtyard, in fact. Where the fountain is now. It's been filled in for years, of course."

But it had been there, and may have been the well Gagnon had been looking for.

"There's something else," I said. "In the hospital you told me how Sophie Clare saved people on the slave ship. Do you remember?"

She nodded. "The believers were saved. Just as we all are saved through Christ's sacrifice."

"With Christ's blood, you said."

"Of course. 'This is my blood of the New Covenant, which is shed for you.' You go to church, don't you, young man?"

I sidestepped the question. "She saved them by giving them Communion?"

"The miracle of God's love. His only Son gave his life for us."

Blood. Sister Marguerite's journal flashed in my head again. "*Le sang de ma sœur.*" Sister Sophie Clare. Not "the blood of our Lord," which I'd expect from a nun, but "the blood of my sister." The slaver's captain never would have given her any of the ship's store of wine to share with slaves. Sophie Clare had used her own blood. Immunizing the Communicants from the disease on board? Was it possible that samples of *both* disease and cure were what Gagnon was after?

I spent another few minutes chatting with Florence about other things. When I saw her flinch in pain, exhaustion playing across her face, I excused myself and told her I'd visit again when I had a chance.

In the car, I called the number Reyna'd given me and paged her. I drove straight from the rectory to the pack-and-ship store up near Northgate. I pulled into a slot across from the store with a view inside. A young kid, maybe eighteen or nineteen, worked behind the counter. The girl from the day before was nowhere in sight. I watched him walk around and pick up a box on the floor, a lock of long dark hair flopping down, hiding half his face, shirttail hanging over his belt in back. I thought of Cole. Even on meds as a teen he'd been incapable of keeping his room neat and organized, his appearance well-groomed. Even when he cared enough to try, he attracted dishevelment like a magnet.

The kid straightened and lugged the box behind the counter and placed it on a scale. I sat unmoving for a moment, and considered how to play it. I had an unobstructed view of the wall of mailboxes, so I stayed put. After thirty minutes, my bladder was full. Another twenty minutes later, the seat grew teeth. I wedged a pill between my incisors, bit down, and swallowed half to help keep from drifting off. I leaned back against the headrest, scanning the parking lot, watching cars come in and out and people flowing through the strip mall like ants on parade. How Charlie could take patrol duty, or how cops on stakeouts handled the boredom and discomfort of long hours in a cramped car, beat me.

Distracted by an obese man squeezing through the space between his honker pickup truck and the SUV wedged into the next spot, I didn't see the woman walk into the store. When I looked in the store again, she stood bent at the waist, peering into an open mailbox, wearing a puzzled look. Maybe midtwenties, she had long, dirty-blonde hair pulled back into a ponytail that dangled over the limp hood of a Huskies sweatshirt. I got my cell phone and snapped a photo. When I lowered the phone, the kid behind the counter was staring out the window at me with a peculiar expression.

A gray SPD cruiser swung into an empty spot a couple of doors down from the copy shop. I slouched as a middle-aged, heavyset cop got out and hitched up his pants. Expecting him to head for coffee, he surprised me and walked into the copy shop. The kid looked just as surprised. The young woman glanced at the cop nervously, closed the box, and removed the key.

She quickly headed for the door as the cop walked up to the counter. I snapped another photo as she walked out, and shifted my attention back to the kid. He had an earnest look on his face now, mouth moving and finger aimed out the window at me. The cop's head turned, his gaze following the kid's finger until he locked eyes with me. The girl was halfway across the lot to a little dark-blue compact. My palms suddenly went damp. I rubbed my hands on my slacks, started the car, and put it in gear.

The cop pointed at me as I eased the car out of the slot, and headed for the door. I gave him a little shrug and raised my eyebrows. My mouth went dry and my heart pounded as I spun the wheel to follow the woman's car as she backed out. The cop stepped off the curb into my wake. In the mirror I watched him take note of my car and stride back to the cruiser.

The blue compact headed north up past the mall. I pulled out not far behind and closed the gap with the woman's car to put more distance between me and the cop. The cruiser hadn't moved or turned on its light bar. SPD had probably put out a BOLO on my car, not the rental.

The woman turned west, heading for the freeway. She surprised me, crossing under it and turning south on Meridian. I checked the rearview for any sign of SPD and breathed a little easier as we wound down past the North Seattle Community College campus, taking surface streets into the Green Lake neighborhood. I held back far enough to keep her in sight, closing the distance only when I thought I might get caught at a light. After another five minutes of twists and turns she pulled up to the curb outside a small bungalow.

I continued on down the block and turned around in a driveway. Easing the car back the way I'd come, I snapped pictures of her striding up the walk to the front door of the house and letting herself in. An empty spot beckoned at the curb, where I still had a view of the house. A big picture window reflected gray sky in the milky winter light. Movement played on the other side of the glass.

I pawed through the papers on the passenger seat and found the invoice with the number I'd called the day before. I dialed it and watched the plate glass across the street. As the phone rang in my ear, a shape crossed in front of the window. A woman's voice answered on the second ring. I cut off the call without a word. Brass street numbers were nailed to a post on one side of the porch. I jotted them down on the invoice next to the phone number and pulled away.

My thoughts traveled down a hundred little side roads at breakneck speed only to dead-end or take a twist in some other direction. But I made sure I kept an eye on the road, an eye on the speedometer, an eye out for cops, and drove to a branch library not far away.

Five minutes later, an open computer terminal gave me access to King County property tax records. Using the county's parcel viewer, I zoomed in on the house I'd just left and pulled up the ownership history. The owner's name at the top of the records felt like a slap in the face with a wet towel—Dan Whiting. As if my mind didn't want to consider what that meant yet, I dialed Frank Shriver's number. Got his voice mail. Didn't leave a message.

A bunch of little pieces began to click into place instead— the GPS location Reyna had told me about; Gagnon's attempts to find a well, confirmed earlier that morning by Sister Florence— giving more definition to the puzzle picture. I navigated to the Sound Transit website. With a growing sense of dread I finally clicked through a page on ST projects and found detailed maps of the light-rail tunnel route under Capitol Hill with the street grid overlaid on top. I remembered looking at it a week earlier and thinking the tunnel was nowhere near Joyance House. Back then, I'd only wondered why Midge thought Joyance House might have a case against ST over an easement. That was before a naval intelligence agent had told me about two hundred million dollars in gold buried somewhere under Capitol Hill.

"Are you almost finished?" a voice behind me said.

I spun the chair around. A woman in tailored black jeans, lavender cashmere turtleneck, black North Face down vest, and with a Coach bag slung over one shoulder shifted her weight impatiently from one foot to the other. A Green Lake stay-at-home mom.

"Just about," I said.

She looked at her watch and sighed. "I had this terminal reserved."

I glanced around. Two other terminals were unoccupied. "If you can wait about twenty seconds, it's all yours," I said. "Otherwise, I'll move to one of the other terminals."

She sighed again. "Okay, I'll wait." She folded her arms.

I turned back to the screen and focused in on the map.

The light-rail tunnel bored directly beneath the McHugh house—Molly's home.

37

I dialed Molly's direct line on my way to the car. It rang through to voice mail. I left a curt message for her to call me, gave the number, and pressed "End." I tried her cell phone next. She picked up on the third ring.

"I'm glad I caught you," I said, heart thumping in my throat. "I thought you might be in a meeting."

"Blake?" Her voice was colored with worry. "Where the hell are you?"

"Moll, you can't go home tonight. You have to find a place to stay." I let myself in the car and shoved the key in the ignition.

"Half the city's police force is looking for you right now. Where *are* you?"

"I *know* that. I'm fine. You're in danger, Molly. You've got to watch your back. And you can't stay in the house." Checking the traffic in the mirror, I pulled away from the curb.

"Blake, are you listening to me? You need to surrender yourself to SPD. Come down to the office later, and I'll arrange it. It'll be easier if—"

"Molly, *stop!*" I paused to make sure I had her attention. The phone was silent. "I'm not turning myself in. There's too much at stake. Now, please listen to me. You need to make arrangements to stay somewhere. You can't go back to the house."

"Why not?"

I heard the petulance in her voice.

"The man who broke in and attacked you? He'll be back."

"There's been no sign of anyone trying to break in." She'd gone lawyer on me, her voice cold and logical now. "Really, Blake, you shouldn't worry about me. It's gallant of you, but not necessary. I had the door fixed and the locks changed. I even had the alarm company come out and check the entire system."

"You don't understand," I said, trying not to let my voice rise any further. "The guy is looking for something in the house. He won't hesitate to kill you next time."

"What are you talking about? Even if he does come back, he didn't kill me before. Why would he now?"

"He's already killed two people that I know of. I'm serious. You're in danger."

"You're not making sense. How do you know the man killed two people? How do you know it was the same man who broke in?"

"I saw him kill Royer, Molly! He wants me dead!" I practically shouted into the phone now.

"What do you mean? The UW professor? You *saw* who killed him and you didn't call me? You didn't talk to the cops? What is *wrong* with you?"

"I don't have time to explain right now. He'll use you to get to me. Don't you see? He knows who I am."

"Who *is* this person? How does he know who you are?"

"He doesn't *know* me. He knows my identity, my name, probably where I live. If he knows that, he'll figure out who you are, too. He's a rogue agent from the French—shit, Molly, it doesn't matter. All that matters is that you stay away from the house."

She was silent for a moment. "You need to come in so we can sort this out."

I reined in the tightness that welled up in my chest, drawing a slow breath. The more emotion that bled into my voice, the farther she'd retreat behind a wall of iron-clad logic and defensiveness.

"Humor me, please, Molly. I'm begging you. Don't go home. Find someone to spend a few nights with."

"That man knows who I am?" she said quietly. "Deliberately targeted *my* house?"

"That's what I'm trying to tell you."

"I suppose I could stay somewhere else tonight." Finally, she sounded concerned.

"Good. Stay at the office. Have someone pick you up there."

"I'm not at the office," she said, voice so quiet now I barely heard it over the traffic sounds.

"Where are you?"

"On my way home. I left a file case there this morning, but they rescheduled a deposition on me. I have to go pick it up."

"Molly, don't! Turn around now. Send someone else."

"It's the middle of the day, Blake. Even if I buy your story, it's not likely some burglar's skulking around the house. I'm getting those files. Unless you want to pick them up and turn yourself in at the office?"

"I can't do that."

"Good-bye, Blake. Call me when you're ready to turn yourself in."

"Molly!"

She was gone. I threw the phone onto the passenger seat and concentrated on driving, pushing the rental as fast as I dared without attracting too much attention. Her office was closer to the house than I was, but she had to contend with city traffic and stoplights all the way. I could take the freeway at least partway.

If there'd ever been anything buried under Molly's house, Gagnon was sure to make another attempt to find it or some way to get at it. I only hoped he hadn't picked today, but if he'd waited out the weekend like I had he'd be impatient to get in there as soon as Molly left. I prayed I'd get there on time.

Weaving through the slow-moving traffic heading south-bound across the Ship Canal Bridge, I cursed at bad drivers on all sides, wishing that license examiners would stop rubber-stamping applicants who obviously had no aptitude behind the wheel of a car. I thumped the dashboard with a hand, squeezed into an opening in the next lane, and shot ahead, looking for another gap. One opened up in the right lane. I stepped on the gas, angled for it, and slipped in front of a panel truck, earning a honk and an angry gesture but sailing past more slow cars.

On the other side of the bridge I got off, crossed over the freeway, and hauled up Tenth Avenue as fast as the traffic lights allowed. At Aloha, I turned east and went up the hill, engine revving, unconcerned about cops now. They had to catch me, and I wouldn't have minded a little backup once I reached Molly's, anyway. I wasn't sure what to expect—Gagnon and a bullet, or Molly's self-satisfied I-told-you-so smirk.

I wheeled the car around the corner in back of the house, tires spinning on the wet pavement, and parked in front of a hydrant. I ran halfway up the block and cut through the back of Molly's lot to the end of the driveway. Her little white BMW convertible sat even with the side door. *Damn! Too late!*

I hurried to the front and up the steps to the veranda, crouched low, and made my way quietly to the side door. Hugging the wall below the glass pane in the door, I reached out and tried the knob. She'd left it unlocked. I vowed to kill her myself if Gagnon hadn't gotten to her yet. I took a breath and held it, cracked the door an inch or two, and peered inside. Nothing moved. I opened the door enough to slip through and silently closed it behind me.

Front rooms—a foyer and formal living and dining rooms—lay to the left. Just inside the door on the right was a sitting room. A hallway extended directly ahead, leading to the kitchen in the back of the house. I'd had dinner in this house with Molly and her parents so many times when we were dating and first married that I could find my way through it blindfolded. I stood inside the door, listening for signs of habitation, hearing only the muffled tick of the mantel clock in the living room. Scents of cinnamon and toast mingled with those of wood and furniture polish, making the house smell venerable, old, lived in.

I took a step and paused, expecting the oak floor to creak underfoot, but it didn't give me away. I took another step. The sound of hard heels clacking on the tile in the kitchen stopped me again. Down the hall, something changed almost imperceptibly in the dim light. I froze, trying to discern what had caught my attention. *There!* The basement door opened a crack at the same time Molly's face came into view. I put a finger to my lips and saw her expression of surprise and irritation slowly turn to alarm as the opening door obscured her from view.

The pounding in my chest and tenseness in my limbs left no room for thoughts, focusing my mind with laser clarity on a single objective—protecting Molly from harm. Guarding the only other person to whom I'd given my unconditional love besides the son I hadn't been able to save.

Impulse, instinct, kicked in. No conscious thought required, only muscles twitching in response to electrical charges transmitted from the motor cortex. Just like playing ball. Unaware of running down the hallway, I reached the door in just a few strides. Tucking my shoulder, I slammed into the door with as much force as I could muster. It swung into something large and heavy, sending shock waves through my shoulder. Still pumping my legs, I leaned into the door, my momentum and weight shoving it closed. A loud series of thuds from the other side faded as a body tumbled down the basement stairs.

I twisted the deadbolt and turned for Molly. She stood rooted to the spot, open mouth working like a fish pushing water through its gills. No sound came out.

"We have to go," I said, grasping her arm above the elbow. I gave a gentle pull to steer her through the dining room toward the front door.

Her eyes focused on me, and she gave a little shake of her head as if waking from a dream.

"My papers!" She jerked away and headed for the kitchen.

Behind me, the basement door vibrated like a bass drum with the force of someone putting a shoulder into it.

"Molly, we have to get out of here!"

As if to make my point, a hard *thwack* and the sound of splintering wood resounded down the hall as a bullet ripped through the door. Molly grabbed my hand and towed me behind her as she ran into the kitchen. She scooped up the file case and purse lying on the counter and turned back. I stopped her.

"He has a gun. Come on."

I bolted for a door leading to a patio off the kitchen. From the hall came another reverberating thud and then a crash as the door burst open and smashed against the wall.

"This was a bad idea," Molly said as we stepped outside.

I looked around quickly. The only other way off the patio was another door through the sitting room and into the hallway we had just left. Over the stone balustrade was a one-story drop to the ground below.

"It'll do," I said. "He doesn't know where we went. I'll go first."

I stepped over the low railing, crouched low, and gently pushed off, bending my knees as I landed to absorb most of the force of the drop. The bad knee groaned from the strain. I turned around and bit back the pain so Molly wouldn't see.

She stripped off her heels and tossed them to the ground, clinging to the railing with one hand. The purse was slung at her waist, the strap across her chest. She dropped the heavy case into my waiting hands. I set it down and raised my arms to catch her as she pushed off. I got my hands on her waist as she came down, but slipped on the soggy grass and fell under her weight.

She scrabbled to get untangled and climbed off me, bare feet now soaked. I rolled onto my hands and knees and pushed myself upright as Molly grabbed up her file case and shoes.

"Can you run with no shoes?" I said.

"Do I have a choice?"

Movement above her head caught my eye. I looked up at the house and saw Gagnon's face in an upstairs window. His eyes widened in recognition.

"No," I said.

I grabbed her wrist and yanked her down the slope toward the trees. Behind us, I heard the scrape of the window against the frame as Gagnon threw the sash open, and the soft, familiar *phut* of the sound suppressor and the smack of a bullet against a nearby tree. *Too damn close!*

The bushes and bare trees gave us limited cover, but we reached the street and started sprinting. Molly pulled up at the corner with a small cry. I looked back to see her limping. I wrapped one of her arms around my neck so she could take the weight off the hurt foot.

"Pebble," she said with a gasp. "I'll be okay. Just hurts like hell."

"The car's just a little farther," I said. She nodded grimly and hobbled faster.

She pushed away from me when we reached the rental and headed for the passenger door by herself. I didn't waste time with chivalry. As we pulled away from the curb, I checked the mirror but saw no sign of Gagnon. It still took a minute or two before my pulse slowed.

"Was that the man?" Molly said.

I glanced at her. She stared straight ahead, her face grim.

"Yes."

"Who is he?"

I shook my head and sighed. "It doesn't matter. You wouldn't believe me, anyway."

"I can't help you if you won't tell me what's going on."

"I don't want you mixed up in this, Molly. Let's just figure out somewhere you can hide out for a while."

"I'm already involved. If you won't let me help you, then at least tell me so I know what you've gotten me into."

I owed her that much. "His name's Aubrey Gagnon. He used to be a spy for the French government, but he's gone AWOL."

"What does he want?"

Stealing another glance, I could tell she still wasn't convinced but seemed willing to hear me out. "A bioweapon that could cause a worldwide pandemic. And maybe a couple hundred million in gold."

Now she looked at me with incredulity written across her features.

"I know…" I said hopelessly.

"There's a man with a gun in my house. I'm calling the cops."

"Probably a good idea," I said, "but he'll be long gone by the time they get there."

"Christ, Blake, what am I *supposed* to make of this?"

I sucked in a deep breath through my nose and exhaled slowly through my mouth.

"The one thing you always insisted on in our marriage, Moll, was honesty." I said, choosing my words slowly and carefully, trying not to get tumbled in the undertow. "Isn't that the real reason we're not together? We stopped being honest with each other."

She opened her mouth. Closed it.

"No more," I said. "I'm not hiding anymore. You get the truth whether you like it or not."

With a glance I saw her taking measure, filled with uncertainty.

"Do you want to hear it or not?" I asked.

She bit her lip and nodded.

"Is there somewhere you think you might be safe for a while?"

She looked away for a moment. "I know. Take me over to the U. I can hang out in Jane's office. I'm sure she'll let me stay with her and Henry for a few nights."

I checked a street sign to get my bearings and took the next right.

"Weren't you going to call SPD?" I said.

"I can't."

I stole a peek and saw concern and fear on her face along with weariness. "Why not?"

"I'm an officer of the court. You know that. There's a warrant out for your arrest, Blake. Even though you're my client—the firm's client—I'm bound to tell them you're with me. Otherwise, the PA charges me with harboring a fugitive."

"What are you going to do?"

"Call them when you drop me off."

"Tell them I took your phone," I said. "Tell them I forced you to come with me. Hell, a few more charges on the warrant won't hurt."

"Maybe." She fell silent, face turned away.

I focused on driving.

"Did you kill that homeless kid?" she asked my reflection.

"No."

I anticipated her next question, but hoped she wouldn't ask, for once taking me at my word.

"But your prints…"

I wondered if she could read my disappointment. "Someone is trying to frame me. I'm not sure who."

I could read the disbelief on her face in a glance. "I don't have all the answers yet."

"Give me *something* to work with. Some reasonable explanation like, 'They're not my fingerprints, Molly. The cops made a mistake.'"

I ignored the sarcasm. "They're mine."

"Then I don't see any way around this." She sounded resigned.

"Don't you think I *know* that?"

She recoiled, pressing herself against the door.

"Shit, Molly, why do you think I won't surrender myself to the cops? I can swear up and down that I didn't kill anyone— not Midge, not the kid, not Royer even—but everything points to me. If I don't figure this out I'm as good as dead. Don't you get it? Is that what you want?"

She clenched her jaw, stony-faced, but an unbidden tear rolled down one cheek.

"We were married for twenty years, Molly. Do you really think I'm a stone-cold killer?"

"I don't know what to think. I don't know you anymore. Not since…"

"Not since Cole died."

The tide had turned if I could finish that thought and she couldn't. A thought of him popped into my head, how he used to make fun of my ADD tendency to interrupt conversations by speaking random thoughts aloud. "Purple!" was his way of calling me on it, his code word for saying, "What's that got to do with the price of tea in China?"

"We both changed after that, Molly," I said. "How could Cole's death, our only child, *not* change us? But down deep, aren't we essentially still the same people?"

She didn't answer for a long time. When I glanced at her, she'd taken a tissue out of her purse and dabbed her nose with it.

"I didn't protect him, Molly," I said finally. "Did we love him too much? Did I love him so much I didn't care enough?"

"No, no, I…" Anguish and confusion furrowed her brow, drew the corners of her mouth down. "Didn't care enough? I don't understand."

"I just wanted him to be happy."

"We both did."

"I didn't care that he was gay. Maybe I should have."

"Why?"

"The bigotry, the hatred he must have faced every day. We accepted him so completely for who he was I forgot that." I gripped the wheel. "I didn't protect him."

Her head slowly turned back and forth. "We couldn't protect him forever."

"I couldn't let anything happen to you."

She put a hand on my arm and squeezed gently. Withdrew it and looked out the window.

"We were good parents, damn it." She sniffled, swiped at the tears making snail tracks down her cheeks, collecting herself.

"So, what *did* happen?" she said after a moment.

"You mean my prints on the knife?"

When I caught her nod from the corner of my eye I told her about looking for Mary Jackson, how I interrupted the mugging on Broadway and tossed the knife in a trash barrel in the park.

She digested it slowly. "You suspect this French agent—Gagnon?—you think he followed you and took the knife?"

I shook my head. "I think someone followed me, but it wasn't Gagnon. Something else is going on."

"I'm confused," Molly said.

"Gagnon's a pro. He's got no reason to kill a street kid as far as I can tell. But whoever killed Midge tried to implicate me. I think the same person killed the kid for some reason, and saw another chance to make me take the fall."

As soon as I heard the words come out of my mouth I knew I had it wrong. Whoever had tried to frame me knew my prints were on the knife. They'd seen me handle it, throw it away, and had killed the kid with it to focus the cops' attention on me. Who hated me that much?

"What does that have to do with whatever you think's buried under the house?" Molly asked.

As soon as she said it another piece of the picture fell in place in my head. "Someone else knows about the gold," I thought aloud. *Framing me was a bonus. Someone had killed Midge to prevent the gold from coming to light.*

Molly stared at me, bewildered. I told her what I knew, starting with Royer's murder. About Gagnon chasing me through the park and Reyna coming along just in time. I was about to tell her my theory about the biological sample Woodworth may have buried when flashes in the rearview mirror attracted my attention.

"Uh-oh," I murmured as I glanced up at the mirror and saw the cop car behind us. I wondered how long he'd been back there.

Molly swiveled in her seat to get a look.

"You have to pull over," she said.

"Shit!" I slammed a palm against the wheel. "Shit, shit, *shit!*"

"You've got no choice, Blake. Please. I'll do anything it takes to keep you out of jail. I'll mortgage the house. I'll help you, I promise."

I checked the rearview again. The cop burped his siren to make sure he had my attention.

"Please, Blake."

Something in Molly's voice made me glance at her. The lawyer was gone. It was just Molly, the redheaded girl I'd fallen in love with in my teens. Fiercely strong and independent but somehow tender and vulnerable, pressed into the seat like a small child. I relented then, a surge of emotion washing away the remainder of my resistance. I was tired of running. Maybe it was time to see how good the lawyers at Molly's firm really were.

Reluctantly, I let up on the accelerator and flipped the turn signal to let the cop know I'd seen him. I looked for a clear spot at the curb on the busy commercial street. Half a block up, I swung the wheel and eased to a gentle stop in a loading zone. The cop pulled in behind me. Molly reached over to the wheel and covered my hand.

"It'll work out," she said. "You'll see."

I didn't reply. I lifted my gaze and watched the cop in the mirror. He sat in the cruiser, moving his arms as if organizing his gear. He leaned to one side, raising his left shoulder to reach for the door latch. As he popped the door, the squeal of tires filled the air. The cop's head jerked around. Molly turned for a look, and I quickly checked the side mirror. A black sedan came out of nowhere and screeched to a stop alongside the cruiser, breaking off its side mirror with a loud crack and tinkle of shattering glass, blocking the driver's side.

The cop pushed futilely against his door, banging it against the side of the black sedan, but it wouldn't open more than a few inches. In profile, the cop's surprised face barely registered fear before it caved in on itself in a spray of red that stippled the inside of the windshield.

38

The black car began moving again as Molly screamed, prompting me to decisive action. I shoved my foot to the floor and spun the wheel before the car behind me could box me in, feeling a thump reverberate through the car as the nose of the black sedan caromed off our rear bumper. A defibrillating shock of adrenaline hit my heart. I shot into the street, the other car close behind.

"Is it him?" Molly screamed. "Is it Gagnon? How did he find us?"

"I don't know," I swallowed hard to keep the taste of bile down. The suddenness, the shock, nearly overwhelmed me, even on the meds. Sensory stimulation—sights, sounds, smells, motion—were like cocaine to my brain. Everything demanded attention, but the sheer volume of sudden stimuli threatened to overload the system like an overdose. I thought my brain might short-circuit.

Focus! Block it out. See the play. Watch the court. Not the stands. Forget the cheerleaders. Only the court!

The light ahead turned red. I blew through the intersection anyway, checking for cross traffic, my head wagging back and forth like a Wimbledon spectator. In the mirror, a car jerked to a stop in the intersection as the black sedan yawed around it, avoiding a collision by inches. The sedan gained on us. I moved over a lane in front of it and pushed the accelerator harder. We made the next light on yellow. Two more blocks and we'd hit the University Bridge. We'd never outrun him.

"He's getting closer!" Molly's frenzied voice cracked. "Can't you go faster?"

The speedometer showed we were already doing close to sixty on a busy commercial street. Oncoming traffic whizzed by, dangerously close. I swung out to pass a car and ducked back into the right lane. *Damn. How had Gagnon found us? Police scanner? He couldn't have gotten there that fast. The cop hadn't been following us that long.* I scanned the traffic ahead, behind, to the sides, the black file case on the floor of the car suddenly catching my attention.

"You said you didn't take that case to the office this morning," I told Molly.

She looked at the case at her feet and blinked, a blank look on her face. I checked the mirror and clutched the wheel tightly as the black sedan came up fast on our bumper. We lurched forward as the sedan smacked into us with a bang. Molly yelped as the seat belt snapped tight and she recoiled back against the seat, the fear on her face now all-consuming. I rammed the pedal to the floor, swerved into the left lane and back to the right, trying to shake him. I gained a few yards and blew through another light, green this time.

"Molly! Stay with me! Did you have the case with you or not?"

She jerked her head toward me. I risked a quick glance and saw her eyes clear. The lawyer was back.

"I left it on the kitchen counter," she said. "I told you, I didn't think I'd need it."

"Throw it out!"

"What? Why?"

"Get rid of it! Toss it out of the car! It's the only way Gagnon could have followed us!"

Reyna had used a tracking device. Why not Gagnon? He must have figured Molly would eventually lead him to me.

She pulled the case between her knees and bent over it, frantically yanked files out and stuffed them next to her seat.

"Christ, Molly! Throw it out, for God's sake!"

The pewter sky suddenly wept, freckling the windshield with tiny raindrops, coloring the ash pavement a darker shade of charcoal. Gagnon's car came up behind us again, slower this time. I tapped my brakes hard. His squealed in response to avoid a collision. I stomped on the gas before he made contact and pulled away, flying down the last block to the bridge at close to seventy. After weaving around two slower cars, we hit the open bridge ahead, one car only about midspan in the right lane. Gagnon kept pace.

Molly screamed again. The black sedan pulled up on our left, its windshield post slowly inching even with my window. Using both feet this time, I hit the brake and the accelerator at the same time. The car momentarily slowed and Gagnon immediately reacted to stay abreast. I took my foot off the brake and the car rocketed forward. I wrenched the wheel to the left and we clipped Gagnon's bumper again as we veered in front of him, the car's rear end fishtailing and tires buzzing loudly on the wet steel mesh grating of the draw span in the middle of the bridge.

Wind tore through the car like a cyclone as Molly put her window down. I pulled close to the curb. With two hands, she shoved the case through the opening. The slipstream instantly yanked it backward. In the side mirror I saw it take a high bounce, hit the railing, and go over the side. She twisted in her seat to check on Gagnon.

"He's making a move! On your left!"

I swung back to the middle and straddled the lanes, blocking him. I swerved to avoid the slowpoke in the right lane. Gagnon followed closely and slewed in front of the slower driver, nosing into the right lane before I had a chance to cut him off.

The end of the bridge rushed toward us. We'd never outrun Gagnon on city streets without causing an accident, killing a pedestrian, or getting killed ourselves. The sign for the upcoming exits flashed by, giving me an idea and a glimpse of hope.

A tight cloverleaf that circled west was first, I knew. A hundred feet farther, the second exit dumped onto eastbound Campus Parkway. I checked the mirrors. Gagnon inched up on my right and eased the side of his car into ours, forcing me toward oncoming traffic. I cranked the wheel a few degrees right, scraping the paint off his doors, and straightened out. He put some daylight between us and accelerated, trying to pull ahead. I judged the distance to the exits.

"Put your head down and hang on!" I yelled over the wind rush.

Molly bent toward the floor. I let Gagnon pull almost even, tapped the brakes once, and then rode them hard. Anticipating my earlier trick, Gagnon didn't react fast enough and overshot the first exit. I stomped on the accelerator and wrenched the wheel hard to the right, sending the car into a four-wheel drift angling back toward the exit, and crossed both lanes.

Molly raised her head and gripped the dash with both hands, knuckles white with the effort.

"Hang on!" I said. The car sped into the cloverleaf, the g-force plastering me to the door.

"He made the next exit," Molly said, her voice controlled now, but scared.

"He has to go up a couple of blocks before he can cut us off. I won't give him the chance."

Molly's voice rose. "He's on us again."

Twisting to look out the rear window, she clutched the seat back. In the rearview I caught a glimpse of the black car bouncing down an embankment toward the cloverleaf. Fear ballooned in my chest, squeezing the air out. I forced a breath in, pushing back against the foreboding.

It hit me then—it wasn't just about good or bad choices, about screwing up or not. There was a difference between civilians and people like Gagnon, a different mindset, a different set of values. Gagnon didn't play by the rules, didn't navigate with the same moral compass. He'd killed a cop without hesitation. He'd do the same to us if I let him get too close. But I had a weapon that could be a match for such a monster—anger. Rage from as primal a place as the killer behind us.

Focus! Don't let it blind you.

Ignoring the "Do Not Enter" sign, I wheeled left onto the first little side street, tires sliding on the pavement. The car roared down a short incline, bumping over a bike path so fast it nearly went airborne. A quick jog put us in a large parking lot fenced on the far end.

"It's a dead end!" Molly said.

"There's another exit," I said, gritting my teeth. "On the other side."

I threw the car into a skidding turn at the end of the lot, rounding the center island of parked cars, catching a glimpse of Gagnon's sedan making the jog into the parking lot. The other exit was just ahead on the left. I cranked the wheel. *The best defense...*

Slamming on the brakes, I shoved the gearshift into reverse and stomped on the accelerator. Molly screamed. I twisted in the seat and maneuvered through a gap in the parked cars, foot to the floor, tires smoking. The car shot backward out of the gap just as Gagnon's sedan passed, T-boning him with an ear-splitting *whump* and horrendous clangor of crumpling metal and break- ing glass. We bounced from the impact, but I didn't let up the accelerator, changing his forward momentum to a sideways slide across the pavement.

I saw Gagnon's face shift from surprise to fury in a blink as he tried to accelerate too late. Holding the car steady, engine whining in protest, I slowly forced him over the asphalt parking blocks at the edge of the lot and down a grass embankment. Gagnon's arm came up, his hand filled with a length of ugly black steel.

"Get down!" I yanked the gearshift into drive and pulled away with a screech of rent metal. The rear window exploded in a shower of glass, two big holes in the starred web of cracks.

I jerked the wheel to the right and peeled out of the lot the way we'd come in, cornering around a building onto one of the narrow streets through the campus.

Molly faced forward and looked out the windshield. "Take a right!" She gestured wildly.

I spun the wheel and we ducked into another narrow street between dormitory apartment complexes.

"Doesn't this dead-end?" I asked.

"We can get through," she said, sounding more confident now that Gagnon was out of sight. "There's a footpath that will take us to Pacific." She saw my incertitude. "You can get through, I swear! You can jog onto Boat Street from there. I've done it. We can get down to the medical center that way."

I followed her directions, nervously checking the mirror to see if Gagnon had picked up our trail. We seemed to have lost him, for the moment. At the end of the street, metal posts barricaded the path from vehicle traffic. I swung into a small staff lot and saw a gap in the curb leading onto the lawn behind the complex. I aimed for it and drove across the grass back to the path. It was just wide enough for a car. A couple of startled students stepped aside to let us pass, one of them exclaiming his annoyance with the flip of a finger.

A hundred yards across the lawn, Gagnon cranked the ignition of the stalled, wrecked car. When he spotted us, he levered himself out of the driver's seat and ran on a diagonal toward the street below, gun swinging in one hand. He was trying to cut us off.

"Shit! Molly!"

Her head swiveled and she yelped. "I'm sorry, I'm sorry!"

I reached for her, found her shoulder, pushed her toward the floor. "Just get down, damn it!"

The path dipped past a line of trees, and I lost sight of Gagnon. We bumped over the curb at the bottom and turned onto the street below, veered around an oncoming car, and pulled into the left-turn lane. We swung onto Boat Street, and two 124-grain chunks of lead punched holes in the car's sheet metal with loud *thunk*s. The road curved to follow the waterfront. We roared down the street, quickly moving out of his line of fire.

I slowed just as quickly, heart leaping into my throat at the sight of three or four patrol cars lined up at the curb ahead. Distant sirens echoed down the glass-walled canyons of the city from all directions. Any second now, the cars at the curb would join them as they closed ranks around us. But the light bars didn't flash. The cars didn't move as we rolled past. Their color and markings were different: UWPD was lettered on the side, not SPD. Parked in front of the campus police headquarters building. They hadn't been mobilized—yet.

Molly didn't seem to notice any of it.

"We need to dump this car," I said, disturbing her reflection in the window.

She started. "What? Oh, sure."

She had a faraway look, and I knew she still smelled the fetid breath of the monster on our tail. It would take her time to shake it, air it out like clothing after eating in a greasy spoon. It reminded me of the distance between the Capitol Hill she lived on and the world I'd called home in the past year. Light-years apart, but separated by only a few city blocks.

The gatehouses to the medical center appeared in the windshield. The car would turn heads, even if campus police didn't already have the plate number. I quickly pulled into the entrance of a small marina before I ran out of options. Slowly cruising the narrow parking lot, I found a space at the end and backed in. A hedge screened the lot from the street behind us. Some boat owner would eventually raise a stink, but the car wouldn't be spotted too quickly. I left the keys under the seat and didn't bother locking it.

Molly scooped up all her files and climbed out unsteadily, brushing a strand of hair out of her face. She tucked the files under one arm, hung her purse on her shoulder, and teetered resolutely toward the street like a drunk in a field sobriety test. I hurried and caught up, lacing my fingers in hers, reassurance that she had someone there to protect her, to fight for her. I felt her heart still beating fast through her fingertips. She glanced at me and offered a wan smile then disappeared down a wormhole again, working it out in her head.

Fighting the temptation to run, we covered the remaining ground to the medical center at a brisk walk, alert. My shoulders tightened at the sound of passing cars, wincing in anticipation of a siren's blurt or the crushing blow of a bullet in the back. Though little more than a long block, the med center's main entrance seemed miles away.

A guard in a gatehouse watched us as we passed, eyes tracking us, a sour look on his face. I waited for him to reach for the phone, to call for backup that would roar up with guns drawn to put us in chains and drag us away. But his discomfort must have been something he ate, or an argument with the wife. He finally looked away, boredom wiping away any vestige of his temporary interest.

Inside, Molly navigated the halls on autopilot, quickly leading us to Jane Thompson's office. Jane stood at a reception desk, her back to us, the crook of one arm filled with books and papers, a valise in the other hand. A black leather purse hung over the shoulder of her lab coat. She listened as the receptionist relayed messages.

"Jane?" Molly trembled, close to tears.

I didn't know this woman, had never seen Molly lose her calm reserve. She'd anchored me all those years. I wanted to put a protective arm around her, tell her everything would be okay.

Jane turned at the sound of Molly's voice. She saw me and frowned. One look at Molly, though, and she waved us both into her office. She shut the door behind us with a foot, dropped her things on the desk, and turned to put a hand on Molly's shoulder.

"Are you out of your mind?" she said. "What are you doing here?"

"We're in trouble," Molly said.

I heard the "we" and squeezed her hand gratefully. Jane looked dubious. Her normal salt-and-pepper pageboy was pulled back tightly from her face and pinned on top of her head, making her thin, acerbic face appear more severe. She stepped around the desk to her chair and motioned us to have a seat. She picked up the phone and dialed.

"Jane?" Molly stiffened, her face pale.

I looked from one to the other, nameless unease growing in my gut. Jane ignored Molly, eyes on me, flicking down briefly as someone answered at the other end.

"Yes," she said into the phone, "I'd like to report a fugitive."

"Jane!" Molly said.

"Jesus!" I leaped out of the chair and slapped a big hand on the phone base, cutting off the call. "What the hell are you doing?"

Jane blinked. "Give me a good reason why I shouldn't."

"There's a man chasing us," Molly said. "Trying to kill us." Her cheeks reddened, as if the words sounded preposterous even to her. She looked at me.

Jane's eyes followed. "You owe someone money?" she said to me.

I leaned over the desk and stared her down while I took the handset from her and replaced it.

"This is serious, Jane." Molly's tone won Jane's attention.

"Oh, please. What's this really about?"

Molly turned to me. "You were about to tell me what Gagnon was after before—"

"Before he shot a cop and tried to kill us?" I said.

Jane sat upright as if jolted with electricity. "Who's Gagnon? He shot a cop?"

I faced her. "You heard about Bill Royer."

She went white and her nostrils flared. "Why do you think I called campus security? I understood you had something to—"

I stopped her. "I was there. Right *after* it happened. This guy Gagnon killed him. Gagnon's a spook of some sort. A spy. Gone bad. He was with an intelligence agency in the French government. There's reason to believe someone buried a biological weapon under Capitol Hill before the Civil War. Gagnon wants the bio-sample, whatever it is. He killed Royer to prevent anyone from finding out about it. That's why he's after us."

She held my gaze for a moment then dissolved into laughter. "It's a joke, right?"

Molly shook her head solemnly and Jane's smile slowly disappeared. She looked at me and back at Molly.

"It's another story, Moll!" She leaned forward. "Do you know how absurd that sounds? It's more of his bullshit. Another excuse for screwing up. You know that. It's never his fault, always someone else's."

"Stop it!" Molly stared at her, the weight of her anger pressing Jane back into her chair. "One more word, Jane, and we're through as friends. Whatever you think of Blake, you couldn't be more wrong. You of all people should understand that, knowing what I went through with Cole when he was little. The heartache until he was finally diagnosed. Where do you think he got it from? I can't change how you feel, but I don't have to listen to it.

"I've just seen a police officer murdered. I've been chased and shot at by a cold-blooded killer. I played demolition derby with no crash helmet, threw my best file case out a car window, ruined a good pair of pantyhose, and got mud all over a new suit. Look at me. I'm a mess. You think I went to work today looking like this? He's not making this up, Jane. And if you don't believe *me*, your best friend, you can go screw yourself." Her eyes brimmed and she sniffed. "Now are you going to help or not?"

Jane's mouth hung open. A clock on the desk ticked loudly. Molly still hadn't let go of my hand. She squeezed it tightly. I felt my heart beat in sync with the pulse in her fingers.

I sat down and went on as if nothing had happened. "I'm afraid this biological agent may have already gotten loose somehow."

"You're not kidding," Jane said softly.

"We haven't always gotten along," I told Jane, "but I didn't know you hated me this much. You know I've always wanted the best for Molly."

"Like when you walked out on her?"

"*Especially* when I walked out. You think I was in any shape to give her what she needed?"

"Both of you, stop it!" Molly's voice was quiet but firm. "It's old news, Jane. And not really any of your business. I know you mean well."

Jane's eyes widened.

"We're wasting time," I said. "Gagnon might already have found this thing."

Jane dropped her gaze to the desk, sulking. "There's no immediate danger."

"What do you mean?" I said. "Why not?"

"I told you before, bacteria or a virus wouldn't survive. The only thing that would survive that long is spores, and *Bacillus anthracis*—anthrax—is the only spore that causes symptoms even remotely resembling plague. If that's really what we have here...Blake?"

Molly looked at me. "What do we have?"

"I don't know. All I have is a journal reference to a pestilence, and a story about a beatified nun who somehow prevented people from coming down with it with her own blood."

I suddenly realized what Gagnon was after. "DNA," I said. "He wants to replicate it, whatever it is. Jane, is there natural immunity to plague?"

Her forehead furrowed. "Sort of. Researchers think the herpes virus, of all things, might offer some natural protection against the bacteria, but—"

"And viruses?"

"Of course."

"Think about it. If I'm right, it came from Africa. What if this thing is some sort of hemorrhagic fever virus?"

"Depending," she said slowly, "it could spread quickly. Ebola-type viruses usually don't travel far before burning out. But…" She shrugged and frowned.

"Some people survived this thing, whatever it is. They may have carried a natural immunity. If Gagnon gets to it first, he'll get the antibody, too. He'll have both—disease and cure."

"There are samples of both? The virus—if that's what it is—and the antibody?" Jane's pupils grew large.

I nodded.

"In the wrong hands…" she whispered.

That was good enough for me. I turned to Molly. "I have to go. You'll be safer without me."

"What are you going to do?" She bit her lip.

"Find whatever he's looking for," I said. "Before he does."

I was pretty sure I knew something Gagnon hadn't figured out yet. I stood.

"How do you know about all this?" Jane said suddenly. "About the CDC's concerns? How did you get mixed up with this…this Gagnon? How did you know he was a French spy?"

"From someone who works for Naval Intelligence."

Her demeanor changed almost imperceptibly. As if her estimation of me had been transformed somehow. I saw grudging respect in her eyes instead of her usual scorn. Her head bobbed a fraction of an inch. She knew. She'd been briefed.

I turned for the door at the same time someone knocked loudly. I froze.

"Dr. Thompson?" A man's voice. "Campus police. Are you all right?"

I looked around wildly.

Jane caught my eye and put a finger to her lips with a warning look. "I'm fine," she called. "Just a moment, please. I'm on the phone."

She motioned toward a side door. "That connects to a lab," she said in a low voice, pawing through her purse. "There's a connecting door to an office on the other side of the lab."

"Dr. Thompson?" the voice said through the door again.

Jane's head jerked toward the sound. "Be right there." She tossed a set of keys at me, a regretful look on her face. "Whoever this guy is, he won't be looking for a Volvo wagon." She gave a short, sharp laugh. "I still have the old soccer-mom car. It's in the reserved lot. I know I'm going to regret this."

I moved for the side door. Molly followed, a hand on my arm, pushing a wad of cash at me.

"I figure you're probably short," she said. "Take it."

I hesitated, then shoved it in a pocket. "Thanks, Moll."

"Go save the world, cowboy." She leaned in and kissed me then, lightly brushing my lips with hers, a faint echo of what we'd once known together.

"Dr. Thompson!" Loud banging reverberated through the door. My heart jumped.

"Wait!" Jane said. "I'm coming." She jerked her head toward the side door and mouthed the word "Go."

As Jane came around the desk to let the cops in, I paused midway through the side door. Looked back at Molly with one of those purple thoughts.

"You know who Cole was in love with, don't you?" I said. "The one who broke his heart?"

She shook her head, a sudden rush of profound sadness flooding her eyes. "No. I don't. But I could take a guess."

"Who?" It came out more sharply than I intended.

Her mouth tightened. "You figure it out."

The campus cops started banging again.

39

I moved across the empty lab space silently. Loud voices came through the door of the office behind me. Jane's rose above the deep male voices, angry, authoritative. I gritted my teeth. She was a piece of work, but Molly couldn't ask for a more loyal friend. I still wasn't sure if she'd just helped me or wanted me away from Molly when the cops caught up with me.

I grasped the knob of the door on the other side of the lab and twisted. It opened soundlessly. Stepping through, I pulled it shut just as the door from Jane's office opened with a soft click. A white-haired man sat behind a desk wearing a blue dress shirt and striped tie, a tweed jacket slung over the back of the chair. Head bowed over papers strewn across the desk, he peered up at me over half-frame glasses, then checked his watch.

"Did you have an appointment?" he said.

"No," I said. "I've gotten myself turned around. I'm very sorry to disturb you." I headed for the door that led to the hall.

"In a hurry?" he asked, stopping me.

I turned and smiled. "Yes, actually." A muscle near my eye twitched.

He sat up, took his glasses off, and looked at the door I'd come in. "Lab's usually locked. Which means you came through Dr. Thompson's office."

I shrugged, the smile still pasted on my face. "Like I said, I'm lost." I raised my empty palms. "I didn't take anything. Honest."

He cocked his head. Sounds came from the lab next door. I gave him an oh-well shrug, and yanked his door open. A beefy cop in a blue UW uniform came through the lab door behind me.

"Excuse me, sir!"

Every fiber in me screamed *run*. He didn't have his gun drawn.

He doesn't know who he's looking for.

I paused and turned, flashing the cop the same polite smile. "Yes?"

Confusion played across his face. His gaze bounced from the man behind the desk to me. The man showed no concern, only interest.

"Everything okay in here, Dr. Cowell?" the cop asked.

Cowell's eyebrows rose a notch. "Fine. Why?"

The cop eyed me. "We got a call. We're just checking to make sure everyone here is okay. Does this man belong here?" He gestured at me.

"I've never seen him before." His voice was neutral, matter-of-fact. He seemed almost amused, as if waiting to see what would happen.

My heart sank as the cop's face turned to granite.

"Mind telling me what you're doing here?"

He took a cautious step, leaving space between us. I shifted my weight to one leg.

"I got lost," I said. I could barely breathe.

"Could I see some ID, please, sir?" His hand casually went to his hip.

"Sure."

I held my hands out. His eyes shifted to watch them. *Now!* I transferred my weight, pushing off with my back leg into a round-house kick that caught him above the ear. Using my momentum, I twisted over into a crouch and put a back kick square into his chest, the solid blow sending a satisfactory jolt up through my leg. He went crashing backward over the desk. Cowell smiled as if this was the most fun he'd had all day. He waved as I bolted through the door.

I raced down the nearest stairwell, taking them three at a time. Stumbling near the bottom, I caromed off a wall and burst through a door into a wide hallway, pain shooting up from my shoulder. An elderly woman pushing her husband's wheelchair looked up, startled. His chin hung on his chest, and his head bobbed erratically as she jerked to a stop. I nodded and smiled. She shrank away from me.

Desperate to be away from that place, I forced myself to breathe and slowed to a walk. My size attracted enough attention without running like a madman. I focused on the glass doors fifty feet away and the sullen gray freedom that beckoned beyond them. *Forty feet, now thirty. No alarms.* I pushed through the doors into a cold Seattle rain and hurried across the street.

I ran through the parking lot, jogging past rows of look-alike cars. Sirens wailed nearby, muted in the sodden air but dangerously close. Swallowing the thudding heart that threatened to bubble out of my throat, I pulled up short and took a deep breath. *Asato ma sat gamaya. Shanti. Shanti. Shanti.* I turned around, heart pounding slower now. *There!*

Thirty seconds later I backed Jane's Volvo out of its space and nosed it toward the exit, scrunched down in the seat, looking like the driver of a clown car. The day's absurdity had almost turned comical. I turned onto the street behind a white compact. It slowed, rolling up to the gatehouse. I pulled into the right lane to pass.

Four UWPD patrol cars swept by in the opposite direction, lights flashing and sirens whooping, flowing around the gatehouses like salmon past boulders in a stream. The startled booth attendants turned and stared, paying me no attention as I slid by.

I headed north, dug my phone out of my pocket, and dialed Reyna's number again. At the beep, I thumbed in my cell number and tossed the phone on the passenger seat. I drove like a grandmother, staying below the speed limit, eyes flicking from one mirror to another. I wondered what would happen to Molly. At least she was safe. And she hadn't really been helping me. The PA couldn't charge her with aiding and abetting. Jane, either, if she didn't mention anything about steering me through the lab door.

God, what a mess.

But it wasn't my mess this time. Little comfort, since I'd still gotten stuck with cleanup. Thoughts of Cole sprang to mind, memories of a mess or two bringing a brief smile to my lips.

Purple.

I swiped at my eyes with the back of a hand and checked the mirrors again. The phone rang. I snatched it up and answered.

"What?" Reyna said flatly.

"All hell is breaking loose, that's what. Where the hell have you been? I paged you earlier. Gagnon broke into Molly's house again. I barely got her out of there in time. He—"

"I can't help you."

"What do you mean you can't help me? Gagnon's still out there. He chased us all over hell, but we finally—"

"I can't help you," she said, louder this time. "You're too hot. You're radioactive, you're so freaking hot."

"Damn it, Reyna, what the hell is going on?"

"You screwed up, that's what! The locals have you up on the murder of some street kid."

"I *know* that. For *chrissake*, Reyna, I didn't do it!"

She didn't reply for a moment. "Even if I believe you, there's nothing I can do. SPD has the murder weapon with your prints. That's two. Bad luck for you."

"God*damn* it, Reyna! I'd have to be pretty fucking stupid to make the same mistake twice, wouldn't I? Gagnon just *shot* a cop! He's not going to stop until he gets what he wants. And he'll hunt us down. I won't let that happen. Not to Molly. If you don't want to help me, fine. But do your job. Get this asshole off the streets."

She was silent for a moment. "He killed a cop? Where is he now?"

"I don't know. Last I saw, he was near a parking lot on the UW campus taking potshots at us. We trashed his car and barely got away from the guy. He may have gotten it running again. But you can bet he's long gone. What the hell are your people doing?"

"We're working on it," she said peevishly.

"I'd have thought you'd have the navy, the army, hell, the coast guard looking for this bioweapon before Gagnon gets his hands on it."

"We're working on it." Her voice was cold.

"What if this thing is still live? If Gagnon gets his hands on it—" Her words suddenly registered. "You're aware…you believe me. About the bioweapon. What changed your mind?"

She didn't answer, shifting gears instead. "Where are you?"

I glanced out the windshield and had second thoughts. "Uh-uh, no way. If you're not with me, we've got nothing more to talk about."

"Wait! Don't be stupid."

"Christ, I wish I had a dime for every time someone said that to me."

"What are you going to do?"

"I've got a killer on my case, every freaking cop in the city looking for me, and you want to know what I'm going to do?

You're the one who asked me for help. And now I'm expendable? Too big a risk? All that talk about my patriotic duty? Get fucked."

"You're angry. I understand that. Come in. Give yourself up. We'll work something out with the locals. Let us handle this from now on."

"Too late," I said. "I can't do that. I know where the bio-sample is, Reyna. And the gold, if there really is such a thing."

"Where?" Her voice gave away too much excitement.

"I'll let you know when I've found it."

"Blake—"

I closed the phone and focused on driving, letting my mind work on the question of what to do next.

Think! Concentrate, damn it.

The phone rang, startling me. I ignored it, figuring it was Reyna trying to get a fix on my location. It kept ringing. I eyed it, curious now, and picked it up to check caller ID. Frowning, I took the call.

"Now's not a really good time," I said.

"I love you, too," said Frank Shriver. "What? You on a date? Still in bed? In bed with a lady friend?" The questions came in rapid-fire.

"How'd you get this number?"

"You called me, remember? Little while ago? Didn't leave a message?" He sounded put out.

I sighed. "What do you want, Frank?"

"You definitely want to hear this, buddy."

"I'm listening." I checked the mirrors and pulled into a parking lot behind a bank.

"You may have put me onto a great story. I checked the list of contributors to Acasa's campaign fund like you suggested. Amazing how many of Lenny Damien's drinking buddies showed up."

"That's no crime. A shame, maybe, but no crime."

"Yeah, but the contributions are all at the limit. More than a lot of these guys can afford, I'd say."

"We're talking, what, seven hundred bucks?"

"These are working stiffs, not businessmen."

I chewed on it. He had a point. I couldn't afford to drop that kind of money on a political candidate these days, either. And I couldn't see the guys Frank was talking about writing a check for more than twenty-five or fifty dollars.

"Get this," Frank said. "You know contributors have to list their employers if the contribution's over a hundred bucks, right?"

"Yes, I know, Frank. You want to move this along?"

Images of the cop's blood on the windshield, the car chase, Gagnon's face, and more flashed by in a blur. I checked the mirror, scanned the parking lot, anything to push them away and focus on what to do next.

"Sorry. Anyway, a bunch of the companies that pop up do business with Lenny's company. You know, suppliers, business buddies, that sort of thing."

"You think Lenny's handing out favors in return for campaign money for Acasa. Why? What good does it do him?" I struggled to stay with him.

"Use your head, Sanders. Lenny's company has work all over the city."

"Sound Transit's not the only trough, you mean." His ramble finally started to draw me in. I wondered what other projects Acasa's political influence could boost.

"There's more," Frank went on. "I'm working my way through the list and see a bunch of Hispanic names. I figure that makes sense, you know. And a lot of the addresses are in Delridge neighborhoods down where Acasa lives. That's only natural, right? But these contributions are all at the limit, too. For the hell of it, I drove down there, cruised a few neighborhoods. Looked up a few addresses. These folks might like Acasa, may even vote for him, but they're definitely not in any position to be chunking down change like that."

I thought furiously. There was a lot of development going on in West Seattle, gentrification, from the environmentally friendly High Point subdivision to Westwood Village shopping center down near White Center, one of the poorest neighborhoods in Seattle.

"How do you think he's working it?" I said.

"I don't know, but he's raising a lot of money from people who don't have it. Smells to me like campaign fraud."

I didn't say anything.

"You may have been right," he said. "Acasa looks dirty. Kind of tough for you to have played a part in this. I guess you really didn't have anything to do with those missing funds last year. I owe you an apology."

"I'll settle for a beer one of these days." I paused. "Hold off on this, would you, Frank? I haven't quite made up my mind about Rafe."

"You've got to be kidding."

"I wish I were. Gotta go."

I knew what to do. I patted my pockets for a dose of meds.

Darkness would fall soon. I'd be in my element then.

40

Gagnon fumed. *Le géant* should be dead. He'd never seen some-one as lucky as Sanders. The man was an amateur, a fucking ama-teur. Gagnon had assassinated dozens of men in his career. None had been as troublesome—or as blessed by angels—as Sanders.

Gagnon had searched the area for the couple block by block, but there were too many places for them to hide. And they could have easily slipped away entirely, though some instinct told him they were still in the neighborhood. After all, Sanders had come to the university to ask Royer for help. Perhaps he had other con-tacts here as well. Gagnon considered simply parking and wait-ing to see if the pair showed themselves. But where?

His cell phone vibrated on the seat next to him. He looked at it, startled, as if he didn't recognize it. As far as anyone knew, he was Alain Dufours. The phone belonged to Aubrey Gagnon, his alter ego, and only one man knew the number. Gagnon picked it up.

"Yes?"

"Have you accomplished what you set out to do, *mon ami?*" the familiar voice said. His former boss at DPSD.

"*Non.* Not yet. But I'm close."

"I'm afraid you're out of time. I tried to protect you as long as I could, old friend, but now the dogs are nipping at my own heels. If our cause is to survive, I must not be exposed. You understand."

"*Mais oui.*"

"Baroche's body turned up a few days ago. The *Police nationale* are quite sophisticated these days. Based on the state of decomposition and the river's currents, they estimated the point at which his body had gone in and dragged the bottom for evidence. You've gotten sloppy, friend. They found the weapon you used."

Gagnon cursed silently. "How much time do I have?"

"They know your new identity. They're tracing your movements to find out where you are now."

"I understand. *Merci.*"

"*Au revoir*, old friend. *Bonne chance.*"

Gagnon hung up. He couldn't waste any more time on Sanders. Or his bitch ex-wife. The cops would get Sanders eventually, anyway. Especially since Gagnon had called in an anonymous tip about the cop he'd shot, blaming it on a man fitting Sanders's description. And by then Gagnon would be long gone, anyway.

He'd gone about this all wrong. Woodworth had buried Sophie Clare's talisman deep. But somehow the burial site had been disturbed. There could be no other reason for the old woman to get so upset in the first place—so upset that she had called the order in Montréal and set everything in motion. Gagnon had found no sign of a well at the church or the location indicated by Woodworth's survey notation. Which probably meant that it had been filled in long ago. So something else had disturbed the site, which meant construction of some kind.

He needed to find a construction site where they were digging a deep hole. It shouldn't be too hard.

* * *

Reyna stood outside the UW Medical Center entrance and dialed Hinson's direct line.

"What've you got?" he asked without preamble.

"Sanders knows where it is, sir."

"Where is he now?"

"In the wind. We scared him off."

"Damn," he said softly. "Any ideas?"

"He's definitely innocent, sir. He got caught in the middle of this. I tracked down the ex-wife. Sanders practically told me where she was. She saw Gagnon kill an SPD officer."

"Do you think Gagnon knows where the gold's located?"

"No, sir. Otherwise he wouldn't still be after Sanders. And Sanders thinks he's after something other than the gold, anyway. I'm inclined to believe him at this point, sir."

"What's the something else?"

"A bioweapon. The ex-wife was with a friend when I spoke with her, an epidemiologist with CDC connections. She's worried, and she's no fan of Sanders."

Hinson's silence spoke volumes. "What do you want to do?"

"You told me to trust my gut on this, sir. Sanders can lead us to the location, unless he gets killed or arrested. Every cop in the city is looking for him. I need to find him first. Do I have your support, sir?"

"Whatever you need, Commander. Keep me posted."

"Thank you, sir."

* * *

Rafe lived in a small, refurbished craftsman in West Seattle not far from the High Point mixed-income housing project. It was a long way from the poverty of White Center, and even farther from the apple and cherry orchards in Yakima. Perched near the top of the ridge that ran south from Elliott Bay the length of West Seattle, the house had a panoramic view of Puget Sound and the Olympics to the west. Lights twinkled on the north tip of Vashon Island and Southworth beyond that under a dark sky heavy with clouds. A ferry crawled across the black surface of the water, a phosphorescent water bug from this distance. The rain had let up for the time being, the air scrubbed clean.

The house stood dark and silent, along with half of the houses on the block. The city hadn't rolled up the sidewalks yet, but Seattleites tended to turn in early. Rafe was attending a holiday concert at Benaroya Hall according to his staff. With time to kill, I'd run a few errands before driving to West Seattle to stake out the house. A couple of hours in the cold car had stiffened my joints and fueled the anger that had built since the narrow escape from Molly's house earlier. It felt clean, righteous, untainted by bitterness. Jeri often reminded me that anger salted with grief had its place. But bitterness infects you, festers, and eats you up inside, leaving you empty as a rotted corpse.

It was after ten when the interior of the car lit up with the sweep of harsh blue-white high-intensity discharge headlamps. I blinked and closed my eyes to slits so I wouldn't lose my night vision. Darkness closed in again as the car turned into the drive at the side of Acasa's house. I got out and walked across the street toward the house as Rafe killed the engine and doused the head-lights. He climbed out, pulling a briefcase and topcoat behind him. Without a glance in my direction, he rounded the trunk of his car and crossed the grass toward the front door. I picked up my pace and angled in between Rafe and the car, cutting off that avenue if he harbored any thoughts about running. I shoved one hand in my coat pocket, index finger extended.

"Rafe."

He spun around, features jaundiced by the orange glow of a streetlight up the block. Shock and fear dissolved into peevishness.

"What do *you* want?"

I thrust my pocketed hand forward. He saw the movement, and I let him wonder.

"Let's go for a drive."

"What for?" His jaw jutted belligerently.

"We need to talk." I shrugged. "Come with me, maybe I help save your ass. Stay here and I guarantee your political career goes down in flames."

Night, darkness, sap the color from the world, leaving everything in shades of gray and black, but I could still see his face darken as his temper flared like a match.

"A cop was shot today," he said. "A good cop, the chief tells us. Rumor around city hall is you were involved somehow."

I should have known Gagnon would find a way to implicate me. Probably figured the cops would run me to ground for him. The news had little effect at this point.

"I guess I don't have much to lose then, do I?" I said.

His eyes flicked up and down the block as if weighing the odds of running for it, and settled on my face again.

"Make a sound," I said, "and I'll pop you before anyone has a chance to look out the window. Your choice, Rafe. What's it going to be?"

He glanced at my coat pocket again, more nervous than fearful. "You've got to be out of your mind coming here. With all the charges you're facing, you'll never see daylight again."

"I barely see daylight now. Won't make much difference, will it? You, on the other hand, might have a problem with jail. I don't think you'd like it much."

"What are you talking about?"

I motioned toward Jane's Volvo. "Shall we?"

He lifted his shoulders and let them fall. "Hell, why not?"

I followed him across the street. He strolled with bravado now, his back straight. He got in the passenger door and laid the coat carefully across his lap.

"Where are you taking me?" he asked as we pulled away from the curb.

I answered him with a question. "Why were you so quick to believe I stole campaign contributions from you?"

His mouth opened in surprise. "You're still pissed about that? Is that what this is about?"

"Answer the question."

"What are you going to do? Take me somewhere out in the country and shoot me?"

I didn't reply.

"No one else could have done it," he said. "That's why."

"*You* could have." I gave the thought time to sink in. "You had access to the account. After all, you were the candidate."

"Steal from myself? You're nuts."

"No one considered any other possibility, and I just let you all roll over me."

"What's your point?"

I shook my head. "We never should have set it up the way it was. Christ, Rafe, it was a conflict of interest from the beginning. Even when we separated everything, the firm was still your issues consultant. We—I—never should have agreed to serve as your campaign treasurer. Old man Dreier should have known better."

"To trust you, you mean." His voice held disdain.

"Fuck you. You took advantage. I'd just lost my *son*. You have any idea what that's like? I could no more think clearly enough to steal from your campaign than I could have realized it was happening in the first place."

"Well, we fixed the problem," he said, sounding smug.

It was my turn to be surprised. "You went outside?"

"Of course we did. You're right about the ethics. Campaign finance law is tough. We needed to clean up our act. Found a woman fresh out of UW grad school who'd been a campaign volunteer to take over as treasurer."

For a moment, the news threatened to yank the King of Hearts out from under the house of cards I'd constructed. I felt bony fingers of desolation reach out of the shadows for me.

A woman? Of course, the one McIver had mentioned.

"Candace Wilder?" I said.

He snorted. "Hell no. We fired her after a month. No, someone else."

I took a stab in the dark. "About five five, five six? Long dark-blonde hair?"

"Rachel Horton." He turned sideways to look at me. "How did you know?"

I drove in silence for a minute, the brightly lit downtown skyline spreading out in front of us as we headed down the hill from Fauntleroy to the West Seattle Bridge.

"Lot of people convinced you're a Boy Scout, Rafe. If so, you've got big problems."

"What do you mean?"

"I mean whoever set me up to take the fall back then hasn't stopped ripping you off. And if you're not careful, history will repeat itself. Only this time, you're the one who'll take the heat."

"No way. You really are nuts. That shit ended when you got caught."

I shook my head. "I can prove it."

"Bullshit. I don't know what you're trying to do, but it won't work. You can't shake me down. And you can't drive around forever holding me hostage."

I wormed my cell phone out of my pocket, flipped it open, and scrolled through the screens. I handed it to him.

"She look familiar?"

"Rachel…" He let it hang a moment. "So what?"

"Look at the next one. That house? Belongs to Dan Whiting."

"So, she's meeting with the strategist on the campaign. What's wrong with that?"

"You're in serious denial, Rafe. The girl went to a mail drop to pick up a check from a supplier who doesn't exist. That's how Whiting's been pillaging the account all these years. He submits invoices from ghost suppliers and cashes the checks. I'm guessing he's moved way beyond that now. I think he's peddling your influence behind your back and making you think you're the one doing good works for the community."

He looked away, staring out the window. I'd hit a nerve.

"Tell me I'm wrong," I said. "Tell me he hasn't been your shadow since they fired my ass."

He didn't move. I let him stew a while before I ventured another thought.

"He wants more than money, you know. More than wherever riding your coattails will take him."

His head swung around, a baleful look on his face. "What?"

"He wants you."

"He's got a funny way of showing it." He stared aimlessly out the windshield, suddenly sitting upright. "He wants me? As in sexually?"

"At that fundraiser? He looked at you the same way you looked at Molly."

"Oh, Christ, just what I need." He made a face then flushed. "Not that I have anything against gays, of course."

"Not that it could hurt you politically," I said.

His head jerked toward me. "I don't see how. It's no big deal anymore. Tim and Janine both have gay partners."

Two other council members. "No, it's no big deal. Unless you're married. You're not married, are you, Rafe?"

"Hell, no. And for the record, I'm heterosexual."

"Doesn't matter to me, Rafe. But that's probably a good thing. Whiting would have found a way to use an affair against you." I paused. "You need to get out in front of this campaign finance thing. Blow the whistle on your own campaign. It's the only way you come out of it with any political future."

He shook his head. "I can't believe this. Rachel wouldn't do this to me. She couldn't."

"And Dan?"

I could see him working it out in his head, considering the possibility that his chief strategist was mercenary enough to steal from his war chest and turn on him if things didn't go as planned. The thought hadn't occurred to me until I'd pulled up Whiting's house on the county plat viewer in the library. But then I'd been blind to a lot of what had happened around me.

"You have no choice, Rafe. Frank Shriver's digging up enough dirt on this to refill the U Link tunnel."

He looked ghostly under the passing streetlights. "Shriver? I'm as good as dead."

"It's not that bad. He actually defended you."

"The guy's a fucking pit bull with a bone. He won't let this go."

"One more reason to get ahead of the story. Give Frank the exclusive."

I could see the wheels start turning as he thought about how to spin it.

"If it's any consolation," I said, "I don't think your girl knew. I think Rachel did whatever Dan told her."

We rode in silence. The two big sports stadiums crouched in the dark, silhouetted against the water and sky beyond like bullfrogs on lily pads. They blotted out the left half of the wind-shield. Lighted skyscrapers filled the right as we came up I-5 from the south. Light and shadow, the ribbon of concrete poured in between a tightrope walk to freedom or disaster, I wasn't sure which.

Rafe lurched in his seat again. "Why are you doing this? What are you after?"

I'd wondered when he'd get around to asking.

41

Reyna walked into SPD's East Precinct and handed her ID to the front desk sergeant.

"I need to see the watch commander," she said.

"Can you tell me what this is about, ma'am?"

She weighed the quickest option to break through the red tape. "I have information about your cop killer."

The desk sergeant stiffened. "I'll see if the captain's available, ma'am."

He reached for a phone, punched in an extension, and spoke into the receiver. She fidgeted, biting a nail. Less than a minute later another sergeant came through a door into the small lobby.

"How can I help you?" he said as he walked up to her.

"You can stop giving me the runaround and take me to see your watch commander, now."

"Ma'am, if you'll just give me the information, I'll be happy to pass—"

"Perhaps you misunderstood me, Sergeant. This is urgent. I need to speak to the watch commander. I'd ask for your chief, but I know he's at home and doesn't work out of this building, anyway. I'm a lieutenant commander in the US Navy, so technically I outrank you. But this is your house, not mine, so I'm trying to be polite. If you need to verify I am who I say I am, then your boss can speak directly to the head of ONI, even the chief of naval operations if he wants. Now, take me back to the watch commander's office."

A minute later, she stood in front of the Captain Jim McDermot's desk. He wore a pleasant expression, but she saw a cop's wariness in his eyes. Her escort remained in the doorway.

"You've got a tip about the shooting suspect from this afternoon?" McDermot said.

"I need your help, Captain. The man who killed your officer is an agent for the French defense ministry. We don't have time for a long explanation; I need you to put out a BOLO on a rental car, and I need to monitor your dispatch calls to help pin down his location so you can catch him."

Reyna turned to the sergeant behind her. "Now would be a good time for you to call Captain Hinson at ONI."

* * *

I turned off an exit ramp onto a downtown street.

"It's simple, really," I said. "I want to make you a hero."

The look I caught was filled with suspicion. "What the hell are you talking about?"

"I need a Get Out of Jail Free card. You're it."

"Why me?" It sounded more like a complaint than a question, his earlier bravado sapped.

"I've got no credit left, Rafe, no chips to play. I've been charged with murder. I'm wanted for questioning in another, and they've got an arrest warrant out for me on a third. I'm at the top of this week's *America's Most Wanted*. You're still credible. People will believe you. And, if people think you're a hero, it'll put you that much farther out in front of the shit storm that's going to break when the news about your campaign finance problem surfaces. Especially if you're the one who leaks that news."

"So, what am I going to do?" he said acridly. "Die while apprehending you?"

I barked a short, sharp laugh, relishing the irony of the thought that leaped to my lips. "Don't be stupid. That'd make you a martyr, not a hero. You still believe what they're saying about me."

"Why wouldn't I? Grief makes people do strange things."

"Grief doesn't *make* people do anything." I reminded myself that grief was a process. Part of my process involved channeling the anger roiling beneath the surface. "I need you. Alive."

"What for?" His whining began to get on my nerves.

"To uncover a little piece of history buried under Capitol Hill."

I gave him a short version of the events that had brought me to the verge of kidnapping him. If he bought into it, I might just manage a way out of the muck. If not...

I found a place to park on the street a few blocks from our destination and shut off the engine. Silence crouched in the back-seat like an unwanted guest. Acasa squirmed in discomfort.

"Look," I said, "you do this and you may come out of it in pretty good shape. But you really don't have a choice." I patted the imaginary gun in my coat pocket. "Let's go."

I climbed out and opened the lift gate in back. Rafe got out more slowly and shrugged into his topcoat while I retrieved a hard hat, work gloves, and reflective safety vest I'd bought with the money Molly'd given me. While waiting for Rafe to get home, I'd had plenty of time to make it look worn and dirty. I pulled up the hood of the sweatshirt under my jacket and clamped the hard hat on top.

"This'll never work," Rafe said when I rejoined him on the sidewalk.

I smiled broadly. "Sure it will, councilman. You're a politician."

I checked my watch, put a hand on his shoulder, and gave him a small shove of encouragement up the street.

The Broadway Link station hummed, a generator on steroids, lit up like a stadium for a championship game. Night didn't exist for this small piece of the city. The work never stopped, and the banks of work lights up on poles did their best to dispel the darkness. Outside, at least. Underground, no amount of light could prevail. The earth absorbed it like a black hole, sapping its brightness and energy only yards from the source.

Men and machinery flowed in constant motion on the site. We arrived right at shift change as workers streamed in and out of the makeshift gate in the security fence enclosing the construction. My palms felt sweaty despite the cold, and my stomach tightened as we drew close. I steered Rafe to the far right behind a group of workers headed in to work. We passed a string of men filing out singly and in pairs. A security guard idly scanned the crowd, a look of boredom on his face, not bothering to check IDs. He stifled a yawn as we walked by.

My breathing eased. Acasa headed for one of the trailers parked on the perimeter to check in. I went inside with him so he wouldn't get ideas, but hung back while he stepped up to a counter and signed a visitor's log. A man at a desk behind the counter reached up, lifted a hard hat off a wall peg, and placed it on the counter.

"Surprised to see anyone here so late," he said. "You know you need an escort, sir?"

I raised a hand. "That'd be me," I said before Rafe could respond. "I'll take him down. Shift super said it was okay."

The man rose far enough off his chair to peer at me over the counter. "So they know you're coming?"

"That's what I just said, isn't it?" I put a little aggravation in my voice. "Like I don't have better things to do?"

"Just checking," he said, apologetic. "You know how they are. You brassed in?"

"I'll do it on my way down."

Numbered brass tags hung on a pegboard outside the entry to the headhouse. I once asked my father what it meant when one hundred eleven men hadn't "brassed out" of the Centralia mine. Each worker down in the shaft or the tunnel, according to the old mining tradition, was assigned a number and moved it from "Out" to "In" at the beginning of a shift. When they left for the day, they moved it back to an "Out" peg, signifying they'd made it aboveground to safety one more day. My grandfather was one of those who'd never brassed out that day back in 1947.

The man nodded to Rafe. "Enjoy your visit."

I waited for Rafe to precede me out the flimsy aluminum trailer door, and we walked abreast across the site into the headhouse. On the way in, I moved a brass tag from second shift to an empty third shift "In" nail. Several men stood talking and laughing in a tight knot in front of the elevator cages, waiting for a car to ascend. They quieted quickly at our approach, nervously shuffling their feet until the cage doors opened.

We squeezed in with them and rode down in silence. A couple of them cast sidelong glances at Acasa, recognition registering on their faces. No one broke the stillness until the cage doors opened at the bottom of the shaft more than a hundred feet below. The workmen piled out, jabbering to one another as if someone had thrown a switch. They scattered in different directions. A few stood idly at the edge of the station platform.

With a nudge Rafe leaned in. "Okay, we're here," he said in a low voice. "What do you need me for?"

"This won't work if you don't help find what we're looking for." I walked up to one of the men. "Waiting for a supply train?"

He nodded.

I jerked a thumb over my shoulder. "Councilman wants to see the TBM in action. I get to babysit. Mind if we hitch a ride?"

He glanced back. "Suit yourself. No skin off my ass. He's likely to get a little dirty, though. Who is that? Acasa?"

I nodded, grinning at the thought of Acasa ruining a good suit. "He won't mind."

I waved him over. He shuffled up, looking disconsolate, like a small child who's been sent to his room.

"It's not that bad, is it, *sir*?" I said.

Rafe grimaced. "I'd rather be home in bed."

"Checking us out?" the other man said, making polite conversation.

"Right."

Rafe almost left it at that but saw the man's curious stare. "All the dignitaries come down during the day with a lot of advance notice. Figured I'd come see what happens on graveyard. You're the guys with the tough jobs."

For an ad lib, it sounded pretty good. But then that was the quality that Rafe had used to get where he was. It might take him a lot further, depending on what the night brought us.

Less than five minutes later we sat facing each other on the rim of a muck car surrounded by a half dozen other workmen, our feet tucked down inside. Rafe's tasseled leather loafers were already streaked with gray mud. The train pulled out of the lighted, open space of the station with a small jerk and accelerated to a decent clip into the black mouth of one of the twin tunnels.

Temporary tracks had been laid behind the TBM to supply the concrete liner sections put in place by the machine itself. Here in the Capitol Hill station, entrances to both north and southbound tunnels had been excavated sequentially at each end of the platform area after the main shaft was dug. The southbound tunnel running parallel to us ended only a hundred feet or so past the station, waiting for the TBM's second pass in about a year and a half.

We passed through pools of light every hundred feet or so, traveling from brightness to near darkness, lending the ride the feeling of a roller coaster moving up and down humps of track. Four flatcars stacked high with curved shells of precast concrete tunnel lining pushed through the tunnel ahead of us. A squat locomotive behind us propelled the whole load.

High up one wall, supported by rollers on steel scaffolding, a belt conveyor rattled and bounced, carrying tailings away from the behemoth up ahead. The conveyor snaked more than a mile back to a staging area in the stub tunnel where the spoils were loaded on trucks for transport to a disposal site. I scanned the concrete walls of the tunnel behind Rafe looking for anomalies, something different, but saw only a constant stream of gray turning lighter and darker shades. A low rumble slowly grew in volume to a steady roar and hum of equipment grinding away at a wall of earth and rock.

I leaned across the car and yelled over the growing din at the workman we'd spoken to on the platform. "How far has the TBM gotten?"

He shrugged. "Not sure. Under Volunteer Park, maybe." He looked around for confirmation. A couple of men nodded. The others weren't paying attention.

"Sounds like pretty good progress," I shouted. "Twenty, thirty feet a day or so?"

He nodded. "More, usually." He left it at that, communication difficult over the constant noise.

The alternating shades of gray came faster now. Lights were spaced closer together, as if the train were approaching the outskirts of a town. A few moments later, we slowed and the train came to a gentle stop. The men piled out of the muck car. Rafe and I followed alongside the train at a little distance toward the head-filling growl of the earth-eating TBM. The tunnel floor vibrated beneath our feet.

"What now?" Rafe shouted into my ear.

"Play the politician. Take the tour. Shake hands. We'll go from there."

We threaded our way through the maze of supply tanks, electrical support, and exhaust fans that stretched half the length of a football field behind the TBM itself. The flatbed cars rolled into machinery at the back end of the TBM that lifted and placed each precast liner shell in a designated spot and locked it in place with a keystone, giving the TBM something to push against as it ground steadily forward.

A steel-grid staircase led up into the bowels of the TBM. A workman met us at the top of the stairs and led us on a center catwalk deeper into the machine. The near-claustrophobic surroundings of hard steel reminded me of the German U-boat I saw as a kid on a class field trip to Chicago's Museum of Science and Industry. Near the front, workmen read the dials and gauges on control panels and made adjustments, "steering" the giant borer with hydraulic jacks. A steel ladder bolted to the bulkhead led down to a lower level.

One of the men—captain? pilot? driver?—turned to Acasa. "First time on the TBM?" he shouted. I lip-read the words more than heard them.

Rafe shook his head and held up two fingers.

The man nodded. "Questions?"

Rafe leaned in and shouted something I couldn't make out. The man pointed one way then another and shouted something back. After two similar exchanges, Rafe nodded and took a step back, slowly pivoting to take in the enormity of the machine. Nodding once more, he shook hands all around. No one bothered to accompany us out.

We backtracked out the rear of the TBM and down the stairs into the tunnel. Then waited while workers finished unloading the last concrete shell off the first flatbed car and cautiously made our way past the trailing gear into the open tunnel. The train had pulled out, moving back up the track to wait for the flatbed cars to empty.

I headed up the tunnel. Acasa hurried to catch up.

"Nicely done, Councilman," I said loudly into his ear. "You were good back there."

"What now?"

"How far would you say it is from Molly's house to Volunteer Park?" I saw him hesitate. "Don't tell me you haven't been there, Rafe. Discretion may be the better part of valor, but I'm not stupid. Not as stupid as I act sometimes, anyway."

He tipped his head. "Two blocks."

"Call it three. Say a few hundred yards? Maybe a little more?"

"And you think whatever we're supposed to find is under Molly's house? A hundred and sixty, maybe a hundred eighty feet underground? That's a hell of a deep hole. When was this supposed to have been dug?"

"Eighteen fifty or so. I don't think they dug a hole that deep. I think they dug a tunnel."

"A tunnel?"

The Sound Transit website had given me the idea that maybe Woodworth's crew had tunneled under the hill. Reyna'd said Woodworth's logs contained a single chart location—longitude and latitude in degrees, minutes, and seconds. A note in the logs with a direction and a distance had led me to the second location—Molly's house. Maps of the U Link tunnel route on the ST website showed the horizontal placement of the tunnel on a surface map. Below it, on the same page, a line chart showed the tunnel's depth along the route.

Woodworth's crew must have started digging where the church rectory's fountain was now, a quarter mile east. But instead of just dumping the gold in a pit, they'd bored a tunnel that gradually sloped down to the depth of the light-rail tunnel. It was the only scenario that made sense. The engineering it must have required was even more mind-boggling than what we'd just seen aboard the TBM.

We came up behind the motionless train. Easing alongside, I waved to the engineer as we passed. I set a brisk pace down the center of the tunnel between the rails where gravel holding the ties in place had been tamped down. I counted my steps, trying to keep track of how far we'd gone since leaving the TBM. The noise abated to a tolerable level. Rafe's breathing came hard enough to preclude talking, anyway. He huffed to keep up. Not more than twenty yards farther, the short toot of a horn turned us both around to see the train coming up behind us.

The engineer nodded curtly as he approached. Didn't bother to slow or offer us a ride. We hugged the wall and let it pass.

Light and shadow shifted in the tunnel up ahead as the train pulled away. About a hundred yards ahead the train appeared to slow and pause for a few moments. Motion along the wall caught my attention. A shadowy shape moved to the side of the train and hefted a large container that looked like a garbage can up over the edge of the muck car. Heavy, from the way he carried it. He leaned over the edge of the car for a moment, then turned around and disappeared into shadow. A moment later he reappeared and dumped another load into the muck car, going through the same motion. He ducked back into darkness once more, and when he stepped into the light again the container was gone.

He slowly diminished in size as he walked to the head of the train. Stood still a moment, then his silhouette grew larger again as he worked his way back to the muck car, something bunched in one hand growing more distinct in the light by the door. Cloth, like a canvas tarp. Shaped more like a duffel bag. But limp, empty. He slung it over the side and climbed in after it. The train pulled away, slowly vanishing from sight.

"Come on," I said, breaking into a trot. "I think we just found what we're looking for."

With a groan, Rafe matched my pace. Less than half a minute later, I pulled up short and slowed, looking for the spot where I'd seen the man's shadow meld with the tunnel wall.

"There."

Quickening my step, I pointed to a rectangular metal door set in the tunnel wall. It had no lock. I pushed down on the handle and the door swung inward easily. I ducked under the low header. Inside, the chamber was nearly pitch dark, the only light filtering in from the closest fixture in the tunnel. Even that was momentarily blotted out as Rafe came through the door behind me.

"*¡Mierda!* It's dark as a hooker's bedroom in here," he said. "Not that I would know, of course."

My eyes began to pick out shapes. Suddenly a small ice-white beam of light swung around the interior of the chamber, lighting up equipment and tools. Rafe turned around, shining a little key-ring flashlight on the doorframe behind us. Tracing a cord up a wall with the beam, he reached up and switched on a work light hanging over the door. The sudden illumination revealed a utility room, about fifteen feet square, littered with tools and equipment, tanks and motors.

The room was unfinished, roughed out, concrete walls not yet completely sealed, exposed wiring dangling from a bank of conduit leading to a big electrical panel. Four six-inch water mains capped with bronze valve wheels protruded through the cement wall. Hoses and loose cables snaked across the floor.

"This is your big treasure?" Rafe said.

I bit my lip. A response would only encourage him. I'd only trip over my tongue while my brain sorted the dozen replies whizzing by. Better, I'd learned in twenty years of marriage, not to say anything at all sometimes.

I did a slow tour of the room, waiting for something incongruous to jump out at me. The mess defied a logical sense of order. The workmen who used it probably knew exactly where to look for what they wanted. Sort of like the piles of paper that used to decorate my office. In the end, something familiar, not out of place, caught my attention. A plastic trash can stood in one corner next to a pile of construction materials—lumber, open bags of cement, lengths of conduit pipe. A muddy canvas tarp covered part of the heap. I wondered if the workman had simply been dumping some of the trash that had collected in the utility room.

"Bring your flashlight over," I said.

Rafe turned and crossed the room, curious.

"Shine it in here."

I tipped the trash can, and he aimed the beam inside. The plastic was scuffed and crusted with dust and smears of dried concrete and paint. Inside, a few small dots reflected the light like flecks of glitter from someone's discarded party decorations.

42

Rafe peered into the trash can. "What's that?"

My focus had already shifted to the pile in the corner. I took off the hard hat, pulled the tarp away, and started dismantling the stack, moving it to a clear spot on the floor. Rafe watched me in silence, not offering to help. I'd transferred about half the pile when I heard him grunt. I followed his pointed finger to see the black edges of a hole in the wall down near the floor. I cleared away more bags of cement, my pulse quickening from more than exertion.

When there was enough space, I got down on the floor and peered into the hole, seeing nothing but inky blackness.

I held out my hand. "Light."

Rafe bent over and handed me his key chain, hovering over my shoulder while I shone the tiny beam into the hole. Past the jagged six-inch lip of concrete around the hole was another foot of packed dirt. Beyond that appeared to be some open space and what looked like wood—timbers or boards, hard to tell. Maybe two and a half feet high, the hole looked big enough to squeeze through sideways. I pulled work gloves out of a hip pocket, put them on.

Raising my arms over my head, I reached through the hole, got a purchase on the dirt wall on the other side with my gloved fingers, and pulled my torso through. Wriggling my butt free, I sat up and shone the little light over my head, revealing a low chamber hollowed out of the earth, shored up with old wooden timbers. Wooden boxes banded with rusted metal straps filled the space. The small cleared area gave me just enough room to stand. I got up carefully but still managed to crack my head on one of the low beams. Boxes were stacked two high, nearly reaching the ceiling, with narrow aisles between rows. Several open boxes sat askew in a stack—all empty. I peered into an open box on top of a nearby row. Startled by the gleam of light reflected back at me, I jerked reflexively and cracked my head again.

"Damn!"

"What? What is it?" Rafe's muffled voice came from the other side of the wall. "What happened?"

"Nothing. I'm okay." I ruefully rubbed the sore spot on the back of my skull, wishing I hadn't left the hard hat behind.

I shone the light again on a layer of glittering rocks: shiny, milky-colored pieces of quartz streaked and seamed with gold. Mixed in were nuggets of pure gold ranging in size from peas to large softballs. Mesmerized, I suddenly realized I wasn't breathing. I closed my eyes and pinched the bridge of my nose with a thumb and forefinger. They opened again at the sound of scuffling behind me. Rafe poked his head around me and peered into the chest.

"*¡Madre de Dios!*" Rafe sucked a breath in between his teeth. "Is that what I think it is?"

"Don't get any ideas," I said, thinking how easy it would be to pocket a few nuggets. "You're going to be a hero, remember?"

"How much is here, do you think?" He scanned the chamber.

"A lot. Literally tons."

I worked my way down a narrow aisle between stacks of the wooden boxes, getting an approximate count. A perpendicular aisle at the far end of the chamber led me around another row. A third row beyond that was covered in dirt where a portion of the ceiling had collapsed.

"I don't think we should stay long," I said, sudden queasiness knotting my stomach into a sailor's hitch. "Ceiling's caved in over here. No telling how rotted these timbers are."

"How did this get here?" Rafe called from the darkness.

"A tunnel from somewhere over near Eighteenth Avenue. It's a long story."

"Then there should be an entrance somewhere."

He had a point. I scrabbled carefully over the mound of dirt into the last aisle over and sidled back toward the wall closest to the utility room. A gap in the crates appeared halfway down the aisle. I shone the light into the black hole in the wall. Five or six feet in, a sloped wall of dirt blocked the passage.

"It's here," I said, "but it's blocked. Either a cave-in, or they deliberately blocked the passage on their way out."

"Anything else here besides boxes of rocks?" He laughed.

I did, too, giddy with apprehension. Images of old episodes of *The Flintstones* ran through my head, Fred pulling rocks out of his wallet to pay for a new TV.

I eased my way back, panning the light from side to side to see if I'd missed anything. At the top of the dirt mound I nearly banged my head on a timber again. Squeezing through the tight space my foot slipped in the loose soil, and I slid unceremoniously on my ass down the other side. Feet splayed, I dug in my heels and came to an abrupt stop when one foot hit something solid under the dirt.

"What the hell are you doing over there?" Rafe said.

"Hang on. I may have found something."

Metal the color of brass gleamed dully in the light. I brushed more dirt away, slowly uncovering a small, carved wooden chest with brass fittings. I found a handle on one side and wrenched it free. Dirt covered a brass padlock hanging from a hasp on the front. I wiped it off and tugged on the lock—secure. Tucking the box under one arm, I stood and scuffed back over to Rafe, hunching to keep from cracking my head on the timbers.

"About time," Rafe said when I reached him. "Never did like being in the dark."

I motioned at the open crate with the little light. "You pocket a few of those?"

He didn't answer for a moment. I shone the light on his face.

"I was tempted," he said, "but no, I didn't."

"You should." He looked surprised. "Proof," I told him. "Who'd believe you?"

"I see what you mean."

He stepped closer to the crate. I handed him the light, and he pawed through the top layer of rocks. He came up with a couple of small loose gold nuggets and two pieces of quartz smaller than a fist laced with gold veins. He slipped them into a deep pocket of his topcoat.

"What have you got?" he said.

"Don't know," I said. "Let's go see."

He turned and got down on all fours, not giving his suit a second thought. I had to give him credit. He scooted through the hole into the utility room. I shoved the chest through and followed, blinking as I emerged into the relative brightness. Rafe was searching through the pile of construction materials. He brought back a length of iron pipe and a short-handled sledge.

"Try the hasp hinge," I said. "It doesn't look as sturdy as the lock."

Placing one end of the pipe against the hasp, he banged on the other with the sledge. After four or five swings, he got into a rhythm and put more *oomph* into each blow. The hasp finally broke free with a clink. I raised the lid and aimed the light inside. Nestled in a piece of sepia-toned oilcloth lay two small medicine vials with cork stoppers, about three inches tall and half an inch wide, the thick, green-tinted glass wavy, irregular. Rust-colored flakes coated the inside.

Rafe reached for the one of the bottles. "Old wine?"

I swatted his hand away, breaking into a cold sweat. "Are you nuts? You haven't been listening. This thing could make people sick. We may already be exposed."

"What the hell are you talking about?"

"Look, we don't have time for the long version. I already told you, this is what the nuns wanted hidden, the bioweapon that Gagnon's after."

He jumped backward and crabbed away from the chest. "You mean we could catch whatever's in that?"

"Maybe. I don't know. But I'd rather let someone else find out what's in it, wouldn't you?"

I picked up the leather book and pulled the string. I tried to read some of the flowery script on a dry, brittle page yellowed with age. Dates, positions, notations on weather all suggested a captain's log—Woodworth's log. I tucked it into a jacket pocket.

"What are you doing?"

"It's not that I don't trust you, Rafe, but I don't trust you. My freedom's on the line here."

"What about that?" He gestured toward the chest.

"Leave it here. Let the guys in the hazmat suits deal with it." I closed the lid and hefted the little box. I hid it in a corner and turned to face him. "Come on. Help me put this place back the way we found it."

We reassembled the pile of building materials in front of the hole in the wall. When we finished it was hard to tell anyone had been there. Rafe brushed his hands off and stood admiring our work. I walked to the door and opened it a crack, peering out to see if anyone was close enough to notice our exit. Nothing except the distant rumble of the giant TBM grinding its way north, and the rattle of the conveyor rollers. I opened the door a little farther and eased out, motioning for Acasa to follow. Out in the tunnel, we walked abreast in silence for a few minutes.

"What's your plan?" Rafe said finally.

Exhaustion rilled through me, clouding my thoughts. Stifling a yawn, I pushed it aside. I was improvising. In the hours I'd had to think about it after leaving Molly with Jane I still had no clue. But I'd made progress. I'd found what the US government and a rogue French agent were looking for. I'd found maybe two hundred million reasons to kill someone.

Images, memories danced in my head. The crunch of gravel under our feet, the clammy air against my cheek, the shadows on the walls, the rattle of the conveyor dangled like bait, convincing my attention to take nibbles, tugging my concentration away from the problem.

"We take it to the naval intelligence officer in charge," I decided. "Tell her what we found and let her set up a surveillance team. We don't know how many people are involved. Two that we know of. Maybe more. They catch whoever's stealing the gold. You take the credit. I get the cops to look at someone else for murder. Maybe stay out of jail. And somebody figures out what's bottled up in those vials before it kills us all."

The tunnel ahead brightened where it curved to the south, and the syncopated *clackety-clack* of train wheels rolling up the tracks reached our ears. Shadows shifted and danced as the sound grew louder, and the engine's single headlight hovered in the darkness, turning the bend until it shone directly in our eyes. I moved close to the wall as it approached. Rafe followed me. The engineer—a different one due to the shift change—looked at us curiously as he drove by, but said nothing.

Once the loaded flatbed cars cleared us, we meandered back to the center of the tunnel and kept walking. Rafe was subdued, head down, silent, and seemed to be thinking something through. I let him stew. I had my own issues to ponder. The meds were wearing off.

"You didn't have a clue, did you?" I said.

His head came up. "About Dan? I knew he was ambitious. He's good at what he does."

"Would you put him on your staff if you got a chance to move up?"

He was silent. "Higher office, you mean. Never thought about it."

"Bringing Whiting along? Why not?"

I saw the outline of his shoulders rise and fall in the dim tunnel.

"Look, I had no idea he could be behind those missing funds. He's always done the job. Done it well."

"But…?"

"He pushes too hard. Looks for expediency instead of doing the right thing. Tries to cut corners, work the system. Playing politics is my job description. For me, that means finding workable answers to tough questions. For Dan, I think it means getting what he wants."

"He wants it all, Rafe."

"Maybe." He fell silent.

I'd underestimated Rafe. He wasn't the egotistical moron I'd made him out to be. Shriver's initial assessment may have pegged him right. An *oxy*moron—an honest politician.

* * *

Reyna had to hand it to SPD. So far, they'd been speedy and efficient in complying with all her requests. And it wasn't solely due to the fact that the department had been on heightened alert since one of its own had been killed in the line of duty. But that had certainly honed their focus and nerves to a keen edge. The precinct squad room swirled with activity.

"Got it!" a unit sergeant shouted over the buzz. "Dispatch says they found the rental car!"

The room quieted.

"Where?" Reyna said.

The sergeant walked to a precinct map on the wall and pointed to a location. "Here. Parked on a residential street. No one in the car."

"Give me the lay of the land," Reyna said hurriedly. "Landmarks, type of neighborhood…"

"Main streets are commercial," he said. "Side streets are residential, apartment buildings mostly. Seattle Central here, Seattle University campus here."

"Any major construction projects nearby?"

"Sure. Light-rail station is a couple blocks away."

Reyna tensed. "Get me a ride over there, Sergeant! Now!"

* * *

Less than ten minutes later, the muck train caught up just as we approached the bright lights and cacophony of men and machinery in the enormous cavern slowly being transformed into the station platform. I steered Rafe toward one of the cage lifts. We rode up the way we'd come down, wary and silent.

At the top, I opened the cage door, feeling for the first time in weeks as if waking and shrugging off a terrible nightmare. Cold night air wafted through the steel skeleton of the headhouse. I took a deep breath. A puff of breeze billowed a huge sheet of translucent plastic wrapped around the girders and snapped it taut with a gentle crack. My eyes followed the sound, and a face just beyond the chain link construction fence sent my heart into my mouth.

Gagnon!

Gagnon looked at the gate as if considering whether to bluff his way in or find a way through the fence somewhere. Without thinking, I turned back around, bumping into Rafe. As a confused Rafe tried to protest, I shoved him to the back of the cage, where he lost his balance and sprawled on the floor. I yanked the doors closed behind us and stabbed the "Down" button as a voice shouted from a different direction.

"Sanders!"

Dan Whiting stood on the steps of the office trailer, vulpine face twisted in a snarl. He broke into a run as the cage started its descent. Before we dropped out of sight, a last glance at Gagnon showed him following Whiting's path with his eyes until they reached mine. His mouth slowly widened into a wolfish grin.

Rafe picked himself up and thrust an angry red face at me. "What the hell was that for?"

"There's a very bad man up there with a gun," I said. "He wants me dead."

"So what? You've got one, too."

I shrugged, palms held out, and gave him a wry smile. "Sorry."

"You bluffed?" His face turned a shade darker. "You fucking bluffed?" He dug into a pocket. "I'm calling the cops."

"Be my guest. Sounds like a good idea about now."

He held a phone to his ear. "Who was yelling at you, anyway?"

"Whiting."

"Dan?" He looked startled. "What's he doing here this time of night?"

I wondered the same thing.

He pulled the phone away and studied it. "No fucking service. Just my luck. Stuck on an elevator with a nut job who's being chased by a killer. Who'd you say the guy is?"

I shook my head. "Doesn't matter. What matters is that he's already killed a couple people, and won't have any compunction about killing a few more to get to me. He's after those bottles we found. Or whatever's in them. The gold, too."

It was all coming apart. I felt sweat break out under my arms.

"Rafe, this guy doesn't know you. I don't think he saw you. You have to get out of here and call Reyna Chase. Lieutenant Commander Reyna Chase, with ONI."

His anger flared. "Why?"

"Look, if your pride's wounded, take your best shot. Hit me. But I need you to do this. It's the only way I get off the hook with the cops. Reyna's the only one who knows what's going on. She can find out who's behind this."

"If I don't?" His chin jutted.

"If the guy catches me, you're screwed. Shriver writes the story, and you go down."

He hesitated, finally nodding. I gave him Reyna's number and watched him program it into his cell phone.

The cage jerked to a stop at the bottom of the shaft. I yanked the door open and walked out, not bothering to look back.

"Hey, wait!" Rafe called. "Where are you going?"

For a moment I felt trapped, a cornered animal, heart hammering, mind furiously churning, looking for a way out. The twin tunnel entrances excavated by the huge machinery and armies of workmen yawned blackly at both ends of the cavernous space. *South!* The tunnel had been bored clear through from downtown. I headed that way. I heard Rafe's footsteps behind me.

"Go back," I said. "They'll be coming down after me in the other car. You get out of here. Take this car back up and maybe you'll miss them at the top."

"Wait a minute!" he said. "That's it? What do I do?"

I didn't bother turning. "Call Chase. Tell her everything. Don't call SPD. They'll never believe you."

The footsteps stopped. "What about Dan?" he called after a moment.

"Fire him," I said over my shoulder.

After only a few hurried steps into the tunnel entrance I heard my name shouted over the din of construction. Without pausing, I glanced back and saw Whiting walking down the platform toward me, ignoring Rafe. Rafe sidestepped, intercepting him, and I caught snippets of his angry voice over the constant hum.

His problem now. Time to move. I broke into a slow jog.

A sharp *pop* echoed from the chamber behind me. I slowed long enough to turn and see Rafe slump to the ground. Whiting stepped around him, a dark object in his hand held low, close to his leg, glinting metallically. Workers at the other end of the platform had stopped to see where the sound had come from, too, but they were too far away to stop Whiting even if they figured out what had just happened. It was enough to jolt me into a sprint down the dark tube already gently curving east on its way to Pine Street and the Westlake station downtown.

Darkness thickened around me as the lights from the platform disappeared from view. Lighted fixtures on the tunnel walls sat farther apart here since much of the work in this part of the tunnel had been completed. I welcomed the shadows, pumping my legs even faster through the pools of white that exposed me. I stripped off the hard hat and reflective vest as I ran.

Quiet slowly descended, a shroud that muffled the incessant, irritating man-made sounds of progress. Every running step took me farther away from the dissonance of the worksite. In the growing stillness, my breathing rasped loudly, lungs heaving to send more oxygen to swinging limbs. My heart thumped loudly and rhythmically in my chest, each pulse singing in my ears. I heard thoughts again, streaming through my consciousness like salmon returning upriver to spawn.

Had Gagnon found a way into the construction site yet? Why had Whiting shot Rafe? Was Molly safe? Wasn't that my favorite perfume she'd been wearing earlier? Had Cole had any last-minute regrets before he realized it was too late to call for help, too late to pump the barbiturates out of his stomach? Had he, like Liz Tracey, wanted only enough time to see what flying felt like, but not enough to turn back? What did I have for breakfast? When was the last time I ate?

Focus!

The muffled sound of another set of footsteps echoed down the tunnel. Adrenaline surged through my tired limbs. It hit me then. What I should have figured out long ago. I told Molly some-one must know about the gold. Not Gagnon. He was after what-ever the nuns were supposed to protect. Sophie Clare's legacy—*la peste.*

Whiting. Whiting must have stumbled across the gold when he was down here on a photo shoot or a VIP tour. God, how stu-pid I'd been. It had been right in front of me all this time.

Like a funnel cloud descending from an ominous low-hang-ing black spring thundercloud over the town of my youth, black-ness narrowed my vision and a storm exploded inside me with the force of a twister. Blood flowed in my veins like F5 winds, pushing me into a steady rhythm, feet on packed gravel, arms swinging, running dead center between the iron rails gleam-ing in the dim light. For a moment, the repetitiveness and sheer exertion of running brought a kind of peace, awareness and acceptance of my present, of the moment. And then the storm exploded again. Its winds howled in my ears. Lightning crackled in my brain, filling my mouth with the taste of pennies.

I wasn't running from anything, anymore. I was running *to* something.

I needed a weapon.

43

Over the soft whir and rattle of the conveyor, fast footsteps crunched the gravel heavily behind me, louder now. My knee throbbed with the pounding of each stride. Whiting's age and conditioning gave him a huge advantage, allowing him to eat steadily into my lead. I'd gone flat out for the first quarter mile and now felt the effects, the air sawing in and out of my lungs turning my throat raw, lactate in my legs building to a point of acidosis.

A sharp toot from up ahead shocked me out of my concentration on the ties that flashed beneath my feet. The supply train was on its way back, the lead car not more than a hundred feet away. I leaped to the side, pressing myself against the cold concrete, and awkwardly sidestepped to keep moving away from Whiting's pursuit. The train would slow him, too. As soon it cleared, I broke into a run again.

The tunnel straightened. Up ahead, lights on the wall sharply veered left and vanished where the tunnel widened and turned into the Pine Street stub. Not far, maybe a few hundred yards. If I could make the next curve, I'd be out of sight and range long enough that I might reach the safety in numbers at the Westlake station.

"Sanders!" Whiting's voice echoed in the tunnel.

I threw a glance over my shoulder and saw his shadowy form still a hundred yards back, no longer obscured by the curve in the tunnel.

"Give it up, Blake!" he said, voice loud in the tunnel.

I didn't answer, my attention already focused on some sort of machinery hulking in the shadows where the tunnel doubled in width ahead. A loud explosion reverberated off the walls, knocking my heart against my ribs and sending my legs flying faster. A bullet whined off cement. I feinted left and cut right, angling for cover behind the machinery. Behind it, I paused to lean against the cold metal for a moment and suck in lungs full of air.

Quickly, I eased forward to see Whiting's progress. He passed through one of the pools of light farther back, moving cautiously now, close to the far wall. I ducked down out of sight and took stock. The smell of tar filled my nostrils. I looked more closely at the machinery next to me. The deck of a large asphalt paver loomed nearly six feet high and about eight feet wide. My gaze climbed the narrow steel-runged ladder near the back to a single bucket seat mounted up in the center of the machine. There was only one, not the dual seats on either side of the wide pavers that laid asphalt out on the freeways. This paver was narrow enough to lay a level floor in the bored tunnel. A control panel was situated in front of the seat. The engine housing stretched out a few feet forward of the controls with a long hopper in front of that, hiding me from view. A fat chrome exhaust pipe rose over the engine, providing even more cover.

"You've got nowhere to go," Whiting called. "Let's talk about this."

I risked a peek around the front of the hopper, staying deep in the shadows along the wall. He stood maybe fifty feet away, outlined at the edge of the circle of light spilling from the closest fixture, his face in shadow. I cupped a hand around my mouth and faced away from him to make it more difficult for him to pinpoint my location.

"Nothing to talk about," I said.

"Sure there is," he said. "I'm sure we can come to some sort of understanding here."

"Like you and Rafe just did? No thanks."

I saw him tense, but his voice was honeyed. "He said you told him I've been ripping off his war chest. Now why would you say a thing like that? I thought we were friends."

"Must be true, though, huh? Why shoot him otherwise?"

"You find the gold?" he said, his voice sounding different.

My head jerked up, and I slunk forward to see why. He was on the move, silently treading one of the rails toward me, putting one foot carefully in front of the other, making his way deeper into shadow. When I didn't answer, he stopped, cocking his head to listen.

I tipped my head back and spoke to the ceiling. "Yeah, I did."

"Lot of reasons there to make some sort of deal, Blake. What you're making these days, paperboy, you can't tell me it isn't tempting. How'd you find out, anyway?"

"Long story short, Midge found an old diary."

"Nosy old bitch!"

The venom in his voice jogged something free from the recesses of my memory—the uncontrolled rage that someone had loosed on Midge, carving her up so badly that her blood had spray-painted her kitchen floor. It all became so clear I wondered why I hadn't seen it before. Whiting knew everything about the light-rail project, spent a lot of time on site. And he would have quickly heard about Midge's push for an injunction against Sound Transit; monitoring and containing rumors was part of his job. Midge would have posed an enormous threat.

"That was a mistake, Dan. You might have gotten away with killing Midge. But framing me? You really hate me that much? I mean, I get it. You knew Midge and I were friends. So, you waited around after you killed her until I showed up, and phoned the cops. But it was a mistake."

I put my foot on the bottom rung of the ladder and pulled myself up for a quick glance over the top of the paver. He crept closer. I hopped down and scrabbled toward the back of the machine, ankle suddenly turning when I stepped on a rock. I reached down and groped in the dark, my hand closing over a rough chunk of asphalt half the size of my fist. I took a step up the ladder again, rose up on my toes, and imagined a small forward cutting across the paint toward the hoop as I shoveled a hard pass right at Whiting's silhouette. The rock struck him somewhere high up near one shoulder.

He twisted away with a sharp cry.

"You might want to hold your ground right there. I've got lots more of those."

"Motherfucker," he said, backing away warily. "Fine, but you'll have to come out some time. I can wait."

I needed a better weapon than a chunk of asphalt, and a way to keep him talking while I found it. "You brought the gold out in the muck car on the supply train. How'd you get it past everyone on the other end? All the truck drivers?"

I ducked down and slithered to the back of the machine. Posts mounted on either side of the bucket seat rose toward the ceiling, topped by large square halogen lamps. I saw another pair at the front of the tractor, between the engine and the hopper. Everything was bolted down. Nothing, not a scrap of metal on the big beast, was loose.

I flashed back to the sight of the train stopped in front of the utility room after it passed Rafe and me. "Let me guess. It never got that far. Your guys loaded it into tool bags before the train reached the station. Just walked off site with it at the end of their shift. Nobody the wiser."

I inspected the side and back of the paver again while I talked, eyes burning into the shadows, feeling my way with my hands. A pole of some sort leaned against the tunnel wall a few feet behind the paver. I inched my way toward it in a crouch, hugging the wall.

"We're wasting time here." His voice was impatient.

I crawled close enough to the pole to see a long-handled screed with a three-foot-wide blade at the bottom that workmen used to help spread the asphalt. Useless to me. Too big and awkward. I climbed up a rung and peered over the top of the machine. Whiting had moved a little closer again.

"Looks like it's all falling apart on you, Dan. Who else knows? You going to try to kill us all? The guys who are in on it with you, too? And you don't think at least someone back there in the main shaft recognized you?"

"The others won't talk. I can lay low, let them bring out the gold for me."

"You think so? Hell, I bet you didn't even find the gold yourself. Some construction worker did, and you just took advantage. You don't think they'll talk to save their own skins?"

"How naïve are you?" he said. "They didn't even know what they had until I stumbled onto them in the utility room. *I* came up with the plan to get the stuff out. They do what *I* say."

Rage like molten rock seethed through me, seared my brain, excising extraneous thoughts, cauterizing them, clarifying everything else.

"You think we're the only ones who know about this?" I said. "Where do you think the gold came from?"

He didn't answer. Apparently hadn't considered it.

"Newsflash: government agents on two continents have been homing in on that stash for weeks. They know I'm down here right now. This place will be crawling with cops any minute."

I heard him chuckle again and went up the ladder again to check on him.

"You are so full of shit. Hell of an imagination, though, I'll give you that. Worthless, otherwise."

He'd moved a little closer, increasing my sense of urgency. I climbed up another rung and leaned into the cab to look for anything I could use.

"Worthless? Seems you learned a few things from me along the way."

"From you? How to kiss ass and nearly fuck up everything you touch?" I heard the hard edge in his voice now.

"You wanted to move up. Everyone does. I would have helped you get ahead."

He barked derisively. "*You?* You played by the rules. You never would have gotten Rafe into the governor's mansion."

"It's all falling apart, Danny boy. Too messy. Not smart enough."

I stretched to get a better look at the control panel. Covered with knobs, dials, and toggle switches, the labels and icons were unreadable in the dark. I searched for the ignition switch. Sure enough, no one had been kind or foolish enough to leave a key. But a memory from my youth planted the germ of an idea.

Other memories intruded. I frowned.

Whiting hadn't just wanted to ride Rafe's coattails to Olympia. He wanted the whole package. Money. Power. Rafe himself. All those years working with him, I hadn't seen beyond the usual ambition of a smart associate on the way up the corporate ladder. No one had. A classic sociopath? But he was losing it, his actions bolder, more desperate. More vicious, his rage coming to the surface. He'd killed the street kid, I was sure, not just to make the frame stick against me, but because he'd enjoyed it.

Rafe himself...

The look in Whiting's eyes as they'd followed Rafe around the room at the fundraiser popped into my head. The way Whiting's assistant had watched *him*. And I suddenly flashed back to another memory. A day when Cole had met me at the office for lunch during a break from classes. Poking his head into my office as I wrapped up a short meeting with Whiting. The broad smile on his face slowly dissolving into that same expression for an instant. I hadn't understood it then, hadn't read its meaning.

A horrible realization closed over me like water over a drowning man.

"Cole was your lover." As they left my lips, the words ripped an even bigger hole out of my chest than I ever would have imagined possible. "You dumped him. He killed himself over you."

I held my breath as if to keep night monsters at bay.

Whiting's harsh laughter tempered the molten slag boiling inside me as if he'd thrust it into ice water, hardening it into steely resolve.

"I didn't break it off," he said. "He did."

"You broke his heart."

Desperate now to release all the pent-up energy, to avenge my son, I got down and scoured the paver from front to back again.

"Too bad, too. The boy was a sweet fuck," Whiting said as I searched.

My jaw clenched. The paver cut into my palms I gripped it so tightly. Two steel hooks, half-hidden by the ladder protruding from the side of the paver, finally wormed their way into my consciousness. A bucket hung from one, a straight-bladed shovel from the other. I lifted the shovel, careful not to bang it against the ladder.

"The real joke in all this? Cole didn't kill himself over me. You're the reason he fell apart."

"Bullshit!"

"Cole found out about the dummy accounts I set up. I told him you must have done it. At first he believed me just like everyone else did when it came out. He slowly figured it out, though. He saw my interest in Rafe's career growing and got jealous. Smart kid, Blake. I'll give you that. You didn't raise any dummy."

He was baiting me. Looking for an opening. Trying to distract me. Using my own ruse against me. Big mistake. Now it didn't matter if I made it out of the tunnel alive as long as he didn't. I went up the ladder again, all the way into the cab this time, and crouched behind the control panel, thinking it through. Whiting had gotten closer. I could see his head turn, trying to spot me.

I gave him one more chance to reveal some shred of humanity.

"He cared about you, Dan. God knows why. And you treated him like a cheap trick? He was just a kid. How could you do that to him?"

"What would you have done if you were Cole, I wonder? Who would you have betrayed? Your father or your lover? My, my, caught in a dilemma. Sharp horns on that beast." His voice went flat and hard. "That's what killed him. Not me. He made his choice. Turns out he couldn't live with it. Too bad."

My hands gripped the shovel so tightly I thought I'd crush the wood handle. My ears burned, and my heart ached for my son with a pain unlike any I'd ever felt before. I wanted to scream, to leap off the machine and bash his head in. He was too far away. I'd never reach him before he cut me down. I mustered the resolve to find my *ujjayi* breath, felt its calming influence, oxygen flowing through my body.

I turned to bounce my voice off the wall and dangled some bait of my own.

"You were nothing to Acasa, Dan," I said. With silent apologies to Cole, I let the storm inside gather up poisonous words and hurl them at him. "He would rather have eaten a plate of warm shit than touch a flaming little faggot like you. You think Rafe could ever love someone like you? He was dating my ex-wife! He lusted after women, not you. Hey, I'm glad Olympia finally legalized same-sex marriage, but do you really think even if Rafe had the slightest interest that he would've risked his political career for an openly gay relationship? With you?"

"Fuck you!" He extended his arm and squeezed off a shot that *whanged* into the metal hopper, sending me diving for the steel deck. He fired two more shots in quick succession, the explosions nearly deafening in the enclosed space, one of them close enough to pepper me with chips of concrete and a shower of dust. He fired off a couple more rounds.

When the echoes faded, I rose up for a look, ears still ringing. He stood motionless, holding his head in his hands, gun pointed at the ceiling. I wondered how many bullets he had left, how close I could get before they stopped me.

Shifting shadows behind him suddenly caught my attention.

44

The radio in the patrol car Reyna rode in squawked as the dispatcher came on air.

"All units in the vicinity of Edward-One, shooting reported at Broadway and John. Use extreme caution. Suspect armed and dangerous. All units, vicinity of the Link light-rail station, Broadway and John, shots fired."

"That's it!" Reyna said. "Let's go!"

The officer behind the wheel had already punched the accelerator.

* * *

The moving shadow took form. A man edged stealthily along the tunnel wall, his shoes on concrete, not gravel. I prayed it was a cop. He glided quickly through a pool of light and back into shadow like a wraith. *Gagnon!* He'd finally made it to the party. Now I faced two guns instead of one. That complicated matters.

Whiting stood stock-still, eyes closed as if listening intently. I marked Gagnon's progress. He moved with surprising speed considering the care he took in making a noiseless approach. He focused his attention on Whiting, throwing occasional glances toward the paver. He hadn't looked anywhere near my hiding place yet, but he knew I had to be in the tunnel somewhere.

Silently, I rose up on my knees and cupped a big hand over a bank of toggle switches on the control panel, seeing how many I could cover at one time. Almost all of them. I peered around the panel over the long cowling stretching toward the hopper in front.

Gagnon skulked close to the wall where the paver sat parked, closing steadily. Still keeping an eye on Whiting, he leaned over for a quick look down the space between the paver and the wall, looking for me. He slowed and stopped several yards in front of the paver, still positioned slightly behind Whiting. The thrum of tension in my muscles matched the steady hum of the conveyor belt carrying spoils out of the tunnel.

Gagnon leveled his gun at Whiting and squatted down for another quick look alongside the paver. He stood, all his attention on Whiting now. I tensed, clutching the shovel in one hand and placing my other palm lightly on the toggle switches. I put a foot up on the lip of the cowling, took a deep breath, and held it.

"I think you better put down the gun," Gagnon said loudly.

Startled, Whiting jerked his head up, whirled and fired wildly in Gagnon's direction. Gagnon's gun spit two fat cigars of flame and Whiting crumpled where he stood. Before he hit the ground, I squeezed my eyes shut tight and flipped every toggle switch on the board at once. Bright light turned the inside of my eyelids red. I waited a beat, flipped off the switches, jumped onto the flat top of the paver's massive engine, and threw on a burst of speed.

Three strides took me to the edge of the cowling. I leaped high enough to scrape my knuckles on the high arc of the twenty-foot ceiling. Landing hard, I hit the asphalt running. Nothing felt broken. Gagnon swung toward the paver, gun arm outstretched, the other raised to shield his eyes. He waved his gun arm back and forth wildly, night blind from the sudden glare of the halogens.

Perhaps for the first time in a year, I could see clearly, even in the darkness. I brandished the shovel like an ax, cocking it back over my shoulder as I charged Gagnon with the force of an enraged bull elephant. I brought it down hard, intending to cleave his skull in two. He got his arm up higher and squeezed off a shot. I heard a loud crack as the force of the shovel blow sent a satisfactory jolt up the handle into my hands and arms. Gagnon grunted in shock and pain as the shovel blade bit through flesh and shattered his ulna. I didn't feel the bee sting of pain along a rib on my left side until a split second later, followed by an eruption of searing heat. I gasped.

Focus!

Shoving the pain aside the way I once had on the basketball court before the agony from the osteomyelitis had become unbearable, I gripped the shovel tighter. I swung it sideways, sweeping the gun out of his hand with a loud *clang*. It clattered against the concrete and skittered across the asphalt, disappearing in the dark.

Gagnon backpedaled, retreating out of range of the shovel. He managed a toothy grin despite the pain that had caused sweat to break out on his brow, glinting wetly in the dim light. He held his injured arm tightly against his chest, hand dangling limply, useless. "I was beginning to think you were nothing but a coward, but you bite back. Good for you."

His accent was so thick I almost didn't understand him. I squared off, facing him with the shovel in both hands in front of me, waiting for the inevitable attack.

The first two spinning roundhouse kicks came at me in a blur of speed that sucked the breath out of me. I blocked the first with the shovel, but caught part of the second on the fake hip with enough force to jar me to one side. Before I had time to catch my balance, he advanced again with a leaping front snap kick. I backed away, avoided it. He quickly followed with an ax kick that knocked the shovel out of my hands, letting him chop at my face with his good hand. Blocking him just in time, I stepped into him with a hard jab under his ribs that slowed him. He leaped back into a fighting stance, looking for another point of attack.

He came at me again with a flurry of kicks, forcing me back. My arms flailed from side to side, mimicking the blocking motions from all the *poomsae*, the forms Cole and I learned in tae kwon do. I heard Cole's cheery voice in my head, egging me on. Gagnon's speed was tremendous, but I had a longer reach, and he had to get in close to land any blows. My side throbbed, sweatshirt and jacket sticky with blood.

At the *dojang* my lack of concentration and flailing limbs had sometimes amused Master Han. But he'd also said unpredictability could work in my favor. "If it works," he'd said, "use it." This was no *dojang*. Gagnon was here to kill me.

Attack is your best defense.

I waded in before he had a chance to strike, kicking and punching, feinting and jabbing, regaining ground. He blocked most of what I threw at him, but the few grunts of pain I forced from his lips told me I landed some solid blows. I feinted and stomped his instep, used my momentum to bring my other knee up into his groin. He twisted his thigh into the way. I drove my knee deep into the muscle and he gasped. Close enough to smell his breath, I saw his face grimace into a mask of fury. He threw a knife-edge blow to the wound in my side.

With a roar of pain, I leaped away.

Focus! Ignore the pain. Expect to be hurt.

He advanced, taking advantage, using his feet like fists, whirling and spinning, hammering me with a barrage of walloping kicks. The dimness made it difficult to read his body movements, to anticipate what he might do next. I parried each thrust as best as I could, buffeted by each jarring blow, the aching pain growing too hard to ignore.

Use your rage as a weapon.

The sight of Whiting's body behind him jolted me. Whiting was the reason my son was dead. Whiting had been the catalyst that had sent Cole into a depression so deep there'd been no saving him. For that, I wanted to make him pay, to suffer, to feel the pain he'd caused Molly and me. But Gagnon had taken that away from me, had snuffed him out as easily as a guttering candle. And with Whiting dead, I had little chance of proving my innocence. I'd lost it all—my son, wife, job, my reputation, my pride. All I had left were survival instinct and my heart hammering in my ears.

I planted my back foot, let Gagnon's next kick bring him inside the reach of my long arms, and punched him in the face with a combination of jabs. His head snapped back; he staggered. I bore down, slashing and punching, trying to find an opening, concentrating on his right side where he couldn't use his arm to block the blows. I saw a wide, dark trickle of blood cover half his chin where I'd split his lip. I kneed him as if marching in place, preventing him from throwing a kick. I stayed in close, crowded him, kept him off balance, giving him no room to counter.

Survival instinct consumed me, pumped my muscles full of adrenaline, my psyche full of omnipotence. Gagnon was younger, faster, better trained. I was more determined—to live, to avenge my son.

We traded places now, his back to the paving machine. I could see his features by the dim light behind me. His eyes widened. He didn't face a scared civilian, but some otherworldly creature. I saw reflected in his eyes something I hadn't known existed inside me.

In my split-second lapse of attention, he dropped into a low crouch and swung his leg in a powerful arc that cut both of mine out from under me. I collapsed like an imploded Vegas hotel, toppled down on him with the imaginary sound of someone yelling "Timber!" reverberating through my head. He grabbed a fistful of fabric under my throat as I came down, rolled onto his back, put a foot into my belly and neatly flipped me.

The world tipped upside down as I arced high over his head. I landed flat on my back at the edge of the tracks, air rushing from my lungs with a *whoosh*. My diaphragm convulsed trying to suck in a breath. Paralyzed, I desperately turned my head from side to side to see where he'd gone. Half of Whiting's ghostly pale face appeared above the iron rail just inches away. I twisted my head away from that ghastly vision and saw Gagnon roll across the asphalt away from me. He bounced to his feet with the shovel grasped in his good hand.

I thrashed my arms. The pumping action seemed to loosen my diaphragm enough to finally draw in a huge gulp of air as Gagnon ran toward me, the shovel angled over his head like a tomahawk. I couldn't let him win. Not now. Not this close to getting my life back, to ending my own night blindness.

My hand brushed something metallic and cold. *Whiting's gun.* My fingers curled around the butt, the knurled grip comforting in my grasp. Gagnon stood over me and raised the shovel high. I lifted my arm and squeezed the trigger, the explosion filling Gagnon's face with shock. As the barrel rose with the recoil, I fired once more. This time one side of his face caved in on itself and disappeared in a froth of blood, black in the subterranean night. His lifeless body crumpled in a heap.

I rolled over and heaved bile into the gravel, my stomach clenching like a vise over and over. Breathing heavily, I wiped my mouth on my sleeve and slowly lifted my head. The track gleamed brightly and flickered gently as a beam of light hove into view and drew steadily closer. The single beam of a supply train engine's headlight turned into several as men on board aimed flashlights down the tunnel.

I rose up on my knees and feebly waved my arms.

45

I watched the two of them enter and stamp the rain off their shoes and the cold out of their bones. The younger one cupped his hands in front of his face and blew on them while his eyes roved the room. Charlie and Downing always looked different out of uniform, almost like father and son. Charlie put his hand on Downing's shoulder and gave it a little push as if reminding him what he'd come for. With a start the younger man strode down the aisle between the tables. Charlie followed. Their route took them right past me. As they approached, I caught Downing's eye and nodded. His face reddened and he turned his eyes away.

My gaze slid to the man behind him. "Coffee, Charlie?" I tipped my head toward the two cups of coffee sitting at empty chairs around my table.

Charlie stopped Downing with a hand on his shoulder again, turning him in midstride.

"Morning," he said. "Don't mind if we do." He threw a hard glance at Downing.

"Morning, Legs," Downing said, eyes downcast.

"Officer Downing," I acknowledged, watching him quickly slide into the seat on my right. Charlie eased into the chair opposite mine.

"Call me Craig," Downing said. "We're off duty."

"You don't look too bad," Charlie said, his gaze taking a stroll across my face.

"Feels worse than it looks."

An attempt at a smile turned into a wince as I sat up straight. The raw stitched skin under the bandage on my side hurt like blazes as the slight movement stretched it, and every muscle in my body felt as if it had been hammered with a mallet. I ached in places I'd forgotten I had.

"I heard the bigwigs at Molly's firm were mighty busy over the weekend convincing the PA not to file charges," Charlie said. "Congratulations."

"Thanks. It's not a done deal yet."

"Well, they kept you out of jail for the time being at least. That's a good thing, right?" He paused. "You're still an asshole, you know." His voice didn't hold a hint of animosity, but Downing turned pink again.

"Professional or personal opinion?" I said.

"Both. What the hell were you thinking down there?"

I blinked. "Not a lot besides staying alive."

He shook his head. "I can't figure if you're just plain stupid or have the biggest balls of anyone I know."

I heard admiration in his voice and coughed, putting a hand to my mouth to hide a smile.

"If you're going to go around discharging firearms," he said, "maybe I should take you to the range with me some day and teach you the proper way to handle them."

He looked at Downing, who shrugged, then turned his head suddenly.

I followed his gaze to the door and saw Reyna Chase shake an umbrella before closing it neatly and casting a glance around the restaurant. Charlie craned his neck to see what we were staring at. He let out a low whistle. She smiled and headed our direction.

"Hel-lo," he said, facing me. "You know this one?"

"Naval intelligence," I said.

His eyebrows rose. "Ah," he said, putting it together. "Molly know?"

I gave him a look to shut him up and stood up for Reyna as she approached.

"Didn't expect to see you again," I said. "Get you some coffee?"

She looked radiant despite the early hour, no sign of weariness on her face. "Sorry, I can't stay long."

I made introductions and invited her to sit in the remaining empty chair. "Sure I can't get you anything?"

She shook her head. "I'm on a plane back to DC in a few hours. I just wanted to give you an update before I go. And an apology."

I felt my eyebrows knot. "What for?"

"Not backing you up." She locked eyes with me. "A lot of trained field agents wouldn't have been able to handle that situation down there. I had no right to ask you to do what you did. To leave you out in the cold wasn't right, and I'm sorry."

I accepted the apology with a slight tip of the head. "You did what you had to. So did I."

She held my gaze a moment longer, then relaxed. "You've been busy the past few days. I imagine you have a few questions."

I'd spent most of Tuesday morning in the ER at Harborview under guard, being attended to, and that afternoon in SPD custody answering questions. The feds finally put together the paperwork asserting their jurisdiction late that afternoon. I spent Wednesday and most of Thursday going over my story again and again with everybody but the Pope, at one point in a big conference room that included Hiragawa, Donovan, another detective, and an assistant chief of police from SPD, a King County PA and his assistant, Reyna and two others from ONI, and three attorneys from Molly's firm.

By Thursday night, they all reached a compromise to transfer me to "protective custody" in the naval brig over in Silverdale. When I arrived, however, officers there told me orders had changed. They put me in a big SUV that brought me back across the sound to the safe house where Reyna had taken me.

They finally let me sleep, and when I awoke after fourteen hours, two former navy SEALs burly enough to make even me feel small were on hand to make sure I came to no harm and stayed on the premises. More suits visited at the safe house, debriefing me a few more times, but Reyna never put in an appearance. Sunday evening, my two guards bundled me into the black SUV parked in the driveway, drove me back to my apartment, and dropped me off without so much as a fare-thee-well.

Peter and Chance fawned over me—well, Chance, anyway— glad to see that I hadn't disappeared or died some horrific death. They insisted on feeding me dinner. Then I did the only thing I could think of under the circumstances. I went to work.

"The vials you found did contain biological material," Reyna said, not waiting for my questions. "Blood."

I swallowed and gave her a grateful look. I wouldn't have known where to start.

"Lab people are all over it," she said. "Preliminary results show it's not plague, and probably didn't make anybody sick. One sample is riddled with strands of viral material. It looks like you might have been right. Maybe some type of hemorrhagic fever. They'll pick apart the DNA and see if it could have been cloned and turned into anything lethal. I'm betting you saved us a lot of grief by keeping Gagnon from getting his hands on the stuff. How am I doing so far?"

"Covering the bases quite nicely, thanks," I said.

"Okay, then, the gold. We uncovered one hundred and forty-four crates in total."

"I counted only about half that many."

"There's another chamber behind the first," she said. "The connecting tunnel was blocked. We dug through and shored it up temporarily. Until we can do a proper job we're not sure there might not be more. Right now, though, we're thinking this is it. Each crate weighs about two hundred pounds, meaning there's about fourteen tons of ore down there. But I'm told this is one of the richest finds in terms of yield anyone's seen outside of Australia. Most of the crates contain nuggets of pure gold. The rest of the ore is mostly gold mixed with quartz. Some of it was broken up just to make it easier to transport. We're pretty sure they didn't have a crusher on site where the gold was found in California, so Woodworth's crew must have busted it up with pickaxes. Whatever, they tell me what's there should yield at least six *tons* of pure gold—worth a little over three hundred million dollars at today's prices."

I saw eyes around the table go as wide as mine did. Downing, this time, gave a low whistle.

"For that," Reyna said, "your government thanks you. In fact, I've strongly suggested to the higher-ups that they consider giving you a reward or a finder's fee of some sort for your efforts. My bosses are very appreciative of the way this has turned out. I think they'll see their way clear to do the right thing."

"You'll share with your friends, right?" Charlie said, a rueful grin on his face.

I didn't know if Charlie would ever be able to bring himself around to a direct apology, but he was trying to make amends in his own way. The fact he'd stopped by the table at all said a lot.

"That's generous," I said to Reyna. "Won't matter much if I'm in jail."

Reyna glanced at Charlie and Craig before looking me in the eye again. A corner of her mouth turned up in a hint of a smile.

"Oh, I think your boys in blue will get Mr. Whiting to sing like an *American Idol* contestant."

"Whiting? He's alive?" A sliver of hope lifted weight from my chest.

She nodded. "Still in the ICU, but I'm told he'll make it. The other fellow, too. The city councilman?"

"Acasa?" Now I felt truly bewildered and relieved at the same time. I blinked several times. Took a breath.

Reyna nodded. "Whiting's facing attempted murder. If that doesn't convince him to 'fess up, we're prepared to slap him with charges of terrorism. I think he'll probably cave on the murder of your friend Midge and the street kid if it means taking the death penalty off the table."

I sat silently, trying to digest her news. I'd thought what had happened in the tunnel would weigh heavily on me, but I found myself neither gloating nor feeling guilty. Killing Gagnon had been necessary. What I'd worried about instead was whether the PA would simply add Gagnon to the list of others I was supposed to have killed. Reyna'd just thrown me a life ring, and I was having trouble believing it wasn't a mirage.

"She's right," Charlie said softly. He stared down at the table, idly picking at the lip of his coffee cup. He finally raised his eyes. "He'll cop to save his skin. Donovan and Hiragawa chased down the cell phone that made the nine one one call about the old lady that night. Purchased at a drugstore a few weeks back. Turns out the kid at the register remembers a guy matching Whiting's description. Some stink the guy made stuck in the kid's mind." He shrugged. "Not much, but it could be enough to make Whiting consider a deal."

I stared at him, speechless. Reyna put a hand on my arm. Its warmth spread, filling me with a sense of calm I hadn't felt in ages.

Her eyes searched my face. "Don't lose hope. It'll work out." She stood abruptly and looked at the faces around the table. "Don't get up." She extended a hand to Charlie, then Craig as she said, "Nice to meet you both. Hope you keep an eye on this guy for me."

She leaned over and kissed me on the cheek. Before straightening, she whispered in my ear.

"See you, civvy."

When the restaurant door closed behind her, Downing finally closed his mouth. Charlie faced me and idly tapped the table with a forefinger.

"So," he said, "we going to have to do like the lady says?"

I shrugged. "Hard to say. You know as well as I do, anything can happen on third watch."

* * *

The light had been on in Molly's upstairs window for the past hour, the lights downstairs for more than half that, but I still hadn't mustered the courage to get out of the Toyota. The chill began to seep into my joints, making my knee ache worse than usual and reminding me of all the bruises I still bore. No sense in freezing to death. I heaved a sigh, threw open the door, and climbed out. Forcing one foot in front of the other against my better judgment, I went up the porch steps to the side door. Just as I raised a hand to rap my knuckles on the door it opened.

"Blake!" Molly froze, her face uncertain.

"Hey, Moll."

"I'm on my way to work." She crowded me so she could step outside and close the door.

"That's okay. I didn't plan on staying long."

She faced me. The shiner had diminished to a darkened smudge under her eye, ringed with sickly yellow. The bandage and stitches were gone, leaving an angry red welt on her cheek.

"What do you want, Blake?"

I opened my mouth, closed it, and tried again. "I just want to say I'm sorry. About everything."

She looked at me, her mouth a grim line. Suddenly, her face softened and she nodded.

"I lost my voice when Cole died," I said. "I lost myself. In the process, I lost you. I just wanted you to know how sorry I am about that."

She stood silently for a long moment. I shifted my weight and turned to leave. She put out a hand to stop me.

"What are you doing for Christmas?" she said.

Christmas. Only three days away, I suddenly realized. I shrugged.

"Come for dinner," she told me. Her hand hadn't left my arm. "Please."

I hesitated. "If I can bring Chance and Peter along. It's Christmas, after all."

She nodded and slowly pulled her fingers away. Then she smiled.

Acknowledgments

It's fiction. Made up. A story. But readers demand verisimilitude, which requires authors to check the facts. Writing can be a lonely business, but researching and preparing to write is rarely accomplished alone. I could not have written *Night Blind* without the help of an enormous number of smart, talented people.

For answering innumerable questions about policing in general and at SPD in particular, I'm indebted to Sergeant Deanna Nollette, Detective Kim Bogucki, Sergeant Joe Bauer, Detective Leonard Carver, and Captain Neil Low. Special thanks to Officer Joe Osborne for letting me ride along on one of his patrols, and to SPD CSI James Danielson for telling the real story about crime scene investigation (and how it differs from all those TV shows). Many thanks to Maggie Olsen, community outreach program manager, Seattle Police Department, for putting together a terrific citizens' academy and to all the officers and detectives who present a wealth of information during the months-long course.

For all the helpful information on Seattle's Link light-rail projects and how tunnels are bored, thanks to Calvin Chow at the Seattle DOT and Geoff Patrick and Bruce Gray at Sound

Transit. Extra help with geological questions was provided by Ron Tessierre, a geologist at the Washington Department of Natural Resources.

I learned about newspaper delivery with the invaluable help of Terry Ding, Tim Carothers, Mike Jordan, and Griff Tilmont at *The Seattle Times*. They not only answered my questions, but let me tour their distribution facilities in the wee hours when it's at its busiest.

Selim Woodworth was a real person, and the facts of his life are a matter of public record. I took creative liberties with his story during his two unaccounted-for years in the US Navy. Help with factual information about Selim E. Woodworth and the *Anita*, the ship he captained between 1848 and 1850, was provided by Daniel Jones at the Naval Historical Center and Kim McKeithan at the National Archives and Records Administration.

History professors Bill Rorabaugh at the University of Washington and Bill Woodward at Seattle Pacific University put Woodworth's story in context and made mid-1800s America come alive for me, no easy task.

Information on the plague and other delightfully dangerous diseases came from Lisa Jackson, epidemiologist at Group Health, and Jo Hofmann, MD, state epidemiologist for communicable disease, Washington State Department of Health.

Finally, many thanks to suicide survivors Jonathan Mannheim and Pam McBride at the Youth Suicide Prevention Program (www.yssp.org) for sharing their difficult and heartfelt stories.

I've taken liberties with everything I learned; any mistakes are mine. And for all those I haven't mentioned, for lack of space or simple oversight, thank you, too.

The great group of people at The Editorial Department, especially Ross Browne, Peter Gelfan, Jesse Steele, Kate Steele, Karinya Funsett-Topping, and Jane Ryder, believed in the book and made it better with their insight and expertise. And without them I wouldn't have found agent extraordinaire Lukas Ortiz at the Philip J. Spitzer Literary Agency.

The team at Thomas & Mercer—Alan Turkus, Ed Stackler, Stacee, Jacque, Leslie, Rebecca, Danielle, et al.—has been nothing short of wonderful. They're a delight to work with and have strived to make the book better every step of the way.

Above all, thanks to my wife, Valarie, and my family for putting up with me and supporting this crazy thing I do called writing.

About the Author

Photo by Valarie Kaye, 2010

Michael W. Sherer grew up on a farm in northern Illinois, went to prep school and college "back east," and lived in Chicago for twenty years. After stints as a manual laborer, dishwasher, bartender, restaurant manager, commercial photographer, magazine editor, and public relations executive, Sherer decided life should imitate art and became a novelist. He is a member of International Thriller Writers, Mystery Writers of America, and the Authors Guild. In addition to *Night Blind*, the first thriller in the Blake Sanders series, he has published six novels in the Emerson Ward mystery series, including *An Option on Death, Little Use for Death, Death Came Dressed in White, A Forever Death, Death Is No Bargain*, and *Death on a Budget*, as well as a stand-alone suspense novel, *Island Life*. He's now hard at work on his fourth Blake Sanders thriller and a new young adult thriller, *Blind Rage*. He and his wife and the youngest of their four children now live in the Seattle suburbs.